The Girl From Convict Lake

by

Sharon Shipley

This is a work of fiction. Names, characters, places, and incidents are either the product of the author's imagination or are used fictitiously, and any resemblance to actual persons living or dead, business establishments, events, or locales, is entirely coincidental.

The Girl From Convict Lake

COPYRIGHT © 2022 by Sharon Shipley

Cover Art by *The Wild Rose Press, Inc.*

The Wild Rose Press, Inc.
PO Box 708
Adams Basin, NY 14410-0708
Visit us at www.thewildrosepress.com

Publishing History
First Edition, 2023
Trade Paperback ISBN 978-1-5092-4492-8
Digital ISBN 978-1-5092-4493-5

Published in the United States of America

The guttering candle still cast a subdued glow.

The quilt, a reddish patchwork called "Snakes and Apples" and one of my favorites was different. More red. The pattern distorted. Debbi's foot still protruded. I yanked the quilt straight.

I stood, holding a corner of it, staring at her.

Debbi lay in a soup of blood, one eye staring sightless from a ruined face. The other eye was a grisly hole. Dimly, from somewhere deep in my primitive mind, the determined pounding renewed, booming like thunder over the howling blizzard screaming like a banshee up the stairwell. *"That isn't wind,"* I whimpered.

My own cries would wake the dead as I backed to the banister, half-sliding, half-falling downstairs. I could hardly control my leg at best of times; now it threatened to collapse. Clinging, to the banister, I half-tumbled down the steps using only one leg, dragging the other. Dread was almost a distraction. When I pulled the drapes, I waited, frozen, for whatever to materialize. I blinked and backed my hand to my mouth to stifle a yell.

A six-foot-tall black crow stood hunched on the drifted-over veranda.

Then, the creature turned.

Other Wild Rose Press Titles by Sharon Shipley:

Danforth the Dragon
Sary's Gold
Sary's Diamonds
Sary and the Maharajah's Emeralds
Love, Lust and Peril: A trilogy
The Wylder Ghost and Blossom Cherry
The Dishwater Duchess of Wylder, Wyoming

Dedication

To Skipper as Always:
The Wind Beneath my Wings

Acknowledgments

Ally
A most gracious and patient editor…
Thank You.

Prologue

The Beginning
Grosse Pointe, Michigan

The pretty girl threaded her way through a jungle of struts under gray metal bleachers, unsavory even on the sunniest day. Now, the insalubrious space was cold and drear with the flotsam of many seasons…candy wrappers, old condoms, rusty soda cans—the odd shoe.

A lame place to meet, she moped. Pursing candy pink lips, she looked dubiously up through open steel treads, to slices of overcast sky, seemingly another world away, feeling trapped of a sudden, as if risers were bars to a cage.

Where the heck was he?

Sulking, she fingered her heart locket. The note said: "Under the bleachers." "Meet me under the freaking bleachers!" South side? South side toward the hot dog stand? Her mind nagged. *Farthest away from the school. Down by the trash bins behind the cement enclosure. Where no one can see us…*

She hoped it was that cute Zak, feeling first doubt. Didn't say, did it? Might be that creep, Rodney sitting and farting behind her in homeroom. She hugged her pink cashmere-ed arms. *Shoulda worn a coat, sexiness be diddly-damned. Startin' to snow too.*

Then she saw the thing.

1

Round. Glossy blood-red and startling white against gray filtered light. She stepped closer, bemused, not freaked out. A target? A freaking *bull's-eye* target! Lame place to shoot arrows or *whatever* under bleachers with all these beams and crap.

The pretty girl…perennial cheerleader, prom queen, first pick for the school play, stumbled over crisscross struts to examine it. Then heard *the voice,* turning with a smile curving glossy pink lips, her back flat against the red and white target.

Now *she* was the eye of the target. Her first instinct, when the arrow thumped her chest with the force of a pile driver, piercing the delicate barrier of pink wool, then her skin with ease, scraping off sternum bones and into her heart, was…*all that blood will ruin my sweater.*

****

Winter. It could be any winter—*any* girl *or all of them in years to come*. But it was *her* winter. The girl in the pink sweater. The winter *she* died. She was only fifteen. Now trundled and dragged like unwieldy furniture through a dense wood over felled logs resembling buried bodies, through snow thick as the muffled curses erupting past the killer's bulky hood.

The figure kept heaving, yanking the naked corpse, already rock-solid, therefore uncooperative, off of the road deep into a wood. The pretty girl's only attire now, was the heart locket bouncing against a marble-hard neck.

Rigid fingers snagged each obstruction, no matter how insignificant—claws of brambles, stick-tights, tangles of winter-blasted blackberry thorn. It was like dragging a manikin unyielding as Carrara marble with traceries of purple vein—frozen columns of blood that once coursed warm and red through her arterial highways, had the killer thought about it.

The killer backed into banks of briers with a sort of hollowed-out place beneath, much like a berth on a train. Snow dropped from a tall fir. The figure in the bulky parka whipped around disconcerted. In the arctic blast, wild black hair flew from the hood in long dark flags. The figure cursed, kicking the body with one thick moon-boot until the body rolled like a square log, halfway under.

Concealed—almost.

One last boot. "There. Good enough," the killer grunted.

****

August, Friday 13, 1993

The sleek sexy prototype—DeLorean gull wings, grill reminiscent of the sexy S-type Jag, plus road-hugging lines of a long-snouted E-Type, but more, *oh, so much more,* hurtled down a gravel two-lane that magnificent fall night. Oak and full-leaf maple blurred by, that in daylight would be sanguine-red, and serum-yellow, blazing with life the four passengers would soon forfeit, as surely as leaves brown and decay.

However, on this night, trees limned in silver cast bulky shadows as the exotic car rocketed, ejecting in and out of sight. The dark shattered with screams and drunken laughter. At the wheel, a young woman, exciting in the big-haired way of the late '80s, barely holding rubber to the road. Any other car would have flipped long ago. Flo Lodge stroked multiple gears like caressing a cat's back and passed back the bottle of peach-flavored schnapps. Almost empty now.

The others, a young woman and two young men

enjoyed the edge too, with varying degrees of fear, jubilation, and sobriety as the sexy prototype rounded a bend—*outta sight.*

Flo's face took on an odd expectation—an excited *violence,* then, the others reacted too, as each became aware of the hundred-year-old oak, impermeable as death, encroaching the road and their own fast-rushing destinies. These awareness's snuffed out in a crush of detonating metal and screams, erupting like the fire-ball gilding the night.

Chapter 1

Exactly Six Years Later

August 13, 1999

The sports car with the rusting Lodge Lancer insignia, crawled an alley in the once snob section of Grosse Pointe Woods, Detroit, lights out. From a short-lived line of the now bust, Lodge Automobile Company, the car was rare as Hispano Souza hubcaps. But, that, as the crashed prototype before it, was another story.

At the wheel, Zak Lodge, dangerously handsome at fourteen and Lance, his cousin, a year younger, is skinnier, not so handsome but both owned the same thick dark Irish hair; Zak's long and flowing, Lance sporting a mullet. There the resemblance ends. Lance is without the spark—*the dangerous eye.*

Zak yanked the hand brake and the two crouch-run to a sleeping-den jutting from a flagstone mansion; a screened porch where folks used to fitfully doze on sultry Michigan nights, much like this one, in days before air conditioning.

Through the rusted screen, the boys watched as "*Lugosi and a troika of underfed female vamps menaced a helpless blonde in flickering black-and-white.*" Meggie, twelve, eyed the television with rapt attention.

From the bushes, Lance sniggered, howling wolf-like, *"Owwww - ooooooooooo!"*

"Stifle, loser!" Zak smacked his head.

The girl frantically pushed the "mute" button on the boxy remote. In a frightened little-girl voice, she ventured, her every nerve salsa dancing. "Who—anybody there?"

****

I must have appeared ghostly to them behind the screen. The two leapt out, *hands in claws*. I recall shrieking, collapsing in on myself. I gasped breathless. I couldn't stop giggling until Zak clamped a hand over my mouth and with his other, groped my too-small breasts (over my PJs), and breathed in corny Lugosi-speak in my ear.

"Vant your necka suckeda? Vill, I dooooo?"

Lance shifted uncomfortably. "Holy crap, Zak. I'm her freakin' brother! Cool it." Zak glittered at Lance. "Oy. Got better plans anyway." He threw me off and flipped his long thick hair back.

I swayed with longing I could not conceal. I had no sophisticated graces yet to hide my crush, if indeed I ever would.

"Right, old Lancer-dude?" Zak gave Lance his usual hurtful head-noogie, nodding at the crap car and winking at me.

I checked the house's fusty interior. "Shhh guys. Uncle Dez's sleeping! So, should you be," wincing at my nagging mother-voice. "Almost ten o'clock!" *How lame is that?*

Zak sniffed my hair. "Don't ya just love the smell of stale popcorn in the evenin', Lancer dude?"

"Dunno, Zak. Maybe we should—like—you

know?" Lance was already shuffling away, *distancing* himself, I saw. Something was on though! Real *bomb,* if Zak was involved. And he wanted me!

How could I believe it was the beginning-of-the-end, even if it had been filmed in black and white?

Then, Zak curled his wicked lazy grin and sealed the deal. He nodded at the car. "You in, Magpie?" I recall considering the TV flickering an ad for *Rebel Without a Cause.* The brilliant technicolor crag-race scene. You remember the one. If precognisant of what it portended, perhaps I *would* have stayed home—safe, watching *Old Bella* after all but I raked the shabby lounge— *stale popcorn kernels under shredded wicker seats, wadded up old Kleenex, empty soda cans*...and the lure of a summer escapade with Zak, was *way* too enthralling.

Starry-eyed, I assessed Zak's devil face promising unknown thrills, and Lance's slightly prudish one, the mosquito-chorused night and star-sprinkled sky.

A vagrant breeze of night-blooming jasmine turned the humid night into an intoxicating lure.

That made it perfect.

Gleeful, I dashed in my summer PJs to the car.

Sneaking out and playing hooky, practically the middle of the night!

I felt wild, and free, like one of the popular girls, especially when Zak scooped me up, dumping me in the front seat. I felt Zak's taut young muscles and smelled his man-sweat, though he was only fourteen. Lance barely fell in the narrow rear seat as wheels spat gravel.

Behind us, I recall, the TV brightly flickered exploding cars.

My last warning.

****

After an hour of a red-light-running, corner-skidding, fishtailing, white-knuckled ride, at least for me, Zak slewed broadside into an alley and commenced crawling through a maze of wrecking yards and Quonset huts.

In the humid summer breeze, I remember the crusty oil and rust smell. Something metal flapped and creaked. All else was quiet, except for a dog, old by its wheezing growl. Zak idled the car, playing a spotlight, one of the car's features, outlawed now, but perfect for playing *"spotty"* during commercials and previews at the drive-ins at that time, through a chain link fence while Lance chewed his thumb.

For a flash, Zak's electric turquoise eyes regarded me.

Zak.

I had wished it were only me and Zak and that Zak held me close and safe somewhere among the shapeless hulks of cars and junk barrels beyond the chain-link. Maybe even in the back seat of one. That would be spooky, exciting, and daring...lost there in the shadows. Instead, Zak showed his eyeteeth and swung frayed paper-tagged keys. It wasn't till then, I realized where we were, and why.

He smirked. Through the window Zak knuckle-banged a rusting sign affixed to the chain link: "Lodge Enterprises. Keep Out." And the remains of a guard shack.

"You didn't!"

In the backseat Lance studied his hands.

"You broke in Uncle Dez's office!"

The battered wood cabinet was more a coffin for lost

dreams and family fortunes after our parents destroyed the prototype that night but uncle Dez, guiding light of *Lodge Motor Works Ent.*, kept the cabinet sealed as a sacred memorial, which in a way it was.

Zak scowled. I instantly clamped my jaws shut.

"Only wanna see it!" He wasn't whining. He was disappointed in me. Why wouldn't he be? I was as exciting as a bowl of cold mashed turnips.

"What could go wrong?" Zak studied the Quonset beneath lowering brows. "We're owed."

"Owed what?" I ventured.

He rounded on me. "We'll bring it back! A freakin' test drive after all this time. Doin' him a favor!" He leaned over the seat hooking Lance's neck giving him another noogie. "With me, Lancer-dude?"

"Zak, Uncle Dez will kill us, sure," I nagged. "He'd kill us if anything—happened to us too." I faltered then as Zak flashed annoyance.

"Only way to break bad karma."

"*Only way to break bad karma,*" Lance mimicked. "Tempting fate, asshole! Told ya."

"Teasing fate, pussy!"

"They died," I whispered. "Omigod. It was like—*this time,* wasn't it?"

Yes, I was young, stupid, and impressionable. I admit it.

Zak's eyes turned icy in the lone arc light. I shivered in my shorty jams.

Okay, it was moonlight gave us all that, just-fresh-corpse look.

"Bad shit follows us," Zak nailed me smirking, "like one a Nutmeg here's effin' vampires!" He smacked Lance still studying his hands. "We can stop it. Tonight by—"

"Recreating the *accident*?" Lance sneered.

I had the feeling then, Lance was a turncoat, that before this, he had sided with Zak. Typical of Lance.

"They died! Fuck, man, they died! Damn it! Our parents fuckin' died! We're fuckin' orphans."

"Yah, ya do look a little *pathetic*."

"Not as pathetic as smeared all over the road with our head up our ass!"

"Now that creates an intriguing picture."

"It makes a crazy sense, Lance," I volunteered. "Like a—loop. If we get past the beginning, we—"

"Christ, Meggie! Saturday Sci-Fi Theater strikes again!"

I glared at Lance's scathing look.

"You don't wear skirts do ya, old Lancer-dude?"

Zak swiveled to me. "Old Dez never gets pissed at you, sweet-chips. You're our insurance."

Lance flipped his hair back in imitation of Zak. "Why the hell else, ya think we let ya hang with us, Nutmeg?"

He'd switched again.

"But why, Zak?" I despised the timid wussy timber in my voice.

Zak sighed as if explaining to the village idiot.

"*Why Zak?*" He mocked. "Look. Uncle Dez needs a kick in the keester. He's scared shitless. That old girl," he nodded at the Quonset hut, "was repaired, fixed up almost good as new, sitting there rusting, for what? Ten years? He's frozen as that wreck in there, is *gonna* be. We gotta kick-start somethin' and get the show back on the road, even if it's on that bastard in there."

"You run outta cliché's yet, Zak?"

Zak backhanded Lance. "Stuff it. I'm thinkin' of our futures here."

"What, Zak!" *Darling.* Even then, I hoped he meant, his and my future…

"Look Meggie, maybe you wanna be two toes from bankruptcy alla time; I don't. We get the company goin' again, get some money-men up front—I dunno. Lotsa nostalgia for this line. Make press on the old headlines. *'Heirs bring old car manufacturer back to life. Popular line raises from the dead'.* Something like that—get some interest going. We'll work it out," he flipped it off, as he did his hair.

Poor Zak. Money meant nothing, only how fast he could spend it even then. But at least he was thinking of us—*of me.*

"Don't know 'bout you," he brooded, "but I wanna inherit somethin' more than a bone-yard of unsold cars and a couple derelict factories and *this.* Looks like a bomb site."

I would have said, *The Hound of the Baskervilles,* brayed deep and growl-y then, grinding the night silence to hamburger. Instead, the ancient bull terrier stood like a muscled foot-stool, four legs squared beyond the fence. His gummy snarl showed old fangs, still sharp but its tail wagged.

Zak scratched the animal practically drooling over him, through the fence. *Don't all the bitches?* I thought, feeling stupid.

In a sudden move, Zak boosted me up, the last time I'd have that agility, liberally feeling my bottom. Then he toed diamond links, jumping over the shaky fence with grace…Lance throwing disgusted looks our way, thudded down beside me.

"Hey, girl. Ya lonely?" Zak opened a Ziploc of half a McDonald's. By then, the dog would have unlocked the gate itself.

We three picked our way to the oxidized old Quonset hut with the terrier bitch wagging its stump like a miniature rotor after us.

"Hunh! Nobody cares." Zak pointed. A corroded Master Lock hung open on the wide double doors.

As he creaked them aside, I shivered. Zak's face was all moonlit with black craters for eyes. When Zak was like this, nothing stopped him. Yet, we all stood in awe as the moon spread wan fairy dust over the Lodge Lancette prototype, the late lamented, last sleek hope of the Lodge fortunes.

DeLorean gull wing.

A grill reminiscent of the S-Type Jag.

Road-hugging lines of an "E". Restored—somewhat, to past glory.

Zak fell on his knees, *ala salaaming*, crooning, "*Sweet* mama, come to daddy!" He leered at me. "Gonna love ridin' *this* bitch," and flipped the keys at Lance.

Lance jumped back and let them drop in the oil-stained dirt. "I look suicidal?"

Zak winked. "Magpie? You been drivin' since you were 'bout ten."

True, being in an automotive family, all us kids learned to drive way below the legal age with free access to the many models, past and present, experimental or duds, 'specially on the back roads of the Upper Peninsula.

A dubious benefit…but never-the-less, it brought back *the good times,* when we all felt *special*. Heirs to a fortune. Popular. The future bright and boundless. The one percent. The privileged few. Hah!

I grinned and put shaking hands behind my back and tried flirting. "Uhn-uhn...not even for you, Zachary Lodge!"

He shook his head and grinned wickedly, tossed the keys, caught them, and jumped in the front seat. Dust sprang up like midges. He flipped switches and tapped the gas gauge, chortling something triumphant. Lights popped on almost alarmingly, highlighting broken-backed wrecks, rusting denizens of the yard in all their lurking shabbiness beyond the door. Soon the all-steel prototype would join them if left to the cancer of neglect.

Zak was right as always.

"But how!" I asked, my eyes wide in adulation.

"I make my own luck, 'member? Charged the old battery yesterday."

He had all the luck in the world. We didn't even need the gas can wedged in the backseat. Idly, I wondered who fed the dog, then noted the hole in the fence behind barrels. The yard wasn't even properly guarded. And that put paid to my last apprehensions; plastering a grin, I nodded. We pushed the car out in neutral. Lance creaked the rusty gate back along the fence.

Zak called, "Here girl, you're free." He laughed as the dog stared stupidly at the invisible barrier; timidly walked across the line and sniffed at weeds. Then the dog took off at a steady trot and didn't look back—

We didn't either. Perhaps we should have...but as Zak said, *"Karma was in the wind."*

Chapter 2

Storm Warnings

The sleek prototype with the Lodge Lancette trademark hurtled as if a horse too long stabled, bolting ahead as Zak crashed, mauled, slapped, and slid gears in a blur of hands and feet.

The gritty tarmac was a Michigan country straightaway. Dials spun like a whirly-gig–80—97—110—130! Our long dark hair whipped like three black flags across our faces as Zak in a show of bravado, passed a bottle of peach-flavored brandy 'cause he couldn't find schnaps.

No seat belts. Only tinny-looking rudimentary controls. *Was this what our parents thrilled over that long-ago summer night? This exhilarating freedom!* I hoped so. Gamely, I sipped the brandy. Sugar bear, that was good! My stomach danced the tarantella.

There was much drunken laughter as The Lancette rocketed, barely holding rubber to the road. *Any other car would have flipped long ago.*

A watcher would have a snapshot of my petrified face, then, Zak's—then Lance's as we each became aware of the hundred-year oak with the old burn scar that awaited a hair around a bend. Racing toward it, Zak spun the wheel, insanely laughing, zagging at the last possible moment. We were past it.

Looking back, Zak didn't see the bridge abutment, until way late.

In a crush of exploding glass and metal, a long dull silver door pinwheeled to a beet field.

I silently screamed. A prayer? A curse? Afraid for Zak, or myself in that last split second to infinity?

Lights sliced the dark ahead—two knives cutting across fields.

I heard whirring sounds. Tortured metal…shards of heat slicing open my leg.

* * * *

I viewed a moonscape of gravel level with my cheek, courtesy of the skewed headlights raking the road. When I awoke again, my body felt like broken pick-up-sticks, all awry, neck bent awkward and face kissing grit, for the tarmac gave way to gravel right after the oak tree, still bearing scars of the crash years ago.

Painfully, and afraid I could not, I raised my head.

Missing. Something missing.

I recall even now the terror…*Ah…can't open one eye. Am I blinded? Stuck. Force lashes apart. I see red. That's okay then. No. Can't feel anything. Must not be hurt, but grasped the fact I am. Even scarier. I hurt all over. All except my leg, oddly not—not—there? Then, a searing pain zigzagged thigh to calf. I sensed a hot mess spreading under me.*

I'm in the center of the road sprawled in my own blood. Alone. I wondered stupidly if another car would flatten me like road kill. No, no one else was as foolhardy driving this isolated half-forgotten country lane.

I didn't grasp yet that my leg was shattered bone. Only numb. Nature's anesthetic.

Excruciatingly, I moved my head and saw the

15

Lancette accordioned into the bridge abutment with a wheel still spinning like a game of chance. One of Zak's Air Johnston's poked from weeds along the verge.

I can't see Zak's face! Then, blessedly I heard…

"Meggie? Hurt! Help *meeee…*"

Zak! Digging my elbows and one knee, I hitched over, one foot dragging behind like a dead cat. Nevermind gravel scraped my pajamas, then my flesh and leg bone skinned raw and trailing blood, or that my injury came alive blossoming with pain. *Zak needs me— he needs ME.* Panicked, that I can't relieve his anguish. *Or if he died.*

"Coming, Zakkie! Hang on," I cried.

It was only then, I looked for Lance safe in the hedgerows.

Chapter 3

Twelve years later

January 3, 2021

Well. That was me then. I recall it as if it were yesterday. *August 13, 1999.* How I wish I could go back and rewind that old Lugosi tape...

In ways, I still resemble that young girl verging on adulthood, at least I look like one they tell me. Fragile, pale, blue-eyed, and black of hair, but even back then, with a woman's aching heart and body.

I think of myself as Margaret Anne Lodge now, though no one else will humor me. I sit before a kidney-shaped vanity—called a "Hollywood Vanity," in the late fifties when Flo, my late mother owned this room, watching snow drift past the fake Tudor panes of our old Grosse Pointe mansion.

Great.

Not white fluff balls, like in *White Christmas*. Stinging, sleety missiles in fitful starts and stops. *Spiteful* snow making my bad leg gnaw with pain. Another waning day in Grosse Pointe, Michigan, the once grander edge of a Detroit increasingly resembling a bombed-out Syria.

I closed the faded drapes and sipped wine the color of prune juice. I didn't mind. Whatever was on sale at the liquor shop by Golden Moldies Video, still hanging on thanks to cult "purists" and slumming yuppies. I guess they are still called that. "*Oh look!*" They squeal. "*Isn't this quaint! Imagine! They still have video's here! And one can rent the players!*" Then the cackle of disdain. However, I'm cozy enough and looking forward to the evening's entertainment.

The room behind me is vast, also "late Hollywood fifties." White accented with corroded gilt. Rich brocade faded to blenched beige.

Not shabby chic. Shabby.

The room's true jarring note I suppose, when my mind's eye wanders, is the teetering stacks, shoeboxes under bed, jammed bookcases of black or blue plastic video boxes, most affixed with tacky rental stickers. Ninety-nine cent sell-offs from long defunct Blockbusters or from trolling Goodwills, and garage sales.

The room is a slow slide into neglect, the comforting warren of a young, still pretty, semi-invalid, I like to tell myself when most melodramatic and self-pitying. Greta Garbo perhaps in *Camille*…

Haven.

Lately, I splurged on few DVDs but they aren't the same, breaking into annoying pixels, thrusting me *out of time* with the shock of cold water as I follow Bette Davis, Joan Crawford, or Ingrid glide, vamp, or storm across the screen.

I babied my ancient video player, haunting Salvation Army for more against the time my machine would no longer be coaxed to play, a hedge against the dread day I couldn't revel in my beloved black and white *noir* and treacly '40s romances like *Now Voyager,* but mostly I relished the old scary stuff. Karloff, Lugosi, and Christopher Lee have a lot to answer for.

Yet, I secreted away a few exotic foreign films too, truly frightening, and morbid, and only taken out when I'm especially dispirited.

That wasn't tonight.

I can't wait. My treat at end of day, yearning to dive into the delicious warm waters of make-believe. Groping the tarnished silver brush, the matching broken ivory comb, the crystal scent bottles tacky with perfume and cosmetics from the 99 Cent store, a dusting of powder over all, I meticulously prepared. I have to admit, I looked palely-pretty, even fragilely beautiful in the mirror. A watercolor of a woman.

I looked away. Face it. You are a *runt*. The accident seemed to have stunted my growth as well as my future. I was barely five-two, with a face like a waif from *Le Miz*, I grumbled. Big haunted eyes, long black hair, a face heart-shaped over a long neck, petite but shapely figure rounded in all the right places. Too bad about my leg, I thought, absently rubbing the long, jagged scar.

****

After a few more gulps of wine, I fixed my hair in elaborate twists—very forties now, carefully brushing on thicker brows and a full red mouth before slipping into the long black velvet gown from the Goodwill awaiting on the bed, the closest I could find matching Ingrid Bergman's gown in *Notorious*. My eyes strayed to a fancy framed headshot—*more delayed rewards,* taking time to trace Zak's sculpted lips stretched in his reckless lopsided grin. He had felt-tipped…

"*Nutmeg,
You make me laugh!*

Zak"

Not "*love, Zak,*" but that was all right. That was his way. The modern-day Don Rickles—the provocateur, the Bill Maher, King of Barbs, slander, and innuendo designed to hurt and maim.

No, that wasn't right.

Zak had to be edgy to be noticed. He told me to wait, that was understood. Wait until his Big Break. I'd be manager, promoter, most supportive fan, lover, and sounding board. A team. Live in motel rooms with hot plates, and smuggled in microwaves on tour, if he let me. Wouldn't have given me the photo if he didn't feel the same. That was unspoken. Had been for years. I glanced up. Had to hurry now, though.

Reflected in my mirror, *Notorious,* the black and white thriller is starting. This time on TCM. As I paraded about the room, I drank in Ingrid Bergman's severe black velvet gown, comparing it favorably with my own, while accurately mouthing dialogue. My breath quickened. "*Claude Rains sees handsome Cary Grant kissing Ingrid in the wine cellar...*"

...just as the white and gold phone jangled. "Drat!" I stared at it as if my hairbrush had levitated. Coming awake, I forced a breathy, husky whisper—*okay like Ingrid would sound.* It came out a squeak. *Sugar bear!*

"*Darl-ing.* Is that you?" *Stupid! Stupid!*

****

I could picture Zak on the other end, slumped at a table the size of a hat. The club, badly lit for cleaning, sadly revealing grunge-city, seats and floors patterned with drinks-spills and God alone knew what else. The cleaning crew would be clueless.

"Who are you tonight, Magpie?" He blew smoke at

a passing blonde.

I had so carefully rehearsed what I would say.

Bright, breezy, ready for anything. All Zak could wish for.

"Kinda hoping you'd call?" *Oh brilliant! How needy is that*!

"Nobody Zak…only—dressing to go out," I lied. Forcing a smoky sexy voice, drawled, "Amazing crowd? Dazzled their socks off yet?"

"If ya rank the plumbers' convention, a hot ticket."

****

Zak, checking the thin crowd, picked at his beer label with a sulky little-boy expression.

"Need you, Magpie. Get your cute little ass over here."

He slammed his chair on all fours. Two college guys sat "cool" but embarrassed they were "first," already getting a head on *obnoxious,* by ordering four beer buckets. He can deal with them. Can't wait to skewer their ego and chop them to chicken liver. He stared at the stage, cool eyes taking in everything—*already on.*

"Like Gable needs Harlow—" he heard her purr, matching his husky tones.

Colored lights popped on-off. A combo draggled in, one scraping a bass fiddle. In the club twenty miles away, Zak rolled his eyes, interrupting. "Why not play hooky, climb down a drain pipe or something? The old boy won't know. You're my lucky charm, babe."

****

I bit my lip. "You'll knock 'em sideways, Zakkie."

I thought that suitably clever. My lips brushed the receiver, almost in prayer. "Uncle Dez isn't feeling so hot or—" *Why did Zak always ask at the wrong time? Oh yeah? When is the right time in your madcap life, Meggie?*

"He's using you, Magpie. Old coot doesn't need a baby sitter. Been dyin' ten years. Last a lousy weekend. I need you to rub my—rabbit's foot. What are you wearing tonight?"

The innuendo was not lost. He heard me suck in, I recognize by his silence. "White Diamond perfume," I whispered huskily.

He sensed my rising passion over the phone, the flushed cheeks, recalling our half-delirious, wild-eyed looks when we melded together, all hot and sweaty in the old boathouse, our lips and limbs slipping off each other. My budding breasts sliding beneath his kisses. We went way back.

I was the only one who still stirred him, I felt in my bones, no matter how many other women he had, or chased, or chased him, rather. I was the first. He, my lodestar, no matter we were cousins. The one iron clad anchor in my life of which I was sure, no matter how unlikely to the rest of the world. Sadly, he still thought of me as a child in many ways.

****

He picked the rest of the label and checked the lighting guy. "No, sweetheart, my bad. Look, your cell phone. Got a gizmo that wires funds. Right? Just tap…."

He listened, sighing. "Right. You wouldn't have a 'gadget,' later than an electric pencil sharpener." He shook his head and grinned finally, "Yeah. Yeah. Like Gable loves Harlow. Can't you upgrade your fantasies? Christ!" He laughed. "Gable! How about, like, how Kanye love Kim-mie? Oh, forgot. They split." The snark only made him look dangerously wolfish.

"Kim…? *Who…?*"

Cackles emanated from the mike. Zak glanced over.

"Look. On soon, Magpie."

The lighting was poor. They forgot his blue cell again…Fuck!

Zak strolled onstage. Tried not to notice, besides the college kids there were only three others. A bickering couple bombed out of their skull, and an older guy. Maybe a scout.

The metamorphosis was astounding. In command, not quite late-show material…yet. Zak strolled over.

The barker, feinting like a boxer, waved Zak on. "….and *no-ow*—ZAK THE HACKMAN, aaaaaand the sharper edge of COM-ED-Y!"

Zak ambled around making them wait, hands in pockets, eyes to the floor before zeroing in on his first victim. A party of five looking like easy marks had seated themselves.

They all waited for the kill, some gormless victim straight out of *The Hangover*.

*　*　*　*

My mood curdled no matter how I strived to pick up where I left off; draining my sticky wine like medicine, I reached for a cigarette holding it ala Lauren Bacall in *To Have and Have Not*, miserably watching myself through the acrid pall in the mirror with *Notorious* fading like a gray fog behind me until credits zoomed by and Robert Osborne introduced another Claude Rains film. Looked like *The Wolf Man*. Ordinarily I would have relished it. I opened up another precious bottle of wine.

My fingers fumbled the off button, switching channels instead.

The TV with serious cardboard talking-heads blared

color and sound. I watched dully. *"BREAKING NEWS"* the banner screamed in flashing yellow and red. A hysterically grinning blond announced, *"blabla bla*...another girl missing for six months...found...last seen hitchhiking... yada yada..." The TV flashed to a cute brunette, one hand wearing a class ring with a sapphire-looking stone laid beside her cheek in classic year-book pose.

Another one. I tried to avoid them, averting my morbid gaze from the grisly montage of past discoveries by snow crews, hikers, garbage haulers, once even a Forest Ranger up in the U.P. The montage of photos soon filled the screen—a whole stamp collection of murdered young women.

****

I hitched with a definite starboard lurch to the bath, thanks to the wine I told myself, *not my gimpy leg,* carrying the bottle, shedding my black velvet as I went. Studying myself critically in sections in the small mirror, my figure, though denigrated by me, is quite good, I am told.

Wiry toned arms. Even a tiny six pack. Okay. High breasts, fragile waist, slim hips, and a—thank goodness, pert bottom. My right leg is proportionally long and shapely. The other is a tad shorter marred with the lightening flash of a cicatrize, purple and angry. I usually avoid such encounters.

Proud Flesh, they called it in the old days.

Nothin proud about it, I thought with contrariness.

The bath is more '30s. Original maroon tile, pedestal sink and faded purple towels from K-mart that I imagined would match the décor, but didn't. I scrubbed off thick makeup until my face staring back is achingly innocent.

****

The desk clock nagged its loud *cluck*: 1:45.

In my scruffy terry robe, more a security blanket, and horn rim glasses, I added numbers, chewing a stub with teeth marks all over, rechecking an enormous calculator, stamped *"Compliments of Goodrich Bank."*

"Holy Toledo," I moaned finally sinking my head in my hands. I jerked up from the clump of bills before nodding off. Can't *ignore* them, like avoiding sullen stares from the homeless with their grubby cardboard signs at intersections. Some of these were overdue the second month even, I winced, holding one—third notice. "Gas and water, K-mart Visa...old Doc Summers...can't forget him." I groaned. No insurance after the company went under.

"Meggie! Margaret Anne!"

The plaintive voice was still strong, if shaky, turned querrelsome. *"Meg-gie!"* It demanded. A childish fear-note softened the order.

Plastering a weary smile, I rose. "Coming, Uncle Dez."

****

Next morning, I pushed into the vast dining room. "Kitchen's cozier, Unc," I said as ritual, besides it was easier to keep warm, turning the three-bar heater from two to one. The old man frowned in his oatmeal. I sighed, switching it back. He liked it warm but the old furnace was eating us alive!

Somewhere in his sweet old curdled brain, stirred memories of splendors past. Now, half the chandelier teardrops went missing and the rest filtered dingy light dulled by time and grime over the ancient crocheted table cloth.

I didn't notice any more, or tried not too, limping past the dented metal pot, no-name bread, and jam from the dollar store on the sideboard. Yet a different me; button-down shirt, warm corduroys, a ratty beige cardy over all, kissed the old man's pink forehead, stroking the snowy fluff on top his head.

"Like those striped jammies. Very dashing. Matches your eyes too," I flirted.

George Herbert Desmond Lodge, founder of the infamous, depending on the headlines, *Lodge Motors Ent.*, suspiciously slurped oatmeal, studying every bite with the intensity of a stamp collector eyeing the "*Inverted Jenny,*" as I chattered above a cranky vacuum running somewhere.

Uncle Desmond smiled vaguely and continued spooning oatmeal. He wasn't paying attention, but I had to talk to *someone.*

"Ernie down at Oldie Moldy Videos ordered a rare copy of *The Spiral Staircase.* Half in love with the little weasel. It has *outtakes.*"

I smiled inwardly.

George Brent actually strangling the beauteous Rhonda Fleming, in place of the fade away... I cringed. Almost a snuff film.

My face grew serious. *Quit fooling around with your favorite films*, I lectured myself. Still, I panicked every time I went, fearing the "Going Out of Business" signs. On the one side, I could grab a bunch for a buck or two, on the other it meant the dreary task of looking up oldies on my cranky computer. Plus, I'd sorely miss the owner's half flirtatious chitchat over our shared love of classic film.

The old man's turquoise eyes twinkled.

"Pick up your med'cine too."

Anything to get out of the house for a few breaths.

Innocence aroused. "You have enough money, Margaret Anne?" He asked too wide-eyed—too artless.

"Boodles from last month's housekeep, Uncle Dez. Stashin' it for a wild week in *Joisey.*"

The old man frowned. "With the funny man? Don't like that funny man!"

"It's Zak, your grandson! And he is *very* funny, Uncle!" *And I love him.*

The old man dumped three tablespoons of grape jam in his oatmeal and a spoonful of sugar. I looked away. "Want anything?" I knelt by his chair.

Uncle Dez smiled vaguely. "Yes." Fretting and plaintive, he said, "Fetch Lolly. Where's Lolly?"

"Lollypop's gone. 'Member?"

The old man nodded thoughtfully and persisted spooning. Grape dribbled his jammies. I sighed. "We'll go to the shelter. Pick out another dog. A cute little pup. You—would you like that?" No answer. I patted him, wrapped my sweater close and grabbed my purse.

****

Hearing the door slam, the old man tottered from the table. The vacuum sounds were farther away now as Desmond Lodge pattered the long front hall to the vestibule, calling, "Here Loll-girl…"

With a happy face, he opened massive front doors and stepped out barefoot following Meggie's footprints into blowing snow, away from the immense limestone Tudor monstrosity, still impressive with its massive copper drainpipes—a miracle of survival in the changing Grosse Pointe Wood neighborhood.

Uncle Dez wandered the drive, passing broken statuary; slate roof fragments littering dead weeds, the old summer sleep den, his bare chest open to the wind and white hair sailing like silken flags.

"Lolly?" His voice floated away and tears leaked out of puzzled, faded eyes.

Chapter 4

10 Days Later, January 13, 2021

"Mackinac Bridge.
Sault Ste. Marie.
Otsego 50 mi"

State highway signs whipped by as I crossed the massive suspension bridge, entering the wild, remote Upper Peninsula, that peculiar orphan of Wisconsin attached to Michigan, while steering another relic of the Lodge Motor Co. that somehow managed to escape bankruptcy court. Excitement rose in my chest like a soap bubble, iridescent with hope and frightening thrill of an unexpected new life.

Punching buttons, I chinned my phone.

Thank all cell tower Gods. It's ringing.

****

Zak, snapping a chunky gold bracelet, let it ring…and *ring.* The theme from *The Godfather* wove its seductive tune.

Behind him, the room resembled a backstage littered with props and costumes. One sleeve of a white dinner jacket, caught in the closet door next to a Ralph Lauren third-hand tux, jammed in with tennis rackets and yachting gear. A professional crossbow and quiver of shafts propped carelessly in the corner alongside a set of mismatched yet good graphite clubs, as if Zak could be called on, for any occasion, at any opportunity.

He checked the call-name and looked away, then—

*****

"Yo. Got the man."

"Zak. Thank God. Afraid there'd be no towers. I-I mean no coverage. Where are you? Now? I tried to reach…you left so fast." *Like Custer fleeing the Indians.* "I wanted to tell you, I'm on my way to—"

"*Yeah, baby,*" Zak broke in, imitating Mike Myers. "The Catskills, Magpie. Can you dig the Catskills? I'm askin'? Gotta be there yesterday or all the borscht'll be gone."

"Yes, but, Zak…"

In his room, Zak glanced humorlessly outside. "Wakes. Memorials. Real downers, Magpie. Ya know I loved the old geezer. I did. I *loved* that old fart."

Silence.

"Sorry. Bad joke. Top billing Goldstein said. Maybe I can hone that horny, klutzy veterinarian bit."

"Wonderful, Zak! When—when did that come up?"

"Look! A joke. It's a joke, Magpie."

"It's Vegas!" I yelped.

"Something like that. Think I'd play *The Borscht Belt*? Not even there anymore."

"Never tell with you Zak, joking or not. Must be why I…"

He cut in. "Meggie, swear I'd quit stealing shtick, if I didn't have to ask, but…"

He looked outside bleak.

"How soon will the whadoyacallit. The *will* get probated?

****

30

He felt waves of what? emitting like cheap perfume from my silence. Disappointment—disapproval? Concentrating on the slippery road, I didn't answer, at least I told myself that.

"You get me! Money, cash, dough, simoleons—*moolah*. Don't make me beg, for God's sake! Some guys're givin' me grief," he finally mumbled.

"Are you in trouble! It's not cash, Zakkie. Not yet. Even then—?"

Zak despised hesitancy. Anything devoid of absolute certainty, I knew, when it came to what he wanted, needed—or thought he did.

"It's a frigging big house way out in the boonies! On a lake yet! Get a *loan* for Crissake? How hard can that be!"

I could see him now, thrusting fingers through his long dark hair in frustration, his eyes heated to a Mediterranean hue. I winced, part from the exasperation in his voice and my phone cutting out.

The phone's silence held a petulant quality.

"Antiques. Right—*right*? And woods. Lots of woods. Trees are worth a bundle." The phone cut back in, in time to for me to hear—*"read that somewhere."*

"Zachary?"

More dead space. Resentment in place of cajoling.

"You realize…?" I spoke like skirting landmines. "The lake house was left to *me* and…" *I suppose because I took care of Uncle, while you…* snipping that thought before it budded like a blighted rose.

"Don't have to hit me over the head with a rubber chicken."

I desperately tried to think of something clever in return. To tell him I would share. Of course, I would.

Zak, and Lance too!

Too late. The phone *clicked* in my ear.

Even now he was sorry. He'd ring later feeling bad, making me laugh out loud. He tried so hard for top drawer. Edgy before Vegas. If that was where he was going. I frowned then. But Zak wasn't aware of where I was, or why the bad reception.

He hadn't asked.

****

In the mirror over the cheap dresser, Zak swept a black hank slick and straight into a classy knob on the back of his head, so in vogue then. On him, it looked dangerous—piratical. Catching a cracked photo stuck in the edge of the mirror, he turned his mouth down, ruefully thumbing over the three of them posed all gap-toothed.

Damn. Were we idiots ever that young?

A rum team. Himself, lanky, shirtless with hair like Tarzan on a bad-hair day.

Meggie with her cute little face and skinny little legs, *before the accident.*

And Lance, in his usual pathetic scowling slouch.

Zak's affectionate, slightly melancholy grin lit up the shabby room.

He laughed. All three posed with ratty bows and arrows like the hoodlum Indians they were, when not being pirates or super heroes.

His handsome features drew together as he peered closer. In the background loomed the epitome of over-embellished Victorian lake-houses hemmed on three sides by a dense forest and object of the call.

"Christ! Look at all that wood."

He shrugged, for the first time wondering how much

was theirs, *hers* actually, and how much Federal Forest, also if the Feds would miss a couple trees? Meggie might get a few bucks for it. Christ, they were thick as the smoke in his cruddy dressing rooms back of the bar. Be doing them a favor really, he mused. Thinning them out.

Strange. As he was about to call Meggie, there she was. Always happened that way…if he waited long enough. His smile took on an odd quirk, as he gently thumbed her funny little face, whispering softly, "*Magpie…*" And carefully stuck the photo back on the mirror.

He sighed and went to the corner sorting through the archery set and golf clubs.

Big day ahead, maybe.

****

I quickly punched the phone.

No bars.

"Sugar bear! And down to thirty percent. A heater would help; naturally there's no working lighter in this old heap!" Inordinately fond of it as I was, the "Lodge Dagger's" wipers kept going *drudge, drudge,* in place of *flap-flap-dry.*

Just great.

I caught my face in the rear view. Startled and pleased. That *me*? Fresher, younger. Well—rested since Uncle passed away. I almost forgot what it was like not being wakened at three or four in the morning. Poor Uncle Dez.

A car honking in the decibels of the "1812 Overture" *with cannons,* unexpectedly flashed past my vintage Lodge Dagger convertible blinding me with a splat of slush, and nearly taking the driver's door with it. Suddenly aware of fat flakes dancing lazily off my windscreen, I punched the radio on a dash designed to resemble a rocket ship.

The announcer ended a snippet before the train wreck of commercials—"*something something, bla, bla.*" More about the latest dead girl. Didn't catch the name, plus salivating hints of a bizarre murder weapon, "not disclosed at this time."

"So many," I murmured, distracted by static as I fine-tuned Detroit's clear station, WJR, strong as an aural cross-country beacon and very comforting. *Damn. Missed the weather.* Sugar! I watched with first alarm the slush build-up caught on brittle wipers, smear my windshield, praying it wouldn't ice over.

Only 100—120 miles to go…

****

After the last Federal Highway sign, I veered onto a county two-lane. Snow now pranced a *Swan Lake* chorus before my dull twin-beams picking out sagging fences and fields with desiccated stalks poking through snow like yellowed bones. I shuddered. *Put a game face on, girl!*

Twenty minutes later by the still-working clock, I skidded into the county one-lane—a snow tunnel of overlapping firs encroaching the berm such as it was, and white blobs hurled suicidally against my headlamps while the Dagger's tires routinely slipped. Tried WJR again, calculating I still had fifty miles to go.

As the crow flies, the imp on my shoulder nastily reminded. *A dead crow…*

The gravelly road climbed a bit. I checked my cell. *Still no bars.* And of course, the lighter didn't work, even if I had a car charger. Then the car slithered up and over the top of the rise and the radio unexpectedly broke through.

"Thank God, a weather report," I muttered crossly.

The voice stuttered nasally loud when it was not squeaking in terror.

I grinned.

It happened before. I could see him now—a pimply-faced janitor in ill-fitting jacket, terrified before the mike, and the only member of the regular staff who had "made it in" to make the broadcast. My smile faded as I checked my side mirrors, worried now. *Must be getting bad ahead.* Then another local station boomed out, making me sit up and grip the wheel. I must be right on top of a tower. Sure enough, I spied the skeletal rigging of a lone country radio beacon.

"Well Upper-Michiganders! Looks like we're the buckle of the storm belt, tonight all righty! Radar shows a heap a cold wet stuff ablastin' our way..."

The voice was chortling, apparently with a weatherman's sadistic glee.

Static fritzed.

Then I heard, *"— Otsego, Presque Isle, clean up through Mackinac counties— "*

The Voice dissolved into fritzy static.

I glanced from my cell phone to the road. *No joke. I'm running smack into it!*

My boots jammed the brakes, at a flash of something moving from the corner of my eye. "All I need," I muttered, "is hit a freaking deer and smash the radiator." Then I'd be up the crick without a paddle. The mushy brakes compounded with slush seemed a formula for two perfect donuts as I suddenly swirled like a teacup ride at the local fair.

In one of the smeary windows of space I *thought* I

saw *someone*—a girl shivering by the berm, risking a look back mid-donut.

A blur of black and a pretty pale face. Or—only a small fir tree with a blot of snow? There and gone, as the Dagger slip-slid by. I hung on through another half-donut, and by that time my convertible slithered over a rise and around a curve between tall firs hugging the road.

Chapter 5

Deadly Cold

"Damn m'fuckin' bitch! How many freakin' cars out here tanight, anyways!"

The girl stomped up and down, swiveling left-right in the near whiteout. *Wisht my own piecea-crap car hadna went south on me.*

Oh! Wait! Another chance. Thank the Devil!

Goth Girl, unexpectedly sultry under the stark makeup, put her feet on the dash, never mind her mesh stockings had more holes than mesh. *My legs are white and plump and ya never can tell where somethin' might lead,* she hoped. "So, I told skuzzball where to hang'm an' how high! Knowhudi…? Whooopsi!" She broke off. "Gotta piddle. Kin I have a li'l ole pee break?"

Goth Girl fell out the door shrieking, draining, and tossing a beer can where it sank in snow, and staggering to clumps of bushes.

Didn't want nobudy ta see her personal bizniz.

Gotta pay fer that!

She giggled, screeching as she squatted and snow bit her bare butt. "Whooopsi! Gonna pee popsicles out here!" She called. "Hear that? Gonna pee pop—" Her pretty face under all that black and white, looked up surprised.

Not fearful yet.

"Oh! You too? More the hairier," she giggled, hating the nervous titter.

She hitched her tights. Too fast, she realized, sensing the cold wet and rising steam. *Half wet my damn britches. Hope that din' queer things. Dang that was nasty. Wet panties in the cold. Dang! My britches gonna stand up all by them fuckin' selves…*

"Oooh!" She rubbed her hands together all mock-jolly. *Had ta pretend sometimes, don'tya know.* She saw the *need* in the eye. "Le's you'n me get on back where's all nice and warm and have us a little *fun*. I don't mind." Goth Girl rushed the car. Ran toward the light, *the white light, back to tunnels of car beams, the warm running engine, to safety—*.

She stumbled past beams so welcoming-bright, snow sizzled off them, yanking too panicky at the door. *Never show fear!* "Hey!" Her voice came out a kitten's mew. "Why ya lock this bitchin' door?" She backed up, whining. "Whatcha lookin at me like that for?" The girl giggled nervous again. "Playing cowboys 'n injuns?"

She watched something closely, with cross-eyed intensity, sneering, "that's so fuckin' lame!" And stumbled, looking sideways. The woods were deeper there, but the arrow still tracked her. Maybe the driver's side. Maybe get in the car and— She circled and tried to sidle past the hood, swiveling her butt across so's she could keep the psycho in view.

Almost there. Too freakin' easy, the keys 'll be there. Ah well. Too late. *The arrow motioned.* All Goth Girl's senses where focused on that sharp metal tip.

Please! She addressed that sharp point—*please,* waving her hand as if brushing away death. Futile. She could tell by the look, the coldness, the blankness of eyes like two dull stones.

"Take it off."

"If—if I do? This is freakin' weird, ya know?" Goth Girl thrust her chest out and put her hands on her hips and started to stomp over. "You some kinda perv? Will ya lemme back in? I'll like so, do *anything!* Like, ya know?"

"Yes."

There was a finality in that statement, like the first clod of dirt to hit the coffin, a confident inevitability Goth Girl didn't cotton to none. She stumbled but carried on. The voice spoke volumes. As if the deed were done and she already flat out, spread-eagled in sex in the cold, but this time with an arrow in her chest, not a thing up her twat.

She wasn't really a Goth, she wanted to explain, a last testament to her character, or if it might make a difference. In the U. P. she was the closest thing to it and damn sorry now, that Goth Girls fancied skimpy skirts and net hose and that she was quite pretty, even the black lip color, purple shadow, and chalk makeup could not hide.

"Ferget it, sicko!" Goth Girl stalked toward the road. "I ain't a playin'!"

"Hold still. Cunt."

Her bravado was no use against that business-like strong bow, gleaming, polished to a warm honey against the all-white gloom. Goth Girl stood there beaten but not recognizing she was, watching the increasingly agitated tip. Numb, she disrobed naked down to her boots. *Get this over.*

Goth Girl playing her last card, snapped between clenched jaws to keep from stuttering, only partly from the frigid air. "I like k-kinky sex, any ole time but do it got to be in the cold?"

Something, well, not good, but not the worst could come out of this, yet. She shuddered uncontrollably, hoping the damned psycho-sicko wouldn't think she was ready to pee again, so afraid, she clenched her knees and held her sex with one hand, her breasts with another.

"Boots too," her killer answered.

Delay the inevitable. Goth Girl relished the cold as if finally comprehending it was her last earthly sensation—she'd best embrace it with all her skinny needle-marked arms, as Goth Girl kicked off her boots, then looked down laughing at the arrow plunged to its bright red fletch. She viewed it like slo-motion—the metal tip just entering, the first piercing cut, the cold metal barb creating a hole, the burning slide of a wooden shaft through her chest walls, a bare heartbeat after hearing the singing *twanggggg* of the bow-string.

Then a searing pain, when flesh is rubbed hard in an old fashioned *Indian-burn*, as the shaft tore its way clean through. She toppled backward as she thought she would, which thrust the arrow back out a few inches as it hit frozen earth, and waited for the sick assault.

She could scream.

But as her eyes looked up through trees lacey with dead branches, a dollop of cold wet stuff fell on her face—a last indignity and slush melted in her mouth, denying Goth Girl even a last voice.

"Have it your way, then leave..." She thought she whispered.

Her cheeks were slabs of stone, mouth frozen open. Still, she thought—*I can make it to the road.* But only a wet warm gargle gushed out with an upwelling of blood.

The last thing she heard were footsteps crunching away. Her flesh was chilling, matching the snow…

Chapter 6

One Mean Bastard

The road was pure up-country now. *Good old northern U.P.!* Half gravel, half tarmac, half dirt, half nowhere. I laughed then. "And dead as a freakin' cemetery." The last traffic was left behind an hour ago. I remembered the car beams in my face behind me that disappeared. I remembered the girl. Can't be too careful though.

But, sugar, it was cold!

I tried the radio again. More static filled the car like aural barb wire scratching my ears. I squinted through wipers now, blowing my fingers in relief at the blessed sight of a diner/gas/grocery's, red and yellow beacon glowing cheerful through the whiteout.

Heck yes! Might not be the worst idea I had that night. *Oh yeah? Like running off without telling anyone?* I saw a yellow shape move behind wet, runneled glass as the Dagger slued sideways across an acre of ice-coated gravel—and the neon sign blinked out.

"Oh no! Sugar!" I beat the steering wheel, slammed the door, and tottered over a parking lot littered with gritty cubes of ice, hearing distant locks *snick* with finality. "Damned boots!" I cussed. I would have to wear my pointy-heels in the name of vanity. *No limp was going to get me down! Stupid stupid in this weather.*

"Wait!" I slapped the door. The yellow shape loomed. A hand wiped a space in the glass and a ruddy moon-face with wide set brown raisin eyes of a female, about thirty-five with frizzy hair tamed by an old-fashioned waitress cap and a hair net low on the brow, peered out. "*Agnes*" embroidered on a hanky, stuck from her yellow pocket.

"*Agnes*" mouthed—"*closed.*" And started to lumber off. "Oh! No!" I slapped the window, panicking of a sudden—a whim became *need* as I realized I fled the barren house in Grosse Pointe without even a thermos of tea, or coffee. "*Please. Just coffee!*" I mouthed.

Pathetically hugging my politically incorrect fur, thin with age, I stamped up and down. *Have some pride girl,* I lectured myself and scowled. The face loomed again—*oh yes!* behind the door studying me. Perplexity lowered her hairnet almost to her brows. Then the locks snicked the door opened, releasing humid air with a hamburger grease perfume. Heaven.

"Wouldn't keep a mangy old dog out onna night like this!" 'Agnes' boomed cheerfully.

Mangy? Did she look at my coat as she said that?

I rushed in before Agnes changed her mind.

I scarcely paused to check the higgledy-piggledy mess of business cards, notices for barn sales, boats, fishing permits, babysitting, used household items, wood and brush-clearing, posters, or pathetic snapshots of missing teens plastered over each other in the weather vestibule, vaguely registering them in my haste to enter the hamburger heaven.

"Didn't reckon get no business," Agnes boomed out as if I were across the room. "Just goes to show. Keep me company whilst I clears up, guess."

"Thanks. A bunch. I am *ever* so grateful," I gushed awkward. *Shoot was that from a Bette Davis film?*

Agnes lingered doubtfully as she watched me limp to the booths. Both wide-eyed and curious, she cocked her head. "Where'd you get that there gimp-leg at?"

I froze, before slipping into the red Naugahyde booth.

"I was attacked by—" I hesitated "—dogs."

I didn't understand why I did that—made up stories. It made me seem more interesting, I guess. Harmless enough. At times, though I was way too young, I told, "I caught the last case of polio before the vaccine," as if a car crash was shameful.

Agnes squinted. "At's too bad. Bet you was real purty once't though," she added earnestly.

I checked myself in a napkin dispenser. *E-gods. I did look pulled though a knothole backwards.* But Agnes had already turned to a smeary blackboard where most entries were wiped-off ghosts.

"Gottsum real good chili. Bin cookin' ona backburner since yes-tiday."

I said, doubt creeping in my voice. "That'd be good?"

"An here's a little old bitty wedge a pie too small to sell, on the house." She plunked a weepy-looking lemon meringue slice before me, pouring hot bitter coffee, no doubt also on the back burner all day.

A phone jangled in back. Agnes lumbered over and bellered, "You got Aggie!" She guffawed at a joke, chatted a bit and hung up.

Of course, it's not for me. I fumbled my cell anyway, dropping it back in my purse, troubled.

"Jes soon string two tamaty juice cans together as

44

them things." Agnes plunked down an inch-thick china bowl filled with steaming chili. "Don't get no signal in the boonies nohow."

No shit Sherlock.

Digging pockets for crackers, she spilled a handful of jellies out too. Stupidly, I didn't put them in my pocket.

"Do you serve beer? Wine perhaps?" I asked innocently as I blew and spooned a bit.

Sugar that was good. Definitely the way I liked it. Not too spicy, with a hint of sweet. I laughed. "I don't usually drink but—" I waved indicating the night.

"Folks buy in the grocery," Agnes sniffed, "if they feel they have the *need*."

I shrugged at her subtle moralizing, polishing off the surprisingly tasty chili, realizing I was hungry, cold, and starved for company. Smiling apologetically before any more lectures, I rushed to the grocery section through an archway, before Agnes, wiping an already clean counter, could stop me.

Foolishly, I hadn't given food a thought, as I roved gallon-sized jars of pickled-pigs' feet. *No!*

Hard boiled eggs and the grandmother of all dill pickles floated in other jars. *Maybe.* Next to the cash register, a similar jar with a ragged black and white photo of a teen girl taped to the side, was stuffed with dollar bills and coins. I didn't see, "what for," as I raked work gloves, tins of snuff, paperbacks, cheap china dolls, gluten-free diet books, *Prayers for the Day*…

"Look lady. Bin a long day and my dogs is tired."

"I'll be extra quick. I promise."

"Okay. Gotta lock up in back. No checks'r nuthin though," she warned lumbering off.

I watched her head to the rear. Rapidly grabbing up eggs, peanut butter; Jiffy, extra crunchy, Wonder Bread, a brick of cheap spice cake, spam, two cans of tuna, five withered apples, a pound box of sugar, tea bags, browning bananas, instant coffee, powdered creamer, two boxes of cuppa soup, rusty cans of off brand tomato and chicken rice soup, a ramen noodle, dusty on top— put it back, grape jam, two big Hershey's with Almonds, snatching a box of plain white candles at the last-minute feeling mature and capable. A paltry amount at the time, but the selection would manufacture glorious worshipful memories.

One never knew.

Funny, how I had never stopped at this needful establishment before, feeling uncommonly grateful for Agnes.

Curled and overlapping, five posters of missing teens and young women going back years, taped to the counter's glass front caught my eye, but again I was side-tracked by rows of glittering gorgeous dark brown, gold, and russet liquor bottles behind the cash register— *vodka, tequila, flavored brandy, but mostly off-brand whiskey.*

Shining bottles of amber forgetfulness.

No wine. Not popular, I guessed, but pyramids of beer. Not my thing either, yet the glass case of cigarettes, now that was a horse of a lovely shade—all those tempting colors and logos!

I admired the way Barbara Stanwick smoked in *Double Indemnity letting smoke curl into her nose, and out again in soft plumes shading half-closed eyes and a sultry mocking*—giving myself a mental shake. *Focus!*

Yes, the lock dangled. Merely a couple packs to see

me through the weekend or whatever. Vague on that. Yet, I could always return for more, when I had things sorted out— and pay her too.

What's the saying? When Man plans, God laughs. In my case, God must have been having a real hootenanny.

I bit my lip, grabbing three of the whiskies in front and four packs of *whatever*...turned out to be "American brand" with an Indian logo; tossing them in my large bag, quickly re-shuffling the bottles before Agnes's return.

Pinching my slim wallet, I vowed, *I'll make it up— later.*

I placed two more bottles and one pack of cigs on the counter with my groceries as Agnes returned, adding up my bounty. "Twenty-eight dollars...an ninety...two...cents." She waited fidgety.

I pinched my purse—*how appallingly light it was—* reluctantly shelling out the twenty, and eight ones, I scooped up the two sacks, with Agnes shooing me out by her yellow-clad bulk.

At the door I glanced at the two ancient pumps outside. "How much is gas?" *Might know the deeper I travel, the more the cost...idiot.*

Agnes shrugged on her puffy coat. "Don't make no never mind. Pumps locked. Management," she said cryptically, then stopped, staring out. "Hold the phone! At's a Lodge Dagger. My Pop had one a those."

I looked out at my vintage car. Wondered if that would get me gas. Apparently, Agnes wasn't that impressed.

"Might say it's a family car." I began. "Stopped making them in—" and lost interest, suddenly tired, flinching as wind blasted the door.

"Hear 'at?" Agnes doubled down. "TV man sez this is one mean bastard, pardon my *Fran-say*. Socked in 'tween here'n Ironwood. County Mounties won't let Santy Claus through, I reckon," she chuckled. "Where you say you was aheadin'?"

I looked bleak at the sideways-blowing snow feeling like I wanted to hug that bit of me close. "I didn't." Then shrugged. "Just the lake."

She made a noise. "Lotsa lakes out here." Then, Agnes, imitating the Goodyear Blimp in puffy tubes of down, checked my shabby fur and thin boots. "Best be careful now. Don't stop for nobody and keep your..." She studied the Dagger's flimsy rag top through blowing snow. "...self, locked in," she uttered doubtfully.

Thanks for the reassurance. "Of course." I looked at her, curious. "Promise."

"Suit yourself. Sure, I can't take you no place? Town's only 'bout twelve miles from here. Well—okey-dokes." Agnes waved, crunched over and climbed in her stolid Cherokee, as I skated to the convertible; hand-scraping windshield ice, I slipped in the crackling cold seat manually rolling down a window to clear the side mirror, all the while watching Agnes's bloody tail-lights turn pink in the white-out.

Bet her heater's on full blast.

I rummaged for one of the bottles, uncapped it and took a deep pull. *Sugar bear, that was warm and fine....*

Chapter 7

Hazard Warnings

"HSSSST!"

I adjusted the rear view, one hand on the gear lever, the other on my heart, barely making out a girl huddled by Agnes's dumpsters and rushing my car like a linebacker.

"Heya!"

The girl slapped the hood effectively stopping me, yelling through the windshield. "That fat bitch gone?"

While I stared, the girl yanked the door handle and hopped in with blast of cold.

"Don't drive away from me, lady! Not in this crap!"

"Hold on there. Who the—?"

"Nevermind *who,* girlfriend. That cow!" Indicating the vanished Jeep, "hates thumb-riders. Guess who's stuck with me?" She grinned cheekily. "Can't leave me. All kinda shit goin' on. Livin' under a rock? Ain't you heard the radio?" Only she pronounced it, raaadi-o. "I'd be piss'n in my..."

"Enough! I got it! Okay. What in God's name is wrong with you girls? Don't you care?"

"Yeah, yeah, gramma."

"Grandma! Hold on." *I'm the same age as you.*

"Hey! Sor-ry, but you do get that pissy little old lady look, about-cha, ri' now."

"Sure know how to sweet-talk. But I'm not moving an inch. How do I know—?"

I flashed a spooked look past the girl, all skin, and bones, hoping I didn't show how nervy *I* was. Sometimes they work in teams—one distracts, the other robs you blind and slits your throat. Then, I saw the torn jeans, more holes than jean, thin flannel shirt and faded windbreaker with a "Detroit Tigers" logo, plus a flabby "Hello Kitty" duffle riding her back.

"You nuts!" The girl smirked. "We just met. Course ya don't know me. Geeesh! Not like you invited me to a pajamer party. *Not.*"

She settled back, huffing. "Brother! Kinda people I let pick me up these days. Well, let's go!" She made little shooing motions. "This heap got any thin' like heat?"

I thrust the car in gear to stop the barrage. "Don't get where I'm supposed to let you off…"

"Like I'd give this dump a rep." The girl scowling back at the diner, overrode me. "Not!" She unwrapped a sucker, slurping it noisily and that apparently gave word to thought.

"Givin' this big ole trucker *lap candy?*" She rolled her eyes.

I rolled *my* eyes.

The girl continued. "An uh—said he'd brung me outta burger. Cause he ain't sposed to carry riders…*of any kine*," she giggled.

I made a face as I carefully eased, more like slithered out on the road. "Yeah. Not!"

"Got that right. I skip inta the john an when I come out—? Hey! My belly's touchin' my backbone." The girl leaned over and snatched a bag. "Whatcha got here?"

I grabbed her, swerving. "Hold on!"

But the girl's jacket rode up revealing her bony ribs. "Bread?" I offered weakly.

"Bread, hunh? Okeydokey. Guess in a beat up ol shit pile like this, can't expect *'Little Debbie's.'* That's my name. Debbi. With a 'i.' Hey—"

Debbi babbled on. I tuned her out. This train was going off track, *fer shure,* imitating the girl's twang in my head.

****

It *was* a real bastard, as Agnes had warned. Twiddling the radio, a hair at a time, I concentrated more on the road than my unwelcome rider. After Jimmy Haggard faded, a male commentator grated through the crackling… *"hindering search—female…dangerous… Picked…night for it…pity…local patrols…"* then, final-sounding screeches and I could not fiddle the knob to a clearer station to save my life.

I flashed a look at my passenger, eyeing the thin rabbit coat fitting her like a second skin. I made a tiny snort Debbi missed. If this girl concealed anything bigger than a nail file under that get up—spying her skinny rib cage once more, as she stretched and the waist-length jacket rode up—I'm a jumpy old maid.

*Well, I am, but…*I shook my head, smiling grimly. *Sugar! What was wrong the me. Don't be lame. What? Is she carrying a cleaver in that Miss Kitty rucksack? A gory baseball bat, with bloody hair still clinging?* I laughed involuntarily.

"Watch out! Jeeeese, Louise!"

Debbi shot scathing looks at me, as I slued past flares on either side of a skewed Patrol car. We both watched a petite female deputy in bulky olive-green pick her way over, then Debbi dived under the dash. I threw a frown her way and un-cranked the window.

"Nother accident down thata away, ma'am. Nigh impassable." She waved her arm with concern. "Don't see how you're gettin' where you're goin'?"

"You said nigh? How, ah—nigh?"

The petite woman, plain as a mailbox under her Mountie hat shrugged into the dizzying snow. "This stuff? Live down there do ya? Not much down—"

The deputy's manner stiffened as she heard me say, 'The lake.' Hooting, "Lake Champagne? That what rich folk call it. More like Convict Lake, reckon I recall. Either way, better skedaddle on back where you come from, know what's good."

I was desperate for warmth and a roof over my head. "But I need to get home!"

She shook her head and scanned the forest.

"Your kind never do. Well, no doubt the roads will part for *you*. Jes like Moses." She headed smartly back and waved, more a—*get outta here,* than *good luck.*

"Wait!" I yelled against the hurtling snow. "I always liked the name, *Convict Lake!*"

The deputy briefly saluting, gunned around us.

Debbi uncapped my whiskey. "Stuck up Pig-bitch!"

I grabbed the bottle, struggled for the cap, and screwed it back on one-handed. "Don't! Just don't!" *Sugar!*

****

I eased two more tedious miles through a clinging wet blanket of wooly white. Peering through the blizzard, I fishtailed another U-ie within inches of a big-bellied figure in a smokey bear hat looming foursquare by a whited-out Dodge Ram truck, with its lights glowing sickly yellow. I made out a Forest Ranger logo as my poor car slid to another unscheduled stop.

Stone-faced, the Ranger looked like he'd rather die under my slick tires than give an inch. I roved the guns racked in back, flicking over an industrial-strength crossbow in the rear—a hunting bow I supposed. To complete the picture, a row of kills—silhouetted deer heads, marched under the window below a Michigan State Seal.

"Cripes! Don't frickin' buh-lieve this! What is this? A frickin' *Pig* convention?"

I threw Debbi a grim look. "Me neither, but something's sure not Kosher. He's not a policeman anyway. Hang tight."

"Think he'll hit on me?"

I threw Debbi a scathing glance while un-cranking the window. Snow bit my face. The Ranger leaned in with a wave of beer, onions, and acrid piney aftershave.

"Ma'am? Registration? Driving pretty erratic back there, were'ncha?"

"Certainly. I mean—no! Under the circumstances…" I waved. "All this *white* stuff. I missed my turn," I lied. "Uh…" I checked his insignia. *Forest Ranger?*

"Officer. Umm, what department are you?"

"And what turn might that be, ma'am? I'll ask the questions." The big black-mirrored glasses reflected my face, white and scared. He didn't wait for an answer. "Not much, this neck of the wood, 'cept the prison cross't the ways. Road's socked in."

"So, I've been told." *Many times.* "Didn't realize you fellas had jurisdiction—"

"Papers, ma'am."

I groped for my bag. For a sick minute, I feared I left

it at Agnes's and shoved Debbi desperately aside. Laughing, I joked, "Guess that's why they call me, Magpie!" As I reached over Debbi digging side pockets, I could sense the Ranger bending his big body and poking his head in, flashing the open glove box with a torch, leisurely shining it over Debbi, and then the open bottle. His face stiffened.

"Ma'am, mind steppin' out of your ve-hicle?"

"But I have it!" I waved the crumpled registration.

The Ranger lingered on Debbi's bare knees and cheeky face. "Sit tight, sweet stuff." His meaty lips curved a toothy grin. He studied my papers as if deciphering ancient Aramaic—back at me—lingering on Debbi a couple heartbeats while Debbi opened her coat to show her tight sweater and jiggly little tits.

He winked at her, then turned to me, barking, "Open the trunk, ma'am," never taking his appreciative ogle off Debbi.

"The—the…? You think I'm hiding *what*? A convict?"

****

A mile off as the crow flies, a gaunt Indian and a burley bald white guy both draped in prison-gray blanket-ponchos, one belted with lengths of rope and one with duct tape, plowed fitful drifts around Convict Lake. They avoided the lake's darker spots, where springs welled up turning the snow to thick clingy mush. Sometimes their bound feet splashed through the tiny rim of open water and lacy ice crawling the shore-line, before the true, thick lake ice began. Stuck in the makeshift belts; knives, from hand-crafted screwdrivers and razor blades embedded in toothbrushes wrapped in more masking tape, to a claw hammer and a rusted railroad spike.

****

"Funny you should ask, miss." The Ranger waved to the dense mass of trees surrounding us. "Federal land. Most of it. Outsiders pretend the Fed Pen over there don't exist." The mirrors studied me. "Proceed to the rear please."

"This isn't right," I whispered to Debbi.

"What ain't?" Debbi blurted pawing my purse and checking out my lipstick.

"Never mind." It was futile taking Debbi away from *herself.* I grabbed the lipstick, got out and resenting the Ranger swaddled in his sheep-lined bomber jacket, braced against the wind taking icy bites of my ratty fur, as always, trying to control my limp with feet like wood weights and watchful eyes on my back, I lurched around the rear and popped the massive trunk lid.

As the Ranger leaned over the trunk, piney aftershave reminding me of toilet bowl cleaner insinuated up my nose making me sneeze. With his hand on the lid, which threatened to close anyway, he played a light between lumpy blankets and Debbi flirting through the rear window.

Brushing my breasts, he poked about prodding an old lap robe; hearing the clunk of tire irons and odds and ends, slammed the lid.

The black mirrors on me again.

"Don't wanna scare your little friend none," he whispered as if Debbi could hear. "But a bunch a loonies from the Rez, high-tailed it again. Hom-i-ci-dal Killers."

"Thought most killers were, uh, *homicidal.*"

He reddened. "Don't get sassy, missy. The worst

kind—*if ya get what I mean*," he said heavily. "Ain't safe, two gals on their stony lonesome. Two-three gals missin' right now since summer!"

He was getting angry. Louder. Bellowing against the blustering wind.

"One a month a while back! And one recent. *Real recent,*" he hammered home. His face was growing red, seeming to swell.

I eased to the car door.

"Don't you gals get it? I happened to be familiar with one of 'em," he hissed, nailing me with the black mirrors. "May. No better'n she should be." He glowered at me as if I did it. I felt he must have known her better than he admitted.

"I'm s-sorry," I stammered.

"And ain't all—" He stopped abruptly. He seemed lost, staring blind into the woods so long I checked around to see what he saw.

****

Ten years ago. High summer. Humid air black with mosquitos deafening with their whine. A car eased to a weedy berm. A young woman in cutoffs, little more than a Band-Aid between her legs, got out rubbing her arms, scratching, and slapping.

"All right, I'm here! You said someplace nice. Nice to me, means refrigeration! Air conditioning. An upscale mo-tel!" May kicking at dead pine needles snapped. "What is this?" She sneered wrinkling her nose. "You're cute, honey but not that cute. And bloodsuckers are eating me alive."

"Not the worst of your problems."

A hint of burbling laughter she didn't like.

"Out there, May."

"I said I don't wanna make it out here in the woods, cheapskate!"

"Gotta surprise."

May glared at the gloomy woods. "Seen enough trees to last me a lifetime. Why do you think I'm doin' this? For fun? With you!"

"You don't listen."

May, A pretty blond, other times, other places, a slam dunk for Charlize Theron, save a missing side tooth, sighed. "Crud! Let's see your money and get it over with."

Instead, she found herself pushed deeper into the trees.

"That's far enough! Ow-wah!" May slapped her arm.

"Know what I like?"

"No! What?" May snapped. "Gettin' et up by skeeters?"

"Bare shoulders in the moonlight. In fact, bare everything."

"With these bloodsuckers? Get real!" May tried to push past. Then she saw it. And looking into the woods, backed on her own accord.

"Nothing like a body...pure. White. Sculpted by moonlight. Marble tombstones. Beautiful. Pale. Bloodless. Hard."

May's lips trembled in a rictus grin. "Crazy...you are crazy as a frothin' at the mouth dog. I had a dog with distemper once, acted crazy as you! And I'm not removin' my clothes no matter your fancy-shmancy talk." May giggled nervously, but all her bravado leaked out at the sight of that sturdy bow, the arrow drawn from behind her tormentor's head, the arm quivering, nock fitted on taut string, the red fletch, and most of all, the lethal point aimed straight at her, mesmerizing her into inaction.

"Undress."

"No!" May stumbled back.

"Ever see an arrow stick out of a head on both sides? Funniest thing. Ya gotta laugh. No? Steve Martin? You don't know Steve Martin?"

"Yeah, sure," she placated. "I know old Steve…good ole Steve…"

The arrow motioned. "I don't believe you, May. Move."

"Yeah, yeah. He was on Saturday Night—" She wriggled out of her short skirt.

"Shoes."

"Shoes?" Her face twisted. May flipped her jeweled thongs off. The better to run.

The arrow raised higher, head level, and motioned again.

May hip-hopped backward barefoot on dead leaves, stickers, glass fragments, over whatever flotsam was spat out by passing cars. The mosquitoes and no-see-ums were a welcome distraction from her bubbling fear as they feasted on her fear-sweat.

"Run!"

You got that right. May eyed the road.

"Not that way."

The arrow wavered past her.

May turned and ran heedlessly over a crackle-crunch of leaves, swatting firs leaving scratches on her legs, arms, scraping her face, yanking her hair in league with the devil back there.

Fearful anticipation lifted like an acid bubble in her

throat, only to pop with the twang of the string and hissing whirrrr *of a shaft rocketing through the air.*

She even heard the thunk, like a car hit her, the split second before her skin pierced with a silken sigh. The jolt didn't register until sliding between fat and muscle, skittering off her backbone—could even hear and feel the grate of the tip shearing off bone a hair from her heart, lodging deep in her lung.

Her murderer paced to May, loosely holding the bow, placed a foot on her back.

May tried to speak, feeling the hand...the excruciating tug. Hearing the wet ripping as gloved hands began to yank the arrow out.

The barbs caught tearing muscle, lacerating the heart, loosing precious gouts of blood. Mosquitoes whined a crescendo zeroing in, hundreds sinking their own barbs—gorging...

Then in a swift reload: as promised the second punched through her skull right above her left ear.

May gasped and slumped gazing sightlessly with eyes that bulged out like a cartoon character.

"Funniest thing..." was the last she heard.

Chapter 8

Frost Bite

Squinting through the blizzard, I scanned the woods encroaching the country road, expecting thugs in striped pants to come plunging out, realizing I had a cartoon image in my head. *Focus!* While I was looking, away, the Ranger pinned the big mirrors back on me. *Okay I get it! Now can I get back in my car?*

"Rez?" I mumbled instead, jamming hands under my pits, and stamping up and down. *Get the hint?*

"Officer, it's freezing. I really need to get home. I got kids…and…"

The ranger barked a laugh, over-riding me. "Rez away from *home!* So many Indians locked up in the old days, all liquored up, now it's more prison ward for the DTs. Can't help their nature," he said jovially. "Have a weakness. But it could be anybody, just ta be po-lit-i-cally correct, as they say." He poked me with his elbow. "Could be you."

"Is that supposed to be funny?" I bit my lip, thinking of that open whiskey bottle. That was my business, but Debbi made it his! For an instance, I wondered if I could palm Debbi off on him, but the moment passed, or something made me not trust him. I don't know. Lord alone knows what she'd spout off about me. It was cold. I was miserable. Agnes's chili was making a repeat performance in my angst. Call it brain freeze. Far better I had.

Shut up or you'll be here all night.

"Unless you think it is, Miss." The black mirrors scanned the woods. "Only happens, most in-digenous up here, *is* the Indian. One scarpers ever now and then, goes on a well-oiled warpath, hatchet'n all."

"Well, I harbor no Indians, drunk or sober." *And, I'd like to discuss Politically Correct sociology with you till the cows come home, but...*

I scooted past him, diving in the haven of my, now frigid car, punching the lock.

"Good notion, ma'am."

"Pig in a blanket!" Debbi smirked.

"Shush!" I fingered the window crank, but he clamped the window frame with a gloved hand resembling a ham hock. "Keeping yourself locked safe inside your ve-hicle." He eyed me coldly with the big black mirrors, and rummaged a tin, stuck a wad between his lip and jaw, *all the time in the world.* "Yes sir! Lotsa killings, these parts. One last year, froze solid as a rock. Looked like a ice sculpture!" He seemed pleased with his description, droning on while I watched the cold wet stuff mounting on my windshield, barely hearing... "Animals of some kind, got to another though...that warn't so purty."

At that, I began cranking, regardless of his fingers. *This was getting way weird.* "Enough bedtime stories, officer, sir," I smiled—*like Hedy Lamar,* I hoped. "We got the message. *In spades.* We'll scurry on home now, if you—umm—?"

The Ranger effortlessly kept his gloved fingers in an inch of open window, halting the upward slide.

Scowling, he motioned me to crank it down again.

Fudge!

I elbowed Debbi pressing me as she grinned up at the Ranger through the window.

"Now—now, now." He smirked at Debbi. "Where wuz you two a hurryin' this time a night, in this shitstorm anyways? Pardon my plain talk. Good to be tuckered up all warm in bed!" He oozed with a big shit-eating grin. "Why not I follow you on home? Or, heya!" He snapped gloved fingers as if he just thought of it. *Right.* "Gotta idee. You hop in my truck here. Know a place slaps a slab a beef that'll set us up right. Twin Pine Mo-tel down the road. Couple drinks and a nice warm—"

"Why sure, Officer. I just loves big ole slabs of beef," Debbi simpered. "And purely what Sis and I was aplannin' if you'd quit hittin' on me!" Then, right when I thought Debbi would follow him to the ends of the earth for a drink and a warm bed, no matter whose, even this Nazi, Debbi gave the Ranger the finger. *Oh no, Debbi.* But it did the trick. The Ranger backed, palms up with a face hard as red granite.

"I don't think we have anything to worry about, Officer…but I really appreciate—the warning and pardon my sister. I can't do a *thing* with her, since she left the institution," I said, earning a kick in the shin. My bad leg, already aching from tromping on the gas and stomping through snow. This promised to be a *long* night. Cannot wait to get home. *Home.* A strange word.

Not, *The Lake House* now, but 'home.'

Suppose I had to take her along too.

I gunned around him as fast as bald tires and slick roads permitted.

In the rear view, the ranger still watched us, great

booted feet wide, arms curved like reaching for a gun. Black rounds of glasses were two holes in the blizzard. No doubt remembering my license, until snow blotted him out.

* × * *

"That was smart!"

Debbi uncapped the bottle smugly, taking a long swallow. "Lard bag! Worked didn't it? What was all that about Indians? I'm kinda Indian."

I yanked the precious bottle. "Thought Indians didn't talk much!"

"That there's a *stereotype!*" Debbi huffed.

I rolled my eyes and swerved hard, almost missing the old logging road-cum-shortcut. Slithering broadside between an overgrown gap, making a sharp left in the recalled forest trail, I plowed on, firs brushing the car on both sides for two miles or so. As suspected, snow lightened here.

"Let Loverboy Ranger try and follow us," I soothed as Debbi kept swiveling and looking anxious. "Don't worry, I know this place like the back of my hand. Shortcut."

As promised, the trail petered out near a wooded slope, with a ragged path for the foolhardy leading down to an acre or so of clearance. My dubious inheritance, *at last* hulked large, turreted, and many-gabled against a vast moon-struck Convict Lake shimmering a platinum welcome at us.

Debbi stared down goggle-eyed. Her reaction would have been humorous if the moment hadn't meant so much to me. "No way, girlfren!" Debbi yelped. "Ain't goin down there!" Scandalized. "Looks like that *Munster* house I seen on TeeVee-Land!"

To nail her concern, an inhuman groan rumbled from the ice like a giant belch.

"Damn. Lake's yellin' at us."

"Maybe it's saying, *welcome*," I mocked.

I wouldn't tell her the lake manufactured wails, groans, and cracks like booms of thunder time to time. Something to do with air and temperature changes I thought vaguely.

"Not!"

I smiled grimly and thrust the car in gear, more sliding than driving the fire trail down the grade, sluing across the "lawn," right before careening into my boathouse. Debbi watched me sourly as I switched off the ignition and sat back savoring the quiet and beauty of star-spangled night, until my feet screamed, they were turning into two blocks of ice and Debbi started making grumbling noises.

"Take that suitcase"

"Ain't your servant, neither."

"Freeze then." I grabbed two cases and the grocery bags shuffling through shin-deep snow, to an old latticed-in porch. Hipping the groceries, I groped for the key above the door. Behind me, I glimpsed Debbi checking the eerie yard, leaping gingerly through white stuff and yes, bitching, but carrying a box. I hid a smile...*but really, did I need this*?

I gazed up the sheer side of the old house with the black eyes of windows. Maybe company wasn't such a bad thing.

****

At the end, though, I so wanted to be alone.

Walk the rooms.

Have the old house wrap me in a blanket of

emotional memories. I smiled as I stepped into my kitchen. Sweet lazy mornings with Lance, Zak, and Uncle Dez over burnt pancakes, gallons of maple syrup, enough butter to launch the Queen Mary, and Dez's bitter black coffee when we were too young to drink it. Fishing expeditions. Our first matching archery sets, and when I won the county fair competition beating out the boys...

As a slant of moon highlit the kitchen's homely features, gelled in the aspic of time, I forgot Debbi breathing down my neck.

Plus, I had plans. Already I could see the antiques to keep, and changes to come...Then grinned. That simple notion of a future seemed so alien until now. I had been wedded to Uncle's care. I dare not think of a life, let alone, a rosy one, as my hungry gaze roved the old '30s Kelvinator Fridge with the generator on top still grumbling away.

I didn't register it was on, at the time. Outside of manufacturing outstanding cars, Uncle Dez wasn't the most forward-looking soul. I ran a fond glance over the beige and green porcelain high-topped gas range, ditto the porcelain table edged in a thin red stripe with a tin shaded light dangling over all.

A galvanized tub still hung on the wall. I always fancied the red handled hand-pump hunched over the zinc sink resembled a broke-neck animal. Still did, I grinned. Even the scrubbed-white, wooden drain board, and caddy of mismatched knives, all endearing. I yanked the chain. Wan light shone a soft moon, not quite reaching the open servant stairs leading to the fourth floor, or half-open cellar door right beside it.

I frowned at an upended glass on the drain, fingering

a spoon in the sink. These homely objects seemed sinister somehow, ominous in the drear light as if the ghost of the last user still lingered. Who could that be? Funny? Then, Debbi, grumbling as usual, dropped the box on the table and I forgot the anomalies.

****

The Indian and Bald Man straining against the wind biting through flimsy ponchos, turned as one toward the faint glow leaking through trees from Meggie's kitchen window. The lake curved outward at that point and they were behind the house. It would be shorter going through the woods than following the shore.

****

I tossed car keys skittering under the wooden drain board, when Debbie poked me on the shoulder, complaining. "Cold as a bitch in here! Barrel of laughs for little Debbi tonight! Not!"

Sugar bear. Almost forgot the despicable girl.

True enough. The house was a solid box of chill straight from the house's bones and jealously retained I recalled, even when July outside. Going to close the cellar door, not liking that slice of night through its opening, or chill must of coal dust emanating up like sour breath I ignored her. Peering into pitch dark, I called back, "Cold as a bitch out there, too. Which d'you prefer?"

Debbi watched me wide eyed. "Like I'd go down there."

"Spare me—*not!*" I shot back. Reaching blind in the dark, I punched a button switch on the wall by steps leading down to a 'Michigan Basement'—a foundation of native stone, stumps, concrete block, all three, or whatever was on hand, and a beaten earth floor, usually clammy with the essence of mold and coal dust—still not unpleasant, rather like truffles...*or a grave*.

Shivering, I punched the button again.

A dead *kluck!* answered. I struck a match from a box kept for that purpose on the steps, intending to check the furnace when Debbi's voice floated down.

"Hey! This where some dude grabs ya from under the stairs? Hey! Don't leave me up here! Alone!" She amended with an accusing whine. "Kinda creepy up here, ya know?"

Down here too, girlfriend.

True, my ankles tingled. I felt hands grasp them between open treads and almost ran into the hoary 'mastodon' of a furnace, so eager was I to get to the bottom.

I stared at the massive oxidized bulk, so old, it was probably, *most likely*, dangerous, not that I had the brains or courage to light the monster at any rate. Wasn't difficult to imagine odorless poison seeping through those fat asbestos-wrapped pipes snaking out in all directions to upstairs vents, which probably, in my memory had not conducted sooty heat for over twenty years. No fear, even if there *was* a dusty heap of coal under the chute.

I gave the "mastodon" the wide respect a cave man must have done to the real thing, and so did not see, at least at that time, flicking over blackened bones like twigs thrust up from the coal bin mummified with coal dust, and blending right in. Plus, the match died.

Coal, or something, rattled in the dark. I admit, I leapt for the stairs as fast as my bum leg would allow. *Shades of all those creepy films I watched.* What a ninny I was. To add to my vexation, the precious matches plinked through open treads to the dark beneath. Groping back down, cursing words worse than *sugar bear* or *ginger,* I felt between the bottom treads probing clammy dirt and Lord knew what.

There. My fingers touched thin sticklike things. "Gotcha!" *Dang, what was that?* My fingers cringed. The thin shafts were more skin and bones. Suppressing a yelp, I explored rough desiccated fur.

Yuck! Dead rat? I drew my fingers back. But, dang, I *needed* those matches. I'd need *all* my resources was the sick drowning sensation. I recalled Agnes and her small grocery. Why had I not presence of mind to grab a box of big old kitchen matches? Gingerly, I probed further, finally touching scattered wood. Definitely thin sticks, *with matchheads,* thank God. One, two, three, four, all together. The rest could wait. *So, could the dead rat-thing*—whatever.

I backed up more panicky than I'd admit, at least to Little Debbi of the bon mottes, and insults.

I crawled up on all fours. It was so black I couldn't see my hands. Should be *some* light filtering down. "Debbi? Hey!" My head banged the door. "*Ooow-wah,*" I yelped, yanking the knob. My hands slipped off the cold china knob. Had I not crashed into the wall, I would've tumbled clear to the bottom, arse over tea kettle.

"Dang, the little nuisance. Trying to spook me, closing the darn door." Something odd about her. What the heck was she doing hitchhiking in this weather, practically buck-naked? I picked up a total stranger. Lesson one. Do not pick up hitchhikers! *Running away, escaping prison? No that was for male offenders across way.* I grabbed the lead pipe banister, hauling up again,

my bad leg on fire. Dank air pressed my face—*can't breathe—can't*...

Wait! If Debbi locked me in, what was she planning? Sugar bear! She could take the car...rob me blind. *Rob what?* I answered myself. Or leave me helpless, trapped, and starving. Worse than alone. Or burn the house down. Then recalled the coal chute and slanted storm door, feeling foolish. My thoughts were moths batting at a bright light.

"Yeah, girlfriend," I muttered, "you do watch too many crummy movies." But damned if I go out that way! "Open!" I demanded pounding the door.

Silence.

Then, I detected a sort of rustling sound like mice through paper on the other side.

"Debbi? Not funny. Let me OUT!" I hammered the flat of my hand against wood abruptly falling through, blinking in wan light to find Debbi munching peanut-butter and bread—*my peanut butter bread.*

Debbi scowled up at me. "What's your prob? Scared the bejeebers outta me, man!"

"Gimme that." I snatched the sandwich, bite and all, intent on stuffing it back in the bag. I looked at it. "Never mind. Eat it!"

"Your fingers were all over it."

"Eat that or I swear you will wear it all over your face. And don't touch another bite!" With that, giving her the stink eye, I stuffed my groceries in a tall cupboard. Before losing it completely and swatting her one, I thrust through the kitchen swing door, to what we always grandly called, *The Great Room;* fumbling for another of the house's antique button-switches, I eyed the interior fondly.

Broad curving staircase, huge rock fireplace, and tall veranda doors. Unconsciously thinking rewiring costs, I assessed the room unfiltered by memories. The antler chandelier illuminated the same homey/shabby maze. Retro-cool. I could keep those. A half-finished puzzle on a crappy card table, the splendid river stone fireplace was wall-sized, fronted by a wide flagstone hearth with hefty brass stag-head andirons, perfect for sitting in the warmth of a blazing fire, sipping hot chocolate.

My gaze swept the piece-of-crap rifle on hooks over the mantel, from the French and Indian wars it seemed like, but the old thing lent character—*yes, that will do nicely*—next to cheesy milkmaid and shepherd figurines. *Those could go.* I admired French doors with heavy drapes pooling the floor, fronting the deep, wide veranda overlooking the lake. Another elegant retro touch. I could picture Adirondack rockers and wicker tables.

Caressing the handsome newel post, I peered up the curving formal staircase disappearing in the dark— movie star elegance. My favorite part of the room. I could picture Clark Gable or Loretta Young descending those stairs! I scowled at my silliness, striding over to build a fire, but lingering over a haphazard group of photos flanking the fireplace and littering the mantel with no notion of décor.

There was one of Uncle Dez holding a fishing pole. *Was he ever that young?*

And Zak and Lance, grinning back at my old Instamatic, Zak making devil's horns on Lance's head.

And one of myself gap-toothed over a melting birthday cake, clutching a barbie doll and my brand-new pink, bow and arrow set.

I moved on to three scabby-kneed hoodlums

drawing bows, aiming at a raggedy-assed homemade cardboard target. And the same three, holding bows and quivers of arrows, posed ramrod straight with crow feathers in our hair.

I stopped at candid shots of my parents, Flo, and Landon Lodge, lingering over Mom's wild gypsy beauty, with her hair billowing a dark cloud around her face.

My hair.

Mom stands hip-cocked, slightly apart picking tobacco from her tongue. Her lips are dark red. It appeared *that* woman laughed often, a full-throated breathy laugh promising secret worlds.

Everything I was not.

Flo Lodge, with her foot on the racy bumper *of the car that killed her.*

I averted my eyes, fingering another of my dad, Landon, kneeling with his arms about a small tousled-haired *me*, and older brother, Lance. Lance also inherited the wild gypsy hair, but our father's pale irises, ringed in black. Ghost eyes.

"Hello, Dad. Hi, Mom." I greeted, shyly, touching the glass. Glancing over, my eye caught the hefty tarnished brass replica of "The Lancette" on the mantel. *"This* sad reminder is the *first* to go," I muttered.

"Who's the weird old dude?"

I jumped, holding my chest. "Sugar! You scared me! My uncle! I lived with him."

"Why? Was he a *funny uncle*?" Debbi put her nose nearly to the glass peering at him.

"Hardly!" Feeling mean, I snapped. "Bedroom." I pointed dramatically up the formal stairs. "Top left. Bath across the hall. Good night! And, I don't want to see you

again, until morning. Then—we'll sort something out."
I punched the button switch at the bottom, hearing
another hollow, *klack!*

*Damned fuse box. Not tonight. Not in that bloody
beastly cellar.*

"Here." I thrust Debbi a lit candle from the mantel
piece. "I'll be right down here."

"Why kin't I kip by the fireplace? That big old arm
chair?" Debbi whined.

*Because that's where I want to be, curled in Uncle's
chair.* I didn't say I was sick of her and wanted time
alone—*to try Zak.*

"Because you can't!" I felt my nerves snapping like
twigs. "They are proper bedrooms with plenty of quilts.
I said I'll be right here!"

Debbi studied the well of darkness. "Crazy,
girlfriend. Dark as a bitch up there."

"Anybody hitchhikes, can't be spooked of a little
dark!"

I was impatient, but tired, and sad and really wanted
to make sense of the last few days.

****

Skirting the lake, knee-deep in snow dense as
concrete, the Bald Man and Indian kept to the narrow
trail between thin shore ice and impenetrable scrub
doggedly making for the house, even though a span of
wild woods lay between it and them.

The Indian's head jerked up. The Bald Man ran into
him, groaning. "Fuck ya heathen. Don't fooking stop!"

The Indian grunted, waving a stiff arm. The Bald
One saw the light again—literally. They stumbled faster,
keeping the wan glow steady on—a compass-heading,
through the firs. The Indian wobbled pinwheeling his

arms. One foot plunged in thin ice covered with mush where the lake thrust swampy inlets into the woods; his poncho flew up and away in a nasty gust. He fell back, his lower leg locked in ice and bottom marl. Shivering, he faced the stars and then simply closed his eyes.

Rest a minute. Good to lie here, even in the wet and cold.

Baldy bent his head against the wind and kept going. He stopped. He trudged back and without looking at the Indian, rescued the poncho, shrugging it on over his own blanket poncho.

The Indian's eyes blinked open against the wind. The final act of betrayal gave him the impetus to extricate himself, gazing with murderous intent on the bald man.

****

"So? Go!" I said crossly.

"Okay. I'm goin'! Seen scarier stuff before breakfast! Takes a bunch ta scare this girlfriend. I seen *Friday the 13th* seventeen times!"

"Say hello to Freddy." I muttered.

"That's *Nightmare on Elm Street*. Bitch!"

I snapped my teeth shut, watching the light dim. *Can't back down now.* "Almost there," I coaxed. "First door, left. Blankets on the bed!"

Bitch. Huhn!

Were there? Find out soon enough. Too weary to go up. I had driven over three hundred miles into a gale. Let her find her own blankets. Turning, I tossed twigs and dead branches from a wood box willy-nilly into the enormous maw of the fireplace—a proper Girl Scout. "Ain't," I muttered, snatching newspapers yellowing quietly in the kindling box, wadded them underneath, reaching for the small hatchet to chop stuff that wouldn't fit, saving the ax for outside.

"Where's the bloody ax?"

"Oh. There's the bloody ax." I giggled, light-headed. Wished I eaten more at that diner.

As I groped for it, my hand stubbed against an elderly suitcase squatting in the shadows by the box. Sucking fingers, I drew out a case with corroded metal corners. Hunh? "Where'd you come from?" I pried the rusted-in-place snap-locks with my fingernails; the lid exploded knocking my hands painfully aside. I started to suck my fingers but thought better and made a face at the smell, "*Euuuugh!*"

Gingerly, I probed black plastic heavier than a trash bag. A musty coppery odor wafted out as I spilled old tools, a broken knife haft, a rusty saw, screwdrivers, a corroded scaling knife, pliers, duct tape, tangled in stained rags stiff with something brownish on the hearth.

And there was that smell.

I lowered my face sniffing, waving the odor away.

Like old meat. Ugh!

"Yuck." I threw it all back and shoved it aside. "Another thing to toss." So much to do; instead reached for an ancient Bakelite radio, the kind made during WWII before plastic was new. *Probably worth a mint.*

Miraculously, the old vacuum tubes yet glowed. I had a feeling that was pure grace, and not to last. Lord knew when the last time we used it, more an overlooked sentimental ornament, regretting I was a Luddite, and hadn't brought my clunky old computer. Not that it would do any good without wireless. I was savvy that much.

Haven't exactly planned this have you girl?

But before the old radio gave out, I caught snatches of words... *"continued bad weather"*... "Great." Plus, scraps of garbled announcements... *"escaped convict yattatayatta"* ...sandwiched between *hissing* and more *Hank Williams,* stirred with classical snippets from WJR, Detroit's clear station.

The land-line shattered the silence.

My hand jerked off the knob. I stared wildly about. *"Who could that be this time a night?"* I mocked, like from a bad movie, but my heart stilled.

Zak.

Of course not, idiot!

Doubted he even recalled there *was* a land-line, *even if he had an inkling where I was.* That's right. No one did. No one besides Lance and Zak, guiltily recalling I hadn't bothered notifying my irritating bro. Hesitant, I picked up, amazed someone still paid the phone bill. Probably fell through some estate-planning cracks, such as they were. Desmond's elderly lawyer likely kept some utilities paid year after year, with the sinking feeling they'd be cut off at month's end. More expense. The old lawyer passed away within a week after reading Uncle Dez's will.

"Hello? Hello? Zak?" I practically yelped into *dead air.*

"Zak? Don't kid, now."

I *click-clicked* the cutoff buttons.

Lame, Meggie, really lame.

It never worked.

It merely cut connections. A holdover from Hollywood Noir films where heroines with homicidal maniacs in the house *slash, attic, slash, basement,* attempted in vain to reach a *live* operator, and of course the heroines were bedridden, blind or *whatever*, hysterically punching cutoff buttons of a clunky ancient dial telephone.

Like this one.

I glared at the ugly black plastic receiver.

Live operator, hah!

I searched for my old cell phone.

If it was Zak, he'd call my cell, I thought agitatedly, dumping my bag.

****

My old cell phone, after searching coat pockets, handbag, the kitchen, and porch, even retracing steps to the car, was nowhere. Darned cheap old thing! If he did ring, I'd hear it wouldn't I? The dread thought I probably dropped it either on the road, wriggling in and out of the car dealing with the looking-for-love-in-all-the-wrong-places ranger, or perhaps plowing to the house juggling groceries. It could be anywhere under the snow.

A long day. Uncapping my whiskey, I pulled deep— the hot spice flavored my courage and renewed strength. "Just the whiskey and the road." I giggled and hiccupped. Sounded like a country song, I thought and slugged more whiskey, no ladylike sipping tonight; *with silent thanks and apologies to Agnes,* I replaced the bottle on a top shelf. Removed it, took another pull. Noted the level, put it back and firmly shut the door.

I wasn't drinking too much.

I wasn't.

It was a few seconds before I registered new noises, jerking my face to the ceiling. As I peered up *creaks* and invisible cracks seemed to radiate right over my head; revolving until dizzy, I muttered crossly. "Not funny, Debbi. Go to bed!"

Probably searching for something to steal. What an idiot I was.

I slumped back to the Great Room, lighting the wadded-up paper. All my hard-won confidence and serenity struggled to survive as I knelt by the fireplace and rested my head against the warming stones. My eyes closed despite myself, dreaming of the lake and cracking ice.

Ice cracking?

That wasn't ice.

"Now what?" I checked the dark well of staircase leading to the warren of upstairs bedrooms. I'd identify that sound anywhere. A careful squeal of a stair-tread. Yes. Nailed it! Damn, Debbi! I was so tired. Behind me, a dead branch caught, flared, and crackled. I jumped as shadows danced up and down the steps, *but no Debbi.*

"Deb-bi? Are you there? Is that you?" I called anyway.

Carrying the kindling ax, I climbed the steps as if testing thin ice. My stupid imagination. Probably a branch cracking from the weight of ice. "This old house has more creaking joints than an old folk's home," I groused, uneasily aware of increasing wind for the first time. It was turning into the promised blizzard warnings "*'in the buckle of the snowbelt,'*" I mimicked.

I found myself at the top, checking both down the stairs and flickering fire making a warm circle of safety and then the black well of silence ahead. The upstairs wall-switch still clicked hollow, yet low light leaked from Debbi's room from the cracked open door.

"Debbi, quit playing games!" I snapped. Not sure I wanted to wake her, *or anyone,* I checked the fire still burning a Halloween glow, casting spiky claws up the steps. It took that moment for a shutter to bang loose *somewhere* in the four-story warren.

I rolled my eyes. *Somewhere.* Sugar, I was spooked as a goose. My imagination sure rode a wild horse tonight. *Get a grip...This is your house, now. There are no secrets. A place of fond memories. Sanctuary.* "Better get used to me old girl," I addressed my new home. "You are going to be tarted up like it or not."

I stared at the dim glow from Debbi's room, resenting her all over. Sugar bear. I did not want to share my homecoming with her. Sleeping like a baby probably, while I was turning into a psycho. I stood in the doorway, fists on hips. "Glad *you're* all comfy!" The candle by her bed flamed fitfully in a draft of unidentified origin thinly illuminating the lumpy bed.

Debbi's toes stuck out from the quilts. The lone white foot looked cold and vulnerable. I resisted the impulse to cover it. Fixated, I cocked my head and watched the girl in the glow from the flickering candle, thinking wistfully it would be nice to have someone to chat away the night, with the wind blowing outside and the loneliness.

I had been insulated, too long.

Debbi scarcely breathed...Her face flickering in the softening effect of candle light, appeared smooth-cheeked and childish. I watched her. She really was a *very* pretty girl under all that crap she plastered on her face, wondering idly what Zak would think of her, shaking my head at my weakness. Zak would think any girl was pretty, at least with his irresistible charisma, make them think so.

Sugar bear. So, she was sleeping like the dead, or the sleep of innocence, while I had a feeling my own night would be filled with terrors, jumpiness and hollow let-downs after Uncle Desmond's funeral, and the pitiful number of attenuated cronies attending his memorial.

The resentment built up again…So tired.

Even Lance couldn't make it. For a fleeting second, I mulled renegade thoughts.

Was it a merely a week ago?

****

Not getting a grip, I hitched down to the kitchen, still shaky. Wind scratched twiggy fingers on the window over the sink; that did not help. Rubbing frost off of glass black as a dead TV, I checked the dark; impossible to see anything beyond snow battering like white birds against panes.

****

The Indian huddled against the lee side of the boathouse staring back with longing at the kitchen window after he saw a pale face looming against the glass, and shivering uncontrollably, crept inside.

****

"Getting worse. Maybe I should get out, while the gettin' is good." I ducked below the black square of uncovered window. Something was out there. I don't understand how I identified it, but I didn't imagine that faint cloud on the pane, like a breath, or mist instantly freezing.

Frantically searching for my keys, simply in case— *where the heck was everything? —was I losing my mind?* I finally raked them from under the drain board, muttering, "Oh, there you are!" I couldn't avoid my face in the window again, pale but resolute. "Probably my own breath," I muttered. "Nothing's out there." Still, I snatched up the hatchet where I laid it on the table.

"Okay, get your game face on, girl."

Checking my car from the lattice porch, silently swallowed by snow, and listening to a chaos of thrashing pines, I tossed the keys back not extra certain I wanted to brave icy blasts again, after the relative coziness of the house. Besides, I was vexed at that wretched girl. "Can't just leave her. Not!"

I climbed for the bottle. "Screw that!" I giggled unscrewing the cap and headed in the Great Room. Feeling sorry for myself, I checked the half empty bottle and defiantly took another deep pull... "Antifreeze!" I chortled, then sobered recalling Uncle Desmond's memorial attended by a scattering of old friends and business associates from his salad days looking rather smug. The rest, morbidly curious. One reporter I recognized, but from a third-rate local network.

Elderly relics milling about the cavernous room— myself, sedate in black, a simple bow securing my long jet hair, face with a slapdash of makeup not even pretending for once to be Bette Davis or Loretta Young, as I limped among the guests, watching them pick at their plates of limp canapés—hah! trying not to stare at empty walls and a threadbare Persian rug once owned by Gloria Swanson.

My face flushed again with the memory of how *they* sipped cheap wine even I thought tasted like vinegar and made faces. The canapés white bread triangles. Tuna and Swiss cheese. I made them myself. Somehow, I should have honored Uncle better. It should have been a catered affair for the curious—*the vampires of pain*, I sniveled, if I had to go in debt until I found out *what,* if anything was left over—or even mine, no matter how scant.

I wiped my nose, honking histrionically. Zak had

come late, practically *hoovering the place,* staring at the high ceilings, already envisioning reaping the profits. My face warmed with the remembrance of how we toasted Uncle in my bed for the last time with the remainder of the bad wine, after the mourners and the elderly lawyer, so anxious I was to be alone with Zak, I scarcely took in what he said, recalling his mild vexation and puzzlement—and not much was discussed later, after Zak swept me up, racing me up the stairs two at a time, *like Rhett Butler did Scarlett O'Hara.* My cheeks burned at the ambiguous memory, or was it the whiskey?

Poor Zak. Even now I saw him eyeing his flute of sour white wine going down like battery acid, with a hint of puzzlement and felt a flush of anger. Why did I need to be the strong, prudent one?

I had watched the mourner's mouths, fascinated— *talking, chewing, braying.* Did they care that I picked up what they said—as if each word was broadcast deliberately in my direction, their words still echoing in my head? Even the crony who whispered, as through a megaphone as only the elderly can. I watched her brilliant greasy red lip-sticked mouth, as words spewed out between chomps of tuna and bread.

"... if old Dez didn't have bad luck..."

And then moustachio-ed mouth finished her thought: *"Would he have had any?"* Accompanied by titters. And the one with large capped teeth, chiming in, as she gazed about. *"Wonder what this huge place will fetch for the family?"*

The one with crooked teeth sniping, *"...a tear down surely."*

"...play poker with Desmond's lawyer..."

"...mortgaged to the rafters, I hear." From another.

A deaf woman in pearls holding a hand behind her ear had broken in. *"Who? The lawyer?"* The old man repeated quarrelsomely, *"George Herbert Lodge! The founder of this—"* He looked askance at the white triangle. *"Feast."* Shaking his head, he lay it back on the tray. Tarnished in spite of the polishing.

"So, what do they live on?"

"Cheese the rats refused, or as Meggie would say..."

And the clump of mourners all chuckled, most saying in unison ala *Bette Davis*. *"Christ! whatadump!"*

I drifted by with a fixed tight smile, but burning inside.

They too were aware of my pathetic penchant for drowning myself in old films to ward off reality. And it was too true. I stared about the kitchen trying to see beyond nostalgia for what it was. After triple mortgages were paid and lawyers fed, Uncle Dez willed the "proceeds" to me such as they were. Antiquated lake houses were popular up to the 1950s or so. Then, came international travel and other lures more exotic than an up-country, cold in winter, sweaty in summer, family fishing retreat.

This, my dubious inheritance.

Still, it was *mine,* and whomever I wished to share it with. It was *my* house.

I blinked. The long day and brutal drive caught up with me...so much to do. I wandered back staring blankly into the fire and hearing the hiss of unrelenting snow, trying to quench it.

Chapter 9

Whistling Down the Chimney

I had fallen asleep; my head was pounding. *BAM BAM BAM!* No headache. I peered about, groggy. That was outside my head. I stiffened at the relentless hammering too regular to be a branch slamming the house. Sounded like it came from the French doors. It stopped. I heard wind wailing round corners of the house

Where to go, where to hide? No one was aware I was here!

I looked wildly for a weapon. Didn't see the kindling hatchet, *anywhere* The shepherd and milkmaid knickknacks lay shattered by the fireplace from the pounding. Their sharp angles and mincing bodiless heads glittering orange in the light, winked slyly up at me. I stared at them blankly and crunched the milkmaid, heedless underfoot. Reaching down, I tossed shards in the fireplace, feeling the prick of shards, snatching up the tongs, hefty, with the bronze stag head's suitably sharp points.

Conscious of wind thrusting through every crack, hooting down the chimney, ripping slates, and muscling though the slanted coal door below, I wanted to shriek—*Stop it! Stop it! Had enough!* The pounding renewed. The French doors seemed to bow inward with each blow.

As I neared the drapes, my mind whimpered. *Get it*

over! I glanced down. There was blood on my hands. Can't deal with that now. I surveyed the remains of the shattered milk maid. Her simpering glossy china head watched me slyly with milky blue eyes. I ripped my attention away.

Keening wind now sounded like distant calls, even cries. I screamed again; I couldn't help it, covering my mouth, pressed my other hand to my groin. My knees were knocking so. I wished the lights weren't on. I tossed a boot at the parchment shaded table lamp flickering on and off anyway. I kept hearing my name in the gale howling about the corners of the house, but it was a false note. No one, not even Lance guessed I was here.

Unless it was the ranger.

I raked the rifle over the fireplace, a split second. Useless, unless you wanted a house-breaker or murderer to laugh himself to death. Swinging the poker like a Louisville slugger, I focused on the veranda door's flimsy brass locks, more for show than anything secure. Soon, whoever it was, would smash the panes. That decided me. I thrust feet in my boots and hitched to the kitchen. The pounding stopped abruptly leaving my ears ringing.

I peered through lattice. Swiveling the poker, I slipped to my car keeping my feet in my former boot prints with hair whipping about my face blinding me. I shoved the keys in the ignition, not with the easy slide, but reluctantly with haste.

The starter groaned. I pumped gas darting looks everywhere, eyed the convertible's flimsy roof five inches overhead. *An ugly knife slashed the rag top, stabbing repeatedly down! Down, down! With a coarse riiiipping....*

I blinked.

No knife slashing through.

Still, the canvas top had huge rents letting in gusts of snow. Petrified at the implications, I pumped gas, inanely appreciating at the same time I was flooding it. The engine turned over making a tooth-gritting grinding, sluggish as a teenager told to get up for Sunday Mass— and then *klucked* dully.

I focused past the boat house on prison lights far across the lake, winking between respites from gusts, watching mesmerized until cold crept in my bones. Bet they were warm and cozy. Wished I put back on that ratty old fur. If I stay here, I would never leave. My old car would make a swell icy tomb. "Don't be morbid!"

I tumbled out and lurched backward to the tree line, fanning the poker. From there, I checked options.

The wood was a ghostly labyrinth, even in daytime, easy to get lost and freeze to death.

No way I could climb the slope anyway and walk the logging road—and even if I did?

Roads were even more socked in, even if the car *did* start.

The proper entry road leading from the two-lane looked like a formless wallow.

I considered the boathouse, yet looking at it—it seemed a trap.

The back door was wide open.

The wedge of faint light welcomed me back.

"I can't," I heard myself whimper.

But I had run out, without even a hat and gloves.

I'm freezing.

It's the only place I can go.

Stupid to leave.

"Bolt the door!" I muttered grim. Barricade windows." I backed to the lattice porch still swinging the poker.

There!

I locked the flimsy screen.

Fat lot of good that will do.

Lock the kitchen door too.

Shove the white enameled chair under the knob.

Forgot the cellar.

I felt an itch. A breath on my neck. Sly fingers, or a very thin blade tickled my back.

Blinking, I whirled, my eyes wide, limping across, rammed the cellar door latch home, then checked the yard over the sink, dropping back down breathing regular again.

That's all it was…only the storm. Still, I grabbed the butcher knife with a bleached handle and huddled back into my ratty fur. What an idiot.

Silly!

Ride it out. Leave tomorrow.

First thing.

Am I losing my mind? My head felt all wobbly from my stupid imaginings. Whiskey didn't help either.

Back in the Great Room, I frowned a moment studying the dark well of stairs curving gracefully upwards. Stupid girl. Not a care in the world!

Almost in a trance, I again trod the steps. At the top, Debbi's door was still open.

I peeped in.

The guttering candle still cast a subdued glow.

The quilt, a reddish patchwork called "Snakes and Apples," and one of my favorites was different. More red. The pattern distorted. Debbi's foot still protruded. I yanked the quilt straight.

I stood, holding a corner of it staring at her.

Debbi lay in a soup of blood, one eye staring sightless from a ruined face. The other eye was a grisly hole. Dimly, from somewhere deep in my primitive mind, the determined pounding renewed, booming like thunder over the howling blizzard screaming like a banshee up the stairwell. *"That isn't wind,"* I whimpered.

My own cries would wake the dead as I backed to the banister, half-sliding, half-falling downstairs. I could hardly control my leg at best of times; now it threatened to collapse. Clinging to the banister, I half-tumbled down the stairs using only one leg, dragging the other. Dread was almost a distraction. When I pulled the drapes, I waited, frozen, for whatever to materialize. I blinked and backed my hand to my mouth, to stifle a yell.

A six-foot-tall black crow stood hunched on the drifted-over veranda.

Then the creature turned.

****

Black hair whipped from a mob cap, obliterating a face of a figure in a long, black, collar-up, topcoat stamping and blowing on thin white hands, hunched, shivering, and looking out at the lake. The figure turned. The frozen mask creased into a stiff grin. "Magpie!" The *crow* yelled through the glass and I near yanked the door from its hinges falling into Lance's arms, *even then, wishing he were Zak.*

Chapter 10

Cold Welcome

"Meggie, what f—! What the hell? Only me! Judas Priest! Been pounding and pounding! I went round and round this freaking place, calling. Where the hell were you…?"

I stared back. My face felt cold and white as the snow he let in.

"What?" Lance laughed uncertainly. "Did I *skeer* ya?" He fluttered hands ghostlike, before my face like an idiot, hooting…"*Whoooooo!*"

I still looked through him. But Lance, thrusting past, didn't see. Yanking his mob cap, he released a profusion of black hair and opened his coat to the fire as I looked on like a statue.

"Ahh, heaven!" He rattled on. "Sorry, sis, but dang! It's a witch's cold white butt out there." He glanced about. I noted his jeans showed snow up to his knees. "God, this is great! Fantastic! That fire could use some TLC, though, but hey!" He rubbed his hands. "I freakin' guessed this is where you'd come to ground, Magpie. Anything to eat? Whew! Check these hands."

He turned frowning at my silence.

I backed wordlessly to the staircase. My mouth seemed frozen too.

"What now, Nutmeg? You could at *least* act as if

you're freakin' glad to see me. *Gee, Lance so relieved you made it!"*

He sneered, wearily thrusting long slightly greasy hair back with nails that I saw were bloody and cracked, reached for me palms out. He laughed uncertainly, then checked his own blood-caked sweater and stained cuffs.

My cry caught in my throat as Lance came closer.

"Hey! Don't go all postal on me!" His voice was peeved. "It's blood from the clinic, dammit!" His long black-clad body gave a rippling shudder. "Bloody tired too, I can tellya. Too cold to take this damn thing off and wash up. 'Sides, I wanted to beat the storm. Crap, Meggie, I drove all the way up here, thinkin' you might need company 'bout now." He scowled and stuck his lip out in a way I recalled well.

At my continued silence, he muttered. "O-*kay*! Didn't mean to spoil your sensitivities."

With that, he dragged the blood-caked sweater overhead and flung it on the embers. As the sweater flared, the thick smell of blood and burning wool smogged the room sickeningly. Lance burrowed back in his black coat as sweeping as an old plains-duster.

"Lance," I whispered hoarse. "Not that." Words still stuck in my throat. I pointed up.

Oblivious, Lance tossed on my precious wood. "God, I'm wasted," he threw over his shoulder. "Crack mum. Young. Thirteen maybe. Dumped. The clinic delivered her kid, but I..." He shrugged. "Needed a proper hospital. Judas Priest. I chewed up the list and pulled in a ton of favors to get her in fast." Lance sighed and stretched his back. "Finally drove her to Saint Jo's myself." He grimaced. "She bled like a..."

He saw my face and stopped dead.

"Yeah, well. Start actin' the proper bro tomorrow, Nutmeg. Yo promiso."

With my mouth open and eyes wide, I still pointed up.

Lance glanced queerly at me. "Hey—hey! Magpie. This is over the top, even for you. Still watchin' those spooky flicks?" Stiffening mid-chuckle, he followed my fixed gaze.

"S'happening, Meg?" His pale gaze flashed around the room.

I jabbed ardently at the stairs.

"Upstairs? Someone upstairs?"

"Uh-huh," I managed. "Oh. God, Lanny. Thank God, you're here. I sent her up there." I hung on, holding him back. "Don't go!"

He started to grin. "Christ! Meg?" His eyebrow waggles always made me laugh. Not now. *"Her?* You gotta girl—for me? You shouldn't have. Must think I'm like—you know— Zak." The edge to his voice was a paper cut.

Lance, hands on his waist, eyed the stairwell. His grin faded when I didn't react. He looked down at my own bloody hands still wet from the quilt. "Christ, Meg!" I watched numbly as Lance bounded upstairs.

****

I hunkered outside Debbi's door as my brother took in the ruined quilt, the bloody patches already browning and stiff, *not* part of the *Snakes and Apples* pattern.

I peered in. He took in the too-white foot sticking out and followed blood dripping like syrup on old floorboards onto a thickening puddle. I felt my throat close. I could smell blood above the chill air.

"Judas Priest!" He yelped. Still, I noticed Lance's

inspections were more clinical in place of horrified.

"A girl. At-at the d-diner," I stuttered from the doorway. "A hitchhiker. Cold. It was so cold! Oh Lance! I was so very cold. Couldn't just leave her. You can help her. Can't you, Lanny?"

He stared at me, incredulous. "This ain't a *movie*, Magpie." He said it angrily and risked a glance at the corpse again.

"Tell me about it!" I snapped.

"I can't—" he shook his head like a dog shedding water. "What the hell happened…Christ!" He paced the small room, rubbing his neck still flicking glances at the bed. "I can't believe this!"

I peered around. Again. Couldn't help myself. I heard him lifting the quilt. Lance felt her carotid, I think it was called—what was left. With the cut veins and tendons, the right side of her neck resembled a mass of spaghetti swimming in blood. I swallowed bile at the thought as he closed the one eye stuck with mascara smeared like a raccoon down her cheek. Finally, clinically, he studied Debbi. I pinched my eyes tight. Futile, anyway.

"Pretty. You can tell. And young under all that…" He started to say *blood,* but instead said, "make up," dropping the quilt over her face. Underneath his blank expression, I saw his mind racing for explanation, and a way to leave. "I'm no bloody coroner, but Christ Himself couldn't have helped her." Lance circled the room aimlessly, fisting the walls and staring back at the bed.

"What we gonna do, Lan?" I asked miserably.

"Outta here for starters! Jesus. How could you pick up a freaking stranger! Then, we gotta call—Christ— *someone.* Let somebody else sort this mess. Jesus,

Meggie. Anybody followed you guys? She may have had enemies for chrissake. She was running away from something!" He scowled at me as if it were all my fault.

I nodded, numb. He stood helpless. "Maybe we could like—dump her. Nobody knows she was—" Then he saw my haunted face. *The ranger.* "Okay. Right," he sighed disappointed-like. "Tell me later, kiddo, start to finish. But first—"

"I'll be all right," I whispered. "Just—let's leave!"

Lance threw me a look and checked his cell for bars, waving for a signal. "Like there's a tower within a hundred miles of this dump." He flashed a look. "Sorry, Meg."

"Land line's dead too."

"Of *course,* it is," he said heavily checking the room with disgust.

****

"Can't freakin' *believe* this." Lance paced the Great Room, nervously checking out the French doors, letting drapes drop only to lift them again, peering into the night. The snow had stopped. "How long you been here? See anybody—*anything?*"

I hesitated. "Only you. I mean made the noise. Nothing besides that." I didn't comprehend why I didn't tell him about the kitchen ceiling creaks and groans, or ghost breath on the window, if that's what it was, and not a bloom of frost.

"Anybody follow you? Another car?"

I waved it away. "One, but I lost it, somewhere. And the ranger I told you about?" I waved my hand like swatting a fly. "Not him either."

"Ranger? Did you tell him where you live? He may be on his—".

"Way?" I laughed mirthlessly. "Not a chance, I sighed. "The—the—*Debbi* and I weren't exactly *friendly* to him."

Lance listened to fists of wind pounding to get in. "Bastard could still be here, somewhere. This house is a bloody maze." He checked over my shoulder and up the stairs.

"Let's go, Magpie."

"Yes. I wanna go *home*, Lanny." Aware I sounded like a wimpy little girl.

"I get it. Home. Home, bloody sweet home. From what I *hear*, you already *are*."

Of course, I was, then I heard what he *really* said.

I had inherited over the two boys.

****

Lance slipped a knife from the caddy. Me gripping the fire tongs to his amusement, with a—*what do you think you are going to do with those?* expression. I fumed. I wasn't *that* helpless!

"You cool? Chop-chop kid. Where's the car?"

"Didn't you see it?"

"You mean your canvas tank? No. And all I got's the crap clinic van. But, bloody hell. Meant to get go-juice at that diner. Damn thing closed. I'm out. Freakin' hiked the last bloody mile."

Chapter 11

Dark Side of the Moon

The Indian, with narrowed eyes, tracked Lance from the dirty boat house window as he scanned the yard from the latticed-in porch through the rusty screen door. He made it this far. He was turning to stone he was so cold. Thoughts of killing and holing up in the inviting house with the two girls was the top of his goals...until the intruder arrived. Shivering, he searched the boathouse. Nothing he could use as a weapon. That pair of rusty ice skates? The flaking rusting scaling knife? Doubtful. Had to get that poncho back and stick to his plans...he saw the way the traitorous bald-headed bastard headed...

****

"Over there," I pointed. "Guess it got covered up. It's under all that snow!" I don't understand why I felt contrary. I suppose I did not want Lance to see how scared I was. I wasn't sure I wanted to enter the real world yet, or endlessly explain. It all seemed beyond me.

Lance squinted. "Never mind, Meg. You and me? We're gonna make it to your car. It'll be all right. 'Kay?" I wasn't sure who he was assuring, me or him.

Huddling at his back, I nodded sourly.

"We'll blast our way outta here and drive to hell and break in, if we have to. With me?" I shrugged. "Sure, Lanny." I could scarcely make out the boathouse let

94

alone the way out. I frowned. It seemed something stirred behind a dirty window. But then, Lance half-carried me—I felt like a kid bundled in my scarves, and too-big fur—to the mound shaped like a car. My mood softened. Lance was trying. I was the ingrate, yet it took five minutes of cursing, flicking the lighter and holding the tiny flame to thaw out the door handle, while I stamped my feet and checked the house as if expecting Debbi's angry ghost. It didn't help.

After thawing and popping the handle, and climbing in the icebox, I avoided the ripped canvas top as if somehow, it was an embarrassment. Lance, fiddling with the frozen ignition, only flashed irritated looks at the gashes, muttering, *"Come on, you bitch."* The starter obliged with a leaden, *ratataitaattatata.*

Lance felt the light above the dash. "Kinda warm. Interior was on."

"Guess I—I, didn't close it. The door."

"Christ! Poor kid."

"Don't know who she was."

Lance threw me a pitying—*I meant you look.* "Could a been you, Nutmeg," he muttered checking a snowscape resembling the dark side of the moon, blew on his hands and leaned forward, his gaze darting around like a crazed squirrel past the frosty windshield.

"Whatever maniac, he's long gone. Probably."

"You don't *know* that."

He rubbed his hands. "Okay, okay! Think fast, before our brains need antifreeze. Can't try for the road, till morning. That boat house," he nodded, "is cold as a morgue in Alaska. At least we can barricade the house. Keep warm."

"I can't, Lanny—"

"Sure, you can. Where's my little Nutmeg, ready for…" he sighed. "Well not this. Don't think of…her."

"Debbi."

"Yeah, whoever." He chewed his thumb, checking the back door.

****

Lance half dragged me to the house, latching the flimsy screen. I rammed a chair under the knob and locked the servant stairs' door: shuddering, flicked over the cellar door.

That could wait.

"Room to room," Lance said behind me. "Smoke'm out if they're dumb enough to stay." His laugh was all mock hearty.

I faked a shaky grin. "Do we want them to?" *And don't patronize me!*

"That's my Nutmeg,"

Chapter 12

Deadly Frost

"Look. No prints."

I played the flash over a football field-sized attic, lost in murk, oddly empty of the usual flotsam, the plank flooring thick with dust, plus the trap door with the short ladder leading up into the low-raftered ceiling.

"The Widow's Walk!" Lance laughed. "Dang, almost forgot that. 'Member? You, me'n Zak played those yucky video games? No one found us."

"Ever," I murmured wistful.

"Probably on purpose. We were creepy little shits." He motioned. "Let's go."

I tarried. "Yeah. Uncle Dez thought they'd warp our already twisted little brains full of mush." I smiled faintly at the memory.

"Too late! That was School for *Muurrrr-der,* Sis." He made a hokey laugh, then seemed sheepish. "Sorry. Way stupid." He sighed gazing at the trap door. "Zak sure ate'm up, though. The gorier the better."

"Only the truth, Lanny." I looked rueful. "Zak loved those blood and guts games. Mainly to torment me."

"He'd be lovin' this, then."

We were distancing from Debbi. I recognized that and maybe that was a good thing.

Already *it*—seemed less real and what we did no

more than a game when we were kids.

The servants' rooms on the fourth floor, right under the attic, disused for at least sixty years, were mostly warrens of iron headboards, and faded ticking mattresses rolled up like sausages on rusty sagging springs.

With a start, I checked a lone uniform rotting in a tiny closet. Lance snorted and motioned me out. "Quit mooning, we got a lot of territory."

Securing each room, armed with the poker, Lance's flashlight, and a ring of skeleton keys; Lance closed the last door on the servant's floor, twisting the key forcefully, crowing with a triumph I did not feel.

"All eight, plus the two bathrooms!"

I waited at the head of the stairs going to the next level.

Uncle Dez's private domain and finest suite in the house, owned sweeping views of Convict Lake through wide triple windows; a vast bedroom, ensuite bath, dressing room, a massive four poster, plus sitting room, facing a gingerbread porch overlooking the lake itself, took over most of the third floor. The vista was unrelieved white and gray, with clouds like cement trucks rolling in from the north. Outside of looking under the bed and checking the closet, we locked it, and a smaller ensuite bedroom next to it, untouched and belonging to Desmond's late wife, Helen, I was too young to recall.

The second floor held smaller spaces—our old bedrooms among a slew of guest rooms.

Zak's and mine were side by side, and Lance's across the hall. I smiled ironic. *Yeah. Me, Zak, and Lance, and our* rare *sleepovers. We didn't need guests, we said. We had each other.* I wasn't ready to check them. With one accord we locked them without opening, giving Debbi's room a wide pass.

"What about—her?" I belatedly hesitated at the top of the broad formal stairs. "Can't hardly *leave* her."

Lance flashed annoyance. "Can't touch anything!"

"It—he—could be under the bed!" My face flushed and had a set look I'm afraid Lance knew well.

He shook his head heaving a gusty sigh. "Under the bed. Right. Of course. How could I have not thought of that? Don't budge." He threw me a sour regard. "Back in a jiff."

Checking the dismal hallway, I nodded. "Hurry."

He grimaced and ducked in the room. I waited, girding myself for calamity, a cry, groan, or shout for help; feeling like the coward I was, I peeked through the doorway watching Lance gingerly lift the quilt off the floor, not looking at the bed, or what was on it. I heard him mumble…*"Damn, Meg's gettin' to me. Thought I saw something…damned dark under there… Why the hell she made* me *come in here again! Like I need this."*

I stepped back.

"Nada but suspicious-looking dust bunnies," exiting, he answered my look.

"Closet?"

He sighed. "Died of mothball inhalation. Can we *go* now?"

"Don't joke! And leave her night-light on? 'Kay?"

He groaned and went back in.

"Night-light on! Now. Pretend she's sleep-ing."

"*Sleep*-ing?"

"Dammit, Meggie! I'm trying! *I'm* dead beat. I felt like caterpillars with little icy feet, crawled down my neck when I walked in on that!" He made wiggle fingers.

"And Christ, I can't make out *what* to think! Give me a frickin' break! Just cause I'm around sick bodies, doesn't—"

Lights flickered and browned.

Debbi's night-light blinked and stayed out.

He shook the flashlight, slamming the door. "Shit. Christ. Fucking hell!"

Then, a lone sconce wanly lit the hallway again.

"Some clown hit a pole. See? A bounce!" He banged the flashlight. "Damn! Battery's old as Moses. Let's get this done, f 'Christ's sake!"

Meekly, I followed him down. Only the vast dining room with a table one could skateboard on, next to a butler's pantry now used as a closet for odds and ends. I scoured it hopefully for anything edible. Coming away with a thousand-year-old tin of artichoke hearts, and a jar of maraschino cherries. Perfect.

****

Lance slammed the cellar door against the kitchen wall, releasing the familiar wave of must, coal, mice, faint whiff of apples and something undefinable.

He snapped the switch button. Of course, it was dead.

"Oh! The bulb is shot or something," I whispered unaccountably guilty.

He threw a sardonic frown. "In this place, of *course,* it is." Once in the basement, I watched him fan a dying flashlight behind the oxidized furnace, and thumped a warped door leading to another room, I vaguely recalled, as sort of a fruit cellar, and where old paint tins and broken chairs were kept.

"Nothin got through that." Lance pointed at the narrow coal chute, and banged the slanted storm door giving off a tinny rattle. Raking the coal bin behind the furnace and under the steps, he tripped over something, scanning the ground. "Ugh. Desiccated rat!" I turned, watching him brush coal crumbs over something with his toe. Then, the flash dimmed and couldn't be coaxed back.

Wordless, I handed him matches.

Lance held one to a cobwebbed window last letting in daylight twenty-five years ago. "That either," he muttered. "Okay. One more thing."

He held the flame close to the ancient fuse box to the right of the furnace, checking an empty slot next to a grid of old-type screw-in fuses, each labeled with clunky faded descriptions: *Livingroom, Servant's Quarters, Main Bedroom, Kitchen & Porch,"* etc.

"Maybe one's dead too. Do they even sell these fuses anymore?" He held up a chalky screw fuse with a copper end.

I shrugged. "Probably Uncle stashed enough for the millennium. Somewhere."

He checked around probing a small shelf. "Don't see any. Got a penny? Pennies bypass—complete the circuit. I think. Electricity arcs. Copper content or somethin'. These old boxes are fires, just waitin' to happen. 'Specially with pennies," he added.

"Gee. Thanks."

My brother shivered, checking the cobwebby rafters. "May need a fire, before this barbecue's over, anyway."

"Not funny, Lanny."

"Wasn't meant to be. Insurance."

I bit my tongue wanting to stick *his finger* in the empty fuse slot, and watch him light up.

"These old boxes, Meggie. Like old Christmas lights. Kinda. One goes—they all go?"

I distantly recalled the caretaker, a fixture for years, sort of magically took care of all that before we arrived. Anonymous, paid by the elderly lawyer. Shamed now that we took all that for granted. He must be a hundred by now. He would not have been here for years. I wondered if he had ever been replaced. Recalling our circumstances, probably not.

"But Lanny, we had lights. They were on."

We gazed at each other, neither wanting to go there. I shrugged. "Guess you were wrong."

He laughed but the humor wasn't there. "Wouldn't be the first time. More expense. Probably everything down the line's, toast, Magpie."

"Comforting."

"One stupid penny." Lance pounded the fuse box.

I struck another match fanning the dirt. "Got one!" I held out two pennies, one bright, the other corroded and dated 1972.

"Appears like we're not the first."

"Think it fell out?"

Lance shrugged as clueless, as he slipped the new penny in the empty socket, rewarded by a glow from the top. We did a high five. "Back in business. Haveta get up early to catch the Lodge brats, hey Magpie?"

I made a sour face. Lance was nervous but trying to hold it together, that's why all the jokiness. I wished he'd stop, pocketing the old penny against the day—one cent between us and having the lights on. I watched Lance pound bent nails into planks from an apple crate over the coal chute and the slanted storm door to the outside.

"There. Safe as houses." I studied the flimsy

measures but didn't say anything. Still, I lingered fixating on the square furnace door with the little isinglass window.

"Wha-at?" He sighed. "No one's hiding in *there,* Meg." But didn't appear too sure as he eyed the dull smoke-stained door.

"Just for you." Lance tugged at the iron door flaking rust on the dirt.

"Go on—look!" I wheedled.

Together, we peered in the beast's huge sooty maw. Lance lit a match revealing a cavernous space large enough for a body, but empty, save for ancient clinkers on a corroded grate.

"Okay. That's it. Not much we *can* do till first light. Whoever did—*that* if anybody," he motioned upstairs, "is long gone and we're locked in tight. Let's hunker down, stay close to the fire and—gut it out."

I threw him a glare.

"Right. Wrong choice, but you see what I mean. We can go all to pieces or…"

"Act normal?"

"Yeah," he said defiant. "Yeah! But Magpie… Seriously. Stay put. Don't come down here anymore. Ain't nuthin' to see, folks. Move along." He glared at the insalubrious place, before shoving me ahead. "This can't last. Soon, we'll be rid of—" he gestured up "—*it* and get back to normal. Whatever that is for the Lodge clan," he snorted.

"Sure, Lanny," I shrugged, hugging my arms. *You be the man.* I hoped he was right.

****

To be prudent, I juggled candles—fat wax emergency, to old birthday, and hauled in the grandmother of all tea kettles to the hook in the fireplace. I did a double-take, mugging, "Glad you found *something* age-appropriate." Lance now wore a too-small *Scooby Doo* sweater. "I nipped upstairs while you filled the kettle," he said sheepishly.

"How were our old rooms?" I asked, too casual, hoping my panic bubbling up wasn't too noticeable.

"Dark. Cold." Lance cut me off. "I grabbed this and left." He checked the sweater with a wry expression and then waggled his soggy sneakers.

After rummaging a coat closet, I knelt, yanking them off. "Jeeze, Lance. Baby shoes got thicker soles. Try these." I held out Doc Martin's, stiff with age. *Try to be normal.* Lance stomped about pleased. "Never thought I'd fit Uncle Dez's boots."

"Fit fine, Lanny."

"Better than, Zak?"

I looked away. "Of course."

"Why wasn't I in the will then?" He watched me intently. Trust Lance to bring up sore subjects. I stiffened. "Not now, Lanny. What does *that* have to do with anything! *Neither* of you idiots were." I added pointedly, smiling to take the sting out.

"Ahhh. Just kiddin'. You deserve the leavings. Probably thought you needed it more." Tellingly, he did not regard my damaged shorter leg, and grinned to show it was a joke. *More he ate a sour pickle.* I wasn't fooled for a nanosecond and stared at him.

He studied the boots. "Ya know, I think I like my old high-tops better. More *comfortable* and who knows? These might be part of your *inheritance*?" He eyed me equally barbed, and began unlacing the Doc Martins.

I sighed. So, it was to be this kind of evening.

"Water's hot. Made tea." I said shortly, handing him a mug, and hugging my knees, stared into the fire.

"Nevermind the will. It's you and me, Lanny."

"What about good ole Zak? Good old sex-on-wheels, *Zachary*?"

I brooded into the fitful flames. "Our darlin' cousin would feed this house, brick by brick to the ponies in a De-troit minute," I replied somberly, meaning it—not to placate. "And that ain't hay."

Lance murmured, "Money ain't hay."

"Guilty, not stupid."

"Yah. You're right. Zak is *Vegas!*" Lance made dazzle fingers. "Florida dog tracks. Atlantic City. Vegas!" He chuckled falsely. "He sent a joke postcard once. From Bermuda! So jazzed he won a packet off of a bunch of broken-down mutts he picked a Playmate Of The Week—" he made quote fingers, "and whisked her off to *de is-lands*."

"Why should I care!" I snapped. "Why tell me? It makes no difference."

"Re-ally."

"And it's your business, how?"

"Hey, back off. Didn't mean to rain on your *doodah* parade."

We were both edgy but striving for normal—for us, to keep the wolves of hysterics away. So far, it worked. "No more pity parties, moron!" I biffed his shoulder. "Tea with a stiffener." Throwing a pillow at him, I limped for the kitchen.

"Effin *A!*" He began to say—"*don't go in alone...*" when I pushed through the swing doors into the dark kitchen groping for the chain for the tin-shaded light. At first, my scrambled brain couldn't register the black-against-black shape silhouetted at the table. I closed my eyes. *Not going to jump like a frightened mouse over every little thing.*

I opened my eyes.

The figure moved an arm-shape followed by a rattle of the chain before I could react, and a sickly glow drowned Zak in a sharp waterfall of cold brilliance over his handsome face all peaks and hollows, which did not detract from his model looks. I stifled a yelp, clasping my mouth with both hands. At the same time my heart beat a glad tattoo.

Zak!

Zak's here!

Zak once again playing the sweet fool, pretending he had a gig!

The man in question gave his dark mane habitually falling from a widow's peak, perfectly framing his sharp cheekbones, and strong jaw a casual back-flip as my knees turned to Jello per usual over my cousin's, *my lover's,* stunning beauty. Electric turquoise eyes fringed in double lashes, a phenomenon all of us Lodge's owned, the black Irish hair so like mine and Lance's, but somehow sleeker, thicker, and those photogenic features, as if lit by a New York fashion photographer. *Gorgeous lips I yearned to have kissing me...I blinked.*

Zak grinned lopsidedly with his bewitching aggravating charm. I reached out to steady myself— wanting to run to his arms, and nestle in his lap. Not to be. At my startled *yip,* Lance barged in with the stag head poker over his shoulder like a baseball bat, gave a furious disgusted glance, smoothing to blasé indifference at the last second and flung the poker to the floor.

"Didn't take *you* long, *cuz!*"

Zak didn't flinch. "Meaning? Your subtlety's lost on me Lancer old son, since I see *you* beat me here."

"Stop smirking you idiots"

But I made the slur a love tap. "How *did* you?" I ran to the window. "And why scare the bejeesus out of me! You don't know what…" I almost sobbed with emotions long-caged like dangerous beasts, breathing deep before facing him.

"Zak!" Lance snarled with bitterness that would put gall to shame, flashing an accusing look at me—*did you plan this! I stared back, "no."*

Zak grinned ferally, raising a wicked black brow. Hooking a chair with one foot, he skittered it to me. "Si' down, my gimpy little Cuz, 'fore you fall down."

"Cute, Zak." I grinned like an idiot though. I couldn't help it.

"What *are* you doing? Merely passing through?" Lance sneered and flashed a quick knowing look at the ceiling; widening his eyes, stared meaningfully at me. I shook my head. *Not now!*

Why explain? And what if I had? My house. Now. My lips seemed frozen and pinched even after Zak stood close, and dragged a wisp of hair from my mouth running his thumb over my lips, piercing me with turquoise fire and speaking only to me. "Our little Meggie, didn't mind my presence—or playing house, at least when we were sprats."

I swatted his hand away. *He's hurt that's why he's so mean.* Uncomfortably aware of Lance, fists balled, steam practically coming from his ears. Zak persisted, relentless. His long hair made a curtain around us as he leaned over me; shutting Lance out. "My personal fave was the boathouse." His gaze bored into mine.

" 'Member listening to the water lap the sides and the rocking of the—*boat?*" He yanked me closer cocking a mocking eye on Lance while murmuring huskily in my ear. Lance stood seething. "Now the boat-house! How we…"

Some things never changed.

Zak's eyes held me like a magnet. *He loves winding me and Lance up. Can't cry. I can't!*

I struggled to be free. "Stifle it! You're here one minute and already—stirring things up. You love to do that." He released me with a crooked grin, hands up.

"You got me."

"Shush. He's pulling our chain, Meg." Lance echoed putting a protective hand on my shoulder. Zak leaned and with a genuine sweet smile that undid me, held my chin, and looked deep into my eyes until the room, Lance, the cold, faded out. "You got my number, my heart and any other odd bits and pieces. You realize that. Money or no money. Now, how about a rewind."

I blushed ignoring Lance's resentful face. "I-I am glad to see you, Zak." How stiff! How formal! Lance pretended not to care. Always the looked over, last picked, at least he thought so, and that made it so. I couldn't help it. I adored Zak with all my heart. Blood-family, true.

But, cousins.

It was legal.

All my children will be born with two heads, I half-joked to myself.

Once again, I wished Lance hadn't come, daydreaming of Zak and me, alone in the vast house and all its possibilities…like a Hallmark movie, an idyllic, *us-against-the-elements-survival tale…* Something to tell our grandkids. Even under the circumstances, standing in a freezing kitchen under Lance's scathing approbation, Zak drew me like a magnet. I was shameless.

Then, Zak threw a sardonic regard my way in place of affection, drenching my dreams in cold water, there and gone. "Oh. What am I? Why am I gracing your presence with my vulgar…?" He pressed long fingers against his expensive Patagonia jacket"…*presence*? Ain't this *Ti-juaner*? The flesh pots a Vegas? The Black Hole of Calcutta? Why, it's your dear Cuz. Childhood playmate. Your *sweetheart*, Magpie."

It could have been more hurtful, if Zak hadn't said it with a lazy drawl.

"You listened," I cut in. "How long?"

"Long *enough*," he said heavily.

"Zak. I would never cut you out. Only talk." I felt my face draw up, ugly and miserable and worse, terribly guilt-ridden.

He slanted eyes at me.

"Enough, Zak!" I pleaded. "It's not *you*…!" I began.

"Surprise. For *once*."

"Hush up, Lannie! We've got to tell him!"

Zak returned his attentions to Lance, still curling fists into white knuckle balls. "Shut up Zak. Just, shut-the-hell—up!" Zak, shrugging, changed his cynical face like waving a wand. "Ah! You're right, though. Love getting the wind up with you too."

"Oh, Zak!" I said with a sob in my voice. "Lance, shush! We've got to tell you—"

However, Zak was glancing around the kitchen as if seeing it the first time; tapping the light chain, he watched it swing as if already somewhere else. I could not read his expression. The shade made weird shadows across his face and dark hollows of his eyes. And Lance didn't shut up. "You ass!" Lance spat out. "A no-show when your grandad was dyin'. Didn't even…"

"And Duncan the Wonder Horse was…?" Zak cupped his ear interrupting. "I don't hear you. 'sides, I *was* at the memorial. Where were *you*?"

"Stop it! Stop it both of you! *I* was the only one there *all* the time, in sickness, Uncle's good times, his bad times, the disgusting messes, his dying, his funeral. *All of it.*"

I trailed off, wincing inwardly, hearing the self-serving pity, the old maidish-ness, yet thoughts unwillingly flew back to Uncle Desmond's bleak, depleted, cavernous Grosse Point mansion, and the weedy memorial. The funereal flowers few. Even before, bare spots popped up like cancerous mushrooms showing how faded the silk damask wallpaper. The handsome tarnished Georgian silver serving pieces, forever in place on the massive 1920's Spanish credenza, oddly missing, among other hefty pieces of silver, like the two-foot-tall candlesticks…

No matter now. I bit my cheek, swaying, fighting off a wave of panic.

How could I forget that girl?

Zak had that effect.

We had to tell him but it would make it all *real* again.

****

"*Hey.* Earth to Magpie."

I shook myself, raising my eyes traveling Zak's super-expensive Patagonia jacket, *gift from an admirer, no doubt*—up to his face, delaying what would come, meeting his beguiling innocence before backing off. The expensive jacket was streaked dark-red, initially thinking it a lightning-flash design.

"That's blood." I said wonderingly while I saw Lance narrow his eyes, ready to spout off, when Zak forestalled his eruption. He looked down with his charming smirk, brushing his chest.

"Wandered into a damned thicket! Couldn't tell where the effing road was. Bled like a freakin' pig. Ruined my new jacket," he said with rueful charm and showed off a shallow gash—a scratch actually from the heel of his thumb to his wrist.

Lance and I bounced looks off each other, aware Zak eyed us closely, masked by his amused demeanor.

"What?" I snapped. "What's so hilarious?"

He lifted a broad shoulder in a careless shrug. "You seem more gormless than usual, Lancer. If humanly possible. And what's with you, Meg?" He checked me close. "Hey? Sweetheart?" He lifted my chin again. "Didn't mean to frighten you. Only a—lame joke."

"Got that right!"

He ignored Lance. "Your hands are ice, where are your gloves, babe?"

"We need your car," I said bluntly, refusing to be mollified.

Zak gave a—*what the hell?* look. "No really. What are you and old Lancer-Dude cookin' up, Magpie besides running a cottage morgue? Judas. It's colder than a—"

Lance jutted out his chin giving him a shove. "Shut—up, Zak! Give it a rest! You have *no* idea what's happened here! Ass! Does he, Meg?" Lance, closing ranks like always.

My face crumpled like a wadded tissue, as if I would dissolve into tears.

Chapter 13

Chill as Death

Fascinated apparently by Debbi's corpse, Zak obsessively flipped his lighter.

"Wild! Never seen a body up close. At least—*dead.*"

I hovered near the door, sickened at Zak's levity on one level—only Zak trying to be an unflappable arse.

Blood on the quilt patterns merged with Zak's jacket, melding into Lance's bloody hands, to a sea of blood, washing from one shore of my mind, to another. My vision shrank to a tunnel, catching myself. Hungry. That's all. The scalding, spicy chili seemed a lifetime ago. Before Debbi. This was not helping. Must stay strong. Who for? The boys? They should be here *with* me. Not squabbling. The usual squall-lines threatened to make this even more intolerable. Zak exceptionally caustic, even for him. Lance could be fussy as an old maid, but Zak didn't need to goad him.

All this waded through a swampy morass of my mind.

Wearily I heard, *"Let the party get a little out of hand?"* I watched Zak lift the quilt again, sneering, "or another botched op?" He leaned closer, cocking his head before dropping the quilt.

"Might've been hot once."

Lance smirked, casually lifting the cover too, all macho, studying Debbi as if clinically.

"Think so? And how would you have knowledge of that? A layman?" He snorted superiorly. "*Forensic Files*?"

I hugged my arms hating them both.

The two trying to outdo each other in macho B.S.

"So that's how you get your jollies, Doc-tor?"

I closed my eyes. Zak never quit needling Lance over his low-on-the-totem pole, status. After graduating from an offshore med school, he ran a—if truth be told—cheesy clinic. Something Boris Karloff, Vincent Price, or Laird Creger might preside over if it were a black and white film, instead of Lance's attempts at empire building with a string of emergency clinics.

My mind was wandering. Concentrate. Get back to what's important. Then, Lance shoved Zak hard. Zak caught Lance around the arms and ribcage twirling him to the door—when Lance hooked Zak's ankle after an awkward tussle. The two spun back, Lance trying to break Zak's bear hug, kicking him with his sneaker. Zak over-tipping, fell hard against the bed frame. As the two idiots grappled, the bed jolted. Lance stumbled into Zak.

Zak swiveled, slamming Lance into the bed in turn.

Unbelievable.

Amid curses, grunts, and charges of "moron!" I watched Debbi's wrapped body rock to the edge, numbed and outraged as the body teetered before falling, dragging the quilt with her, and landing with a horrible squelching *thump*. Unable to make myself move, I screamed.

The two men looked stunned, then down at what

they had achieved.

Sidestepping, Zak released Lance, while Lance's feet tangled in the quilt. He went down hard beside Debbi's body, crying, "Fuck you, Zak!"

I shrieked like a harpy. "Stop it! *Both* of you! What's wrong with you two? Have some respect! You are both acting like jerks!" The shameful terrifying part was, my emotions were stuck between laughing and crying.

Zak regarded Debbi's body now tangled in stained bedding, with aversion.

Lance kicked the quilt free, panicking. "Get it off! You freak!"

"Lance! I said, *quit*."

Zak scrambling up, threw a look, warning me— *better be a great explanation!*

I did not own one. And this whole scene was bizarre—something from a surreal Tarantino film.

"What the hell, Meg? Why didn't you tell me! Christ we were having a damned cocktail party down there! And this—?" He pointed with disgust at Debbi's body still enmired in quilt. It was taking on all the qualities of a farce. I could feel feverish laughter still tugging at my cheek muscles. I nodded wearily, biting my inner cheek. *Why try to explain?*

"Please, put her back." I demanded quietly, instead.

Lance stooped, untangled his feet, and tossed a clean flap of quilt over Debbi's face. The two had the decency to grapple her back on the bed, Zak trying not to touch any part of her, while Lance wiped his hands down his jeans. *Surreal.* Then Lance smiled cocky at Zak. I wanted to hit him. "Little blood never hurt nobody. Knee-deep in it most times." Lance's bragging about his macho status, ground on my nerves like never before.

"So, you keep telling us, ad-nauseam. But blood, man! You don't know who she was, where she's been!"

"Man-up yourself. Like I said, I deal with it every day." As he left the charnel house of a room, Zak threw over his shoulder, "Bully for you, slugger. What med school you say you ma-tri-cu-la-ted from? Haiti was it? Chad? Outer *Mongolia*?"

I crossed my arms and threw darts at them both.

****

"So. *Don't t*ell me." We had gathered in the Great Room.

"—that's all I can say," I finished wearily.

"You pick up a total stranger?"

"We've been through this! I wasn't thinking. You have no idea how bad it was."

"Never saw her before? No one watching, following you on the way? Nothing strange here?"

Only that glass upended in the sink...

"I *told* you. No one. A couple of patrols stopped us, but—"

Zak strode to the kitchen testing the cellar door.

"Oh, not to worry. A *rat* couldn't get in, with your exception of course."

I threw Lance a look, then Zak. "How *did* you? Get in?"

Zak dangled a key. "Jiggled the chair loose too by the way. Bad move, Prancy."

"*Please,* Zak." He knew how Lance hated nicknames. *Nancy, Fancy-Lancy*, etc. Those stupid juvenile labels still sticking like crazy glue on the fingers.

Lance scowled at him. "Car, Zak. No joke."

"Don't get all *manly* on me." Zak mock-cringed and

116

lit a cigarette. *My ciggies* I noted. "Snow-plowed in a drift about a mile back with my usual élan and skill. Why?"

"We siphon Meggie's gas and run for it. Your car. Or mine. That's what, you ass!"

Zak yanked the veranda doors' dusty drapes in answer. Throwing an amused glance, he pulled tongs from the door handle. The French doors blasted open spitting ice-spicules in a hail of wind scouring the room in a whirlwind lifting the carpets. Three feet of white stuff wedged the jamb. Forcing them closed, he faced us down. "After you, sports."

"You're history, once it melts." Lance glared at me. "Right, Meg?" I acted like I didn't hear, as the monster storm blew artic breaths down the chimney, and soot spattered the hearth. To me, the blizzard was personal. A wild beast circling, sniffing for weak spots. Me. I was the weak spot. I came willy-nilly, and drew them all for whatever reason, into this white hell. Even Debbi would be alive. "*If she didn't freeze by that dumpster,*" my lesser angel whispered. I cast the notion aside as weak, observing Lance fiddling with the old Zenith television.

"Makin contact with the other side? It's *analog.*" Zak cast a sardonic glance, including me in it.

"Oh, yeah...forgot." Lance brooded into weak flames, seemingly out of the combat zone.

Zak next fondled the hefty tarnished brass replica of the ill-fated *Lancette* from the mantelpiece, with an unreadable expression. "Wonder why Granddad saved this sad piece of drek?"

"Happier times. We all lost. Drop it."

"Not quite. Old Dez was *my* grandpappy. A bloody saint taking you two in," he winked showing it was joke.

"You and Lance here swallowed the cream," he finished musingly. "And I got sour milk." I studied him. That wasn't like Zak. He always seemed to land jam-side up no matter how cash poor, usually by his cheeky charm.

"Whatever. Said you didn't care." I felt snappish. And yes, slightly guilty. True, enough. Lance and I were under sweet Uncle Dez's wing, while Zak got sucked into the lackluster embrace of Flo's sister, Madge, who maybe not as madcap, but drank as much after both sets of parents died. Maybe that's why Zak was a comic with a cynical edge.

"Truth is, you're a trespasser," Lance butted in. "Isn't that right, Meggie? Tell him. To the point. It didn't take you long to sniff out money."

"What's family for?" Zak asked carelessly. "Wasn't here much. But you two? Tight as ticks on a *dawg*. Couldn't wait to pull the rug out and roll old Zak up in it." He stoked the fire. "No matter. Maybe I can wait tables."

"Why *are* you here, Zakkie? You never said?"

"Why same as our boy here. To look after our little Meggie's interests." Flashing gorgeous expensive teeth, Zak ran a hand down my cheek and dropped it carelessly to my breast. I sat like a deer before a hunter's gun while Lance looked on prissy and disgusted.

"Not necessary, Zak."

He got my message, casting a careless glance as he moved off. "Don't stay on the shelf too long, Meg. One tends to get—dusty." I was hurt; he was the one placing me back on the shelf! "Too late to look after me own interests it seems," Zak resumed, glancing out at the storm. "Now if little Nutmeg hadn't made herself so *gol-darn* indispensable to poor old Grandpappy."

His lazy smile soothed the hurt.

My ringing slap didn't.

Zak felt his jaw. "You work out?"

My glower would have stripped paint.

"Leave her alone! I'm weepin', Zak," Lance yelped. "You pick up every slut waggling her tits. Every bookie and loan shark's gunnin' for you." Lance jabbed Zak's chest. "Uncle Dez shelled out plenty."

"Slut? That's huge coming from the son of a drunk, slash hooker, slash, barmaid, crazy as a Brazil nut! Who, in an alcoholic *stupor* managed to assassinate *both* our parents in a death-defying act of gravity, when the Lancette there," pointing at the mantelpiece, "hit the *fan!*"

Zak punctuated that last by tossing a profligate amount wood on the fire. He turned glaring us down. I had never seen Zak angry, or lose his cool. "And 'sides, I gamble *online*. Where you been the last twenty years, Lance? In a cave, enjoying your hair shirt?"

Then, Zak twisted the knife.

"Yeah. Good old crazy Flo and your pappy. Old Landon, knocks up a boozer, an gotta marry her up, all nice and hog-tied."

"Name Lodge'll do it every," Lance said too offhand. "Beside we wouldn't be here."

I listened sickened. *It was all true.* It was like lancing a blister, releasing the pressure of pain, too-long ignored, but I wished they'd stop before it was too late to take back.

"An, then, and then—listen up kiddies, I'm lovin' this. He lets old drunk as a sow, *Flo* behind the wheel of a million-buck prototype. Brilliant!" I had no clue Zak was that bitter. Yet his own parents died horribly too.

That sad girl upstairs, made it all come out like a hot towel on a boil.

Lance turned even paler. "Mom couldn't help it! Your dad didn't have a gun to his head. He didn't have to hand over the keys."

"Pop had reason all right. A little—" Zak leered, spreading his blue-jeaned legs. "A little *wiiiide open reward*, just beggin' for it." I intuited it would happen. Zak deserved it.

"It takes two! Asshole!"

Lance rushed Zak managing a roundhouse swing.

Zak barely moved, smirking until I spoke.

"If it was so *terrible*. Why did you want to do it again, years later?" I asked quietly.

Zak stopped. If I hit him with the stag head tongs, he could have seemed no more stunned. Could he have forgotten that ghastly night that changed my life?

Zak at last seemed stricken. "Sorry, Nutmeg. God, I'm so sorry. I never quite said that did I? Thought you— guessed."

"Typical," Lance muttered.

"Let's lighten up, kiddies. A little anesthetic in order. Right? Let's get wasted. Your department, I believe, Lancer." He made a drinking motion, swiveling his gaze at me. "Or is that you, Magpie?"

"Can't you stay nice for one second?"

Lance motioned upstairs.

"Really? Like—*party*?"

"Fall off your puritanical pulpit, Prancer." Zak clapped hands. "Toga—toga! To whatzer name. To Debbi! Debbi's wake!"

"Un-believable." Lance shook his head. "Or wake the dead!"

I pleaded with my eyes. "I'll go nuts, Lanny. We're safe. What better way to—to wait it out?"

Anything to change the poisonous atmosphere.

Chapter 14

Eye of the Storm

"So, he sez. Get this." Lance snickered helpless at his own shaggy dog story. "*Oh sir! The koala tea of Murphy is never strained...*" and collapsed into drunken giggles. "Qual-ity of mercy? Get it?"

Zak and I groaned. Zak made a mock toast. "Truly awful."

"Yes, it was, wasn't it?" Lance said pleased.

We three cousins lounged on scrounged pillows. The hearth was warm. Litters of odd gift-liqueurs in lurid colors, wine turned to vinegar, an ancient decanter of sticky sherry, my whiskey, and a half bottle of scotch found below the sink, surrounded us.

"To the lovely lass upstairs, whoever she is."

Zak lifted his jelly glass of something green.

"To Debbi," I whispered queasy.

We had trudged reluctantly upstairs, and covered Debbi properly while discussing what to do. What was appropriate. Soberly, in the spirit of a memorial we began our drinking-to-oblivion, ceremony. At first, the sugar gave me a rush. After checking the whiskey level, I had presence of mind to slip off with it, cap it, climbing a chair, and stow it back on a high shelf. I only had two bottles left.

My drunken gaze strayed to the ceiling, a foot above

my head—then the servant stairs.

Still in a *happy place*, I lit a kitchen candle, and tiptoed up the dark narrow back steps. *"I can play games too."* I giggled. *Wouldn't the guys worry? Like hide and seek. They'll freak out and wonder where I am.* "I'll make noises." I smothered a drunken laugh sobering as I stared at Debbi's room from the landing across the short passage connecting to the hall. A flickering glow from the fire bounced up the broad stairs to her door.

"Poor Debbi," I recall mumbling, all maudlin. Then, somehow, I was outside Debbi's door, and my hand turning the knob.

After hesitation, I stepped inside, falling against the door as I did so when my bad leg flagged. *"Shhh,"* I giggled knowing at the same time how wrong that was, but liquor sat heavy on my stomach screwing with my head, filling the void where solid food should have been. At least I told myself later.

The room was dim beyond the wall of candle light. I couldn't see the bed. *Funny.* Not afraid. Pleased at that. I think I was sobering a bit, when something touched me.

I screeched to wake the dead, even the wrapped body on the bed, with stains inexorably showing through the clean sheet, and whirled thrusting my candle in Zak's face.

"Zachary! Sugar! Don't creep up like that! What are you *do*ing!"

"What game are *you* playin' at, Magpie?" He asked quietly. "Your candle freaked me out, moving around up here."

Of a sudden, alcohol and a sugar low caught up. Resting my head on Zak's chest, I mumbled, "she seemed so—lonely." Not sure if I meant it...something to say to make me not seem so stupid and lame.

"Lone-ly?" His grin was a little off.

"Go 'way," I grumbled. "Don' need you."

"A little smashed. Come on, sweetheart."

"Quit placating!" I shoved him. Like shoving a tree. "You have no right to follow me, or judge. I take care of myself!"

"Right." Zak sighed heavily. "But let's not make a night of it. Say a little prayer—or whatever. One for us, while you're at it." He turned to the bed. The quilt had slid down revealing Debbi's hair, not her face.

I giggled, pointing. "You look like Lance."

"What? Oh."

Zak dropped a thin grayish wrist sticking out from the quilt. The wrist made a *thunking* sound on the bed frame. "Almost frozen. Don't have to worry about *that.* You know."

"Don't." I looked away.

"What's rigor mortis like anyhow? Like when does it start, or end for that matter? Lance'd be acquainted with that stuff."

"What does it matter! Is it a guy-thing? You are all morbid!" Awkwardly, not really looking at her covered face, I felt compelled to gingerly smooth Debbi's hair, neatening it.

Zak grabbed my hand.

"Gotta keep everything *as is.* Remember? What would Perry Mason do?"

I clenched my jaw, still queasy from the mix of alcohol. *Humoring me again. What a weird conversation.*

"*Ironsides.* He was a detective in a wheelchair!" I grumped.

"Iron-sides. In the dark ages. Ever hear of CSI? Dateline? Let's go!"

"Too real. "I kept my eyes riveted on the body. She resembled a mummy now.

"Why didn't I think of that?" He gave me an impatient amused glance. "Your funeral."

"You coming, or still post-death bonding?" He waited. "Come on Magpie. Let's go," he said it softly.

I nodded grateful and for once did not wait for his arm, but sped out ahead of him.

Chapter 15

False Spring

Pulling down an ancient Christmas sweater with a dyspeptic reindeer, over a faded flannel shirt snagged last night, from a closet, I staggered in the kitchen, yawning. Packing had been woefully inadequate for the U.P. Gray sweat pants completed the ensemble. I squinted. My brains were scrambled, and head throbbed from the nightmare, the storm that kept me up, and liquor consumed.

I blinked grumpily at Zak, whistling, busying himself at the gas stove. Sugar! Did he need to surface so perfect in the morning, conscious of my thrown together get up in the name of warmth. The kitchen was relatively pleasant though with brilliant sun painting everything golden. Something smelt good. *Normal.* Yesterday suddenly seemed distant as a silent film. Hugging my arms, I sniffed the air appreciatively.

Zak was frying a mess of eggs on the ancient gas range. Vexed, I noted a wasteful litter of coffee granules surrounding my tiny jar of instant I'd purchased, next to his steaming cup. Deftly scooping eggs to a warming plate, where four slices of toast dripping with butter already resided, Zak settled back like a visiting prince at the porcelain table, sipping coffee and puffing one of my cigarettes from the pack I had stupidly left on the table.

I eyed him balefully, raking the three egg shells, open bread bag, the spilt coffee. Snatching my cigarettes, I shoved them in my pocket and made a prudent cup of coffee. All I could stomach at the moment anyway.

"Too bad you didn't get *real* coffee." Zak made a face. "Have some toast. I made too much."

"Ya think? Sugar bear, Zak. That has to last." *Did it?* Hating my mother tone, eyeing the toast hungrily. *But dang.*

"Defeatist. Do as you want it to be, and it'll happen." Zak airily waved the toast. I shot him a look. Winding me up again.

"Then I'll be expecting that pizza delivery any second now, and snow will have melted."

"Now who's the comic?"

I wandered to the window searching for the yellow yolk of sun, swallowed by a monster cloudbank, to reappear and begin its job of melting. Scraping a wedge of glass, I studied the yard. Same difference. A blinding snowscape. Soon we could leave though. Can't last forever. The sun would come out again, if not today, tomorrow, ignoring a low fast-moving train of clouds puffing away east to west. After some unpleasantness with investigators, *vague about that*, I'll pretend all this never happened.

I ignored drifts to the boat house roof and firs drooping under wet snow-weight, plus the fact the lane to the house was a formless wallow...*jumping* to the *thud* of an ax, habitually rusting in the chopping block. The withdrawn ax screeched like the teakettle *shrieking* at the same moment behind me. Sucking in a breath, I turned the flame down, feeling my heart beat faster. Hated feeling this goosey. Everything was going to be *fine.*

With a fresh cup of joe, I watched Lance heft the axe again. It skidded down the side of the log almost taking him, and his favorite sneakers with it. I sighed. *All wrong, Lanny. Hold it upright for kindling.* I threw Zak a look, nodding at Lance.

"And save some, pig." I snatched at his plate.

"Oh sure, where's me manners?" He grinned, offering me his half-eaten eggs.

"Don't even."

"Yah. Didn't they tell you eggs're bad?"

I bit my lip as Zak ground his cigarette in the unfinished egg's shiny yellow center.

"These too." Reaching in my pocket, Zak removed my ciggies. I grabbed at them, but he held the pack out of reach, snaking a strong arm about my waist, bent his beautiful head to mine, giving me full benefit of his electric smoldering gaze and grazed my cheek with his mouth.

I glared up at him, taking in the bluish stubble. Even unshaven it only added to his rakish appeal. In any other age he would have been Tyrone Power, the bad boy of the golden age of cinema, or more recently I conceded, Jude Law. Zak might be broke and indolent, but his religion was keeping fit. Biking, hiking, boxing, *or bedroom gymnastics.* He illustrated by clamping my body, hip to breast to his, reaching down, with my neck arched to meet him, he kissed me with a tenderness that undid me, spearing warmth to parts I did not want to awaken at that moment, hoping desperately, that Lance would not take that time to enter all hale and hearty, censoring us with a scowl.

Pushing away with more effort than I wished to show, while Zak eyed me as if I amused him, I almost wavered, but instead threw out the egg. Zak tossed the pack back, winked, and tying a muffler around his head, like an old a nanny, headed outside. Funny, on him, it didn't seem ridiculous.

I watched as Zak said something. Lance, pinched with cold, flushed scarlet, mouthed something back; chucking the ax close to Zak's feet, stomped back to the house.

Zak effortlessly steadied the log upright, cleaving it with one blow. A few *tunks* and it split into kindling. I turned as if I hadn't noticed, when Zak toted in an obnoxious stack of wood, a blast of cold trailing him that smelt of snow, instantly changing the kitchen from ice box to Sub Zero fridge, bellowing from the Great Room. "Hey, Nutmeg! Tried to get your battery up. Still dead as road kill."

My car was a near shapeless mound after nightly gales re-sculpted it. Fat flakes drifting lazily past the kitchen window, thickening as I watched—when I felt the first niggle of doubt worm its way, that we might be forced to stay with our unwanted guest, a bit longer. And I really hadn't heard Zak try to get the battery to turn the starter over, or whatever it did.

"If you're going to leave the door open, I need to find something warmer!" I snapped, feeling unkind. I hated going upstairs again but darned if I'd ask *them*. 'Sides, a quick trip to my old room, to dig more sweaters, back in a flash. What was I? I was only five feet two, but my *age* wasn't *two*.

****

At the landing, I darted a peek at Debbi's door averting my face.

I turned back, whispering, *"But, we locked it...!"*

The door was swung back against the wall.

Wide open.

Smears marred faded wallpaper beside it, and what seemed a partial rusty foot print on the old hall runner. I grasped the brown china knob to quickly slam shut the door. Against my resolve, I risked a sideways glance inside. It seemed morbid to keep dwelling on her. The room was like a morgue. She was safe until—?

Forget her, I lectured myself.

I wish I had listened.

****

My shrieks shattered the cold like ice shattering rock—high and cracking. Lance and Zak collided in their race to the top to find me crouched by the banister, whimpering. Lance had snatched the tongs and Zak the hefty bronze *Lancette* replica. "What happened!" Lance yelled. "You okay?"

"She's *gone.*" I observed them wordless. My mouth was gaping, my eyes wide and staring, yet I could not see them, *only the empty blood-crusted snarl of sheets.* "Not there! Left f-for p-parts unknown…" I managed through chattering teeth and began giggling.

"Dammit, Meggie. Stop with the damn games!" To my sick regret, even Zak appeared mildly disapproving. He of the dubious jokes. "Meggie. Dammit kiddo. I told you to stay away from up here."

"No, you didn't!" I had my stubborn face on to match my mood.

"Hell. I should have. Of all the…"

I doubled over gulping for air between gasping laughter, pointing at the open door. "S-see for yourself, He-men!'

Lance and Zak threw a—*what's up now!* look, in

manly fashion over the folly of women in general, and me in particular.

"Jeeeze, Meg! Really lame!" Lance threw at me. Reluctantly, the two stepped inside, self-consciously holding their weapons, when I stumbled past hiccupping and trying to keep from shivering, I stood in front of the bed. "See!" Before they could stop me, I ran my hands over sheets stiff with blood with the imprint of her body apparent, as if trying to prove my argument. Flicks of dried blood spat in the air.

Zak shoved me away and gazed dispassionately at the depressed shape on the ruined mattress. Grabbing my waist, he pivoted me out of the way. I struggled, accidently scratching his cheek. "Ow! Dagnabit, Meggie! Hold on to her!"

Lance grabbing me, still gazed poleaxed at the empty bed, while Zak stupidly checked the hall.

Swinging back, he tipped the closet door poking hangers, making tinny irritating music till I wanted to shout at him. I broke free and walked slowly to the bed whispering her name as if Debbi might rematerialize. Zak lifted me, bodily dumping me in the hall.

"She's losing it, man. Hang on to her, I said!" Zak closed the door behind him. "Get your nutty head out of those shitty films, Meg for once in your miserable life." I flinched as if from a blow.

"Don't, Zak!" I faced them with my hands as clenched as my jaw. "She's alive. Don't you see? She's after us! Hiding. And really-really mad…and…" I put my head in my hands, sobbing. I recognized I sounded insane, like the stereotypical hysterical female.

Lance swerved on me piling on. "She's not a flesh-eating zombie, Nutmeg! She's not one of *Lugosi's* bloody-fanged wives, in case you were wondering! It's not bloody, bleeding, Night of the Living Fucking *Dead!*" Lance bellowed more undone than I'd ever seen him.

"*Now is it!*"

I began weeping great honking sobs, horribly aware I looked ugly. I knew I sounded crazy.

"Oh. Great help, Lance." Zak crouched by me, brushing my hair. I shook off Zak's hand and pushed Lance aside. "Leave me be! Both of you! She's not *dead! Not dead notdead...!*"

"Got it. Okay. Not dead. Probably tapdancing in the dining room as we speak." Zak studied me as if I had bats circling my head.

Lance watched too as if I were being fitted for a straitjacket. "Meggie? How? She's way past dead."

"Where is it? She? The *body*?" He spoke so gently, my teeth ached. I contemplated him as if he asked me to name the presidents in alphabetical order. I shook my head, mumbling, "Okay. I'm all right."

Zak leaned against the wall, blocking the door, I noted, arms folded. "Better?"

"Yeah. Hunky-dory." I glared up wiping my eyes with the back of my hand.

"Right. Back to reality, or real as it gets." He threw an inscrutable look at Lance. As he turned, I made a run for it, limping fast, my voice dimming down the dark hall, calling, "*Deb-biiiii.*"

I don't get why I did that. It was a stupid act. I did not believe she was a *ghost,* or some creature found only in slasher novels, or bad, late night black and white TV. Mainly, I wanted to be alone. I wanted to be worried about. I wanted to rile them both.

"Oh crap! If Meg's on a four lane to Loony-toons, I'm gaining on her," I heard Lance spout.

"Watch out for that short cut. It's a killer," Zak gritted. And I felt even more insane if possible. What had I accomplished? They were as spooked as I, if they only admitted it.

I was at a dead end. The only why out was through the attic. Dumb. *Dumb. I checked back.*

"Christ ona crutch!" I saw Zak thrust fingers through his long hair. "Like we need this. Go get her. Go, go! I'll check the house."

My face burned. I only wanted to hide myself.

"Sure thing. One of us gets to play Super Hero."

"You wanna check?"

Lance sneered and loped off after me.

****

"In the freaking widow's walk."

Lance bundled a sullen me to the fireplace. "Your turn, for God's sake." Glaring, I shock him off, bitterly aware I acted irrational.

He darted a glance at Zak… *find anything?*

Zak gave a jerk of the head.

"Sorry, guys," I glanced up contrite. "I blew it. I freaked out."

"No kidding?" Lance muttered under breath.

****

It was midnight if anyone cared. Lance and I sat, backs to the fire. I held the stag head poker so tight my knuckles showed. Lance gripped the kindling ax. Zak whapped the hefty *Lancette* with the sharp fins and angles against his palm. No one commented when he left. My vow to not drink lasted a day as I nursed a jelly glass of whiskey, listening to banging and hammering about the house. I tried not to think of how hungry I was.

"I scouted outside," Zak said, tossing a hammer aside. "No prints or anything not kosher. What I couldn't lock, I nailed the bugger shut. Split that side table in the dining room to nail over the two big windows. Sorry Meg."

I looked startled. I wanted to keep the antiques but admitted it was an ugly dark Spanish piece that even a shabby-chic whitewash wouldn't rescue, amazed Zak apologized for destroying *anything*. It was needed though. The dining room boasted long windows reaching the floor.

I shuddered, smiling wanly. "Take whatever. Such a—cavernous house. So many rooms with defenseless windows," I muttered.

"Kinda rough back there, Nutmeg. Got to me too." For once Zak seemed to mean it. "This is not a drill. Stick close." We three awkwardly stacked hands even though Lance threw a sour glance. "Zak the hero. Who watches the watcher?" We eyed each other and away, when abruptly the two sconces beside the fireplace flickered. Somewhere a socket made a sizzling sound. Lights stayed off for good…and that was the beginning.

****

I huddled against still-warm stone, trying to separate dark from dark, in the room's vastness. The half circle of orange light, extended only a short way. The overstuffed chair seemed a hump-backed beast. Tongs glittered malevolent eyes. The antler chandelier made wicked pointed shadows on the ceiling, and something kept moving in the corner. I was sure of it. None of us wanted to dwell on the inconceivable. We would go mad.

I tightened my grip on the poker. Zak watched

Lance—then me. Lance and I eyed Zak as he dozed. Snow fell—silent malevolent creeping snow, layer upon soft soundless layer replenishing any melting that happened during the day's feeble warmth.

Chapter 16

Whiteout

As we checked skies resembling dirty gray wool socks and a yard shrouded in clinging fog, Zak kicked a four-foot drift encroaching the screen door. Bundled to the max in a raffish assortment of sweaters, mufflers, gloves, and coats; a moth-eaten fuchsia ski cap with flaps and tassels for Zak, Lance wrapped a sweater over his mob cap, tying the arms under his chin, and me stuffed in so many sweaters and my ratty fur, I couldn't bend my arms.

We were reality television.

Zak surveyed me, trying to stifle a laugh. "Not the fur, sweetheart. It'll only slow you down. I pointedly observed Lance's floor length black duster, but conceded.

To the right, the lake, lost in a chill layer of mist, skirted the lawn, a steep forest shrouded in white climbed to the old logging road. Before us past the boathouse, the formless wallow of the lane was defined by a faint saddle in the middle, that eventually led to the main road, such as it was—only a quarter mile if that. Surely, we could make it, once a sun showed itself. Zak and Lance both put the kibosh on venturing over the logger's trail.

"A three-mile hike, most uphill through heavy snow with too many hungry critturs about, Magpie," Zak winked and nodded at the lane. "Least it's warmer. Cloud cover's holding the heat in."

"We didn't notice," Lance soured. "Must be two whole degrees. A heat wave. Wasn't aware you were a meteorologist too."

Zak ignored Lance. "Gotta better idea? Either go or not. Which is it, Cub Scouts?"

I checked the rusty thermometer by the screen. Ten above. *Right. Warmer.*

"Magpie? Your choice. If we make the road, we might meet snow plows, even traffic. Or not."

I mumbled through the red scarf. "Been through that. Food's giving out," I said pointedly. "Harder to gather wood. It's been a week, guys!" I didn't mention Debbi. As if Debbi was from another silent film seen long ago.

"I can go solo."

Lance dug at Zak. "And leave us behind? *We* can starve! Not to mention bodies floating around. Somewhere!"

He threw Lance a sour stare. "Yeah, that too. So, we all go."

Neither mentioned I may not be able to keep up. Bless them for once.

Zak thrust off as if from the top of a slalom run, and it was decided.

I waddled after until we reached the marshmallow wave of white stuff topping the boathouse. Beyond, I saw drifts engulfed a telephone pole halfway up. Trees seemed stucco-ed and snow clung to my boots like white mud as we waded to the nonexistent path; Zak forging ahead showed no mercy, with Lance close behind in what seemed a deranged race.

Puffing mightily, I trailed, head down, keeping in their tracks, ignoring my leg. It throbbed, but cold numbed the shooting pain that I feared would come. Good exercise, I told myself. Get the scar and muscles limber again, however, my weak leg made me wobble off course about twenty feet into the lane.

I sank sideways to my waist, struggling flailing, I tried to turn on my belly to crawl out, until I was in danger of losing them. I hollered my throat raw. Lance finally twisted round. Contrarily, I waved him on shouting, "I'm fine! Keep going," and face down, finally clawed out, dragging my good leg atop the packed snow. When I raised my head, I couldn't see them, even Zak's fuchsia cap.

"Drat." Dismally aware, with the first flicker of alarm…all appeared the same—a blank white sheet; dimly sensing snow camouflaged invisible firs lining the path and the tiniest dip in what I hoped was the middle path.

Gaining my feet, I plowed on, in what I thought was a faint trail. My scar burned now and muscles, jumping like a frog, seized up like a vice gripped my leg. Opening my mouth to call in anger this time, a tug choked my words off, jerking me backward. "Ginger! Sugar bear!" I cursed, yanking my scarf that had snagged on a pine bough. I rubbed my neck, and massaged my aching leg. The cold seemed to *relish* the damned metal plates holding my tibia together.

I raised my head, alerted. Thought I heard Lance, detecting panic in his voice. *"Damn…! Zak. Which way?"*

"Back there. That way. No. This way. It's this way."
Lance's voice again muffled in layers. *"Where's the*

friggin' trees?"

I put my mitten to my mouth stifling a giggle. Nothing had been humorous for a long time; even giddier after spying a red flash before my nose. A scarlet thread from my scarf swung on a pine bough of one of the blessed trees flanking the path.

Leave me behind will they? I floundered over. Plucking the thread, I made out the next tree lining the lane like ghostly soldiers…and the next…Ten minutes later, I ran onto the boathouse. *"Ollie ollie oxen free!"* I laughed through wooden lips stiff with cold.

****

I was lounging before a fire sipping something hot, water really, but it was the effect I wanted, when Zak and Lance stomped in like characters from *Frozen*.

"Christ, Meg!" Zak roared, "Not smart. Coulda been *stranded* out there."

"Who?" I peered up wide eyed and innocent. "Me, or you?"

"Oh haha, funny as a crutch, Magpie!" Lance sneered.

"Lighten up, Iron Men."

Contrite——*somewhat,* I made soup that night, tossing in a found can of pumpkin from a top cupboard, an orphan destined for some long-ago Thanksgiving pie, with a splash of milk, stirred in peanut butter, and toasted scraps of bread for dipping, vaguely supposing it was "Eastern." It proved to be our last "gourmet" meal.

Unchastened by the aborted run, at least on the surface, Zak blithely suggested games. Even Lance agreed, half-joking, sending daggers at Zak. "Let's play *murder.* I remember where there's a dart board."

We laughed and said, "Good one, Lance." I look

back now on how frenziedly we tried for normal.

Giddy. Like camp. Or when kids summering with Uncle Dez. None of us wanted to think on dropping temperatures, dwindling food, or a vanished body. Grandly, I opened the closet of galoshes, moth-riddled mackinaws, fish poles, and enough old magazines to decoupage Grand Central Station, announcing, "We here at Meggie Lodge's Freeze 'n Starve, Bug 'n Bed, strive for excellence, serving each guest according to one's plea-sures. We have a most excellent Chinese Checkers, and vintage puzzle stock—"

I kissed my fingers, "*Nonpareil* with only a few missing pieces at the utmost."

Zak rubbed hands. "Superb choice. One gets so jaded in one's travels," caroling, "ah, the simple life," and shuffled a raggedy-assed deck of cards, dealing them. "All accounted for as I recall, save the four of clubs, and one ace."

But then Lance had to be an old maid. He tossed his cards, nailing us. "Aren't there more productive items on our agenda? Shouldn't we be combining our energies? Come up with some agenda! Some strategy!"

"Don't know 'bout you Lancer Dude, but my maxim is live good, die old and leave an ugly corpse."

"Hard to live *gooood*, if we're dead first."

Zak shook his head in mock dismay. "Lance-Lance-Lance. Some would call this enforced quality time." Zak smashing me up against him, arching wicked crow's-wing brows, bussed me on the forehead, releasing me. "In the bosom of one's family."

He continued dealing. "Saint Lance-a-Lot here hasn't had a break in donkey's years. Right, Lancer? 'Nough ta make a man go bonkers. All that blood and guts. 'Sides, a few days and poof—all the snow will vanish like coke at a Shriner's convention."

He paused. "Along with me. So, chill."

I hid my disappointment over his casual manner, pretending to sort my cards.

****

The Great Room rocked with the Polar Express rushing French doors; yet cozy with drapes pulled and fire battling the cold and dark, all of us bundled like abominable snowmen as cards flew across a rug; cut throat poker with impossible to recall wild cards or rules. Old Maid, Crazy Eights, then Parcheesi... Finally, we lay back and reminisced over long lazy lost summers with uncle Dez.

Later, though, Zak, sprawled by the fire slugging *my whisky,* morosely fooling with cards, shut us out. Lance, hands behind his head, leaning against the warm stone, stared into the dark. Each of us, I realized, privately brooded now the din of modern life was stilled. Each expected more from life, much as I had. Mine was a given. I would never be a ballerina. I made a face. Lance yearned for a proper doctor's, or even surgeon's, vaulted prestige. He had the hands and the knack, but perhaps not the drive—I never interrogated him—ending up at an off-shore island medical college, with a questionable degree after four short years and a dingy clinic in the cheap rent district.

And *gorgeous* Zak. Model perfect. With his eyes on Saturday Night Live, or his own comedy show on HBO for all I knew; Zak the perfect weekend guest, the witty handsome dinner extra, month-long arm candy for wealthy widows in exotic places, the five lines or less extra, whenever casting was in town. Yet he wasn't vain.

He could have made a bundle by taking Vogue by storm.

His affairs never lasted, and I hadn't asked. Glad the widows drifted away, or I had an inkling it was Zak who bid fond, cleverly worded adieux, leaving the divorcees, the middle-aged career gals breathless and grateful in place of resentful.

I shook my head, safe in the knowledge that Zak was mine, no matter how it appeared, as soon as that first break blasted him into stardom, and pride would allow him to make me, truly *his*...Somehow, by what unkenned chemistry, we were linked.

I jerked up aware he depleted my whiskey at a hurtful rate. "Strictly BYOB from now on, *Cuz,*" I smiled. *"Give."* Zak enigmatically regarded me, making me conscious I was now decked in a maroon muffler, bedraggled red sweater, gray socks, rust cords, and over all, my ratty fur, the warmest stuff I could rummage that didn't smell of mothballs.

"My, you do look fetchin'..." I flushed, shrugging. "Still masses of stuff—upstairs. I'll try harder to become a fashion icon."

"Upstairs? Interesting thought." Zak slowly peeled the label. "Promise something, Magpie? You won't go up there again—alone?"

"Get over yourself," I snapped tugging my sweater straight. I had a feeling he didn't want me to fly off the handle again, as if I had no control.

Zak tightened the cap and after a feint, gently lobbed the bottle at me. I almost dropped it. I won't show my need. *I won't.* I carried it to kitchen. My relief was raw as sandpaper.

****

I sat at the porcelain table in the dark relishing my

martyr role of *freezing to death* and rolling the bottle between my palms, then placing it gingerly in the top cupboard—denying myself with an effort I hated after another short pull. The sugar hit my stomach and my head.

I awoke not sure where I was.

My cheek was an icy slab when I raised my face.

"Sugar." I had dozed with my cheek against the table's chill porcelain top. Even my *nose* hurt. Damn, I'm in an icebox of a kitchen with only a slice of moon for comfort. "Where are the guys?" I muttered crossly. My bleary gaze hit the bread bag left on the drain board. *Making love to it.*

I tried not to eat overmuch. Wish the boys had the same compunction. The bag, one of those extra-long Wonder Bread bags of white sponge, was over half gone, no matter how hard I tried to ration it. Sighing, I double-twisted the top against temptation. *Not after all my lectures.* I brooded awhile about the Donner party and that plane crash in the Andes.

"Stop it. We only need to ration," I muttered. *Ration what?* I made a rapid inventory. Two nights ago, we had half a can of Spam for what was laughingly called supper. Couldn't believe how ambrosial the smell, as we held slices dripping grease over the fire. A couple eggs. Half of that cheap cake I managed to squirrel away before the boys gobbled it all. That had not changed since we were kids. The jam jar was depleted, almost all the peanut butter. Still had some of the soup…what else?

I sighed. Think about it tomorrow. Shouldn't drink so much. I dug out the empty jam jar from the trash instead; sucking my fingers until the cheap grape was only a memory. As the sugar high hit me, I tucked my hands under my cheeks and gently laid my head back on the table.

Doze here awhile in solitude, before going back in with those two idiots.

Chapter 17

Reap the Whirlwind

The Indian was so cold, his body juddered uncontrollably. Now, *he* had *both* ponchos but it didn't help much. Twice, he circled the house seeking a way in. To his burning anger, they, whatever heathens inhabited the house, boarded up most downstairs' windows with furniture, even as he paced outside, by a white man with long black hair much like his own. To his obsessed mind, he did it deliberately to taunt him.

He peered up the steep clapboard walls of the monstrous house, at windows, at least twenty feet above him in these grand old houses with high ceilings. He considered the veranda doors, flimsy with thin dividers, and glass panes. Infuriatingly weak from hunger, the prison's beef stew and boloney sandwiches seemed a wisp of a dream. But he was a hoary old warrior, and had a few tricks if he could get one of them outside, or find a way in.

He crept back to the kitchen window away from brutal wind scraping the lake, before bracing himself to cross the icy funnel back to the boat house. There, undetected, and out of the killing cold, he could plan what desperate action he could take. His thoughts lingered on the smelly can of old motor oil he found. He could burn them out. But what good would that do? A searing heat source—a fire next to a federal forest would bring the pigs faster than a police barbecue. His mouth watered. That would get him revenge, not food.

The gaunt figure started as he made out the shape of a woman through blooms of window frost slumped over a table...Meggie dozed on.

He ducked as she stirred. Not that she could have noticed the ruddy face against the night sky or that she frightened him. He had survived torments of brutal inmates and wardens for ten years tacked on his life sentence now, all because of a little misunderstanding regarding a plastic knife melted and sharpened into a needle point.

Scarred hands rubbed the glass free. Fierce black eyes roved the room, racing back to the white blotch of a bread bag with the colorful circles laying on the counter, *right below him*. Maddened with hunger and powerlessness, the Indian tested the flimsy porch screen. Savagely twisting the rotten latch, he eased through— didn't care how much noise. Didn't care about the squeal the rusting hinges made. He would kill the bitch for the bread, and whatever else he could find.

She was alone. Dead to the world. Still, it might be suicide to make a racket. Hugging his arms, he stared through the half glass of the inner door closely watching. Did not know how many were inside, furiously recalling his stupor while they apparently left the house, only arousing as they straggled back.

She's still as death. Never mind if she awoke. He raised a lip reveling cracked teeth. He looked forward to it. He was beyond starving, beyond caring, beyond sentiment. He could kill silently with a quick jab of his railroad spike tucked in his rope belt, in her neck. Or strangle her as she lay oblivious already feeling soft warm flesh throttled between his calloused fingers; never to waken but for a brief terrifying second as he squeezed the life out of her. He curved one side of his mouth. His usual grim smile.

Escaping from a charge of rape and multiple murder—what did he have to lose? She, his reward. He eyed her long dark braid, briefly wondering if she were of his blood. He strangled his urges, instead. The bright yellow, red, and blue plastic bag was more alluring than any female—for now. After. That was different.

* * * *

I shuddered, hearing a squeak of fingers on glass through the fog of stupor. Stirring at a sudden chilly gust, I crankily peeked over my shoulder at the open door. "Bother! Darned wind!" I grumbled. I was asleep! Frowning and still drowsy, stiff with cold, resenting being brought back to the real world, I stumbled up to close it, my hand trembled braced for the icy feel of the brown china knob.

I felt the ghost of warmth on the knob.

Odd. I clutched my arms.

A goose walked over my grave.

* * * *

The Indian, reaching for the knife block, stiffened as the door was shoved closed. He didn't mind if she saw him standing in the dark, where he had crept, outlined by the milky moon frosting the window behind him. Even relished the idea, but where were the others? His frigid scouting told him there were at least two men, but there may have been three, or even four, but he thought she was the lone female.

His loins quickened...but other hunger won out over

147

lower desires.

"There! Stupid wind!" He heard the woman grumble. Gusting so hard to cover any sound he made; it rattled the window frames. Thin lips pinched a smile as he snatched the bag with numbed hands, fumbling it in the dark. Two slices of bread dropped out, making soft plops on the floor.

He froze in place, glanced at the woman ready to spring, darted looks at the swing door at a sudden sound—merely a log dropping in the grate; snatched up the slices, dropping one. The girl/woman sat up, and turned from him, stood up quiet from the chair. She stilled, as if her entire body listened. But he saw her ears were stoppered by earmuffs. The woman slowly revolved, scanning the kitchen, gravely contemplating the door as he moved stealthily behind her matching her steps until reaching the door. With sorrow, he eyed the fallen slice on the floor, but then she moved.

****

I looked to the Great Room first, feeling *something*—a stir of air, a different smell, a tiny warmth where none should be. A *noise*. I lifted my earmuffs. *Nothing*. Imagining it. There. Gone. So, freaking cold though. Behind me, the damn door had swung open, flapping *again*. Sugar! I *knew* I had latched it firmly. Obviously not!

I studied the dark porch and quiet yard. Something about the moon shining so bright after the fusty house making the lake a sheet of wrinkled platinum satin under soft blankets of shimmering lavender, I sucked in fresh crisp air after the stale dead air of the house. I gazed down.

Something caught my eye. Depressions marring

virgin snow, seemed to lead to the boat house, from the porch. I shivered examining the snow with keener eyes. An animal most likely. I studied the holes for a long time, seeking patterns, but gusts whipping around the corner from the lake, swept the prints clean as I watched. Stupid standing here, vulnerable and shivering. On cue, snow plopped off shingles sinking deep along the eves. That was it, I thought doubtfully...even so...

****

Inside the boat house, avidly checking the grimy windows, and half-open door, the Indian crammed bread in his mouth; so intent on feeding his ravenous hunger, and ashamed of his weakness, he regretted needing to leave the whole bag.

****

I stared at the dim white square on the floor, and the bag with grayed colors. "Must have dropped it, or you fell over," I grumpily addressed the bread bag. Picking up the slice, holding it to my nose breathing in the yeasty fresh scent, I tucked it back with effort, and twisted the bag shut.

As I did so, I glanced up, spying the galvanized tub habitually hanging by the sink, glinting dully in dim light. It tugged a smile out of me. When we were young, dunking ourselves in that old tub, on humid Michigan summers, coated with bits of grass, until the water turned to slurry was considered the most fun on earth. I grinned. It might serve another purpose now. *Still big enough for me.*

Stiff lips stretched a smile. *Ow!* I touched my lower lip. Chapped and rough, it had split from cold. I desperately needed comfort. I felt itchy all over and shivered spasmodically. Snow had gone down my neck

from the porch roof.
I eyed the tub again. Days since I had a bath!
The need became obsession.
I was so cold.

Chapter 18

Squall Warnings

I limped into the great room with the tub sloshing water, sponge, a slab of soap and a rough kitchen towel. The huge kettle puffed steam from its hook. I checked Lance sounding like a buzz saw rolled in a cocoon facing the fire, and Zak curled in the wing chair under a pile of blankets with his back turned to the room.

I'd die of mortification if they awoke, but the promise of warm water and the heat of fire on my icy skin, seemed worth the risk. Cold had taken residence in my bones.

Quietly I fed the fire. Tip-toeing and speedily shucking my clothes in shadows, pouring from the kettle always left filled over embers, the water scalding and steaming into the tub, I lowered myself into the blessedly warm water, rechecked "the boys," sighed luxuriously, and sank down with my pinked knees jutting up. Slowly ran a soapy sponge over my face and arms. Ah! Bliss...

Steam rose. I felt ringlets curl softly about my neck. I raised one leg, *my good one,* lazily soaping and admiring my smooth skin—the symmetry...

"You'll catch your death..."

Gripping the sponge, I stilled, slowly turning my head, instead of jumping up in fright.

Zak's eyes glittered from the shadows. His teeth

flashed an appreciative grin from the depths of the wing chair.

I grinned to myself. *What a slut I am.* I had not planned this. *Of course, I didn't,* I told myself. Still, not regretful, kenning I was appealing as only a woman can—I saw it in his eyes. Perhaps I *had* hoped this. My small breasts breached the water in rosy gleaming half-moons. My hair curled in charming tendrils; my skin dewy. Here, my leg made no difference. His gaze never turned to sympathy, or pity but then, it never had. I tore my look away to judge Lance.

Why did Lance have to be in the room, asleep or not? But here, the bitter-sweet prospect. I had no forbearance left. My lust rose like fermenting wine, bubbling up from my groin to my head. No longer a child experimenting with need. But a woman's passion, endlessly fantasized over and explored. Always, Zachary, my cousin, my beloved, my perfect and beautiful man…the one who made me laugh, overlooked my infirmity, made me desired, forget slights and troubles, real or imagined, as I waited now for our childhood ardor to be resumed as of old.

The best of us.

I watched helplessly as Zak rose from the chair like the graceful panther he was. He knelt, gently removing the sponge from nerveless fingers, never taking his incredible half hooded eyes, hot with his own need, from my face. In a fever, I lifted myself, trembling to meet him.

When he cupped my face in both hands, I moaned with want and happiness. "I'm not entirely made of stone," he murmured in my hair. "It has been too long Little Magpie." Then his mouth on mine felt sweet and

warm, charged with desire, I shuddered not from cold,
but long withheld desire as his hands smoothed my soap-
slippery breasts, kneading the nipples with his thumbs,
groaning as he did so, slipping his arms about my slender
waist crushing me to him. I kissed him back feverishly,
hooking his neck and drawing my naked body closer,
slamping my body, my sex to him feeling his ardor, stiff
and hard with his own want, his mouth still on mine as
he struggled to rip off his sweater. Then drew back as I
unzipped his jeans, scootching the legs down his
muscled thighs. He wore nothing beneath. I held him,
soaping his hard hot length, longing for him to be in me.
Desperately looked about over his shoulder for
somewhere we could go. *Haven't exactly planned this,
have you girl?*

Reading my thoughts, he gave his lopsided grin and
held back, hands holding my arms, staying me. I admired
every part of him, glistening shoulders danced across by
flames from the fireplace, one side of his face glowing,
dark eyed and dangerous, the other in shadow, his erect
staff ready to be used. Helpless with need I closed my
eyes. Delirious with yearning I no longer cared if Lance
was in the room, only my savage primitive body thought
for me. The need was obsession—immediate. It was Zak
who retained his sanity, I am ashamed to say.

With the sponge, Zak roughly traced every part of
me—belly to back until I quivered with heat, cold—lust,
no longer separating the sensations, feeling I would
shatter with conflicting emotion as he cupped my back,
running lips down my soap-slippery neck, to my small
bosom, tonguing my nipple, teasing, as I teased him.
Fear of discovery, aware Lance was in the room, aware
of my own need, fearful of what would happen if we did

not stop, fearing he would stop, and I'd be cold and alone once more with desire intact and raging, all the while reveling in the warmth of his body, the scratchiness of his chest, the flame heating my body on one side, and blissfully drying it, his powerful muscles as he lifted me out of the tub in one motion. *"Yes, yes, now!"* I moaned against his bare warm chest, but he reached for the towel, wrapping me in it.

"Where can we go?" I breathed in gulps. He nodded upstairs. His room of course. Why had we not before? Propriety. I had to laugh.

"It's like before, Meggie. Nothing has changed," he breathed in my ear.

I looked up in his face content and lustful as a cat spying a full saucer of cream. His was tortured with need, matching my own. I nodded.

Still my mind nagged tainting the moment. Before? Before what? When I was twelve? And he fourteen? In the boathouse? Both of us exploring this heretofore unidentified sensation of hormones and heady unbridled lust scorching minds and bodies. Slipping nude in murky July waters with dragon flies sipping cooled wet flesh, water-striders skimming on stilted legs by our mote-filled trysting place under secretive willow screens…Unseen, clandestine. But chaste, still. Heavy petting only.

I looked back with nostalgia. The real miraculous joining of our bodies happened later, after the accident, still under the age of consent as adults put it. But not *my* consent. I gave it willingly over and over…then things changed. Whether Zak's awareness, a latent misbegotten conscience over my age—he left for far flung venues and uncle took more and more of my time, and even though we made love, it had not the passion, the reconnection of now...

But bitterly, we didn't have time to wonder—when, or *what* would happen next ..

"What do you think you two are doing!" Lance's accusation was an icy slap, sharp with disbelief and spite quenching desire like a match doused with cold sand.

I clenched my jaw to keep from shattering, then exploded. "Lance! Leave it! What are you? A sneak! A creepy spy!" I sounded shrill and desperate. I heard it, feeling Zak's hand on my nape. He whispered, *"let it go love—not worth it."* Immediately chastened, I was acting all wrong. *We* were the offended ones, aware too, Zak shielded my naked body with his.

"Sorry, Lancer dude. You know me. Totally irresistible."

Zak threw a charming lopsided grin at my brother. *Just us boys together,* diffusing the awkward affair enough for me to draw clothes over a damp body, and he to zip up. I felt my cheeks redden like a school girl with my knickers down behind the gym.

"No, Zak," I tossed over his shoulder. "We were— wrong, but I can always count on you, bro, for rotten timing!"

"And I can count on you, acting the slut!" His pallid face reddened and his fists balled. "The dirty apple doesn't fall far from the tree, does it, *Nutmeg*?" I flinched, still dazed by the fever of Zak's mouth—the tingle-point deep between my thighs.

"That's enough, dude." Zak said quietly. "It was my doing. Leave off. Find you jollies somewhere else."

I wouldn't hurry. Over Zak's broad shoulders, I faced Lance down as I dressed in my rags. I'd pay later.

Lance would freeze me out, for a while, like when childhood squabbles overboiled into true rancor. But then, I vowed, so would he be left out. Immediately, miserable. What had happened to us? Cabin fever, or had this underlying treachery crawled like a snake in the grass waiting to strike when we were vulnerable? But sugar! When had he gotten so puritanical? I feared deep down I *was* acting like Flo "The Slut." Dear God, how can I be in the same room with either? So obvious so— easy! Seeing the betrayal in Lance's eyes, the hurt.

"I expected better from you, Meg."

Good. it goes both ways. I closed my eyes. Then, heard the kitchen porch door rattle and slam.

I peeked up grinning, expecting to be enfolded and passionately kissed where we left off. Zak merely bussed my forehead. "That was certainly, *mmm*, entertaining, kitten. Should do it again, sometime."

He winked. "Without the audience."

Sure. Any time…whatever. It was all a lark. Maybe even a way to jab his javelin wit, at Lance.

I wrapped my sweater tighter.

"You needed it."

Zak deep dimples worked his jaw. He thumbed my mouth, giving me a light kiss.

"Pity for the three-legged *dog*?" I shot back, narrowing my eyes, I studied him for meaning.

"Pity's a piss-poor reason for loving, Magpie. Didn't mean to hurt. My humor sometimes—isn't." He cupped my cheek melting my bones with his limpid azure magic and warm fingers caressing my skin. "And brittle doesn't become you, my gimpy little kitten. I meant it. I *wanted* you, so I couldn't breathe! I get it I can't show it like you…"

I scorched him with my stare. "Like *I* said, I'm not twelve, or thirteen anymore, Zak."

He nodded, blank faced, retreating, which could have meant anything.

****

Zak threw on his parka, unlatching French doors; doused whatever heat the room managed to contain. He looked back at me, expressionless. "Don't get frost-bit."

I slopped the tub out before the doors closed, dumping the water down the porch steps after him. Zak loped off into the clear frosty night. If he heard he didn't look back. Holding the tub, I gazed at the sky searching for weather patterns, yearning to run after him in this clean fairytale world of frost and sparkle, with the moon bouncing off the ice where nothing was quite real.

The sky was dazzling as only a rare clear cold night can be. Stars so piercing they hurt. It was too lovely to go inside, or waste alone. Bleakly, I scanned the vast eternity of Convict Lake to the far shore of the irregular shaped body of water, vaguely like a champagne bottle, hence its vulgar soubriquet, making out the prison camp's twinkle of lights from across the long end a least a half mile, *or the bottle neck*, a feature so familiar I rarely speculated on it before now. The camp now seemed an unattainable Eden.

In between, my eyes sought out the ugly black blot of a small island, with the old hunter's blind, musing if it was still standing, habitable, or had fallen down.

****

Zak blindly rounded the house with nowhere in mind—to breathe, clear his head, chill both body and emotional temperature. Why did that little scrap of a kitten with the big hungry sad eyes, and soft kissable mouth touch him so? He, whose bottom line usually summed up—Zachary Lodge, and preferred full-busted curvy women, slightly athletic. It was *crazy glue* this feeling that Meggie, for his sins, would be the only one for him. Hugging his arms, he leaned against the latticed porch. Throwing his head back, he studied the same night sky.

The imprisonment. His proximity to Meggie. Lance's insufferable whining presence. *God that was lame. Embarrassing for little Nutmeg...Why had he indulged his needs and not her's? Yet were they not the same? For such a tiny thing she had the ferocious hunger of a tiger.*

He felt his mood soften, recalling her elfin face, hair all awry and kinda curly, the damp kisses, her sweet, trusting compliance, and womanly passions that would put a siren to shame. If she only realized how desirable she was. He was a jerk! It was a few seconds before he registered a motion against snow. *Christ! Lance.*

To avoid him, he turned for the porch screen, when something struck him as odd. He halted, watching his cousin backing from the boathouse, with an ax loosely gripped in his hand—the one from the chopping block.

But more—the short ax glistened, dripping blackish red on white under the dazzling moon, as if red was the only color unnaturally garish in a black and white world. *Where the hell had that come from? Why the boat house? Or had Lance brought it in—?*

He let the thought perish in his sudden sense of dread. *Now what!*

"Overreacting, are we?" He studied his cousin's expression, so like a dazed deer in the headlights. *If the deer had been nibbling weed.* "What the hell?"

Lance worked his jaw. Eyes wide and staring blind. No words came out.

Zak warily eyed the ax, sliding past to peer inside. Looking queerly at Lance, still with a death grip on the ax handle, he stepped back. "After you, cuz."

"Lookin' for a fishing pole. Only a pole!" He was babbling.

"A pole? Right." Zak, doubtful, humoring him, peered in with one eye still on his cousin. Moonlight misted a shrouded dusty space with a recalled scent of old creels, dried earthworms, motor oil, and rusted paint tins, muted in the chill, but there.

"What?" He looked warily back at Lance who raised the ax, not to strike but point with a trembling arm inside.

Zak squinted.

"Over there in the corner, man!"

Zak frowned. Lance's reactions were off. *Theatrical. Made-up. Then, they usually were.* Edging around the scarred plank-turned-fish-scaling-station, he mentally shrugged, searching the dimness for what caused such a bother in his obnoxious punch-drunk cousin. "Where?" About to slug him one and ask later. Lance was giving him the heebie-jeebies to use Meg's expression.

Lance still rigidly pointed with the ax toward what seemed, now his eyes adjusted, a gray lumpy heap tucked in the corner. Hunh! Slowly, the image steadied: what seemed a poncho affair with one broad black stripe over two humps, of what turned out to be knees, judging from rag-bound feet sticking below.

A bowed head emerged. Black and long haired, wrapped in a reddish bandanna—a dark hand clutched a blotch of white. He edged to the figure slumped and bloody beneath a row of old fish traps, still clutching what turned out to be a minute crust of frozen bread.

Zak bent to observe the gaunt face, dark and solidified. Mouth open in surprise and yes—what else? *Resentment? Anguish? Fear?* Zak gagged.

The half not cleaved in two.

"Oh Christ!"

Zak backed into Lance.

"Somebody's takin' Geronimo, way serious."

"You can joke? You can make jokes, man! That's *sick*. And whatdya mean—*someone?*"

"You're the one holding a damn bloody ax, *fool*. What happened here, *Lance*?" He scanned the Indian, puzzled. "Did he *attack* you? What!" He reached down brushing the hand. A marble statue could be no more cold or hard. "He must have come from over there." He nodded toward the unseen prison camp. "Been here awhile, but who can tell in this meat locker?"

Zak walked to Lance punching his chest, heedless of the axe that seem to be a forgotten appendage. "Not a bit squeamish, are you? Maybe you learned to wallow in all that slash and burn, metaphorically speaking—but this poor guy! Why'd ya have to do it!"

He looked away to control his reactions. "Sorry, Lancer, but what the f—!"

Lance shook his head scowling at the corpse in the dim corner. The blood in the body's veins had congealed; only the ax and place it was withdrawn, was still gummy-tacky.

With derision, he watched Zak wipe his fingers, where his hands had touched a splotch of gore. "Christ!"

"Meg doesn't have to go through this," Lance whispered hoarse suddenly limp letting the ax droop.

"Tell me about it. And I do?"

Zak still checked the ax, wary again. Lance focused turning pale eyes on him in a disturbing way. "What's wrong, man? Do you really think I'm capable—*of that*?" Straightening, Zak presented a bland face, but his words were bitter and ironic. "You're the one bragging how knee-deep in blood you are. Always found that penchant a little *off-putting*, now you mention it," he snapped. *Keep your cool.*

"This is different, man!"

He threw kerosene on the fire. "Who can tell what to think!"

Lance flung the ax at the corpse as if to disavow the whole episode. The ax quivered, sunk in an old basket fishing creel next to the Indian's head.

"You're the one always doing the vanishing acts, genius."

"Yah. Getting wood, checking the house—searching for game! I don't see you stirring your scrawny ass from the fireplace much less trying to figure a way out. What do you accomplish, 'sides bitching about me to Meggie! And that was a damn lame stunt you pulled back there."

"*Me?* I'm not the exhibitionist!"

Zak eyed him. "You run a meat factory in a shitty neighborhood. That's what I see, pal. And I haven't seen much of you, either, *cholo*!" He nodded at the dead man. " 'Bout par for a Saturday night, right? Stitchin' up junkies after knife fights?"

Lance soured a face, drooping. "Yah. We're all dying here, if this keeps up. It only takes longer. 'Sides, I'm aware you're yankin' my chain. I quit fallin' for that shit."

Zak grimaced, glancing at the Indian. "Probably from the camp over there." Zak's tone was conciliatory. Lance toed what seemed to be foot prints. "How many you think they were? Guards maybe?"

"Those are *ours*, Sherlock." He shrugged. "How many you need? And he was axed to death, not shot. How many guards carry tomahawks? And why leave him, genius?"

Lance glared baleful at Zak. "Okay, smartass. Maybe not a guard." Lance studied the welter of prints. "An escapee all right though. Ya see under that poncho? Prison garb all right. Could be a fight with another runner. Don't they usually escape in pairs?" He glanced involuntarily at the woods.

Zak snorted. "Been watchin' Meg's old films. The Defiant Ones?"

"That's the second one, man!"

Lance squinted at Zak. "What's that mean?"

"We're not safe! If someone bumped him off, his pal might still be hanging around." Lance hunched in his long black coat making himself small, scanning the yard, scanning the woods beyond. "And that girl? Can't…" He shook his head loosening long hair from his old mob cap. "Can't figure it out. What's goin' on?" he asked plaintively.

Zak began saying something, then said, "Who's counting? But yah. Nothin' makes sense. Gotta be cagy. Alert. Door locked and braced. Maybe someone should keep watch."

"Ya think? Now who's the genius?" Lance soured.

"Damn, this will make hunting harder."

"Hunting? With what?

"Use your noodle, sport. We're scrapin' the bottom.

Meg's trying but she's not Julia on steroids at the best of times. We got bows, arrows too, somewhere. In our old rooms probably. Maybe trapping." He scrutinized the woods doubtfully. "Meg's little hoard won't last forever. Face it. Look around. Might as well be in the north pole, or behind a snow plow, the way we're dumped on. Every damned day. Only wind off the lake scoured this side relatively clean."

Zak jerked his head. "Judas. Meg's alone! And what we doin' out here anyway? Can't do anything. Gonna be frozen as that stiff."

"Cute."

"Whatever."

Lance scowled at Zak, loping to the house without looking back. Zak tossed an old canvas over the body. He returned, wrenching the ax free, shoving it in his tightened belt.

Chapter 19

Killing Frost

I was reaching for the whiskey bottle, needing something stronger than "dishwater" tea, when Lance stumbled in. I jerked my hand back. He scowled. "What do they say? Get a room?" But it seemed forced. I saw strain on his paler than usual face. "Get over it, Lanny. We are all adults here, though some don't act like it."

"Couldn't you wait?" Lance lowered his voice as Zak brushed past into the Great Room with a small stack of wood and out. I followed him with longing, but Lance nagged at our "lapse" like a sore tooth. "You gotta act like an alley cat right in front of me?"

"Lanny—don't! It—happened. I didn't plan it!" *Didn't I?* My brother sneered. "I love it when you behave like a stray cat ready to spit and claw."

"I've waited my life away, Lanny! For *something* to happen. Anything. And I don't mean Zak." *Especially.* I watched my feet. "Let me breathe. I'm weary of toeing the line and keeping you two apart."

"He'll win, Magpie. Don't you see!"

I rounded on him. "And that's so awful? You both have a life. I didn't." I pressed my heart. "Don't deny me these freaking *crumbs* of happiness." The last spoken with a sarcastic bent but ended up pathetic and tearful.

"Used to be we had each other's backs, Meggie."

I studied him. Lanny appeared truculent, lip out like a little boy. True though. I sighed. "Lanny. It's you and me. Like I said. Never *mind* the will."

"Ah! What's the use? Money! Who cares? Right now, sister mine, I'd settle for stayin' alive and scarfing a Big Mac." His voice trembled. He checked the window, flinching or shivering beneath the oversized black coat he never took off. "Isn't lettin' up ya appreciate. We got missing bodies and—"

He stopped short, appearing belligerent and miserable, lending him a half-crazed appearance. I recoiled watching him carefully, placating, "Shhhhh, it's all right. We'll get out of this." I smiled wickedly. "Look. I was going to save this, but…"

…and we were a team again.

I winked. "Close your eyes."

Lance fidgeted impatiently, hearing the squeal and a *POP*. His nose wrinkled, as *tart* and *acidic* met his nostrils. I opened a drawer. His eyes blinked at the sound and I thrust a Mason jar with a spoon sticking out, at him.

"What *is* that!" Lance sniffed the unidentifiable, vaguely tan stuff, pursing his lips as if I offered him a bowl of rancid cat food, scoffing, "Suicide pact? What the hell?"

I checked the contents again. The jar did seem fairly poisonous. More tan, than the sunny yellow they were supposed be umpteen years ago.

"Where the hell you find this?"

I hedged, not wanting to reveal my source, yet. "In back of the cupboard over the fridge."

"Lord knows how long," I half-lied.

"My point." Lance checked the old Kerr jar as if a bomb was ready to blow. He observed me with suspicion. "Thought we checked cupboards?" He scanned my offering again. "Maybe like, for like— *emergencies*?"

"This isn't?"

"Last supper? Hunh!" He still looked askance at the moldering fruit jar.

I eyed him sourly and dipped in, stuffing a dripping spoonful in my mouth, and offered him the spoon in challenge. Lance hesitated, dug in, spoon halfway to his lips. "God, like I am so freaking ravenous, I don't even *care* if I turn radioactive."

"S'all right. I've eaten tons. Well, a spoonful." I grinned. "I'm still kickin'."

Lance swallowed without tasting, checking the spoon with alarm. "Kinda tart ain't it? That botulism?"

"No, idiot bro. *Peaches* are tart."

"Ah! Is that what this is?" He shrugged and dug in. "Not bad, do sorta taste like peaches."

"Hey, save some."

He held the jar away, spooning one more before I could grab it. "God! Wasn't aware heaven was browning peaches," he mumbled through a mouthful.

"Need to keep strong." I regarded the inevitable white pillows of snow growing plumper by the second. "Now more than ever. What were you and Zak doing?" I was still smarting.

Lance scraped frost from the dark windows. "Nothing—much."

I burst out. "I hate him!"

Lance licked the spoon, reflecting. "Nothing for Zak."

Feverish, we spooned browning peaches, emptying the jar.

****

Giddily humming, next morning, I checked the canning jars slowly perishing higgledy-piggledy, God knew how long, on old wooden shelves behind the warped cellar door. A lone smudged window gave me enough light to see what I was groping.

The found jar ignited memories of a cook/housekeeper from Uncle Dez's glory days, hence, these half-forgotten shelves for the bounty of long forgotten kitchen gardens, and the cook who canned them, blessing her as a new Star in Heaven.

Lovingly, I ran hands over dusty Kerr and Ball jars with old-fashioned snap-wires, or screw down lids as if discovering the combination to Fort Knox or the Holy Grail; more crucially, still vacuum tight, filled with stuff, like sour cherries, apples, succotash, wax beans, and what looked like beets, if one could trust faded scribbling on top the jars. Some had no labels, or were too faint to decipher.

As I held one up: "*green beans, 1990,*" gray and unappetizing, to the grungy light, I heard Lance and Zak's bickering from the kitchen. I made out my name, muttering, "Boys bonding. Laughing at me, no doubt." I studied the green beans. "Perhaps I let you try these first, guys." Placing the jar with other questionable offerings; the prize, a crusty glass Kerr jar, labeled "blackberry jam, 1992" on the shelf I felt along the top for any other lost treasure. The clink of jars masked Lance's footfalls.

"So, this's where you get to." The accusing voice made me jump, already spooked and faintly claustrophobic. Whirling, I almost dropped the precious jar. "I'm not *hiding!*"

More than ever, I wished Zak and I had not been

so—open. Lanny, regardless of my peace offering, still snapped. Yet we were all "nutritionally-challenged" and getting a little uneasy, being "city folk" and our survival skills so far laughable, were mostly confined to hopes for an early "spring thaw."

He snatched at a jar. "Let's just see what this is?"

He shook it. I made a grab.

"Don't! It might explode."

Lance held it away from me, staring at shelves. "This is the freakin' mother lode! A whole Thanksgivin' dinner here!" He glared at me suspicious. "Were you gonna *tell* me?"

I snatched at it. "Wasn't going to keep them. Idiot!"

Lance held on.

The jar slipped.

Afterward, neither of us knew who had it last, watching, disbelieving, as green beans and glass exploded in a hundred directions. Dropping like wolverines, we scooped beans from the coal dust. Last night, dinner had been one cup of watered packaged tomato soup each.

I threw them back in the coal dust, smearing my face, ashamed and angry. "Sugar! Lance! Look what you made me do."

****

Lance and Zak, two snarling dogs now more than ever. *Soon as it lets up, I prayed, all this will be over.* The unreasonable train wreck of storms, blizzards, gales, whiteouts, howling, bellowing bitter winds hurling malicious successions of sleet, wet snow and huge pillow-sized flakes as the temperature varied, sucked whatever little heat we managed out the chimney, mixed with the false promise of brief warmups.

After the first week, we all had changed subtly, but it was there. What was an adventure—even with Debbi as bragging rights—a good story to hang free beers on, in Lance's case and who knew how Zak would use this tale for his advantage, if at all, turned all too real. Everything was forced. Our laughter, anger, pretending we weren't hungry. At least we are not starving—yet. Down to precious little grub, even though I insisted we begin rationing weeks ago, to what passed for breakfast and then only a light dinner to get us through the night without hunger gnawing at our rest. *Very light.*

Habitually, I never ate much, however illogically, *maddeningly,* my appetite exploded as supplies dwindled, and I wasn't sure of the boy's lack of forbearance, either.

"I'll take this one." Lance grabbed another jar not checking the label, running into Zak on the steps.

Zak took in the situation in a flash. "For me? How thoughtful. Objections?"

"Quit bickering," I demanded relieving him of the precious jar. "There's plenty, such as they are." I kicked the door closed.

Zak regarded me oddly, if I didn't know better. Couldn't still be embarrassed over—*what we did. Not Zak.* Besides, that was yesterday's dustup. So why so weird? Zak, the cool one?

"Might want to ah—stay close," he muttered helping me with a couple jars, I managed to juggle upstairs. "Like maybe not go down here anymore."

Lance and Zak exchanged annoying glances as I impatiently eyed them.

"Or the boat house." Lance offered.

I threw an exasperated look blanketing both of them.

"What are you two on about, *maniacs*. I found food! And you are on your honor."

They both had identical reactions at the word, *maniac*.

Lance mumbled something like, "Yah. Dirty down there and…"

"Spare me!" I looked irritably at both of them. *They could be more excited.*

I dumped the jars on the table, my surprise ruined. "Stop you two! I'm the only one doing anything sensible," I snapped. "Maybe ya hadn't noticed, but the few groceries I brought *for myself,* you guys went through like a freaking buzz saw."

Zak had the grace to look away, then flicked a smug glance at the off-colored jars. "Past the sell-by-date, anyway, love."

"Yeah. Like me!" I bit my cheek. *Ginger! Why did I say that?*

"Knock yourself out," he tossed carelessly. "Think Russian roulette, with botulism."

Lance swallowed hard and felt his neck.

I slammed out throwing back at them, "I wish!"

I heard Lance say, "That went well."

****

Lance grimaced.

"What should we do with—?" he gestured to the boat house.

"Already taken care of last night."

"Naturally. Now, who's Duncan The Wonder Horse?"

"Tiresome, old son. He'll keep…"

"This place is a fucking abattoir."

"Least of our probs. Meg's right. We should be doing something 'sides sittin' on our arses. She may force us to sample *those*." Zak gestured at the motley collection of discolored jars.

Chapter 20

Thirty-Four Days

The polar express continued to take special interest in my isolated house with relentless pounding to get in, coupled with tantalizing "warm" days when snow cascaded from trees with crashing *thuds,* turned icicles into streams, and warmed faces as we checked the shadowy lane for signs of melting, only to renew its bitter journey, malevolently scouring the lake and hurling sharp daggers of sleet in our cheeks when we ventured out.

Today, I made it far as the widow's walk, staring idly out. *As far as I could get from the boys.* Increasingly we avoided each other. Gone the games, and *never-being-alone,* seemed quaint as we brooded over hunger and secret fears.

Zak took to hunting. Whether entertaining that diversion before or not, I was unaware, yet it seemed an alien concept for Zak, though he took his bow and arrow, a sack, and a knife in anticipation. Day after day, I watched him doggedly slog toward the tree line. Lance was always conveniently ill. I volunteered to hunt with Zak, but one sideways glance at my bad leg told the story. *I would be a drag.*

I glowered as a layer of cement clouds gray and flat as upside-down pavement brooded overhead lending my aerie a vertiginous topsy-turvy look. I felt giddy pressed with the weight of leaden skies pressing overhead.

Another storm front.

It was hunger giving me that woozy feeling. I placed my forehead on my knees to let it pass and scratched under my itchy wool ski sock…as I did so I spied an alien bright spot, wonderingly, digging out a crushed pack. "How long have you been there?" I chortled. Like finding a twenty-dollar bill in an old purse wedged under the bench.

"*Lucky Strikes*," the bullseye proclaimed, plus a half-full book of matches stuck under brittle cellophane. A macho brand like unfiltered Camels. Who smoked Lucky's? Not cool enough for Zak. All three of us had the filthy habit, increasingly unpopular in civilized company making us rather pariahs. Maybe why we did it, when young. Save Lance, who forswore smoking, becoming insufferable, after his brief stint as intern.

I addressed the fragile cylinder leaking tobacco. "You must be twenty years old." Fifteen brittle flaking beauties left. Had to quit sometime, but apparently, the gods of unfiltered death shone on me today.

My secret.

I lit one, sucking in smoke, as if mother's milk—instantly the acrid bite cut off my airways. Mulishly dragging on, my throat felt cut and my head bounced like a balloon; still, I defiantly sucked until I was giddy—a *definite improvement*, fondly regarding the flaming bit of warmth, the crisp *crinkling, the scent* as the paper caught and tobacco flared.

"Maybe I won't feel so hungry."

The harsh tobacco matched my mood, *or penance for being pissy with the guys? What's happening to us?* " 'Sides starvation and hyperthermia?" I answered

myself suddenly startled by my thin pale reflection in the
panes through the gray fug of smoke, as a stray shot of
sun found its way through the cloud layer.

A scrubby lavender knit hat rode my eyebrows,
framing huge purple-smudged eyes. My mouth was pale
to non-existent. *My, I made a pretty picture,* and blew
myself a concealing plume of smoke. Pity, I mused, not
for the first time, Zak was the one blessed with the
genetic lottery. Movie star facial proportions, Lance and
I missed by a marker or two. Lance's eyes were a shade
too close, owned a larger slightly lopsided nose and
coarser hair. Shorter by a hair too, yet Lance had a
perpetual slouch and he *would* encourage that three-day-
old beard thing he considered so macho, but more
incipient bum, I always thought.

I removed my hat and fluffed out my long black hair,
turning decidedly stringy. Ugh! And I? I rechecked my
reflection. Though closely resembling each other, my
eyes were more moonstone than Zak's electric turquoise,
plus the longer lashes I'd kill for; unconsciously stroking
my scar through my jeans. Hardly felt it anymore, like
chronic headache, musing by unspoken agreement, we
never mentioned the accident among ourselves. Zak
suffered a broken arm he used in high-school to full
extent after our notorious return, especially among his
peers. The girls couldn't help him enough.

"Zakie, want me to open your milk carton?"

Boys dazzled by his daring.

*"The million-buck prototype? Ya wrecked it! Holy
shee-it!"*

Lance, unhurt, outside of briar scratches, landed in
thickets of weeds.

Sighing, taking another poisonous drag, I peered

out, when I felt my face warm. A beam of sun appeared like an actor on stage as wind separated cloud curtains. My heart lightened with the skies. What was I doing here, mooning away?

So easy to drift into a slough of antipathy, fueled by lack of carbs as weeks blew past with the snowstorms. I had had such big plans. "But the Gods laugh up their sleeve, right Meggie girl?" I muttered. Then, —"Stop feeling sorry for yourself. Get a move on. Be useful!"

Even then, as if to punish me, I spied Lance crouched over a hole hacked in two feet of ice. As I watched, he tugged out a tiny fish. Must be starving under all that. Lance peered up as if sensing me. His face was ghastly.

I sucked the cigarette to my fingers, carefully snuffing the ciggi-butt. I must be nicer to the guys. Zak was out again trying to scavenge *something*. He had *some* dumb luck, my mouth watering at the thought. Two days ago, he rummaged a dead Canadian goose. Frozen. Like in a supermarket, I told myself. *Thank you, food fairy!* Feeling like a proper girl scout, I stuffed goose down into the lining of a jacket I now wore everywhere.

We plucked and roasted it still half-frozen, over a blistering fire. To say nothing had ever tasted so good was like saying, "Queen Elizabeth needed more tiaras." Too much to hope for, another sky-fall would plop down before him, before foxes or wolves got to it, dwelling once again with resentful longing on the far away prison camp.

So, what if their grub was creamed corn, spam, and watery green Jello?

I tucked the butt end back in the pack and headed down.

****

"Like I swallowed thumbtacks, or glass," Lance groaned. "Think it was, you know—those jars? What was that crap last night, 'sides the goose?" He uttered the word *goose* resentful as if Zak insulted him.

"Beets! I'm fine, Lanny."

"No wonder I hated them." Lance turned back huddled and sulking.

Biting my cheek to keep from booting him down the ice hole, I toed his scattering of what seemed to be minnows.

"Any with my name?"

Lance moaned, gesturing. "Have'm all. Sushi!"

I touched his forehead.

He moved grumpily aside. "Actually, a fever'd make my day."

"Go on Lan. I can do this."

"Tired a being Clark Kent." Lance dry-heaved.

"Bait?"

We both glanced wearily back at Zak.

Lance thrust a bloody thumb and stained strip of cloth at Zak. "That's bait!" And heaved again.

"How bloody brave." Zak dumped a dead loon on the snow. "See what papa found at the lake edge. Poor thing was frozen in place."

I looked at it hungry, yet wary. A loon? Had anyone ever consumed a loon?

Lance lurched off as Zak began plucking, grinning evilly as feathers flew, and not so much reminisced, as needled Lance. "Didn't come winters, much 'cept that Christmas? 'Member? Grandad stuffed this dried up old turkey with angel food cake and—"

"Don't!" I punched Zak, stifling my own grin,

pointing instead to grey splotches dotting the lake. "Mush holes are bigger. Maybe it's melting."

"Spring-fed, sweetheart. Convict Lake's riddled with'm. But you are familiar with all that. Still three feet of ice. Why? You makin' a run for it?" He squinted at the camp, not so much seen as recalled. "Nice day for it."

I shivered on the riprap boulder wall imagining going through the ice, sucked down into Convict Lake's deep gelid black water. No one guessed how far down it actually was. But the water always seemed dark, mysterious, bottomless, even on the sunniest days, with the sounds of loons giving a forlorn—*all is lost*—warning.

Chopping sounds erupted behind me, turning to see Zak hacking a scarily big hole next to Lance, still doggedly fishing, and trying his best to ignore it.

Half resentful on Lance's behalf, I couldn't help admiring Zak. Tall, dark-bearded, and terribly virile with sleeves shrugged, arms rippling muscle, and large hands gripping the ax. "That's how you do it."

"Christ! Maniac! Maybe you fancy bobbing to shore come spring. Or, what's left after fish nibble your eyeballs." Heaving at his own suggestion, Lance staggered off wan and po-faced.

"Come on! Sun and circulation. Bet snow's lighter in the woods. You too, trouble maker!"

Zak dangled a string in the water. "I'll pass another stroll in The Black Forest at the mo. Ta. Watch for bears." Lance looked askance but I tugged him along wishing it were simply me and Zak strolling the woods and he would yank me behind a tree and kiss me and...

We waded past my buried car as Lance muttered, "crazy—ya understand that, Meggie Anne."

"But ya love me anyway."

"With those cheeks? How could I resist?"

I was happy. This was normal talking. Fun stuff. Scuffling snow, I grinned at my flimsy boots. "Mum called'm snow-roses. About all I remember—*nice,* that is."

"Yah, nutty old Flo. Crazy as a bedbug. And what did she call this?" He rubbed my red nose. "Bo-Bo the Clown?"

I swatted him and turned serious. "What's wrong with Zak, always so…"

"Irritating? Feckless lying scum?"

"No! Mean. Like he *hates* us."

"Showing true colors, if you didn't see rainbows shining out his arse."

"You used to be a brat too. Cut the heads off my Barbie dolls," I reproved.

"More interested in their underwear."

I giggled. It felt normal, human, to laugh. The last time, was that game night. Maybe another would get us all back on a familial track. "Raided my sock drawer for Halloween candy too." I accused.

"I'd raid *your undies* for a linty Jujube at the mo."

I studied my boots.

"Lanny?"

"Mmmmm?"

"Where's all the snow plows and salt trucks? I keep thinking I'd hear them."

"An army of plows? Forging a path right to our back stoop?" He snorted. "Won't happen, Magpie. Wouldn't waste a single truck on a backroad for a bunch of rich, no-show summer folk."

"Rich!" I scoffed, almost missing Lance's sharp

glance.

I had to watch that. He was sensitive enough. I shuddered, identifying in my bones our brief happy time was over, yet as things came to pass, that afternoon would seem like Mardi Gras and Christmas all rolled into one.

****

Meggie and Lance shuffled through light snow, past a skeleton stashed beneath banks of briars as if tucked in bed under a soft fluffy blanket. Only the yellow dome of a delicate skull, peeked through like polished ivory in the gleam of a stray sun beam cutting through green, snow-laden boughs, plus a bit of neck bone and spine. Its jaws were open in a permafrost shock. A heart-shaped locket dangled from the cervical vertebrae of a once slender neck, glittering in the same brilliant sun.

****

I halted, feeling a chill breath traveling down my back to my knees, and hairs escaping from my mob hat fan from my neck. I trembled deep in my ratty fur holding it close and looking all around behind me.

I finally tugged up my collar casting a sharp eye at heavy brush. I moved on, feeling cold seep in my boots.

"Come on, Lance," I goaded. "Cars aren't dug out till spring, and Zak's scarfing everything not nailed down." Which wasn't fair. He supplied the only quality protein in three weeks.

"Zak never denied himself much of anything."

"For the first time, I wish I had a gun." I brooded.

"Now that scares me."

"I meant for game, doofus!"

He examined his monochrome surroundings. "We gone far enough?"

As I spun, I ran into a snowy frond spitting cold white stuff, and laughing. "Scared? Bet I'm as familiar with these woods as the back of my hand."

"No worries. Long as we see that—" Lance waved toward the widow's walk. "Wait. Where the heck is it?"

I checked, finally spying a bit of whale-shaped weather vane poking up, rusted north as it had for decades. I turned back to Lance, disoriented, blinking as I detected motion coming at me.

I didn't duck in time.

A hard, cold swinging thump on my cheek-bone, blinded me. Blinking crystals from my eyelashes, I saw a *thing*—heavy, solid, frozen iron-hard, swinging mid-air in front of my nose, like a pendulum where nothing should be. I swatted irritated, without comprehending what it was. The object, bitter-cold, and rock-hard, swayed ponderously back scraping my cheek with a bristly sensation as it lost momentum.

My second impression was—*a side of beef in some old-time butcher's window,* as the object took on focus. I stared. *A foot* swung stolidly back and forth, halting in front of my face.

A foot out of a horror film.

Only this was real. Lard white, near blending in the snowscape. A few feet to the left and I would have missed it. I raised my head an inch, wincing, traveling reluctantly on up. The foot caked with dirt on the sole, was connected to a scaly white marble ankle, thick as an ox shank covered with bristly red hair. That's what scraped my cheek. I gagged, doubling over.

Oh Lord. The other foot swayed beside it.

I couldn't look away.

Couldn't yell, even while I took in details.

Thick fungal nails like cow hooves.

Heels scored with fissures.

Veins like dark purple worms threaded wide flat arches.

A man's feet.

My eyes traveled unwillingly on up.

Beefy legs. Snarled ropes of varicose under reddish fuzz.

Hands calloused and muscular even though dead-white hanging stolid as the feet. Brawny arms, stained with blurry tattoos, heavy and stiff with rusty hair pricked with frost.

I backed wordless. My throat felt glued.

Stepping farther away, morbidly intrigued, I traveled on up past the hard white belly, the furry crotch, and chest mottled gray with rime, or age, and as I kept mindlessly backing, stumbling, I made out a face.

This had color. A deep plum. A wine-red tongue thrust from swollen lips the shade of eggplant. I wouldn't look further. I knew what I might find. Crows and hawks were thick as thieves here in the woods. Still, I got the impression of a bald domed head. All the hair was on his body. No neck, or what was, was buried in the rope, cut deep.

I imagined a scream, *my* scream, shooting through the treetops, and something very bad would happen. The ugly face with the thick tongue would stare with dead eyes and ask for pity, for help I couldn't give. Backing into a tree, I bent over, then looked up, woozily viewing how others would see it was done. Below the hanging man, a branch of oak stuck out, low to ground. Stand on it and toss a rope to a branch overhead and anyone could haul that body up.

All his weight was belly, shoulders, and *those feet*. Enough to make the rope stretch, and twist, making eerie squeaks like a porch swing in the woods' dead silence. The naked body seemed painfully vulnerable exposed to the ten-degree temperatures.

Black dots swarmed before my eyes. I blanked for a second, or an hour. I risked a glance behind me expecting Lance standing, watching. *Where was my brother?* Then, a woodpecker's cheerful machine gun *ratattattta* broke the spell and I caught Lance's flapping black coat disappear between two far distant trees. I ran after him in hitching strides.

Forget this.

Tell no one.

It didn't happen.

What good would it do?

Plenty of time.

Can't deal with this now, anyway.

Zak was right.

If you think it so. It will be.

If you believe it, it will be.

My thoughts skittered like a spider, blasted with bug spray.

"S'wrong? Where ya been! Thought you were right behind me."

I looked through my brother. My mouth hung open. Drool froze on my chin. "Nothin'. J-just cold."

"So, what else is new? This was your show! I can't keep lookin' for ya!"

I scanned behind me once.

Only white against white.

A burgeoning granddaddy of a fir tree hid the direction from where I'd been.

Nothing there.

No tree. No hanging man.

I was starving. My head wasn't right. I saw things.

Mustn't tell Lance. *Think I was crazy.*

"Let's go," I urged desperately, before more scary fantasies filled my head. I was losing it. Lance was waiting! Impatiently holding back a hefty snow-covered bough for me to duck under. "I'm coming!" I wailed.

"Hey, you wanted this!"

"I get that. I don't anymore."

"*Women!*" I heard Lance as he slogged ahead letting the bough sweep back, splatting me in the face if I hadn't swerved.

After ten minutes of hard silent trudging, I stopped near the tree line, breathing hard.

"Zak c-came from—from back *there*. T-that goose."

"Yeah. So?"

I searched the woods ahead. A setting sun speared through pines, turning the snow blood red.

"Let's not come back. Okay?"

"Your picnic! Fine by me."

An animal, possibly a wolf, howled disconsolately as I watched over my shoulder one last time, before hastening inside the flimsy safety of the latticed porch.

****

Each of us held a plate of blackened sprats, sucking and crunching them between our teeth, bones, and all, making them last. We neglected to forage wood. Lance toted coal from the cellar. None of us figured out why we hadn't thought of it earlier. The pungent smoke did nothing for the taste of charcoaled minnows; however, I was tearfully grateful for the heat and we could bank coals for the night till morning. If morning ever came.

We each tried the loon, but the off-flavor, only in our imaginations, Zak heatedly declared, warred against hunger. In honest pique, Zak tossed the remains in the fire. In days to come, that action would seem criminally profligate.

I watched them sleep. I wished I could escape that easily.

I dwelled as always on Zak.

Zak. Losing his model looks even bone structure couldn't conquer. A windburned nose and hollow eyes making him merely, mortally handsome, in place of Jude Law handsome.

Lance came out worse. Always slighter and round-shouldered, his black whiskers against a slum-clinic pallor made him chalkier, rather than merely interestingly pale. Between hunger and ever-present chill like an uninvited guest that stayed and stayed, I decided they both resembled axe murderers.

And I? Probably a big-eyed none too clean, Raggedy Anne with all the stuffing gone.

Zak raised his arm over his face. The kindling ax was stuck in his waistband. We each have our own security blanket, I mused. Good choice though. Lance would be more at home with the cleaver, ashamed I never thought of Lance as a "real doc," belatedly doubting his clients cared much about any old diploma on the wall. Once again, guilt flooded me. My imp of doubt poked me with its pitchfork.

Relief from pain and Lance, the go-to man with the magic prescription pad? Lance did community service for those who had none. What was *wrong* with me!

Chapter 21

Day Fifty-Two, or Fifty-Seven?

They say, little pitchers have big ears.

In that case, I was a very small pitcher with the world's biggest ears.

I had ventured to the kitchen with hopeless optimism; I'd scour cupboards once more, surely *something* was left. Only last week, I scrounged a Christmas tin of stale Ritz crackers from God alone recalled what era, shoved high in the corner of the same cupboard I stashed my haul of filched whiskey. Long ago, I transferred that stash to the widow's walk, digging it out for medical emergencies I lectured my latent conscience. I'd no longer feel guilt. We'd have emergency stimulant when most needed or a celebratory tipple when finally free—until then, it was my solace.

I groaned, opening one door after another, stretching into the far corners, reminding myself, the last scrape of peanut butter and last egg consumed three weeks ago, were distant fantasies. We survived on a few fish, and last of the canning jars now. Zak had taken up hunting weeks ago, leaving with his old bow and arrows at noon after it warmed a tad, after a hearty breakfast of thrice-used tea bags, and miserly spoon of sugar.

It was more Quixotic gesture as he came back exhausted and hungrier than ever, the game scarce. Thin squirrels. A handful of walnuts, acorns aplenty, though I was wary. I heard tales of "acorn coffee" and Indians grinding them for flour. The results were mixed, but we assuage hunger with what we had. I made a sort of flat bread. Salt, water, acorn flour, a few wild dried fennel seeds. We even stumbled on using the tips of pine tree fronds to make hot tea and nibbled the tender tips without undue effect. Zak scrounged a kind of black mushroom found growing off beech trees, and after considerable hacking, according to him, brought the mass back. I broke off some, ground and steeped it in water. It made a tolerable, nutty, and I hoped, nutritious "soup" after Lance was the brave soul to my surprise, to try it out.

By consent, our depleted provisions were long ago, left to me to dole—a dubious honor. Not much, now. I stood before the one cupboard holding all our supplies.

A few used tea bags, a scant amount of sugar. Half a packet of dried soup saved to stew rabbit bones, the near depleted tin of stale crackers, a few canning jars and these, mostly questionable green gray sludge we put off till last. I thought they might be Swiss chard, or spinach.

I made soup for this evening's repast, throwing in a quarter canning jar of browning tomatoes, water, crushed crackers for thickening, salt, pepper, rabbit bones, plus fish bones crushed to powder for calcium. The result was hot and somewhat nourishing, and might last for two days.

I stared at rabbit drippings sizzling on the coals. *Waste not want not.* Inspired, I placed crackers on a tin pie plate under the rabbit drippings crushing them with the fennel seed and reformed into patties with water, setting them out to bake on hot stones.

The result according to the boys in rare good humor,

was a roaring success.

Besides the fennel, sometimes I even dug greenery, after the few false springs from under the snow—what smelled like wild onion, and dandelion leaves. It kept us alive, if not thriving and starved for carbohydrates.

Dwelling on all that, my hand was on the swing door to reenter the relative warmth of the Great Room, when I heard my name.

Curious? Did I really want to hear? But Lance spoke in low intimate tones, guaranteeing I'd listen. I peered through the crack. Eavesdropping. Embarrassing, but I was starved even for this "entertainment." In a conspiratorial manner Lance risked a glance to the kitchen, making me uneased and more single-minded. I ducked keeping the door from swinging closed and like a bad housekeeper, put my ear to the crack.

"She's gotta sell it *some* time, this old wreck…!"

Zak, now. I heard weariness in his voice. "One would think. Meg's…" he hesitated, "…sentimental though. Needs her security blankets." He snorted. "Not as if a sale's imminent. Unless one advertises a haunted house complete with resident ghosts, if we don't bale, soon."

"A waste when you think on it," Lance said as if it recently occurred to him. His next tone was derisive. "All she really needs is one room and a subscription to Netflix!" His scorn came through the door scorching the wood. I waited sick at heart to hear Zak's reply.

"Ah! It got her through. Maybe she watched that old black and white vintage crap, those gruesome old *horror* films to make her own situation better. We could have helped more."

My face crumpled. Was I that transparent and

pathetic? Everyone has a hobby, or guilty pleasure. Wasn't that what they called it?

Long pause. "Think she'll share? Even this old wreck gotta be worth somethin'. You see that? We got nothin'. Zip!" Lance's voice raised petulantly. "Maybe with you. That's why you're so lovey-dovey and sweet on her."

"Don't be lame! 'Sides, this place would fetch what? 250 thou? Hardly a bonanza."

"It is, if you don't have it. I could invest in clinics…rent a decent—" Lance sputtered to a stop. "Why should she have it all! She was taken care of. No skin off her nose all those years." I had a sense this *chat* was bending out of shape ballooning past the initial discussion. "All you'd do is blow it in Vegas, or go roaming!" Lance continued.

"I did okay when I played Caesar's and Bellagio, *Nancy!*" Zak voice was harsh. His use of the derogatory term, meant he smarted. *He lost big.* My heart beat faster. Then with an icicle to my heart, I heard him musing, "Most would go to court over a situation like this."

"So?" Lance's voice rose with anticipation. "So, you're thinkin' what I'm thinking'. We'd could go together…as a last resort. If—if Magpie don't see reason. Soon as we get outta here, right?"

There was amusement in Zak's voice. "You do realize lawyers are bloodsucking vampires?"

"Waste! What a freaking waste!" I heard Lance with a bitterness poisoning his voice. "Don't suppose anything will be left from the sale of the Grosse Point barn?"

"Hardly, old son. It was upside down. I hit grandad for a loan once, never mind what for. *That* was embarrassing! The upshot is, he said it had a triple mortgage and that was, what? —five years ago?"

I smiled bitterly. I could have told them that if any were interested in the house then, or Uncle Dez.

Something struck the fireplace. Did Lance mind that much? Yes. Of course, he did. I thought I explained all that. The will was only probated, a few hours before I impulsively fled. I sighed with despair. How could I make things right?

Their next words caught me in another net of truth.

"Old Magpie'd never appreciate how to spend it! The cash. She doesn't have a sense of fun." Lance continued maddeningly complacent, boring in. His scathing tone made me cringe.

"Meg? Simply out of practice. How could she, caring for old Dez? Not like *we* helped. Now me?" Zak laughed in a deprecating way. "I gotta thousand places to fritter away any spare moolah. You? What would you do with a sudden bundle dropped in your lap?"

I put my back to the wall undecided. I yearned to confront them. My lesser angel halted me. Lance leaned against the river rock with a far-away expression when I peered back, apparently mulling scheming ways to future windfalls at my expense.

I waited, burning, unsure whether to take them head on, *or pinch their heads off.* So far, it sounded like little boys' posturing, proven by his next comment.

"Me? A ship's doctor maybe... Yeah! Meet a wealthy widow. Open a posh plastic surgeon clinic for celebs. Maybe a chain..."

"Isn't there extra med school for that? Sculpting tits—Raising Arses 101?"

"Nah. You don't need special license for plastic

surgery, ya see…"

"I shudder to think," Zak drawled.

I was almost ready to cough, or hum the "Star Spangled Banner," and barge in at that, when I heard what I feared deep down.

"Funny when you think of it. We are most likely, Magpie's heirs." Lance breathed a long airy phony sigh, indicating regret. My heart not only chilled, but stopped in a hollowed-out space where a steady beat, thumped seconds before. I sucked deep, clutching my hands to keep from shaking apart.

"I *didn't* old son, till you mentioned it," Zak replied carelessly. I heard a snort of amusement, while I waited for him to decry it. *Zak, Zak. How can you think that? Even in jest? Why humor Lance?* I clenched my elbows to keep from flying apart.

Then I overheard something even more chilling—

"Ya realize, in Magpie's old flicks what would happen next…?" Lance let the sentence fall in what was meant to be idle speculation, or a joke.

"Don't go there…" Zak. Was he finally aware Lance swam into dangerous waters?

"She'd go wandering off into the woods, or to the basement and…"

Zak chuckled. "Right! And there'd be some lunatic…or phantom…"

Lance. "With a chainsaw!"

"Nah! A bloody axe!"

More giggles from both of the wise guys. I heard enough; it wasn't funny, cutting Lance's speculation in its rotten bud, near sobbing with anger, I eased the door shut falling against the wall, but couldn't shut out the two idiots laughing away my future. They'd hear *me* if I stayed. My knees knocked to wake the dead. My first instinct was go charging in, flailing away at least with invectives, however in my livid state, or even denial, I realized it was smarter to sit back and watch, yet how could I face them?

My chin quivered. Were they really hoping I'd die young? This was perfect spot. And I was trapped—*with them*. They could do *anything*. No one could prove a murder. They'd be in collusion—say I starved and they buried me out there somewhere, or I fell though the ice or—Tears rolled down my cheeks.

I smeared them away with new resolve. Stay smart. *Get a grip*...Simply shooting the bull, isn't that what they say? Maybe they don't mean it! Lance always runs away with crazy schemes...he clearly went too far. And Zak. Zak is definitely a sardonic jokester. Isn't that his calling card? And so, I rationalized, at least on the surface. And we were all half-nutty with hunger. That was it. Sometimes, little pitchers with big ears fall from a great height and get smashed.

But what if it were real? Even if it started with a sick joke. And so it went...

****

I supposed the widow's walk was *cozy*, if cold to the bone and the view unrelievedly white, *and not defendable?* I still could not completely erase the overheard speculation. Sucking in a sobbing breath I composed myself once more. *Stop it!*

Defend from whom, exactly? *Zak or Lance?*

"Fill in the blanks," I muttered, splitting in two and smoking half of one of my unearthed Lucky Strikes and taking a restorative sip of whiskey, feeling the sugary burn followed by lightheadedness. I checked the bottle.

Not too smart. I should stay alert.

I leaned against frosty glass staring at obscuring flakes like a pillow fight softly swirling past. My car was a shapeless hillock, the boathouse hidden to its eaves on the lee side. I murmured seeing the fog on the pane, "Do people still shop, have warm dinners, go to movies, or Starbucks?" I asked the expanse, though not a client, *hardly,* with lattes topping four bucks a pop. I could scarce recall normal life. The time with Dez seemed like heaven, in place of an endless slog.

"No more!" I growled. "No more the weak, helpless, gimp! I had plans at one time!" A fever built inside me to *do something*. Something *positive*. Ignore them. I could not sit like a stuffed goose waiting for the boys to go all Donner Party on me. I scowled darkly smoking the other half and taking another frugal sip of whiskey reveling in the pleasurable burn, lending me courage. Checking the level—a scant quarter left—I wedged the pack and remaining booze under the bench and rose up to do my kind of battle.

The snow had lightened. I frowned down at my brother. He obligingly scraped free a mound of snow from the hood and was holding up a wire.

Fudge! He saw me.

I peered down again. *Lance, trying to start my car?* "Delusional." But Lance still motioned—*come down.*

I was wary, goosey after what I heard, I admit, slipping a kitchen knife in my belt, I stepped out the screen door…As I did so I halted. My mind's eye missed something that should be there. I swung round. The big tin washtub was missing from the wall over the handpump, so ubiquitous only its absence made it noticeable. I shook my head and continued out. Ask later.

Or, was that Lance's not so subtle reminder of my *iniquities*?

Pretending all was the same I limped through snow to my knees. Clutching my arms, I smiled a question, and peered at the Dagger's corroded innards, ready to run back at any trouble. I looked back, half expecting the boys to lock me out. That is how paranoid I was. "You got me. Now what?"

Lance held a stiff fan belt with a ragged break. "And the distributor cap's gone missing!"

"Distributor cap? I'm supposed to get what that is? But where could it—whatever—be?"

Lance waved the brittle belt at me. "Know anything about this?"

"Oh sure! I always sabotage my own cars. A hobby!" What was this? I could see no immediate danger. But all they did held suspicion, now.

Lance slammed the hood. "Where's Zak?"

"Please, not again." Now I was certain he heard me hovering in the kitchen. Distancing himself. Or casting suspicion. "Divide and conquer," I couldn't help saying throwing him a bitter stare.

"You're blind. Who else?"

"How would I know? And why would he?" I poked the radiator belt. A frozen piece broke off, falling beneath the engine block. "It snapped from cold."

Lance huffed sullenly, but slammed the lid, almost catching my fingers.

I wandered to the seawall to scowl out at the lake. Tears were imminent when Lance joined me. I moved aside.

He nodded at the hunter's blind. "Remember? We played Indians, or Robinson Crusoe?"

I was silent too long, not wanting to make nice. He nudged me. "Yes. That old rowboat was a canoe or a pirate ship—"

"And arrows were hand-scraped flint, insteada plastic! Hah!"

I squinted at the faint twinkle of lights even in daytime. "We're the same as them. In prison."

" 'Cept, they have three hots, and a cot."

"How far?" I gazed yearningly at the prison camp and safety.

"Too far…Around the shorelines even longer. Bays and long loops. Never make it."

I nodded at the lake, mesmerized. "Simply keep walking," I murmured to myself.

"Suicide on ice."

Like you cared.

I stared at him until he looked away with an embarrassed cast.

Why? Did I catch you and Zak out, Lance? If so…why not encourage me? Give me a good send off? Could always say I stubbornly wandered off, after a warning… when they found my frozen body out there— *somewhere…*

I think looking back that was where the idea, later, was formed.

A gust plucked my hair from my cap whipping the black ribbons so hard, they cut my face. Lance hunched deeper in his coat. "That answer it?" He nodded his chin. "Cold front comin'."

I remained silent. I did not trust myself to speak. If I had any hope of weather changing in my favor, it was crushed by clouds sluggishly pushing a heavy leaden sky across the horizon toward us. I swiveled to the woods behind us. And Zak was out there, somewhere.

****

Zak poked his boot at a long leg bone–a *femur,* he thought it was called. Lance would identify it. Small sharp teeth marks pitted the polished yellow surface. He scuffled snow exposing foot bones, loosely held with hard gluey sinews. He knelt, brushing, revealing jutting bony pelvic and a long spine beneath a scattering of ribs. Ice encased the skeleton where snow-melt dripped from trees, preserving the skull with strands of red hair still clinging as through wavery glass. Only the thicket of wicked thorny briars encasing it with prickers, saved the remains from being scavenged asunder long ago.

He stood checking the steely sky through snow like feathering ashes. Farther into the woods than he had ever been, in a vain attempt to find *something,* anything edible, acorns, wild blackberries dried on wintery branches, which was how he discovered the bones—*or another goose.* He could no longer spy the whale weather vane.

"As the Brits say, 'a goose would be a fine chance.' " Ah, well, he had a rabbit and a pocketful of acorns for his troubles. They'd feast tonight.

He brushed leaves and snow over the bones in a crude re-burial, and as he hefted a bloody sack over his shoulders, gazed back in the direction of the house.

Something was brewing. He could feel it. Hadn't the energy to delve into it.

****

French doors blasted open. Zak staggered in looking like he rolled in powdered sugar as he hurled a lumpy sack in the direction of the hearth. His head flew back as the old Bakelite radio smashed in pieces on the stone fireplace next to his head, and Lance, coming behind with a proprietary hand on my shoulder, scowled at him. I hopped back from the bloody sack and shrugged my brother's hand off.

"What was *that* all about!" Zak managed through frozen lips. His cold eyes cut me to the bone, with me shrinking under his censure.

Lance snarled. "Where in God's name, or *why* would you take the distributor cap and cut a fan belt!"

I said nothing.

Zak raked us both with pity. "Look geniuses. Not familiar with what little conspiracy you've cooked up— now you're talkin' trash. What the hell's a distributor cap? Wouldn't recognize one if it bit me."

I conceded, neither did I. Even though an automotive family, the only thing we kids were good at was turning on the ignition of the plethora of cars available to us, or used to be, when we could steal the keys. Besides, *Lance was by my car. Lance, the one held up the wires*

Lance who dropped something then ground it in the snow.

You know why, my evil imp prodded. *Lance could get Zak in the soup...* And, maybe both of them were afraid I overheard their plotting. Lance was distancing again. Taking sides. I despised both of them at that moment, but played their game. I could be as good at it.

"Zak!" I cried. "How *wonderful*! I don't see how you do it!" Ladling it on thick as gravy ignoring Lance's fury and balled fists.

But then, after Zak threw Lance an unreadable look, he upended the stained sack. Bloodied rabbits stripped of fur rolled out, ending the disagreement, as I fell on them like a vampire after a two-hundred-year nap in a butcher shop.

Lance threw a disgusted look. "Get stuffed. Probably diseased. Ever hear of *tuia-re-mia*?"

I regarded the bloody purple-veined rabbits. My stomach flipped, but Lance appeared already regretting his hasty words of spite, even though he wouldn't show it, if *his* feet were in the fire.

****

I watched sizzling fat flaring up from the coals, while my brother, ignoring Zak dousing the rabbits on makeshift coat hanger spits, with liberal lashings of salt and pepper, of which we had plenty—poured hot water over a grey tea bag.

Leaning over, Zak wafted smokey redolent steam to his face.

"Ummm. *Swe-eet*, all crusty brown like that." And ripped off a strip, draping it over his mouth, chewed and wiping his chin, gustily swallowed. "Oooh-ahh! Hot!" Zak mumbled through a mouthful sucking his fingers. *Noisily.* "Sorry, kiddies, but this is *so* freaking *good*." Gingerly he ripped into another haunch, releasing roasting meat perfume "accidently" waving it under my nose.

"Enough! We got it!" Lance snapped.

I waited for him to ask me. Be darned if I'd be first. But then, Zak began warbling, "*Here Comes Peter Cottontail. Hopping down the bunny…*" in a wavery Johnny Cash baritone and Lance looked about to stick Zak with his own wire coat hanger skewers.

I threw a pillow. "Going to send *you* down that bunny trail, if you don't quit it."

Lance belligerently waved his mug. "Not

squeamish. And hardly *vegan.* You don't appreciate where those things came from."

"The woods, Lance. They come from the woods. And you never gave a good gosh darn where they came from before."

Lance made a disgusted, *"Tchaaa!"* as I crawled closer, eyeing the rapidly demolished rabbit, watching juice sizzle and flames flare as Zak tore off another haunch, russet colored with cracklings, intoxicating in its aroma. Soon my martyrdom would be wasted. The first rabbit would be gone! Lance was mulish. He didn't really believe they were tainted—it was the *source* that was contaminated.

Zak quirked a glance and held the meaty strip out.

Yes, I nodded. *Oh yes.* It couldn't be worse than the goose. I recalled Tularemia— the rabbit sickness was bad, fatal if one did not get shots. But I checked the bodies as always. They seemed healthy. I was past caring. Snatching the offering, I tried not to mainline the hot succulent meat. Heaven. Oh! I had never tasted *anything* so good. Tossing the meat from hand to hand, I grinned a nod at Zak.

****

Tossing a last bone in the fire I drew a scathing look from my brother. *Don't you dare say it.* "Don't be a frickin hero, Lanny." Shreds of rabbit still clung to the bones left.

Lance was good at not concealing hurt pride. "You win! Satisfied?" he snapped, morosely snatching a scrawny strip Zak tossed him, snarling, *"Thanks!* Don't blame me if you wake up with boils all over and 106 temp!"

I laughed bitterly to myself, but plastering a smile,

gave Zak a big wink. How fraudulent I felt.

"Ah, now you did it. You spoiled it all." Winking back, Zak tore into the next rabbit. "Or not."

I hungered for more, but got up, restless. My tummy wasn't used to rich food anymore. Now, I felt stuffed and slightly queasy thanks to Lance's stupid remarks. Lance, the lead balloon at any party.

"How did you bag 'em anyway." I asked, curious.

Zak quirked his mouth. "Does it matter?"

"There wasn't a mark on them." I marveled like a gushing school girl, despite my former cool intentions.

"Oh, Zak! My hero!" The sneer grated on my ears. I shot a withering glance at my brother. Too bad. Zak was a hero in my book at least for now, whether he liked it or not. As I said, two can play that game.

Chapter 22

Killing Cold

"Hunting's not hard. It's the killin'."

"Yah. Would expect that. Wouldn't think *I'd* have any trouble." Lance laughed, self-deprecating. "Up to my elbows in blood half the time..." Lance babbled on, trying hard, and succeeding in being pleased to be included—*and* outside the chilly warrens of the Victorian monstrosity plus Nutmeg's odd moods: first cold as a well-digger's butt, then she's all warm and gushy toward Zak. The bite of cold, cobalt sky, and hot sun was icy vodka and rum-warm.

"Damn! Could eat my shoes," he burbled.

"Hope we find somethin' tastier 'n your dirty sneakers."

Lance checked for the weathervane, but Zak motioned him farther into the thick featureless snow-blind woods. Between one step and the next, the old weathercock vanished. He turned back unwittingly the opposite way.

Panicking slightly, feeling veins in his neck thumping, Lance rounded a fir, plunging into a brown declivity left by a felled tree; one minute stepping over brush, the next, skidding arse over teakettle into a pit.

Clawing his way back, true panic blossomed. *Where's that stupid fuchsia hat?* "That fat head. Zak

200

could tell Meg anything!" He muttered gloomily. *Like he looked for me*...Be damned if he'd call, though. "Yeah, then he and Magpie, can split the inheritance. Can't tell me that's all there is. Gotta be safety deposit boxes with bearer bonds and old silver, or coin collections, maybe Grandma's jewelry kept back from bankruptcy courts. Uncle Dez wasn't that stupid. He built a damn empire!" Such were his dark rumblings.

At last, spying the cap to the far left of where he *thought* Zak should be, he took a deep breath; brushing snow, hustled without seeming to, before he lost his game face, when a shaft whizzed by his head causing a rush of artic air, thunking into a sheared-off pine. He stared at a thread of his mob cap pinned deep in the bark, at the same time feeling his head. A thin smear of blood came away on his gloves. "Hey!" He yelped before crouching in a hiding stance. "What the hell. Ya *only shot* at me!"

"Stop foolin' around. Where the hell were you? Keep up."

"Here you maniac! I'm right here where you almost killed me, you ass!" Lance tried to calm. Not show fright in front of Mr. Wonderful. "What the hell!"

Ahead, Zak stepped from beyond a fir holding his bow loosely at his side and waited with an offensively bland expression.

Lance blew out a breath. He didn't have to hide in the woods going in circles until he died of hyperthermia. He didn't have to get to the house before Zak. All was cool—except Zak was damned careless. "Yah! Right! You didn't know it. You merely happened to let loose an arrow in my direction!"

"Don't be stupid, Prancer! I was shooting at a

squirrel!"

He walked over and yanked the arrow out of the tall stump of a dead pine. "Keep up pilgrim. I thought you were right behind me. You can get lost here," he announced and stalked off.

Scowling at his back, Lance heard him snort, "never get your badge that way…"

" 'Less I earn one for stayin' *alive*," Lance muttered, checking his surroundings for a landmark. The sky was the shade of old newsprint, trees frosted white. Shrub, and brush blended into seamless ice cream blobs. He hurried ahead before he lost the fuchsia cap again. How the hell was *he* familiar with the woods! How the *hell* did he know where *he* was going? Why was Zak always so goddam perfect!

****

Affecting nothing happened, Lance stared dumbly at an overturned, galvanized washtub. Why the hell was the washtub, the same one hanging in the kitchen for donkey's years by the looks of it, and recent setting for their obnoxious display, doing the hell out here? Lance glowered at Zak. What was he up to? He'd leave if he could find the hell the way out.

"Joke's far enough, asshole! Damned near killed me! And now *this*!"

Zak cocking his head watched him blankly as if studying a particularly dull specimen of bug. "Tub on forked stick. Stick tied to string. String tied to Eve's fave lure. Lesson for the day, Sunny Jim." Zak knelt gingerly tipping the tub revealing a jackrabbit huddling in the dark.

"In this case, dried apple core saved back." And in a move too fast to see, Zak grabbed the rabbit, immobilized in place, snapping its neck in one graceful motion.

Lance winced in spite of himself.

"And that's how you do it, if you fancy hot dinners."

"Yah. Can see that. Thought you shot 'em with your trusty bow and arrow." Lance couldn't help the dig.

"Lose too many arrows."

"Yah! One in my head."

Zak checked the sky ignoring him. "Should have tried this donkey's years ago. My bad. Make tracks. Daylight's in short supply."

"Sure thing, *boss*." Lance scowled at his back while Zak attached a morsel for another unwary varmint. Replacing the tub on the forked stick, he backed, checking it, and trotted off, once again vanishing between two heavily laden firs, sending back sprays of cold mist in his Lance's face, and leading him farther into the woods, it seemed rather than back home.

Sweating under sweaters and the long coat, Lance tromped after him, lifting knees high, increasingly rattled. And damn, his sneakers, no matter how many socks, let in cold and wet. He trotted faster searching featureless ground cover. "Dammit, where's that weathervane? Who needs him!" Lance muttered.

No prints this direction. He circled, quelling panic, striving to pick up Zak's careful trail, before he had to call, aware the sky lowered a shade or two from faded denim to a dirty dishrag gray. Bird chatter stilled, as if even they discerned when to shelter in their hidden nest for the night; perceptively darker too, the snow taking on a city twilight.

"Damn it, Zak," he finally yelled. "Wait the fuck up!" Standing in the midst of frozen silence, he waited to hear. No calls. No cracking through brush sounds. In a frenzy feeling his back drenched with sweat under layers of sweaters and the top coat, he crashed through a thicket fighting prickers and dead creeper tangles.

Zak sat on a stump watching him blunder. "I said keep up, sport. Can't go huntin' for you."

"Yeah. Like you would!" Once again, Zak made him feel asinine as he scanned a landscape now more lavenders and grays, behind him. Thought he saw a flash of light—a glint of something, low to the ground on top the snow, but then it was gone as the sun sank silhouetting black spikes of firs against a mercurochrome red sky.

He shuddered, trotting faster, dragging the coat through deep snow, anxious to get back to the monstrosity and fireplace before another vanishing act. Damn, if he didn't know better, it looked like Zak deliberately tried to abandon him.

Chapter 23

Chill Factor

Haunted and thin, I scraped bones from the fireplace, brushing off ash and soot, feverishly chewing. I fished too, but the fish seemed hook-shy, or were onto the mysterious blessings dropping from the round hole in the ice. Plus, it raged in the night, *what else is new* adding another inexorable layer entombing us in cottony silence past window sills. We're never getting free, I gloomed. We were in the midst of a damned apocalypse film. *The wind that never died. The rains that never ended or drought, take your pick, where water's worth more than gold, or blind monsters with batlike hearing— or zombies…*

I shook my head, dredging composure from the bottom of a very depleted barrel. It was day sixty-three…I thought.

Yesterday, the boys snagged a rabbit and a handful of desiccated berries birds hadn't got to, that I soaked in hot water. A veritable feast. One could call it celebration, by opening the last jar of green beans.

But still, three adults?

Zak hunted again. I fervently hoped for even a three-day-old Canadian goose.

Yesterday, he saw a deer and took the bow again. That's what I should be doing. I wasn't a bad shot myself, I grinned sourly, sometimes even besting the boys in the old days.

Lance pleaded a bad cold. Around somewhere, I supposed....

****

Dragging an empty sack, Zak wearily entered to shouts, and me, limping after Lance wearing a too-small H.S. letter jacket and chewing something.

"Thieving bastard! Cheat! Hand over!" I grappled my brother, screeching, "Zak! He's eating something!" Zak dropped the sack, looking predatory.

"Found it upstairs! In my old school jacket. Kay?" Lance waved a brittle pack. "Ten-year-old Juicy Fruit! O*kay!*" He shouted defensively.

I narrowed my eyes. "You always squirreled away your Halloween and Christmas candy. Sneak! Why am I surprised? Zak shared *his*."

"Yeah, well, and I still *had* mine too after you and Zak gobbled everything like disgusting pigs!" Lance wrinkled his nose and grunted, *"oink, oink, oink!"* He waved a fist. "What about it, Zak? You want it! Come get it." He was spoiling for a fight.

Zak quirked expressive brows, and slanted an icy gaze at Lance that spoke, *really?*

I saw an opening and grabbed the gum. Licking the wrapper, I popped the stick in my mouth, reveling in the tiny sugar rush from a stick hard as cardboard. Then, regarding the chewed wad, I burst into great honking sobs, hiccupping. "We're horrible! I'm sorry, Lanny. What's *happening* to us?"

Zak hugged me, kissing the top of my head. I let him. "Nothin', babes," Zak murmured in my hair. "I hope."

But he didn't hope hard enough.

Chapter 24

Arctic Front

Increasingly, I found myself in the widow's walk. It made no sense. It was an icebox inside and out, with only thin glass to quell the arctic cold. But sanctuary. Safe. Hidden. I had control. I also had two cigarettes and a quarter bottle of whiskey. I can't tell you the comfort that familiarity afforded me, in an existence slipping further from control each hour. We were all becoming demented, or maybe only a distillation of our former selves, the essence of who we *really* were. And conditions were worse. Nutritionally-challenged, I think the politically correct word is, and the wintry feel of the house settled in our bones for good.

Dimly, as I turned foursquare, straining for any changes in the horizon, any sign of melting, sunshine, or even an absence of snow-plow clouds pushing blizzards from Canada, to dump on the U.P. I searched for Zak bringing back anything that resembled *food*.

It took me a few minutes to detect the sounds. I drew my brows in irritation, hearing distant scratching, then a thump that caused my feet to rise, staring down with shock. The trap door shifted. What I heard next, sent the frost on the windows straight to my heart. They found me! The trap door thumped with a harsh clang of metal on metal followed by curses. I stomped on the trap, causing a muffled grunt, and tugged the strap.

Usually swinging wide open, the trap wouldn't budge.

No chance to *starve*, I thought with hysteria bubbling like dry ice clogging my lungs with shock. Only glass between me and an ugly death, leaving a frozen corpse. *The Lady of the Widow's Walk*! A myth, or Halloween tale, my mind gabbled. No weapons, no way of prying the trap.

I tugged at the leather loop trap handle, using all my puny strength. The brittle leather snapped. I flew back, landing with a bone-breaking thud destroying my skinny rump. A shiny tip protruded from the wood. I yanked again feeling the vibration of a hammer pounding the other side and heard the squeal of a nail.

I pressed hands against my temples to squeeze rational thought into my starved brain. Stomp! Don't let the buggers win. Conniving bastards. They'd say I wandered and by the time they found me under a tree, out on lake, or even stuck in here... Maybe disappear like Debbi...The food would go further...*So sad, so close to rescue...so...*

Rage heated me to incandescence.

"You bastards! Let me out!" I hollered, stopping to catch my breath alarmed at how little strength I owned, even for that. Another thud of a hammer shuddered through my feet to my knees. I danced up and down using all of my weight. With a creaking and whining, a nail loosened in the old termite-eaten wood. I heard another squeal and pop and muffled tinkle of metal hitting the floor below. Straining determinedly, I tugged the remanent of the strap and one side shifted.

"I'm still here, you snake! I'm going to make you

sorry you were ever—"

Another nail wretched free and the trap creakily lifted; Lance's red-rimmed eyes beneath his mob hat and one nobbily red-knuckled fist clenching a hammer showed in the gap. His mouth clamped two rusty nails. He spat them out. "Magpie! This where you get up to? What you doin' up here!"

Right! I pushed down past him like a stiff breeze. "*Don't Magpie me*! As if you didn't know! What the Sam hill, Lance!" I darted wary looks at the hammer while backing toward the freedom of the attic door, a mile away. He looked down at the metal wood-thing gripped in his fist as if he had never seen a marvel such as a hammer.

He looked up aggrieved with rheumy eyes.

"You did not *hear* me?" I was determined to get an admission.

"What the hell, Meggie, who would? Listen to that." He accused, as if I committed some embarrassing breach. I became aware of howling and an assault of sleet and snow splatting panes like machine gun fire, out of nowhere. Ice-storm-thunder reverberated in the maelstrom.

"Came up to scrounge wood. Or something?" He shrugged scanning the attic as if a whole face-cord was stacked neatly in a corner.

"Oh," I scathed. "You decided to do a bit of carpentry while at it? Why the nails!" I said with a coldness that might never leave me.

Lance looked aggrieved from deep-set ghost eyes under a shag of hair sticking below his mob cap. "Just— I dunno! Closing off drafts. Gonna seal the attic too," he sulked, "if you must know. How'd I get you were up here playing Greta Garbo?"

"Drafts!" I scorned. "Leave it be," I yelled like a shrew. "Don't you *dare* deface *my* house, again!"

Chapter 25

Storm Clouds

I wondered after the grisly events that followed…if I hadn't looked *too* hard…or, stepped on *that* floor-board to follow my so-called dream—could the fates of all of us have been avoided? Even disowned through ignorance? Yet, what I unearthed was irrefutable. And "you can't put toothpaste back in the tube" was the old saw.

Especially poisonous toothpaste.

Hah! *Dreams!* More a desperate bid to keep sanity from flitting about the ceiling like a demented bat. *I could trust no one.*

My "dream" then, was a raveling end of sanity in order to weave just one more day. Thoughts now, when I had coherent ones at all, were a fritzing lightbulb ready to go out at any second. My mind drifted from one side of the pin ball machine to the other.

The primitives we were becoming was the awakening.

Hibernating before the pitiful fire. Fights over who should scrounge wood, portions of food, theft accusations, the five o'clock shadows on the boy's gaunt faces turning into shaggy black beards. The odd calculating glances we threw at each other. The hours that passed unnoticed as we dozed in a stupor.

Zak resembled a pirate and Lance a homeless person. Me? I avoided mirrors, scrubbing my face pink in the mornings with frigid water from the kitchen pump, giving my long hair a lick and a promise, rebraiding long scruffy black plaits. Yet, I could not ignore, old high school sweaters abandoned in the 10th grade, hung from me as if from coat hangers and jeans slipped off already slim hips.

I saw *us* with horrific re-imaginings of that Andes plane crash increasingly worming its way into my terrors, galvanizing me into action, no matter how rainbow-colored the dream. In another time and place, I *had* plans. Sugar bear. I must go back to *those* rosy dreams! Polish their luster like a corroded copper tea kettle until they gleamed as a lodestar leading me back to life *where future was a given. A last gasp.*

****

With that *noble* goal you can't blame me for the horrors that followed.

Today. I had to do *something* to prove I was viable—sane and had something laughably, called energy.

It was the seventieth or seventy-fifth day, of our ice-bound existence. We fretted last night over whether February had twenty-seven or twenty-eight days, or if it was a leap year, and what month it was anyhow, however, listless, as were most of our squabbles these days.

I secured one of the sharpest knives, to be on the side of prudence, checked the old shotgun above the fireplace, putting it back as useless, besides, there were no shells of which I was aware. The rusty suitcase of tools, I noted that first night, inexplicably vanished.

On that day—that fatal day, I reckoned Zak was in the cellar for *whatever* reason. I heard him rummaging through the scrolled heat registers, concerning me on one level, that I no longer wondered. Probably seeking more canning jars forgotten in dim corners. Hah! Or, the last lumps of coal little more than dust now, no matter how supplemented with dead-fall. Zak still scrounged deeper into the woods when up to it. Storms helped some. When he sank to his knees with a load, I saw how difficult it was to tote back from my aerie in the widow's walk, but felt no pity.

****

Zak *was* in the cellar tossing scattered coal the size of pea gravel in the scuttle, eyeing a negligible mound in the corner he was saving. Later he'd scrounge coal dust. He listened to wind challenging the slanted storm door's hinges. He was avoiding going out. Hated leaving the house into the teeth of another gale rattling the house's old bones. Meg's creativity stretching their meager substance, was magic, but can't dodge they needed another hare for super if there was to be any. Maybe the storm will die later.

He shuddered as gale winds whistled down the coal chute. He checked back. A rare beam the color of oysters found its way through the slanted hatch, making anthracite dust sparkle like the diamonds they would become, in about a zillion years, now flickering the air with silvery motes—when his shovel struck something.

Not coal—slightly yielding.

Shuffling black dust aside, he bent muttering, "Damn."

What seemed like twigs was a clenched skeletal hand thrust from coal as if beckoning. He prodded the thing, revealing a blackened arm bone. Zak perched on the bottom steps thoughtful, until with a sudden galvanic shudder, aware he was freezing to death, creaked up like an old man.

After splintering the frame, the warped door popped open. He tugged the bones through. A small avalanche breaking a wave of sooty grit rattled off them, revealing a clavicle followed by a spine, held with gristle, hardened to amber. The skeleton kept coming. The rest was easy even though the skeleton was more dried flesh than bone, conjecturing coal sucked the moisture out, preserving it. He noted slashed marks—slits in the stiff hide.

Lastly, a dome of a skull bent at a hard angle emerged. Judging from desiccated sacks indicating breasts, it was female. A wonder, Lance hadn't found it. He made such an old maid fuss about only *him* finding the coal, and lugging up the scuttles as if he owned the cellar. More power to him. He shook his head. The thing was at the edge of the pile near the coal chute. Only its outflung hand was in danger of discovery.

Zak's mind wandered as he stared at the shriveled mummy. *Oh, yes. He was hiding it.* Couldn't recall why the hurry, or need even. Not like anyone came down anymore. But still. He hip-wedged the door. It settled since Meggie foraged those canning jars. He noted from wan light filtering through, there were no glints of glass left anywhere. Doubted she'd be back.

****

Unaware of Zak's endeavors or even Lance's at the time, I began. Increasingly. Lance dozed by the cold fireplace huddled in a mound of blankets by a cone of warmth, undetectable two feet off, on the most sensitive register. I tiptoed past to the stairs.

As good a time as any when I could pretend, I had strength and the boys were "busy." Buckling an ancient tool belt about my waist, I hitched upstairs to *do great things.*

I was lost, crawling the long barren halls on hands and knees heedless of the ice box bitterness, beyond blowing on red chapped knuckles, and thrusting a yard stick before me, so ancient from some long-gone hardware store, that one could scarce make out the numerals. I muttered incantations like a mad sorceress, stopping to scribble arcane notes with a stub, in a grubby note book.

With the tool belt from uncle Dez's days, dragging at my waist, I uttered occult words, like—*"ochers— salmon—terra cotta? Or cool marine greys, greens, and blues?"*

My furniture now. The lesser pieces like the ugly side-board, even a shabby-chic coat of white could not save, I had sacrificed in the great stone altar days ago, but stubbornly would not let them toss in other antiques that the boys in manly fashion, designated as rubbish. I gloated; they would give the old girl authenticity.

My brain was still foggy with need after no breakfast besides ground acorns soaked in a cup of boiled water. My body depleted. I recognized I was half-delirious. I should conserve strength to gut it through. Yet, the one spark of lucidity left seemed acutely aware I had to keep the will burning with whatever feeble kindling left, or I'd die, feverish with fright, envisioning the long days marching into gales without benefit of food or heat.

The fire, neglected last night as we fell into stuporous sleep, withered into dead gray feathers without one spark to coax to life. After a frantic search for matches in pockets and drawers, I recalled the few I sprinkled, rashly abandoned under cellar stairs that first night in another time and place. Lance anxiously coaxed a small fire using hacked up picture frames.

I was fretting all this when a high-top sneaker appeared before my nose.

Irritably, I crawled around it.

"Whatya doin', Magpie?" The sandpaper voice intruded.

I started, entering the real, unwanted world. The high-tops stayed in the way and Lanny's voice continued raw and grating, breaking my magic circle. Warily, sitting on my heels scraping stray hair under my cap, I hurled him every look but "*welcome.*"

He waited as if I owed him.

"Can't wait for spring thaw!" I snapped. "If you must know."

Lance considered the hall as if I were up to something nefarious.

"Now leave me alone!

"I'm thinking—bed and breakfast!" I snapped before he asked—if "*I were all right?*" as if he cared. Of course, I wasn't. Crazy as a loon flying over Convict Lake and he didn't help as he raked the tool belt and yard stick with sneering regard.

"Bed and breakfast. Uh. Oka-a-a-y." He inspected the hall speculating with dawning awareness. "Hunh!" He nodded once then turned his suspicious face back to me. "Uncle slip an extra mil we should be acquainted with?" His pale red-rimmed, rheumy eyes slitted in suspicion.

"Eff off!" I barked in ways he was not used to.

"Always money with you!" I threw the yardstick followed by the pencil stub bouncing off the wall. I wanted to say, "Lanny! I'm scared and hungry. 'Sides it's warmer when I'm *doing* something!" But I could not confide the way I had.

"I'll bite."

"I want to be alone!"

"Garbo again?" Lance snorted falsetto, mimicking a tooth-grating Swedish accent, *"Eeeesss, you and me, Lance! Never mind, Zak. Nossing for Zak!* When were you going to let us *peons* in on this?"

"I wasn't!"

"Figures. Okay. So, show me. The decorator-challenged." Lance belligerently stood in my way.

I sighed and sat back on my heels glaring up at him. "If I do, will you leave then!"

****

My *dear* brother mooched sullen and dismissive about the vast elegant room with the lordly view of Convict Lake so appropriate for an automobile scion of the last century.

"They'll love this. Least, it's furnished." I forced myself to laugh.

"Sure thing. If one yearns for *Dracula* or *Fall of the House of Usher.*" Lance tugged a huge tassel coughing at the fog of dust it released. "Might be cash in it at that," carelessly whacking the bed drape jetting clouds with more than a hint of resentment.

I yanked drapes back from the massive four poster, ignoring him. "I was thinking," I said to myself before realizing I spoke aloud, *"The Scarlett O'Hara Suite..."* My mouth opened to scream, but nothing came out, snapping it shut. The lumpy cover and proliferation of pillows resembled a body curled on its side. Lance fingering a civil war sword over the fireplace, eyeing a Chinese vase, and toeing a Persian carpet did not notice my lapse.

Grandmother Laura's suite adjoined Uncle Dez's. I privately named it, *"The Melanie Suite."* To hell with Lance's lead balloon.

As I limped down the hall below, I slapped doors, dully announcing my intentions. Maybe he will get bored. "Down there, I was thinking— *'Casablanca Room'* with the actual film playing on TV when guests—" *Putting the notions to words gave them a new truth. Yes, that would be perfect.*

Lance nodded pretending to be indifferent, but his close-set eyes were sharp with speculation and greed. I smiled inwardly. Tapping other doors, I led on beginning to enjoy myself. "Maybe the *Bette Davis Room?*" I regarded him as if including him in my mission.

"Bette Davis? Do I remember her?"

"You loved *Whatever Happened to Baby Jane.*"

I ignored his *"ugh"* face.

"There was this movie?" I looked wistfully down the long hall, not seeing it. *"Now Voyager.* Bette Davis plays this half-crazed old maid. Eyebrows like caterpillars. She goes on a cruise, and when she steps off the boat, she's Angelina-frickin-Jolie." My face fell. Before I could stopper my mouth, this erupted to my shame. "Wish I'd wake up, and me and this old house would be—*stunning."*

Lance shuffled awkward. "You are, Magpie. Stunning me with brilliance. You really are on to something. Dazzle me more," he said with real interest as his eyes betrayed, he was counting dollars, assessing profits, and judging how much it would cost.

"You got it." I said with dryness constricting my throat. Already it seemed my dream was snatched away. Dirtied. I hid doubts by tapping more doors from the days of illustrious house guests; rumored, even Gloria Swanson, the mega silent film star in Uncle Dez's father's day.

"Maybe Hedy Lamar—Clark Gable…?"

"Holy Silent Films, Meg." Lance jerked his mob cap and scratched his hair. "Anybody remember these old geezers, 'sides you? *Alive* that is."

"Don't spoil it, Lance! I'll have head shots and scenes from their movies, maybe even scripts laying on the…"

"Like the new Gideon Bibles." He saw my face. "I give up. Let me play too." Passing doors, Lance began naming. "Three Stooges. Bela Lugosi. Scooby-Doo… Yup. I can see it now. The Kardashian's are lining up, not to mention the Duchess of Cambridge." He looked at me heavily.

"Your underwhelm is showing. Damnit, Lance!" I pressed my small fist to my chest. "This old wreck will give me a chance to *not* be Uncle's helpmeet, or Zak's girl in the wings! Or—or, *that* girl. You *remember*! The one who *limps*! The one with the bum *leg*! But me. My own business…!" I was shouting raw now.

"Christ, Meg, no one notices your—limp," he began, then stopped, after I threw him a scathing look.

"That it?"

I heard the lack of interest, finally.

"One more." I smiled in my old way with an effort Lance did not see. Pulling him down the hall, I stood malevolently expectant outside Lance's old room.

His grin faded when he stepped through, seeing it for what it was, in a rare glow of chilly sun coming through faded drapes patterned with a cowboy theme.

He sneered brushing the matching wallpaper. "Funny or maybe not so. When I came up scavenging, I studiously avoided all this!" He watched me, accusatory, reluctantly scanning nicked, scarred old maple cowboy furniture with the wagon wheel motif, yet. A quiver of raggedy-ass arrows and bow with a shredded string, dangled from the wall papered with stupid cowboy hats and lariats. He glumly scanned faded 4th Place, Honorable Mentions, and "Participation" ribbons—the cheesy plastic trophies, avoiding garish prom photos thumbtacked to the wall.

I saw his face. *Oh, very classy,* and almost felt sorry, in kinship.

"Who's this room?" He said making light. "Somebody *way* cool. Matt Damon. 007 maybe. Whoever that is these days."

I shivered abruptly. "I've had enough. Let's go."

Lance grinned evilly, pushing me out. "One more."

Outside I frowned at an irregular rusty patch on the hall carpet. "Euuuugh! If we can hide that. Yuck. What *is* that?" I knelt and studied the crusty patch.

Lance tugged me. "Come on! Don't want to feel like an orphan!" He opened a door watching me expectantly. I swayed at the threshold of *my* own old bedroom as if poised on a cliff.

Same cowboy furniture, ditto wallpaper, but with an excruciating pink and lavender spread with matching window ruffles adding to the decor.

He showed his teeth. "The Mylie Cyrus Annex?"

"Might be pushing it a bit, *bro.*" I muttered,

scanning my own pathetic photo gallery.

There's me.

Leg still in a cast a year after the accident, under a pink and purple bouffant prom dress resembling a lamp shade, paired with a short, good-looking boy I couldn't recall, who brought red roses for my purple disaster and had been bribed by Uncle Dez anyway, revealed to be an obscure nephew of his doctor, as the boy sullenly explained, before abandoning me on the dance floor, after I pretended to stump about.

My eyes were riveted on Zak's image though, posed with a striking blond homecoming queen slash cheerleader, in pale yellow apparently glued to her, on his other side.

"What was that old song? 'Purple People Eaters'?" I heard behind me, and felt Lance breathing on my neck. "Very funny. I'll pretend I didn't see *your* prom pics. Did they have a sale on *acne* one year?"

"Touché. God, you still have this!" Lance plucked a pink "*Little Miss Archer*" bow from a peg behind the door.

"Don't laugh! I held my own!" Snatching the bow, I replaced it as he headed out the door, mumbling something about "checking the fire."

"Be down in a mo," I said vaguely.

It all seemed so long ago.

Not much happened since high school graduation. A few online classes. Years in between where nothing happened, when I had to forgo the exhilarating experiment of college and dreams of an exciting future— when Uncle Dez had his first stroke, needing me more than ever.

Somehow years kept drifting by like a sluggish

unremarkable stream, finding myself waking on an unfamiliar shore after his death. In that instance, I saw how spinsterish I had become, how settled with my fetish for nostalgic old films. Films old when I was born.

If it weren't for Zak calling time to time, bringing in fun, cuddles and kisses, turning my bedroom into a trysting place and off brand motel rooms for fevered lovemaking, Shangri-La, making me *desirable,* wanton, madcap, with the occasional joke-surprise filched from some casino, entertaining me with backstage hijinks and small onstage triumphs, relating contretemps with erstwhile managers—*the names kept changing*—or taking me for the occasional meal in fun, funky bars and bistros, like Greek Town near Detroit…

I clouded momentarily—usually the treats tied in with a cheeky attempt to dip into my house-keep money mostly, paid back when the ponies or dogs ran fast enough, accompanied by too-expensive champagne, epicurean chocolate, or a rare prohibitively expensive orchid. Once he even gifted me with a locket he won in a card game. I couldn't despise him, yet often wished for more practical aid, like sitting with uncle Dez, or extra housekeeping cash, yet Zak was into grand gestures.

I closed the door as if sealing a tomb. Praying for early spring snow melt, free to begin again. Surely. I'd never go back to the old ways. All I wanted was a *chance.* It couldn't be all over!

Chapter 26

Blizzard Warnings

I waited for Lance while he still mumbled about *'being cold'*, and something about—*'foraging more wood, since nobody else would do it and he had enough of my crazy schemes'* ...to settle in the Great Room before I invaded Zak's sacred territory.

And that...was my lethal undoing.

If I had only some forewarning from the gods of chance, of the deadly outcome. A niggle of doubt keeping all the deathly dominoes from falling over because of that one simple action of entering Zak's room.

Would I have gone there? I often mull this point...

****

The same cowboy furniture.

I stood at the threshold breathing in the same air Zak inhabited, fancying his cells, his essence becoming a part of me. *Sickening, I know!* So why was his room stylish, with the lingering scent of *Versace Eros*, compared to Lance's and mine, redolent of old sneakers and cheap toilet water?

I fingered his archery set with bright red fletchings, still crisp and neatly hung. His shelves blinded me in the weak sun with ranks of towering, gaudy first place trophies. I installed the shelves long ago. Zak had simply left them in a jumble in his closet. Pictures of enchanting girls, with or without Zak, *with or without* clothes papered pine walls painted charcoal, the bedspread, a shocking teal in Zak's youthful attempt at sophistication. It worked.

I threw myself on his bed. "I'm in your room, Zak," I whispered. "Can you feel me?"

I bounded up as if stung. *How lame.*

Teetering on my bad leg, I stepped wide to balance, stifling a cry when my leg seemingly plummeted through the floor, followed by a loud *thwacking* sound, as a floorboard settled beneath me under a throw rug. *Also, bright teal.*

I toed the boards. One teeter-tottered. Shoving the rug aside, I pried the plank with my fingernails until it popped, grinning with a sense of giddy intrigue. *Oh Zak,* I gloated, *what secret would a flamboyant creature like you think worth hiding!* Plenty as it turned out.

I examined nail holes. Nails had worked loose in their sockets, or missing altogether.

I still could have gone on.

Ignored the wonky board.

However, after spying a faded orange bulk, jammed between joists that separated the floor from the lathing-plaster ceiling below, leaving a sixteen-inch, six-inch-deep cavity stretching the length of the room, I fatally tugged out the scruffy orange thing, the color of a half-sucked popsicle—heavy and bulky—a stained backpack with sharp angles sticking out.

Ripping at Velcro pulls, I frowned, forgetting my hunger. It was chockablock with frayed notebooks, leather journals, legal pads, and multicolored folders, sandwiching yellowed newspaper, and magazine clippings.

"Zak," I breathed, half afraid to delve into the mass. *It seemed so off-putting.* So unlike Zak. *Now if I found a diary or journal—?*

Brushing the thought aside as beneath my dignity, *at least, I told myself that,* I rapidly selected what seemed to be a scrap book with brittle loose pages, the kind with cheap acid paper. In place of pictures of pinups or girls, the pages were pasted, taped, or stapled with newsprint headlines, accounts, and grainy pictures, some on computer printouts with holes at the edges, the kind torn off page by page, ruffled soft at the edges. I didn't read the headlines then.

I set the book aside, frowning, thinking—puzzled. "Uncle Dez had one of those old printers," I murmured. It was the size of a suitcase, yellowed with age and squatting like a troll beside his rolltop desk. He used it in tandem with a relic computer, that would have done the Smithsonian proud.

Be careful what you wish for.

I scanned a page in the middle of the mass.

"Green River Killers... Zodiac..."

Hunh? I caught other half-familiar names, whispering them to myself as I breathed cold life into them, chilling me too. "Edward Geine, Richard Speck...Son of Sam..."

My lips grew stiff. *Richard Speck?* I could hardly get the words out in that empty room. "The killer of all those Pilipino nurses..." I whispered, dropping the folder. "*—one by one, they were led out, lambs to the slaughter,*" I breathed. They all died except the lucky one who hid under the bunk bed.

"Why would Zak *save* all this?" I asked the silent room. I glanced quickly out the window. *Where were the* "*boys*"? "I should get this all back!" I was panicking. I didn't know why. Instead, my body took over my head.

I upended the canvas pack dumping the mess on my knees, twitchily thumbing the contents, with faded to newer covers; some with scrawled dates, a few expensive journals, the type with black leather and red corners showing tastes more sophisticated, while next to it, was what they called, "Golden Rod" pads schools hadn't used in decades, plus two lined legal pads, and last out of the pack, a raggedy-ass, loose-paged steno type spiral-book. Where to begin?

These scrappy efforts did not seem at all Zak's style. *So, what were they doing, stuffed—hidden beneath Zak's floorboards?*

I was of two minds. Leave them be, cram them back as Zak's weird *secret;* besides I was beyond cold and stiff—or ferret out what this all about, once and for all. I recognized this weird stash would haunt me like embers burning holes in my peace of mind.

"*Put it all back. Forget it!*" My lesser angel chided.

Ignoring the notion, I blew on my hands, rubbing frost from my bones, reached in blind, and dug out a manila folder wedged in the bottom. Still troubled by how far back these ranged and why the morbid interest, I picked through random accounts mixed with newer computer sheets, dog-eared from being in the orange bag. "John Wayne Gayce," I scanned grainy newsprint pictures of a fat ugly clown—under that, an account of Richard Dahmer.

*Yes. Dahmer the cannibal they called him...*I shuddered, feeling ill. My hunger was a distant ghost. Adrenalin was rushing through my body like a sugar high as I rifled the pages of newsprint. The latest account, Scott Petersen, was not even taped in, as if the collector grew weary of his occupation.

I dropped the folder as if rotted garbage and gingerly selected a curious thing, unlike any other—crudely, but lovingly bound. Hand-stitched, slick black oil cloth was glued over cardboard stiffener and entitled with a childish pride in gold paint. The work of perhaps a nine-year old at summer camp.

This was more like it.

I smiled. *Zak's secrets.*

But, how long had these been in here, all forgotten? And what purpose, yet the nagging question. Research? School project? And so much? *Spanning years?* Were we ever that young and bloodthirsty? Yes, I conceded, the young can be especially morbid at times, pondering briefly over my fondness for the old Hammer films.

I smiled again and bent my head over the oilcloth book crudely entitled…

"THe ChrOnicles of ZaChary LoDge THE Third."

I smoothed hands down the slick oil cloth, turning pages, reading, and shaking my head over his childish barbarism.

Red paint imitating blood, dripped from the block-print title page writ large in florid childish script, all entwined with flaming cars, skulls, gory knives, and bodies of women by the crude rounds of breasts, and other anatomical detail.

"Oh, Zak! Even then!" Ruefully I shrugged, putting it aside for later, when I could savor Zak's first childish literary efforts.

It still seemed odd. I was unaware of this ghoulish side, but all kids were. I winced recalling the popular, "Little Willie" jokes. *"Little Willie on the railroad track,*

*heard the engine squeal. The engineer just took his spade
and scraped him off the wheel...*"

There were many verses I couldn't recall. Then the
gory video games we played in the widow's walk.
Perhaps those things weren't so harmless. I began
putting the oddments in some sort of order to thrust back.
I'd ask him about *that* stuff too, when the moment was
right. *When we got out of here.*

If we ever left.

I contemplated the scene. Not the first time I openly
feared such a notion. Of *course, we* would get out.
Searching the dirty sweat shirt sky, the endless horizon
of hoary treetops, it was hard to believe the world was
still happening with or without us.

It was, we figured, the middle of March with no
letup. Not a calendar in sight save one from 1990 stuck
on the back of a cupboard door with the inscrutable
listing "*jar rings*" penciled on. I let the poisonous notion
creep in, that it was about par for the Upper Peninsula to
enjoy blizzards till the very last of May into June. None
had broached that possibility, yet.

How long could one last without proper food or
heat? What if one of us caught pneumonia? The less
energy, the less willing, or able to forage food. Already
burning furniture. What would we do when the last five
canning jars gave out and rabbits and the odd squirrel
became shy of our traps?

No one had a clue where I was, except the boys.
Lance's clinic most likely sent out alarms, until his
erstwhile silent partner took over. I must ask Lance.
Funny I had not thought of it, and even some of Zak's
peripatetic friends, who would rightly suppose in his
loose flung community, he was on tour, or a gig, or the

South Seas with the flavor of the month.

Morbidly, I dwelled on their overheard tête-à-tête. The boys might get their wish for inheritance after all.

Grunting angrily, I swam to the surface and the present situation. As I jammed the bag in the joists, it did not budge, feeling a mild panic as if any second Zak would loom behind me, however, something else seemed to be stuck deep in, as I put my foot on it and tried to shove the orange bag in, any which way.

With stiff cold fingers, I dragged it out, laid the bag aside, and put my head to the floor peering in the long dark cavity; reaching in, tugged out a fat book, so wide it barely fit.

Anomalies And Curiosities Of Medicine." More Lance's speed, I mused. The tome turned out to be a bizarre and gruesome accounting of repellant, and sorrowful freaks of nature, unfortunately, fully illustrated.

"Uggh!"

I slammed the ghoulishly illustrated book closed. I intended putting it all back—bury—*hide* my findings, however, I felt compelled to dig out the slick black hand-bound book with the childishly lettered title.

I didn't comprehend why, yet it seemed so appealing, this youthful attempt at fiction—a little glimpse into young Zak's world, another piece I could hold to my heart and make the rest go away.

Feeling the frown draw my brows together, I flipped through the pages of lined paper. "What *is* this!" I breathed, slowly backtracking to make sure I made sense of it.

"...too bad about the othurs. surved daddy right. he - druled over that stupid hore!"

"What on earth?"

With a stiff cold mind, to match my fingers, I read on.

"I saw them. I'm a clever fellow.
They all say so.
glad she's ded.
brakes aren't hard at all.
the skimatiks Skeeematics helped."

I pinched the bridge of my nose and dropped the childish oil cloth-covered book. My fingers had no feeling.

"Brakes?"

Did he mean Mom? And the prototype?

I gazed into space, seeing them. Those schematics were lying about all over the place. Uncle Dez's study. The dining room table, where he liked to pore over them with a glass of whiskey. I could still see in my mind's eye the faint brown rings left on the various prototype's schematics. *Anyone* had access.

Even an intelligent seven- or eight-year-old boy.

Brakes killing Mom and Dad, and Zak's young parents too.

Could Zak really have thought this out, when that young and to do this to his own parents?

It didn't bear thinking.

Not Zak.

How stupid to even *suppose* such a thought. Even if Zak was too young to realize the consequences. Yet the suggestion was here screaming in black and white and red.

I checked the window—*still murky daylight*—quickly riffling another journal—*newer* computer printouts, without the holes.

I'd soon find this was not what it appeared.
An early attempt at story writing or…
I squinted. What was this?
I did not see this.
Still, the devil compelled me to read on…and on.
"The first bitch is dead dead gone…all that alcohol her sodden body sponged, made a lovely pyre.
God! She sloshed when she walked.
On this, the anniversary of dear Flo's death,
another eater of my soul, howled and bawled her innocence blinding me with pity, searing my face with scorn, making my heart eat itself with grief… At least, that is what I tell myself."
The mass slithered off my lap.
A panicky feeling like a red tide blinded me. The lowering sun blazed a bloody streak across my eyes.
Had to get this all back! He'll return soon. Zak will find me.
I snatched another mess before it hit the floor, yet I could not stop catching glimpses of sentences—*seeing* them.
"hello. I am six today.
today's my birfday wonder what my
prezunt is…think I will make my
own. I got me a scowt nife
and a bow and arrow set.
I have my hachet too.
think I will paint my prezunt red."
"Younger again," I breathed a frosty gasp, letting pages slip from my hands, blindly selecting another, and another, taking an armful to the window, rapidly muttering with no inflection—
"June…very young, bud-less I think the term is

sweet as scuppernong grape, woven in the tree outside
my window.

Can taste her now. Wine-blood, an intoxicating
brew.

I'm an addict. Runs in the family don't it?"

Numbly selecting another at random, I recalled an
ancient scuppernong vine with tiny blackish grapes
growing outside, partly obscuring the dining room
window here, at the old lake house, until one harsh
winter stole its life away.

This selection was newer, as was the writing and
penmanship more mature. I reluctantly read on.

"November, 2010! All Hallows Day!

More adult, more controlled.

"...housed in an icy tomb. Nature furnished
flowers... brambles, nettles, thorns...

Hah! I buried a bird with her for cold comfort.

I have my own cemetery now.

I'll name it, 'Cold Comfort'.

Clever isn't it? I think so..."

Chapter 27

Deadly Sunset

By the light and bloody slant on my face and carpet, the day died a fiery death, yet still I squatted, churning through inexplicable material until the red band hitting my face blinded me like a road flare.

Yes. *Danger ahead,* my mind bawled at me.

Red means, caution, stop, deathtrap!

Frantically aware of time racing by, I jammed all the slithery, recalcitrant papers and notebooks any-which-way, back in the orange bag. Rusting paper clips snagged. Thumbnailed pages stuck...off-sizes that would not fit.

As I knelt beside the open space, I was near sobbing with frustration. Behind me, though I did not grasp it then, the sun was in exactly the right spot on the horizon to pick out an antiquated video camera thrust deep under the maple cowboy dresser.

The knapsack jammed. "Sugar bear!"

I dragged it back out and put my face prone to the floor groping deep between joists to find what stoppered it now. Looked like a rammed-in tight shoe box. But way too far back.

I checked the sun.

A deep crimson glow, the color of oak leaves before turning brown, smudged the horizon, yet still light enough to read if I held things to the window.

Stretching as far as my shoulder, I finger-tipped out two crumpled, brittle boxes with the aid of a coat hanger. I tore off a lid revealing it to be stuffed with ancient audio cassette tapes, some with yellowed labels. I ripped open the other. The lid crumbled in my hands.

The next one held hand-labeled videos, and a few DVDs, with what appeared to be names and dates.

No time now...Did I hear a sound...? No. Merely wind scraping firs against the eastern side.

The light was the shade of faded roses now, as the sun slipped farther beneath the frozen west. I scarce made out the label stuck on one of the grubby cassettes.

"Mary Susan Ellenberger, school, sometime June 1"

The name meant nothing.

I switched to a DVD in a plain paper sleeve, labeled:

'Rita Ramirez, August heat wave' 2012'

And another.

'Street-sleeper, Pole Town Jan 3? 2008'

And there, written in felt tip directly on the disc:

'redhead - bar don't remember'

Hard to see now. I squinted at two last video titles, yellowed and peeling.

'Girl from laundromat early may '02'

'Pick-up outside Agnes's. Ug-ly! Summer '16'

I thumbed the name, whispering, *"Agnes'. "My Agnes?"* I never recalled Zak denigrating any woman, no matter how old or unattractive, beggar or highborn. To him, they were all—I frowned trying to come up with the right phrase. Special.

"Oh, Zak. What have you done?"

I bowed my head furiously thinking.

Darling Zak. Dearest, most beloved Zachary. My Zak.

Electric eyes shooting lightning bolts to my toes.

Melting me with tenderest smiles.

Making me quiver, solely by being near, as if even the light hairs on my arms strained for him.

Zak the jokester.

Oh, he loves women all right, my doubting imp intruded. But it is *me* he loved! *Me* he will end up with. *Me,* with the deepest secret connection. Was this to be one of them? I was sick at heart.

"He loves me!" I wailed. "He would never, *ever* do—"

"Do what?" I asked myself, hurling boxes, and discs aside. "Nothing! This is all make believe!" I howled. Tears blinded, wetting my face with irritating heat, turning to cold, smearing them brusquely with the back of my hand.

I should be shot for these horrible thoughts—I should be—

I jerked up clutching the teal bedspread at a sudden *squeak,* searching wildly behind me as if someone was at the door.

That stair tread.

Tiptoeing to the door, I strained to hear more. *Was it?* "Gotta get all this stuff back," I whispered, frantic, jamming the boxes and bags back in the best I could.

That careful squeal again. It was the Great Room stairs!

I recognized it. Fifth and sixth treads from the bottom.

Someone stealthily climbed.

I could sense a foot ease down. Gingerly placed,

then the rest gently settling, before attempting the next step. My own toes tingled.

"Nutmeg?"

Stiffening, still clutching the bedspread, I heard—"That you?"

Zak. Then, it was Zak sing-songing, *"Come out, come out wherever you are..."*

I hunched over my knees still as the rabbit under the tub. How did he know? *But, he didn't, not yet. Get the hell out!* My mind hollered at me.

****

Zak cocked his ear, staring up at his slightly ajar door, hesitated, one foot on the next step, retreating silently to the kitchen. He stared pensively out the kitchen window, then at the back servant's stairs, studied the butcher's block still holding a few odd knives boning to bread, selecting a common, nicked butcher-knife with the cracked wood handle; slipped up the backway, mastered a slow careful climb with the knife in his grip, feeling the ax stuck in his belt.

****

I tiptoed to the back stairs, after jamming the last evidence in willy-nilly, replacing the rug, scuffling, re-straightening it, all the while checking the room to see any telltale signs I had been snooping, ready to slip down the stair when I heard rummaging in the kitchen, detecting a faint noise—then a *new* sound. The door to the *backstairs* now. Without thinking, I acted, frantically rushing back as softly as I could, I dug out the orange backpack, racing across the hallway slammed the thing, any which way in Lance's closet, and raced back for the shoeboxes.

No thought on what I did—it was

instinctive…atavistic, defensive, my brain a hive of disturbed frightened bees darting against my skull. I have no idea where I got the strength or courage, or ability, for my leg never once betrayed me, as if it too kenned the urgency, no matter it made no sense or price later.

In between, the footsteps halted, then continued, a slow steady climb. No doubt, Zak heard my racing footsteps, aware of the noise I created, but unable to halt my frantic activity, I managed one box, threw the rug over the hole in Zak's room, leaving a slight declivity, raced back to Lance's room, and tossed it in after.

The orange bag still showed its dirty malevolent hue. Gasping, more from fright, I yanked ragged garments over the whole mess. Too late. As I spun breathless, from Lance's room slamming the door behind me, all I saw was a dark, broad-shouldered, long-haired silhouette, and Zak's face, blank and bloody with dying light, pacing toward me.

I stared futilely back, guilt plastered all over my face like cheap makeup, barely registering *another* voice, and feet thudding up the broad formal stairs. At the noise of Lance shouting something behind him, Zak pocketed something, held in back, and stared wordlessly at me, in a way I could not decipher.

"Guess what, Nutmeg!" Lance's voice seemed unusually animated in the fraught atmosphere. I nodded, numb, still staring at Zak, now visible by the dim ambience leaking from his old room.

"I shot a rabbit with my old bow!" Lance burbled. "Can you believe it? A real *fat* bastard." Lance bounded around Zak bouncing up beside me holding up a bloody sack, missing Zak's sideways glance of irritation. "Have you cleaned it?" He snapped, still closely watching me.

"Oh sure, your Munificence." Lance's voice took on his old petulant hurt edge. For once he got it right. It was a triumph. "Great Lance," I tried and unstuck myself; pushing between them, I risked a scared slanted glance at Zak.

"Why the back way?" I whispered with wooden lips.

"Thought I heard something." He still observed me oddly.

"Only me!"

I trembled as Zak watched over my shoulder seemingly fixated on his room, even though light was so dusky he couldn't possibly see anything. If he noted the half-cracked door, he registered nothing.

Lance was miffed over our lack of enthusiasm, but I couldn't care less. He sulkily eyed me, darting odd looks at his own door as I kept turning. It was probably my own uncomfortable awareness and of Zak and Lance watching my back.

Each shrugged in their own way.

"Women! Can't live with them…" I heard as I made my hitching way down the broad stairs to the Great Room.

"Can't kill 'em," Zak finished.

"Ya got that right," Lance chortled.

Just us boys together.

Chapter 28

Cold Snap

I hugged my knees close to the fire. We burned
splinters from a door lugged down from the servant's
quarters a few days ago. By now, I hardly gave Debbi's
old room a glance as I went by. When I did, a vague
cloud formed in my head dissipating in a fog of
disavowal. Now, I had a new concern. Zak. Nevermind
constant worries over where to cadge our next food. How
safe were we? Had Zak's apparent morbid taste turned to
reality, forged on the anvil of slow starvation and cabin
fever? Had this strain always been there?

I watched Zak. I yearned to remove the hatchet from
his belt. Zak in turn, I caught watching me, glints, caught
by fire from hooded eyes, and Lance baldly scowled at
me for no apparent reason, then dove back into huddled
apathy. That night even though we distractedly feasted
on Lance's rabbit, a hunger remained.

It was warm within the circle of light; yet beyond,
lay a refrigerator pall. Now the pall was creeping inside.
The only option was to be wary, wait it out. Act ordinary.
Count the days till thaw. Hide weapons. I already
secured a paring knife and a serrated bread knife too
cumbersome though to carry with me and in the end
dropped it back in its slot. As available there as
anywhere. Yet, surely, there was an explanation. The

more hours that dragged like a rusty sled through the chill of the evening, the less real what happened upstairs or what I unearthed.

The weight of hunger crushed my wits. I was reduced to this. Staying warm. Staying alive. I dreamt of daffodils and hyacinths poking through holes in melting crust. Waiting out inexorable blizzards singling us with malevolent ferocity, replenishing snow level between *sulky* bleak days. Gone the brilliant hot yellow disc glancing like diamonds off the lake ice and snow crystals. We didn't even have that for comfort.

I jerked awake. With fitful flames pricking my eyes, I had drifted into blessed oblivion. I watched Lance with envy, snoring on his back, an ancient magazine open on his knees. Zak turned a fire-glittering eye my way as I limped to the kitchen, pushing the hand pump, bringing up sweet water from the artesian well, to make tea, if one could call liquid gray as dishwater, tea. It filled the stomach.

How I still wanted Zak's arms, safe, warm, and comforting about me, telling me it would be all right, no matter my fears.

How I wanted to avoid him.

I could not look in his eyes.

The quaint rule of "never being alone" crashed and burned long-ago I brooded, listening to the rhythmic gush of water into the kettle, as I pumped. Except at night, no one knew where the others were, or much cared as we huddled by the fireplace, or roamed the house, grounds, or cellar, for all I was aware, seeking God knew what. Wood to burn. Old books.

So why was Zak watching me upstairs? Creeping up like that? Could be nothing. My own guilty conscience working overtime. Maybe checking noises. We were all paranoid—when we had the energy.

Those books and papers were *nothing*...a *kid's* scrawl. Creative writing. I could come right out and ask him. Make a joke of it. I *knew* Zak. Felt him across miles in my bones. My body. Discerned when the phone rang it was him, and not another telemarketer, no matter where he was. We had a singular link back to childhood. A meeting of souls, no matter how improbable. Zak was everything beautiful and right saving me from trying days with Uncle Dez. Not an old killjoy like Lance. Zak was *not* what my crazy mind conjured, even if fleetingly. Besides, how could I tell him I poked about his private space? If he was guilty of—*that,* whatever *that* was, it would make him dangerous, a deadly snake ready to strike when I least expected. No, that was not Zachary!

Muddled and troubled, I rubbed the window, revealing a black portrait of night.

Sleet monotonously hit the glass.

I felt I would scream and never stop.

Chapter 29

Iced Over

Agnes looked up from filling ketchup bottles as the vestibule door blasted open along with a hail of bullet-sleet. Blank-facing, she continued filling bottles, a smile flirting across wide lips as the Forest Ranger entered all hale, red-faced, and slapping snow from his knees. Removing his County Mountie hat with the other fur-mittened hand, he strode up familiarly with a big grin, holding his hat over his heart.

"Hey, Aggie?" The big man cooed. "How's my great big beautiful little gal?" And wrapped arms about her to see for himself. Agnes carried on pouring red stuff into the bottle, if a bit shaky.

"Sure would love a hot piece of yer—*cherry pie*?" The Ranger rasped in clunky flirtation.

She finally looked back, pleased. "Only got raspberry. You gotta long-nuff *fork*?" Flirting back.

"Raspberry ya say? Is it sweet now or sour?"

Agnes giggled. "Hot outta the oven."

Then she stuck her lip out looking up at him in mock-pout.

" 'Sposed you liked skinny little gals though. Maybe like that scrawny little crip here last month." Agnes frowned as if counting. "Maybe more'n that? More like two or three. I remember her on accounta, I think she skipped out with some a the store's whisky, maybe a few packs of ciggies!" Then hitched a shoulder, slanting a warm flirty brown glance at him. "Never mind. She's long gone." Agnes moved off, swaying an ample yellow-uniformed bottom.

"Ah. Let's get it together, Aggie." He enveloped Agnes nuzzling her ear. Next to him, Agnes's large body was lost. "Come on, little Agate. How long you gonna keep me waitin'?" His voice muffled as he brushed her flushed neck. "You know how I admire them *sweet-tarts.*"

He stopped cold, releasing her and raised his head. "Crip? That pretty little crippled gal in here? I kinda recollect one."

"Long dark hair. Had a gimp," she said sulkily. "What if she were? Her an her fancy car." She shoved over a slice of pie.

"Hell's fire, Aggie. That car was more'n 30-40 years old. If it's the same gal."

"Told her the weather was gettin' worse," she said defensively. Miffed, she nudged the pie back. "Guess you don't want this. Guess you'd rather talk about that girl!"

"Hell, Aggie. I helped her some. That's my *job*. Christ how long ago was that? Have you seen her since?"

"Your job's puttin' out forest fires, not hers," Agnes doubled down.

The Ranger, knitting his broad face, wasn't listening.

"Huh? Wonder now?

"Lives at the Lake in that big ol fambly house."

"Yeah, I know of it. Used to sneak in an watch them kids' birthday parties. That where she headin'? I'll be."

"Didn't buy nuff to feed a mouse."

The Ranger thoughtfully forked in pie. "Was on out to the prison last week, cros't the ways. Reporting on two runners, bouta month 'r more. Sorta the same time frame. Hadda report back, I ain't seen 'm. Didn't see no lights then. Not that you could. Or smoke."

Agnes shrugged, her mind on other things. "We still goin' to the fireman's square dance on Saturday?"

He nodded absently, finishing the pie in one bite. "Back in a bit, Aggie...keep it hot." He winked, but distracted-like. He looked back. "Naw, I'm sorry Aggie. Meant to tell ya. Got that conference down in Indianapolis. Be there most of a week, then takin' a little time off. Going on to visit Sis while I'm down there."

"Hmmmmpf. Suit yourself."

"Sorry, Aggie. You're my girl. Wisht you was a goin' too. Welp, better check, I reckon." He waited a second, but Agnes didn't turn around.

"Well. Bye now," he said and fitting his hat on his head, hurried out.

****

If one were sitting in a tall tree, or watching from the perch of a full moon, they'd see an Official Ranger vehicle with a V-shape plow slued up behind a boathouse, and a rapidly filling in pathway behind it. And the Forest Ranger heave his bulk out, and struggle past the heap of Meggie's car, rapping on the back-screen door.

He would back off, staring up at the broody house, and raising his face, sniff the faint scent of smoke. He wouldn't see the face at the kitchen window, or the hand rubbing a clean space in the frost.

The Ranger's foreshortened figure thrashed through

drifts to the old-fashioned veranda wrapping half-way around for mosquito-swatting nights…but not for *this* frigid, windswept, bleak setting. Gingerly, he stepped onto the wide veranda; the steps coated in ice under the snow, thanks to Meggie emptying the washtub so long ago.

Without warning the French doors banged open.

A flashlight glared at him. He shielded his face. "Hey! Turn that danged thing off. Blindin' me!"

He waited, squinting, "Hey? 'At you? Is a Margaret Anne Lodge, or a Desmond Lodge here? You folks all right? And turn that dang thing off!"

Met by silence.

Still shielding his eyes, the Ranger automatically reached for his gun belt.

"Say somethin'. Better come on out here, where I can…."

A flying figure exploded out the doors straight at him. The Ranger, too awkward to move, one hand crossed to his belt, the other thrown up in defensive posture, feet break-dancing slip-sliding backwards on ice in place of steps; his spine thudded hard, head striking ice-coated concrete, but he kept skidding backward. His eyes fastened on the knife coming down in a wide glittering arc and then the figure landed hard, knees on either side, further cracking his spine and *whumping* air out from his lungs in a harsh expulsion leaving him depleted as he tried to suck in ten-degree oxygen.

Then, blood spurted with sounds of wet hacking, and bone-crack and hiss of arterial spray turning snow to steaming black slush.

The last sounds he heard was his own body dragged with a *shush-shush* and gasping breaths to the rip rap wall and trundled over and the sound of thin shore ice breaking and first ghostly fingers of icy water clawing at his heavy coat and then from far away, as his dying body sank, destined for the deep marl below, the French doors easing closed. The Ranger eyed the moon before his head submerged for unanswered prayers until snow drifted mercilessly over the vehicle and the Ranger both, and the ice closed round him.

Chapter 30

Icy Graves

A raw day.

A hint of damp, underlay the cold like a frozen dishrag. Nothing to recommend it I mourned, studying the sky for any hint of sky. From the kitchen I spotted Zak, hollow-jawed, raw-faced under his black beard making him appear even more masculine, and thuggish if possible, melting into trees carrying his usual, now brown-stained sack, the hatchet stuck in his belted jacket.

My heart went out to him. Here I was distrustful, while he went out each day, half-frozen, and starving, bringing back the only thing now keeping us alive. Lance was enjoying a sudden cold giving him an excuse to hug the hearth with its semblance of warmth. I smiled cynically. Now, what could I do?

Stay away from Zak's room for a start.

I should find something to offer the *Goddess of the Great Room* though, namely the fireplace, greedily gobbling up anything burnable that I had the heart to sacrifice. Like more of those god-awful dining room chairs, twelve in all, with the sharp carvings that dug in the back bone so deep, they threatened paralysis.

Unwillingly, my thoughts veered to our old bedrooms. That old maple furniture would burn a treat, if we could tear it apart. Worthless anyway in my bed and breakfast scheme as stupid as that sounded now. Unless I yearned for "The Gene Autry Cubicle." Hardly the vintage look I was after. Which at the moment, seemed a million miles from reality. How inane to fret over trivial pursuits? What were our bedrooms anyway? *Shrines to the past?* I should gut them all!

And get rid of all that incriminating trash?

Fiercely nibbling at my composure was a faded orange canvas back pack and slick black oil cloth. And loathsome words. I hadn't fantasized those. With unruly thoughts, I returned to check our wood supply, to find Lance, awake, stabbing me with a stare cold and pale as icicles. I faltered mid-step stumbling back on my bad leg, blurting from confusion and guilt. "Lanny? What's wrong!"

"Okay. Explanation time!" His face wore a pinched slit-eyed look.

I didn't have to ask—*What?* My face said it all, culpability mixed with dread. I could not deal with Lanny's moods or suspicions when I had plenty of my own straining to be unleashed from their kennels of fear rampaging like mad dogs.

"Somethin' was going on yesterday. Everything that goes through your head, Meggie Anne Lodge, is written all over your puss. Always has. I read you like—*that!*" He snapped fingers and tossed an old Time magazine miraculously escaping immolation on the embers. "Think I didn't see? Pawing Zak's room? The door was open! What were you doin'? Hugging his sacred pillow? And what was *my* door doin' open too? What have you been up to? You're pulling *some* shit. I can see it. Quit messin' around my stuff."

Yes, Lance you are so right, I wanted to say, to

249

confide my fears—in that way *dilute* them. Be told I was a hysterical female. Anything but what I suspected.

Lance's face held a paranoid look I identified well. Yet, this expression was icier, more determined than mere sulking.

"Maybe I oughta just tell old Zak. He'd get a hoot! Or maybe *not*," my brother said nastily.

With guilty comprehension, I felt my face drain of color. Lance was a pit bull when it came to his own interests. Could I blame him? He would find that stuff in his closet, if he had not already. *Definitely setting me up.* Why did I do it? It was *safe* in Zak's room, until *I* found it.

Until I could figure it all out.

I should burn all that incriminating stuff, dump it in the lake along with drowning my self-reproach. And now, Lance had to bring it to the surface like a dead body dumped at my feet. And he *would* make the most of that filth, if he found it. I had to get it out of there! Even now, Lance studied me with slits for eyes. "What are you so *scared* of, Mag*pie*?" He snapped, giving my name a searing connotation hurting me to the bone.

"Lannie, please don't! Drop it!" *The wrong thing to say to my brother.*

"You'd *like* me to do that. Maybe I should take a *look-see*. I woulda, if I didn't feel so damn rotten." He rubbed his throat with a hint of whine. My mind raced as I watched him roll over with the parting threat.

"Don't worry. I'll find out, what you two were up to." As I had feared.

Come clean. Divert him like some cheesy magician, or he'll say something stupid to Zak. He can't do that. My head spun like a child's top. *I had to get to the truth.*

Protect Zak? I didn't want to go there. Faster, dizzier, loathsome suspicions whirled by in morbid hues, purple suspicion, red remorse, black mortification over Zak realizing I spied on what could be nothing more than childish fantasies—*yet some weren't fantasies but very adult and dark*, followed by yellow confusion and scarlet anger.

I had to diffuse Lance. He would use any excuse to nail Zak. At the moment his target fueled by resentment, paranoia, and the fog of starvation, was me.

But God knew what hornet's nest he could stir up, if Zak were—I swallowed hard—*deranged,* and we were trapped with him and days grew longer and we all fell into a sort of madness. I turned to study my brother. Better to meet him head on. Let him think I was on his side. *"Why aren't you?"* My lessor angel queried, stifling her with impulsive action.

Perhaps I only wanted to share the guilt.

"Lanny!" I blurted before I changed my mind.

He was half-dozing already! Jealous of that ability. How dare he muddle things up, then blithely sink into sweet oblivion! I'd like to lose myself in dreamland in place of waking every hour fitfully roaming the house, and even outside when feeling closed in and panicky.

I eyed him, sourly. "Wake—up! Lan—*ny!*"

Lance roused as if stabbed with an ice pick. "What now!"

"Upstairs! Quick. He's gone! Can't tell how long though."

"Freezin' my *cajones*, off, Meg. Don' wanna wake up! What the *hell?*" Lance resembling a demented scarecrow, scowled, and rolled back over, cryptically muttering, "Don't worry, still got my eye on you."

"You'll be cold a long time, if you don't *move!*"

"Talkin' trash. Now le' me alone."

I headed to the stairs one hand gripping the newel, beholding Lance peevishly, wanting to pinch the ball ornament off and throw it at him. I grasped I was in a state, and the only way to assuage the wound, was share it. Demented, I appreciate. "Lance!" I barked uncharacteristically sharp. "Come on! You wanted to know!"

It was still not too late, but Lance contrarily stirred himself.

"Okay, okay! Got my attention," he grumbled, making a great show of tossing blankets, shivering, and coughing. Still grousing, Lance stumbled after, abruptly waking to his surroundings. Even then, I realized how hard it was to haul myself upstairs. This might be the last time.

About to enter Zak's room, Lance's gaze darted about suspiciously, as if suspecting an ambush. "Am I allowed on hallowed ground?" He grumbled.

"Idiot. Down here." I stopped at his door.

Lance warily approached his own room, to find me rummaging under a heap of clothes dragging the orange backpack from his closet. He looked on narrow-eyed at me, then the pack. "Where'd *that thing* come from?"

"Can it matter? Zak's room of course. Just look! Listen! Oh, *wake up!*" I fretted already unsure of my plan to divert him. "Can't fool about here."

"Okay. Chillax, Magpie."

I gritted my teeth. "I hate that term! Lance! Stifle the stupid comments and bloody look! Pleeeease." I dumped the same note books on his bed, and lighting a candle thrust a diary under his nose at random. "Read these things."

Lance faked a yawn. "She's lost her mind. I escape this crap for a couple hours. I was dreamin'…"

I snatched his shirt.

Keep all of the plates in the air and he won't notice the wobble.

Lance looked down at my offending hand. His eyes usually insecure, were merciless glassy marbles. I could see he only pretended to be eaten up with curiosity; only a matter of who controlled the information. Let him think I *hated* Zak. He'd put a ferret to shame searching the house down, if not. I bit my cheek to keep from out-crying. On one level, I admitted I needed reassuring. My throat worked. We *needed* Zak. He was the hunter. Still with the energy to split up the furniture. *I* needed Zak.

"I'll look." His face said long-suffering martyred saint. "Okay. Whatever. You want me to read something? *Which* would you like—?" He asked with mock fright, sneering, "*care* for me to read?"

"Stop patronizing. Read this stuff!" I took a deep breath. "He's a maniac."

"Who? Zak?" Lance's eyes gleamed between red rims. Intrigued now, he skimmed the first page…

"…shrill hectoring too is stilled, silent as the wood…."

He shrugged with a—*so what?*

"Don't stop."

Lance rolled his eyes…*now Saint Sebastian with arrows sticking out of him.* "*…teacher said she likes lying in soft green of spring fern, plantain, and may-apple, so I left her there… "*

I interrupted. "Don't you *see?*"

"So? Too sexy-for-his-shorts, imagined or maybe

did fu—*shag* a teacher. Not good. Not good. But hey! Girls practically stapled themselves to *good ole Zak!*" He tossed the writings. "Awkward. We shouldn't…" Then leered, looking anything but saintly, waggled his brows. "What's 'er name was hot though. Least for us randy sixth graders. Jane Brolin. *Whoooo-eee.* Hooters like—" He cupped hands in front of his flat chest, grinning wicked. "Any more of the hot stuff?"

"Plenty." I must have looked authentically grim thrusting a wedge of journals at him. I watched my brother, picky at first reading snippets, sending humorous, then odd glances that changed to frowning puzzlement; his expression avid, then puerile as he raced through the material switching from one example to another. He ignored me reading on.

"So, I left her there—there for the—"

Then looked at me. *"…woodland creatures…"* putting a question mark at the end of the recitation. Resuming, Lance picked out the next words like glass splinters from a finger…

"She was dead of course…"

He dropped the journal.

"Go on."

"Winter." He read aloud.

"They too must eat. Wasn't Teach forever carping about habitat? No one can accuse me I have no bittersweet irony, no passion in my soul.

Let them feast on her bitter bones."

I watched my brother with a curious scowl riffle the journals, the diary-things, and scrappy records for answers. "Nothin' but a date. What *is* this crap? Don't make sense. Wait-a-sec." He went blank. "There was that teacher! That sub. 'Member? Only there six weeks, but long enough to bat her baby blues at old Zak. Christ! He was only—what?"

"Fifteen." I made a face, looking away so he could not read me.

"She kinda like *disappeared*, didn't she? Big rumpus around that time," was said in an excited tone as he scratched the stubble on his chin. The sound was grating. "Then there was that cheerleader, whatzername? Remember? Never could get to first base with her. Rich snob. Always wore those soft fluffy sweaters, and…"

"I get what you mean. Cashmere it's called," I said with the dryness of toast. There was something odd about Lance's reactions I could not trace. His words or meanings behind them, did not jibe. Off. I hadn't energy to wonder at the time.

"Yah." Lance scattered material with manic abandon as if searching an antidote for snakebite and there was an anaconda at his throat, gulping information, tossing uneaten portions messily aside in his increasing unappetizing zeal to take it all in.

I surreptitiously checked the window.

I doubted he recalled I was there.

After a while, I impatiently kicked at the mass. "Isn't it obvious? It makes perfect sense. Zak thinks he's the Poet-Laureate of serial killers. That's what. That's all it is."

"You mean he's a poet laureate—*never appreciated what that meant*—or, he's a serial killer? Which!"

I dropped to my knees. "Oh! I don't *know,* Lanny. I'm all mixed up. He can't be—but, but…" I dropped my head and let out a howl. "Oh, Lanny I'm so hungry, I can't think any more. You do it."

At the time I did not even realize if I meant that, or

it was only distraction. Why had I started this anyway? Chances were, Lance was too lazy to do more than needle Zak and I couldn't deny poking about. Too late now. Stupid-stupid! It illustrated how depleted my batteries were. Not only my ratty car was dead.

Lance sorted scattered journals with one finger as if losing interest. "That it?"

"Isn't that *enough*? Oh sugar!" I wailed. "The videos and stuff."

I could have bitten my tongue. I didn't mean to go that far. Truth, I didn't *want* to see them. *Other girls?* It would break my heart like a stone cracked with cold. Besides, I wanted to distract Lance! Steer him *away.*

Lance winced. "Videos? Sex tapes? Sure wanna see *those.*" He muttered as if I asked him to eat raw snails. Lance studied me closely. "Wait a sec. Like home-made? Okay. So where are these Oscar winners?"

I lifted a negligent shoulder. "Maybe later," I groused. "Besides can't play 'm, anyway. *At least Zak was safe now…I would burn all this! My nosey brother would have a devil of a time, convincing anyone…*

"Can't let this hang over us like radioactive cloud. Where'd you stash 'em?" He began pawing his closet, dragging out one shoebox.

"So, leave it! We're running outta time. He could be back any sec—"

"You think I'm a—*fraid?*" His voice rose dangerously high on the last syllable.

"Don't be silly, Lanny! Merely prudent. We're in enough pickle without…" I let it trail.

Lance threw me a look sour as the pickle. "Maybe. A least get this all back where you found'm, then. If he misses them—"

He let the thought hang like poisonous cloud.

"Sure, Lanny." *And forget all about them.*

****

Light was the shade of dying orchids. In the woods the temperature rose to meet the lowering skies and cessation of wind.

Glancing at clouds, assessing nightfall, Zak gutted a rabbit, now expertly peeling skin and fur, like a glove from a hand, without looking, tossing entrails far away for starving wild life...*and the wolf he felt stalking him,* truth be told. He couldn't shake a weird scratchy feeling. Like something crawling his neck. Or he had a target on his back. He refused to look about.

He saw where a fox or whatever had been digging at the base of a tree, coming away with a handful of acorns and moss—he wondered if green wad was edible. He left it, pocketed the acorns and a bag of tender green pine tips. That would suffice.

Still a few traps to run. Better hustle. Without warning, exhausted and hating the long trek back, and the hinky feeling riding his shoulders, he kept checking the house, or weather vane to be accurate....

Something sure wasn't kosher.

****

Lance reached armpit deep under the floor while I fretted. We both froze at scuffling sounds.

I scuttled to the window peering over the sill.

"Nothing. He's late though, Lanny. Let's go!"

"There's time."

I watched with distaste tightening my face as Lance eagerly shuffled audio cassettes, clunky videos, and the five DVD's. *Too eagerly.* Was it ghoulishness, or wanting Zak in deep water? Probably both.

In the end, I couldn't help peeking over his shoulder whispering the titles with him, until Lance jerked his head at the unmistakable sound of a china knob rattling below.

"No there isn't. He's here!" he whispered with a satisfyingly alarmed look on his face.

Lance would not be revealing anything to Zak, I thought relieved; jamming stuff back the second time, replaced the wonky board and smoothed the rug while footsteps hesitated at the bottom of the wide staircase.

"Hey ya, maniacs. Where ya keepin'?"

We waited.

"Home is the hunter, home from the hill," Zak rang out. His voice sounded like a cracked bell.

We tensed trading looks, hearing his exhausted snort.

"Act normal," I whispered. Lance threw me a wry glance. "Up here," I sang out. "Down in a minute."

We checked the room. I dragged down a corner of bedspread.

****

Zak eyed us all evening. Quizzically, with a touch of insanity in those red rimmed eyes, so I imagined, as he peered slantways from under black lashes half concealing a suspicious gaze, while guilt was painted all over my face, thick as a barfly's makeup. I could feel it.

Lance avoided him altogether, sinking his head between pulled-up coat collars, like a turtle in his shell. *Not too obvious.*

Yet, we all seemed in an otherworldly, *or wished we were,* mood. Zak bagged the one rabbit, which made the evening seem impossibly normal, or normal as we had evolved, coming together each night for our little "feast" of rabbit, the odd squirrel, or a fish or two, when Lance or Zak had the inclination to chop a hole in the ice, plus roasted acorns, or anything we could forage beneath the snow cover— going over the day, future worries, or nothing at all—a familial ritual.

Now hunger and fear, mixed like an eggbeater in my tummy; it was all I could manage to choke down my tiny hindquarter.

Chapter 31

Falling Barometer

Zak foraged again.

Lance and I watched him vanish into the forest from the widow's walk, armed with his bloody bag, and his bow. Part of me guilty he had to go it alone, though I had volunteered, even begged in the past. Lance made excuses after the first few times, with half-baked defenses.

"He felt *hinky* out there, and thought Zak was playing sadistic games." Etc. Perhaps Zak was. This was my brother's justification for not rousing from the fireplace, except when Zak set a line through the hacked hole in the ice, with pointed remarks concerning Lance's fishing prowess. Nothing accepted the lure of rabbit entrails the last three days, yet hope sprang eternal. At least he was doing *something*.

"*Besides snooping?*" My lesser angel nagged.

Nudging my angel reluctantly aside, Lance and I dragged out the lumpy yellow plastic bag from where we stuffed it back between joists, laying it aside. As he did so, he turned his cheek prone to the floor, his other arm out stretched. "In a minute," he muffled, "hold on a sec. What's this?"

He sat up nodding at the narrow opening on the opposite side, ending somewhere under Zak's bed, inviting me to look. I stared at the hole stunned. Somehow, I never thought to search the other side, feeling pique. This was *my* find. How had Lance thought of something so obvious?

Grudgingly, I lay on my stomach. The space between joists dimmed to nothing. "Don't see anything." Somehow, I had hoped hunger and apathy made him forget all this. *Make it go away. Seal the room like an ancient tomb. What now?* My heart was falling off the Grand Canyon as he shoved me aside and reached his longer arm in, grunting, "There!" Waving chaff, he dragged out a fusty, odiferous burlap sack with sharp corners sticking out. I noted the color of the sack and the wood beam were identical.

But how had I missed it? *Why could I not have hidden it?*

I painted false interest on my face. "Oh! What is that, Lanny!" Even to my ears, I sounded phony. Lance tugged a knotted gray string, immediately starting back waving his nose, dropping the bag as it flopped open. "*Euuugh!*"

"What!" I eyed it with alarm.

"You don't wanna know." My brother bashed the bag aside as if it writhed with snakes.

"I'm not an infant!" *What was in there? Something irrefutable?*

Lance upended the bag. "There. Satisfied?" As if I asked for what came next. Out tumbled rusty shackles, stained knives, a pair of dime store cufflinks, a short, corroded pruning shears stuck with brown crust, all tangled with discolored frayed yellow plastic rope.

I scooted back, covering my mouth. "Oh, no!"

"Jesus." Lance dropped the bag staring at the mess.

"Jeesh! Didn't even clean his tools."

I stared at him. "Is that a *joke*!"

"Ah, no! Sorry, Meg. Misplaced Doc-*tor* outrage comin' out," he made light. "Something's still in there." Lance prodded the burlap. Pulling a face, he gingerly groped the interior, immediately withdrawing; started to put his bloody thumb to his mouth but thought better, wiping it on his old navy cords.

"Wait!" I grabbed his hand feeling the cold chicken bone feel of it. I pressed his thumb until blood trickled out. "Now, it won't get infected," I said with no trust at all, aware, Lance smirked.

"What was it?" I asked chastened and smarting.

"Dunno…" He wiped his thumb against his sweater. "It's got teeth."

Tiny metal points stuck through the rough weave. When Lance dropped it, something stuck in the burlap, made metallic sounds. I winced as my brother cautiously withdrew a short hacksaw. Unmistakable, dried blood flaked off pattering floorboards.

We looked at each other with eyes not wanting to reveal what we were thinking. We both lost.

"Ohnoohnoohno…" I moaned not wanting to articulate my thoughts. I poked the bag like it was a beast in a horror movie playing dead, ready to pounce. Poked it again. We both heard dull *clunking*. I nodded, numb. "*Go on!*" I motioned to the bag.

"Thanks." Lance looked at me sourly, both giggling nervous when he withdrew a bulky plastic thing. "Hunh! A DVD player!" He chortled, checking it out. "An old DVD player! And this." Next, dragging out a small cheap VHS player in a dirty cloth bag that turned out to be clanking with batteries of all sizes in the bottom plus owning its own tiny screen, the same as the DVD.

"Well, looka here! Christ."

Lance spilled out both double *A* and *D* batteries on his hand, tonguing the ends. "Bastard! Had these all the time, even after our frickin' flashlight gave out. Jerk!"

I winced. He glared, indiscriminately grabbing two hand-labeled DVDs. Considered the two players, the VHS, and the DVD, viciously jamming the *A* batteries into the DVD player.

I held my breath.

*Maybe the batteries are really dead, maybe nothing's on these things any more. Maybe they got frozen...*I watched feeling a cold snake of fear coiled in my belly as my brother shoved in a disc. To my shock and panic, the screen of the homely plastic player, sprang to shocking vivid color with jerky motion and fritzing badly recorded sound, while my guilty heart lurched a beat.

Oh, Zak...

I cannot stop this. Fascinated in spite of myself. Like a child placing hands before her eyes, peeping through fingers when the monster bites the head off a hapless victim—*I had to see!*

Screeches, shuffles, whimpers, shrieks shattered the cold room with white hot despair followed by wretched, desperate entreaties, ending in drawn-out cries that defied origin.

A female voice sprang out of the raucous mess like a spring flower—fresh, high-pitched, and *terribly* young, that even abject fear had not pulled to shreds, accompanied by a blur of flesh...*an eye wide open in terror—a flash of a bloodied mouth* before the jiggling lens, then the face disappearing in a whirligig of color as if the camera was knocked aside—and picked up once more, accompanied by a roar of rage. Was it Zak?

I hunched into a fetal ball, knees under my chin, rocking and covering my ears, crying, "enough!"

"Grow up!" Lance snarled. "We can't back down!" Lance nudged me aside, as I reached for the player. We owe…"

"Who to!"

"To them." He nudged his elbow at the stack of labeled tapes. "We owe it to *Zak*!" Lance's answer was a nail gun spitting nails. I sat up, nodding dispiritedly, miserably shamed out of my cowardness. If Lance could take it, so could I. Yet I had to make one more stand.

"Isn't it enough we have these? Do we have to…?" My errant head swam with images. I still felt Zak's fevered kisses on my mouth, his hands on my body roaming free and urgent, him *in* me hard and hot, and— I cried out, moaning in shame and regret. All I wanted to do was stop this and destroy them if I could. Zak would never get a fair trial, if Lance had anything to do with it. At very least, I must see these on my own. I had to make my own judgment without my brother's hateful prejudice.

Lance stared red rimmed and savage. "You make me puke, Meg! Do something useful, besides fall apart," he sneered. "Look for Za-char-y!"

The image on the player resumed, sickeningly spinning, drawing me back. Lance held the viewer close to his face. I still saw flashes of another woman. A ticking mattress. Brown eyes in place of blue. The woman, or girl really, on the threshold of adulthood, silently pleaded, her mouth in an anguished square. Lipstick mixed with tears, and a leaky nose smeared across her cheek, making her eyes run all sooty and cheeks red with abuse and smeared cosmetics—a clown face like in that movie folks raved about in another world now. Wasn't sure what the name was, shocked for a second out of my existence in a frigid dreary bedroom looking at horror tapes. All *unreal*...

Still, my lesser angel whispered logically, "*too jerky and unpolished to be professional.*"

"Wait. There was one."

"One what!" Lance grunted distracted.

"*The Blair Witch Project.* All herky jerky handheld camera work! That's what this is." I grasped at the fragile straw as if it were the Mackinaw Bridge back to reality. "Amateur horror films!" I laughed until I could not breathe.

"*Rather short on plot,*" my lesser angel argued.

"They don't have plots, you see, haha—" I giggled. "Short on plot, long on schlock. Nothing like the old horror films—works of art, really compared to—" I babbled with a pleading in my voice.

"*You mean like a porno film? I think they call it gorno,*" my angel sneered.

Lance cast an unreadable expression, part impatience part, scalding derision. "I think they call, this gorno!" He echoed. And if this dame's acting, I'll eat my shorts," as if I mentioned a personal affront.

I shrank keeping thoughts to myself as that segment ended, lost in a close-up of scarred wood—followed by a splinter-flash of a woman's hip, until one vast skin-map appeared, as if the picture-taker was still inept, nervous—excited...

"Maybe all three," I mouthed, feeling like I swallowed cotton balls, resigned, until I could dream up a plan, *a way* to snatch the player from a disturbingly electrified Lance. His mouth hung agape; he never blinked. Obsessively licked his lower lip. I looked away, but not before red drops splashed inexorably across the lens.

I jerked. A hand smeared the wetness until the image turned into a pinkish tie-dye blur. I needed my precious whisky the boys knew nothing about. *Oblivion.* My thoughts turned to the ceiling, reflecting on my arctic haven in the treetops, at least until Lance tried to nail me inside, where scrag-end cigarettes, and precious mouthfuls of whiskey awaited, and I hadn't found that *damnable* orange bag.

I shut my ears to scratchy screams, ending in notes never reached by Maria Callas or Yma Sumac, yearning to be in another time and place—back in Agnes's warm diner—even sharing breakfast with uncle Dez, with happy thoughts toward a cozy evening in my room with a favorite film and bottle of courage. I would not steal whiskey or cigarettes. I would embrace Agnes like a sister, gratefully accepting her caring offer of the warm sturdy Jeep.

I would not arrive at the house…

My whole existence seemed defined by that moment.

Me, in a ratty fur and flimsy boots with a rusting forty-year-old ragtop and Agnes, warm, robust, well fed, loving her place in life, driving a sensible new car. My existence seemed a cheap sham seen in a foggy crystal ball, while I moped and did not make plans. Why allow so many years drift by, unexperienced? It would all be different, I grimly vowed.

Only let me come out of this.

"*Alive?*" My lesser angel's insinuations rang like a gong

I turned a bitter face to Lance. Over his shoulder, from my place cringing by the window, I couldn't help noting the gruesome images had gone gray and grainy. The screams stopped. Lance was removing the disc and casting about for another. How could I trust him to keep from going bonkers? "*Misery loves company, and fear verification,*" my bitter angel intruded.

The new DVD had been slotted in...regenerating with a burst-shot of a tattooed shoulder—sliding down to a "*rose, angel's wings—a boy's name, Daryll or Daniel*" in rapid sequence, with splinter-flashes of a narrow female back. The view spun down to a freckled calf. I winced, seeing a trail of blood trickling to a plump ankle, encircling it like a charm bracelet before dripping to a widening puddle on the floor.

Another woman. Red hair. Pink fuzz on the leg. Young? This one's flesh was pale, sprinkled with cinnamon dots. No sound, but I could tell by the batting hands, the jerking legs and twisting torso, the girl fought with all her might. "How many are there?" I heard myself, morbidly gripped in spite of resolve.

I had to find out who they were.

If Zak was acquainted with any of them, even slightly.

As the badly recorded DVD resumed, I went somewhere else, numbed to the room and cold, sight and sound, yet unable to totally avoid the herky-jerky pictures spiked with resonances, thuds, splashes of slaughter, heavy breathing, the pleading, blood flying in drops on the screen striking charcoaled walls in lightening streaks. Or slashed flesh turning into bloody mouths; hoarse, excited, even exulted breathing in the background from the unseen perpetrator.

Once a glimpse of the heel of a hand wiping the lens dry. I watched too, with morbid fascination, my brother's face change hues as vivid color shifted across the tiny screen, reflecting on his slack-jawed glassy-eyed expression—from shock, revulsion, or sick lust?

Cold sweat coated my arm pits under layers of sweaters and ran down my back. *It was a horror movie, dear God, clearly a horror film. Not unlike ones I viewed in the past.*

Mercifully, the camera stilled as if the killer perched it somewhere. From the corner of my eye, several minutes ran by with sounds of frantic, then haphazard activity going on in the background, footsteps, a rustle of fabric...indistinct muttering. The clash of metal, a *searing sawing,* like the sharpening of knives on the old grindstone squatting behind the boathouse like a prehistoric bicycle with its one great stone wheel.

Blind because all one saw was a blank dark wall. *Charcoal again.* My mind whimpered, trapped in the spiral of malevolence sucking me down. When the screen shifted once more, I *had* to comprehend what happened next.

"A window covered with a sheet."

A hastily wiped screen—a gray rag, like a gym sock smearing it; the monitor splintered and went "*blue.*" I blinked. Lance sucked in a long-held breath. Abruptly, the screen revived. I grimaced back, closed my eyes again, shifting away.

Lance's voice broke in. "Do you remember any of them?"

"No! Nobody. They are...it's—it's probably a—

project…"

"A *project?*" Lance mouthed as if I said, *a picnic in the woods,* snorting, "Scout badge. or school?"

This time the same image stuttered as if the tape was spliced out of sequence. The freckles were still there sprinkling the face of a, yes—red-headed girl. *The one with the blood anklet in the first DVD.* In this one, she was pretty, heartbreakingly young…undamaged, unafraid, smiling at the camera, cupping her hands under small breasts in a chaste white bra. She blew kisses from a plump shining face at the camera, and tried on a sultry look, embarrassing in one so young.

"Lanny!" I clapped a hand over my mouth.

"Yah, I see it."

Glimmers of a maple cowboy dresser—*like in Zak's room.* Or to be fair, *all* our rooms.

It should not have been a shock, yet to see this homely innocent object in conjunction with the blood and shrieking…? I could no longer be in denial.

"It's ours. *Our* stuff." His voice was matter of fact.

"Maybe…?" I trembled as I spoke.

"That is *our* dresser, Meg! *Our shitty* cowboy stuff! It's our bloody *rooms.* Or I should say Zak's!"

I studied my hands. "Turn of off, Lance. *Please.*" I made a move toward the player. Lance struck down my hand, snarling. "Not yet!"

There was a blur of camera-work, then as if the camera was dropped on a bed with a slight bounce—*a glimpse of teal*— then a spinning wall of Zak's trophies, plaques, and sweet-faced girls in prom dresses, as if the video cam fell on its side.

"*Not* ours," he sneered. "*Zak's.*"

I felt woozy. The world jumped forward leaving me

behind, then another splice stole my mind like a pickpocket robbing sanity, as a blurred figure neared the small screen—a girl with short dark pixie hair, a wizened too-old face for one so young and large hoop earrings, heaved up from a *teal* spread, a livid expression distorting her face. Sharp shadows, I mused, so there must be strong light, or the sun shining through a window.

The young woman, or girl's voice muted, not that it mattered. Her chin trembled. She pleaded with her eyes. Then a garbled voice broke in resonating with feedback, and indistinct, *"where...think...get to?"*

Then the unmistakable sound of a match striking.

The dead match hit the floor, as if the camera pitched forward. Cigarette smoke coiled like a ghost-snake before the lens. Through the gray wreath, the girl/woman ardently cried out while a hand jabbed the cigarette repeatedly on flesh. I winced. She twisted away. I saw a splinter-flash of her wrist, cuffed to the bed frame. Angry burns blossomed on arms, stomach, back as she squirmed, silently shrieking and moaning, then the sound blared. "Stop! Why are you *doing* this?" The unknown woman whined and wailed at the same time, like a cat in pain. I said *rough*!" She entreated. "I didn't mean…"

Her head threw back. A hand swished before the camera whacking her face aside. She fell silent, whimpering, and scooting up the bed as far as the cuffs on a short chain allowed, as if thrusting herself through the headboard.

Even more sickening, the tape, for want of a better word, reversed twice—then advanced as if the viewer relished the scene. As the cigarette and hand moved toward the face with the wide bruised eyes, I sucked in, hiding my eyes. Lance grunted like he cleared his throat.

"Put it away! Shut it off!"

"Not happenin'," Lance answered grim-faced; he gripped the machine like a spoiled kid with a favorite toy. "Gotta see this through. May recognize someone, like ya said. Gotta hide it too, but…"

I stood up and shrieked. I snatched the player smashing the off button and made to hurl it to the floor when Lance nearly yanked my arm from the socket.

"No more! Enough."

Anger flooded his face.

"Don't!" Something in his voice, a dangerous edge, stayed me; I dropped to the teal spread matching the one on the screen, bouncing off as if it burned.

Chapter 32

Thin Ice

I wasn't sure how—guilt was not written, but incised with a chisel all over Lance's and my faces, yet after we ate our meager meal, plunged into a stunned slumber, safely passing the night. Zak seemed so out of it, the ceiling could have caved in without comment, leave alone cast spurious glances our way. I had stewed cracked bones we began saving a month ago for marrow and a tiny sprinkling of powdered soup, for a pallid broth, doused with plenty of salt and pepper. *That,* we had.

Now, Lanny and I eyed Zak drag wearily to the woods toting his bow and gory sack. He asked Lance in a *couldn't-care-less* way, if he wanted to go with him. Lance once more pled a cold. Zak shrugged. That worried us more. All Zak did now, carried suspicion. Still, I watched with an anxious frown until he disappeared into the tree line, my heart going out to him unwillingly. He appeared so drained.

Reluctantly, I climbed the stairs taking us to *"Zak's House Of Horrors"* as Lance baptized it. I didn't want to. Let Lance indulge himself, hunched over the tape and video players. He shamed me into it. "What's the matter! Too real! Can't take the mere thought of precious Zak being in the crapper? He'll be in worse than that, after we scram outta this place. I can't wait to pull the plug, and watch Old Zak circling the drain! Revenge *is* best served cold. Zak didn't care if we were injured, or went bankrupt. He had his meal ticket. His face. His charm, his tall good looks." His face twisted with hatred.

Nothing I said, or reasoned made him soften the blow. All evidence pointed to Zak. Why was I fighting it? The best that could happen, was Zak plead mental illness, vowing I would be there for him. Before I could yank it away, Lance rigged the ancient video player, it too, a battery-operated number as if the perpetrator could never count on electricity. Unfortunately, it still worked.

"We have to know," Lance insisted mulishly. "Things!"

Later I smiled with rue, wondering if perhaps he recalled those words, that he found some galling irony.

"Okay, Lance. Glad you are so *altruistic*! Get it over with! Get your *jollies*," I harangued, praying we wouldn't see Zak's room. I closed my eyes after the camera panned an array of tools laid out on the floor.

The same floor in any of our rooms, I told myself.

A garden shears was among the scruffy collection.

I gagged. They had been in the burlap bag.

Looking sideways, I viewed Zak's room on the video player's tiny view screen, but it was his *old* bedspread, with the cowboy motif, covered with plastic, not the *teal* of later years. And floor boards by the bed, were minus the rug. When had he tarted up his room? How old were we?

Lance feverishly jammed another video in without looking at the label, opening with a shot of…"*bare feet advancing to a mattress.*"

Whose feet? And did Lance care if they were

recognized, or was he getting a charge from watching? "Lance? Please, Lanny no more!" His fingers tightened on the player, elbowing me off.

I stopped struggling, struck by the image. Jealousy mixed with pain and horror.

This time, the female was blonde with a long pigtail looking elusively like a girl I was in summer camp with, here in the U.P. High School I thought—when a gloved hand reaching in the frame, snipped off the long thick plait with a familiar-looking butcher knife. I gasped at the sacrilege. But comprehended that would not be the least of it.

"It isn't real!" I cried. *Blood everywhere...pooling—splotching...*"Wait, Lanny! I remember now! Sugar, Lance! Zak was making a film. I knew her! He was only in high school. Remember the film class! Can't you see that! That semester, the video camera workshop in summer school? You guys were all gonna shoot a short, and—and enter it in..."

I was sputtering and stammering in haste, desperate, certain I had proved Zak's innocence. "I can't remember the name. Some film festival for students. Maybe it's..."

"Get real!" Lance's scathing look burned. "Why did we not see this *epic* at the time? Old Zak would have reveled in scaring the pants off all of us, and scandalize our instructor, old prissy pants *what's his name?* Why were these not *showcased* with the *rest* of the class projects? Not that these would have been accepted in a zillion years," he scorned. I could see he was incandescent I took Zak's side.

I looked away, not wanting to meet my brother's penetrating glare. Of course, clumsily-executed shorts, the likes of—"*The Monster In The Woods,*" or slavish

"*Star Wars*" clones, even amateurish love paeons to adolescent angst, that the rest of the film class tackled in order to be the next Spielberg, or Tarantino, was not the sick stuff that these tapes and DVDs were wallowing in.

Miserably, I noted splashes on the wall near Zak's trophies and swiftly checked the pine walls as the tape ground on. *No splashes.* I shut my eyes, not wanting to see someone else I might have known. When had Zak painted the old pine anyway? I thought when he was about fourteen, or so, before the accident. But how had he gotten up here? It was absurd!

My lesser angel whispered in my ear, "*But Mom's sister, Madge was never much of a care taker, just like Flo. It was possible with Zak's mature looks, he drove up in one of the Lodge's superfluities of cars without her wondering, or caring overmuch.*"

I wondered if gore was there beneath the charcoal paint.

Lance nudged me out of morbid speculation. "Look! Plastic on the floor now. Smart bastard."

A palm once again smeared the lens leaving the camera focused on the (bloody) plastic. Was it Zak's hand? The camera swung up again, focused unevenly on a face. Another redhead, but with sleek caramel skin. Strawberry blonde dreadlocks. African-American. About fourteen, I feared judging by the lithe, still budding figure, slim legs undamaged by age, ankles ringed with tribal symbols so popular with the young, hanging from cuffs attached to maple bed boards, with her head slumped forward. My stomach roiled.

A gloved hand grabbed the dreads jerking her head up. She wasn't recognizable as anyone human. I gagged. A shapeless mass of what had been a short delicate nose skewed to one cheek, eyes puffed purple plums, her mouth without form, a *squashed* plum, split and leaking. Small breasts arced once, as she raised her chest with one last gasp. Her head fell forward again, dreads hanging over the worst of the damage. I did not recognize her. She wasn't from school here in the country, or Grosse Pointe Woods.

The video mercifully, *"went blue."*

Lance, breathing hard, jerkily slapped another video in the ancient player before I could protest or back off, holding my wrist in an iron grip. "Can't leave now, Nutmeg! Don't you wanna *know!*"

"I don't recognize *any* of them," I shouted. "Isn't that enough?"

"Yet!" He snarled. "Whatsa matter, 'fraid lover boy might have strayed?" He cast me a surly glance.

"Of course not! You're sick!" Lance cast me an— *I'm* sick look*?*

Lance made me custodian…an unwilling witness. The next tape had its usual "snowy" leader, abruptly entering a scene right out of a gorno film, where sex and porn blended in a grisly unholy union. Some people were whetted by it; turned on by a combination of sex and slaughter, as if sharpening a dull knife. *Not my Zak. No. Not my beloved!*

Yet, it wasn't gory carnage, mercifully silent in this effort, that caught my attention. Robotically, I leaned closer to the screen feeling my face bathed in ice, then flood with heat over *what I next saw.*

My knees dissolved.

I was pitching forward.

Bracing myself against Lance's scrawny back, before I swooned.

Lance shot me an irritated glance, pushing my head away and veered back to the action on the minute screen.

It had taken me thirty seconds to register—

A dubious miracle spying that streak—*that glimpse of faded navy*…I was overcome.

By the time I looked back, the film had moved jerkily on to the bedspread.

Only a blur of blue… Just a blur of blue!

The image stilled, then jolted back.

Only a knee, covered in faded navy cords. That's all!

The video cam dipped, or jiggled, revisiting the image…*an extreme close-up of frayed, spotted, navy cords briefly loomed—specifically zeroing in on a dark, wine-red-soaked cuff and bare foot.*

From the corner of my eye, I realized—I could not deny it, I was seeing a *mirror image of a red-soaked cuff.*

And the image and reality melded, perfectly.

A navy-blue corduroy knee.

A bloody cuff.

"Lanny?" I stared down at his leg.

I couldn't stop fixating on Lance's frayed corduroy-covered knee jutting right below me.

Even a matching wine-dark stain.

"Lance," I said carefully. "Those are *your* pants. The—the ones *you* have on." I pointed to the screen like an idiot, by chance, again offering another view of a corduroy-clad knee and bloody stain.

I realized his head turned as if cranked by a ratchet. I drowned in pale black-ringed irises two inches from my own. The angry red lids. The pouches beneath. Our noses almost touched. The fetid breath. I could feel a prickling of proximity making my own nose itch. I was a mouse afraid to move and he the hawk. His eyes, so close they blurred, hardened into one icy blue stare.

"But not me *in* them," he spoke dangerously quiet. "Meggie? What are you thinking?"

His voice wasn't quite Lanny's. Inflectionless, flat—*dead.* Devoid of emotion, or care for me. I could have been a stranger.

"I found these, Nutmeg," he enunciated carefully. "Like *you* did. I rummaged them from a rag bag on the porch, you see." He spoke slowly as if I were from another country. "I put them on over my *jeans,* because it was *cold* that day we went out, and I barely *saw* them. Thinner now, you know. *Remember*? Here. I am taking them *off.*"

He spoke with the coldness of a robot. Overexplained. I recognized that, too.

Now, I noted his barely controlled anger, the shock of my discovery, my so-called betrayal, and sick suspicions. I didn't want to go there. I backtracked.

"Oh, Lanny, I'm so sorry." I rubbed my forehead as if rubbing away my sins. I had to hang on. I was so confused. My head muddled with images. I had to believe *someone.* "I-I it's all been so—" I motioned, helpless. My brother's shoulders melted downward in a weary, accepted gesture.

"Me too. But jeez, Meg what were you *think*-ing?"

"Said I was sorry!" Tears burst from my eyes from a long held back dam. I sobbed heaving and sucking in air. Fighting off panic, I slapped the "off" button, and hid my face.

But the navy trousers were there! Burned in my head like blue fire.

"Oh, Lanny! What is happening to us?"

"We are both—" Lance finally muttered, shaking

his head..."Sex tapes all right. Sick sex." He was distancing again.

What did I believe? I found I went to a place in my head, where I did not care.

****

We shared a stub of a cigarette in the widow's walk to the literal bitter scrag end, burning our fingers. A sorry peace offering of sorts. I was conciliatory. I felt I had to be and that was the frightening part. Lance waved away the last acrid smoke; rubbing frost, scanned outside. "Gotta keep our heads."

"Difficult on half a stick of gum," I cracked without feeling the slightest humor.

We were trying to bring back "*normal*" to whatever that was, even in our pathetic recent history. Before we learned Zak was a sicko. *If he was,* I amended. *If these weren't all some inexplicable hoax, or misdirection, or school project.*

Yeah right.

The hard part, I didn't care! Miserably accepting I'd follow Zak to prison, hell, or Ecuador, or any other extradition-free part of the world.

"Say it *isn't* real."

I looked over startled trying not to show it. Lance had his reasonable face on. "He could bloody well sue us!" His drawn face quirked comically with irony.

I had to laugh. *He meant it. It worked.* Now, Lance wouldn't say anything—until I could question Zak.

"A lawyer'd probably say this is all—dunno— *research.* A book. A play. Fantasy! Hell, not even *Zak.*"

"Oh Lanny. You don't think?" I heard the shaky relief in my voice. *The need,* hoping he had not detected it. "We'd *never* hear the end of his *gotcha's*—and he'd look for money. You realize he would! We have to keep this buttoned up, until…" I encouraged.

"We finally blow this icebox? You betcha! Seriously, Magpie. Maybe. Not my area. Lawyers are bottom-feeding barracudas, if we were wrong. Zak could get by with—"

Multiple murder?

"Can't believe we're even having this conversation? Zak? Sugar bear! After all we said." I croaked a laugh and rechecked the window. "Almost rather he *were* Jack The Ripper."

"Screwin' with our heads?" Lance looked doubtful. "Rather elaborate? You don't think?"

"Make up your mind!"

Oh, my head hurt, whipsawed between the hard rock of reality and the soft mush of fantasy.

"Hold on. First. That was his handwriting?"

I grimaced. "Late birthdays? Christmas cards scribbled with a freaking, 'Z'? What do you think?" I answered as miserable as I felt.

He picked a hangnail and stared at me sideways. "Why *there*? My room?"

"He didn't. I put that stuff there." I answered, unthinking.

"What the friggin' hell, Meg?"

"Insurance," I stammered. Yet I recognized, that wasn't the reason I impulsively stuffed damning evidence in Lance's closet. I didn't want them found in Zak's room.

"And what cheesy black and white classic did that come from? *Double Indemnity*?" he huffed his scorn.

I stared out, mesmerized by snow dancing a graceful ballet. Soft, soothing…until from my slant-eyed scrutiny—without ceremony, Lance withdrew a triple-folded, black bundle fixed with Velcro, plus a plastic kit from his commodious black coat pockets. The kind of emergency kit one throws in the glove compartment, or trunk, and never used.

Until now.

Next, Lance unrolled the black bundle stroking the shining lethal instruments within with erotic pleasure. Clean, glittering, expensive, I realized with a lump in my throat. These were instruments on which he played, as a budding violinist must dream of performing at Carnegie Hall. Only Lance saw himself as pre-eminent surgeon. I slanted an eye at him, reassessing. Lance really *was* proud of his profession, yearning for way more recognition than earned from oblivious street walkers, or his polyglot of down and outers.

Now perhaps he never would be. Most likely our dreams, hopes and goals ended here, not with a bang, but a tedious struggle for survival until limbs shriveled with cold long after our minds turned gelid. They'd find our mummified bodies in the spring...I hoped. My throat closed with a sob, feeling the itch of cold tears trickling my cheeks, fighting panic and crippling despair, plus, the sharp cold instruments send a black specter of foreboding through my brain like an ice pick.

That bundle was a game-changer from speculation...*to all-out war. Survival.*

I gave a—*where did these come from?* look.

"Small, but handy." Lance continued fondling them. "Grabbed the last minute. Smart hunh?"

I nodded with an unease I could not articulate. "Sure, Lanny."

With effort I scanned his gleaming array of medical

apparatuses, including innocent, blood-pressure cuffs, a stethoscope, bandages, surgical scissors, then, several scalpels, hypodermics, a small saw and sharp tools and clamps, I didn't recognize what they were for, next to vials of viscous fluid.

Oddly, added to the rest, but did not match—duller instruments, with underlying brass showing through the ancient steel; antique, yet lethal and loathsome-looking, as if I viewed an exhibit of medieval tooth-pulling apparatuses, or arcane surgical devices forgetting my revulsion in the wonder.

I raised my brows risking a sideways glance.

Lance pawed them as if waiting to put the disturbing things to use, would be an unimaginable burden. "I collect antiques," he protested reading my thoughts. "Want to keep them the way they are, as they earned the right to be!"

I nodded acceptance to placate, though why I needed to I wasn't sure. None too clean on closer look. Gunk stained the hinges and creases. Could that be—*blood* after all these years? Thoughts flew back to the musty suitcase by the wood box that first night, a lifetime ago…and a burlap bag of crusty tools.

Lance plucked an ancient scalpel pocked with rust gleaming dully under a pale sun crystalizing ice-covered windows, turning it this way and that in a manner disturbing. Those damn things were still sharp, and the way he was weaving it around…? I shifted imperceptibly.

"What's in here?" I said, more to change his focus. Negligently, he tossed the plastic box to me, containing more mundane items: Ace bandages, Bactrim, tiny scissors, alcohol, brown plastic bottles of pain killers, etc.

"You said Zak's auditioning for Poster Child Of Weird, Nutmeg. We gotta—" He let his words fade.

Mesmerized by the shining instruments, I nodded slowly. "Right." Gazing at the ice-fogged world, I expelled a long white breath. My head felt the same. Foggy. Like the gingham dog and the calico cat, thoughts and emotions warred until I could not tell what was real, or important and what was panic-stricken fantasy.

"Insurance," he said with a certain smugness. "Meg? Do you hear me!"

I lifted my chin woodenly, once—twice. "Of course," I answered faintly, uncertain what I was admitting. Equating Zak with those tools of pain? I couldn't bear it. Watching my brother with alarm, as light turned the world gray and one-dimensional beyond the window's walk. I craved to snatch the black bundle and run with it.

Maybe tonight, I could hide it while he slept. I shivered deep in my coat feeling a puff of warmth escape. Soon we'd need leave this glass sanctuary, and upon Zak's return, "act normal" again. Wasn't sure I could. Aware and irritated, Lanny stared at me, smiling weirdly.

"What, Lanny? What's so *funny*?" I began to leave however he still had that tremulous smile fluttering across his face like a sick butterfly, *bursting* to tell me something, my gut told me, I did not want to hear.

His face took on a shy, proud, almost "little boy" look. If he were standing, he'd be scuffing his toe in the sand. I looked down at my arm. His hands were bony white claws digging deep in my coat, staying me.

"Lanny! What is it? You're giving me the creeps!" I

couldn't help it.

He still studied me with that peculiar grin—not answering, as if wheels spun in his head until stopping at a decision like a roulette ball dropped in the wrong slot.

"Lanny! Stop it." I yanked my arm. His response was to grip tighter Dragging me closer. He bent his head as if telling me a delicious secret and released me.

He began slowly, still with that shy-proud manner. "Meg? I-I didn't wanna tell ya."

"Tell me what!" *What makes you act so weird?* Colder of a sudden, I eased an inch off the bench closer to the trap and then the short ladder to the attic floor. I had an icicle for a spine.

Lance still had that little boy with his hand caught in the cookie jar look—*if the boy was a victim of Dachau.* I tried a different ploy, longing to leave a suddenly poisonous atmosphere without his enmity. His eyes held a strange look, as if he had no irises, only black holes, but it could have been the waning light.

"No worries, Lanny. What—whatever it is. It'll wait. We'll make it all right." I babbled desperately. I'd promise anything. I was at the hatch, my foot on the first rung. "Let's go!"

Like a striking snake, Lance grabbed my freed hand hauling me back. He scraped my skinnier hips against the frame. "Ow, Lanny!" My coat rode up releasing hoarded warmth. "Sugar, Lanny! Let go! What's got into you!"

"It was me!" He whispered urgently and dragged at me harder over the sill.

"All right! Okay! I'm coming!" I strived to knee the floor, and gain my feet but he had *none of it,* in his eagerness, yanking me all the way and, plunking me on the bench seat, *hard.* I felt my poorly shielded tail bone hit wood. "Ow! Lance!" I saw in his face I protested in vain. *What do they say? No one home?* His eyes still looked inward, enjoying the drama playing out there. I could smell his sour breath, straining to push back, but he had me in a clutch of bony fingers.

I studied the chalk-white hand scattered with bristly black on the scrawnier chicken-bone back, clamping my wrist as if in a hairy claw-vice. I never noticed how repulsive that combination of hirsute chalk-white skin was before. I looked at him numbly as his words penetrated my mind.

It was me.

He must have seen my revulsion.

He threw me back on the glass wall behind me, I heard a cracking but gladly it was the old frame, protesting. Pallid eyes, sunken, red rimmed, empty until now, sparked as they hadn't for a month. He paced in the small space, casting gleeful glances at me, as if burbling to tell a secret.

"What are you *talking* about?" My skin crinkled. Even then, I had not an inkling, yet the back of my neck prickled.

"It was *me* wrote those dirty, diary things in Zak's room!" He smirked proudful, with a *what do you think about that!* look.

My ears roared as if stoppering up from hearing, or observing, uncomprehending, his self-conscious smile flicker on-off like stuttering neon and he kept mouthing meaningless words.

"D-diaries? You don't mean...?" I gestured downstairs.

"Keep up, stupid! I. Said. I. Wrote. Those. *Diaries!*"

He repeated slowly with an annoying flickering toothy grin like a cheap road sign, as if I were a particularly dull-witted child—alternating fear—regret—puffed up pride? I couldn't *read* him.

"That's what's *stupid*, Lance. Don't joke! I don't *need* this this— this *crap!*"

I darted looks behind him. The trap door was still flapped back. If I could edge around him. Shove him backward? He might fall down it. But then, he'd bottle-neck the trap. He'd be waiting. Angry. Half crazed.

Please understand, the eyes said. Yet underneath lurked deviltry and triumph, as his bland stare turned black and huge with pupil even as I watched, scaring the bejesus out of me. I emphatically wanted out of this icy trap! I couldn't think. Hunger had finally whittled away at my brother's sanity.

"What's the Sam Hill's *wrong* with you!" I wailed. "Quit with the kid stuff. Nothing to fool around with here, Lanny! You and your dumb ideas!" I tried to shove past.

"I shouldn't have said that," he countered with a curious mixture of complacency and disapproving regret. "Knew you wouldn't understand. It's not a *game*! There was some genuinely serious stuff going on here!"

He stopped abruptly. A shade of awareness passed over his face as if revealing too much. He snorted. "You were always slow on the uptake. But in the excitement of the moment—?" He shrugged, giving me that shy look again. "You gotta appreciate, now the cat's out of the bag so to speak. It's—it's *embarrassing*."

"Em—*barrassing!*"

Lance circled the small space, swishing his coat in my face. Like a kid itching to tell Mom what her birthday present hid under his bed was, and bursting to reveal a *huge* secret. Rambling, oblivious as I creaked up, he didn't notice me ease to the trap door.

Then, idiotically, I groped for the bench again, listening in spite of myself.

He whirled on me, his back to the darkening window thrusting hands though his hair until it stuck up in greasy spikes. "Ah, Magpie! I'd be swamped in that grunge clinic. Up to my *pits* in smelly patients who were—so *pathetic!*" His face twisted in repugnant remembrance.

"Patch 'm up!" He shook his head. "Next week. Back with the same old knife wounds, same old gun shots, STDs. Crisis pregnancies! Same old, predictable, boring, sluttish *shit!* I trained! I wanted to do so much more! Then…"

"Then what, Lanny?"

"Never mind." His face took on a sulky cast; he threw a thousand-yard stare through black glass, whispering—lost in some frightening reverie I didn't want to join, *"Who guessed bruises, could be so— blessedly seductive?"*

"Lance." I finally articulated through a choked windpipe. "I don't want to hear anymore, besides…it— it makes no sense." Not grasping what exactly I protested. Was it the tapes, or his so-called confession of despising his patients, or being the author of all those horrible journal things?

He spun with a face twisted with bitterness, nailing me with a—*don't ignore me!*—look. Satisfied, he maintained pacing and railing in an enclosed world getting smaller by the second.

"And there's—" he flung his hand out in an—*I ask you?* gesture, "I'm too sexy for my friggin' shorts, *cousin!*" Lance exploded. "All the time, *crowing* about his *conquests!* The *cool things* he did! Hell, I didn't have time, or ready cash for a *beer* at a cruddy local dive, or a quickie in the *parking* lot, let alone *meet* anybody *hot.* Did Zak think I would *touch* any of those skanky losers I treated? That I had my own harem!" He curled his lip in a snarl.

Still between me and the trap.

I scooted imperceptivity along the bench, not liking the hot purple cast to his eyes. Or, it could have been his hollow-eyed appearance. I was beyond deciphering his moods. He still ranted but I scarce listened now. Where was Zak? Would he not be searching for us— *me,* soon? The windows were opaque showing Lance's pacing figure in the moonlight, all black and white— white face, black hair, black coat, flashing pale hands.

"Only models for Zak! Coked-up sewer rats good enough for Lance!" Darkness enclosed our box of glass as the moon sailed over the lake, leaving his face an unreadable blur. I had to say something.

"But, Lanny, it doesn't have to be like that. You and Zak aren't so very different. If you'd only…"

"What! Be clever and sarcastic. Dress like Ralph Lauren, with maxed out cards? Lie to stupid women?"

He stopped, breathless. Spittle hung from his lip. His shoulders slumped in the dusk. I ignored his careless insult. Why bother? Couldn't believe we were having this conversation—as if we *had* a future.

"Oh, Lanny. Not true! Even my words sounded hollow as the sinking feeling in my chest. "But what has that to do—about…"

"Yeah." He continued brooding almost as if I were not there. "So, I'd write those stupid things. Started out like a novel!" His words were bitter as walnut gall. "You see? Like Crichton, or Robin Cook." I recognized them both as eminent doctors-turned-extremely lauded authors—especially Michael Crichton. *Oh, Lanny!*

"Only—I wasn't *good* enough."

"Lanny. Of course, you are."

"Don't, oh, *Lanny me*! I sent manuscripts! Ya wanna see rejection slips! You could wallpaper this place. Then, I got a better idea."

He giggled as if wanting to share a joke. Yanking off his cap, again thrust long fingers glowing-white in the gloom through lank greasy black hair. "I even made up that crummy oil-cloth book, totally like a kid would!" He chortled phlegmily.

I heard the misplaced pride, while my cheeks went numb.

"What!" My mind sped back to the childish shiny black-clad book, The Chronikles of Zachary *something...*

"You get it? Like it all started when he was a kid-like. Sick, Ya know? Like serial killers when they start out young, messing up animals, then going on to bigger things," he chortled rubbing his hands. "Pretty clever, hunh? Stupid thing, really." This last was uttered with a self-deprecation I did not believe for a second. "Don't ya see? I pretended *he* was a serial killer." Lance hooted.

I felt, more than saw him shaking his head in silent laughter. When I did not respond, he went on in an urging impatient tone.

"I filled it with bad spelling and kid's drawings, and everything, Magpie! It's brilliant, isn't it? You saw it! The other stuff wasn't bad either. I liked the allusions, and progressions in age."

"Yeh. Brilliant, Lanny." I groped for his arm. The image of the black shiny oil-cloth book with childish depictions of bloody knives and fast cars filled my mind. It must have taken weeks to make. God forgive me for thinking… "You must have been planning this for a very long time, Lanny." *What had he planned for me?* "It's really clever, but can't we go down now. I'm so cold."

"Dunno *what* I was thinkin'," Lance answered my thoughts, but not the way I intended. Ignoring me, he chuckled again, wiping spittle from his lip. "Use'm someday," he threw out with a carelessness I did not believe. *He knew exactly what he was doing.* Only this hiccup with the weather, or my decision to come up here, stopped him, from whatever devilish crazy scheme after Uncle died.

"Like I said," he snarled close behind me, as I stared at both of us in the black panes. His face was ghostly white. His eyes dark holes. Mine big-eyed, scared, and thin. "Show him up." He cracked knuckles like pistol-shot in the small space.

I swallowed dry spit. "That's why they were—in *his* room?" I groped for and lit a stub end of candle, wishing I hadn't. His expression was quite mad, eyes glittering, casting paranoia and anger like toxic mold.

Abruptly, Lance plopped tiredly on the bench dragging me down beside him, just as I was poised to ease to the trap. "You weren't the only one liked this place." I felt his foul breath on my face burning ketones. "I used to come up here too," he said it musingly, scratching his scraggy beard.

"Y-you did? I said weakly.

He banged his fist on his chest, once again outraged, belligerent. "Yeah. Me, *princess*! My one refuge, when

I could afford the gas! Hunh!" He curled his lip showing yellowed eye teeth. "I was here *a lot*. You didn't own it *then*!"

He sprang up and resumed pacing.

My mind flew back to that first night.

The lone spoon in the sink. The upturned water glass and yes, too-recent newspapers and magazines in the old wood box.

The moon lifted above the trees, fat and full now, beaming pearly benevolence on the widow's-walk as I followed him silhouetted black against the light, awaiting my move. He placed his hands over his face. Now was my chance. I raised my rump off the bench to scoot to the open trap, when Lance spread his fingers in a weird peekaboo and giving a loopy grin, all little boyish again, yet his whites glittered like an animal in the brush. Thankfully, though they were Lance's, my brother's eyes once more.

"But, Meggie," he pronounced evenly. "Those tapes? I *swear* I didn't! Those *aren't* mine. You have to—"

"Shhh—shush," I soothed. *How long had we been here? Distract him.* "I do. Of course, I do. You stupid dork. You'd never, *ever*—" I stopped and spoke carefully. "You slave countless hours, with no thanks, no money, and precious little respect. It's sucked a lot out of you, Lanny dear. You—you don't deserve that. You n-need rest."

That was wrong, as if placating. Of *course*, he made the films. Too proud, too eager to show them. And the bloody corduroy pants? I didn't recall *them* in any porch ragbag.

But Lanny wasn't listening. He chewed his thumb,

furiously thinking, finally swiveled his eyes set in deep purple sockets, toward me. "Clock's run out, little Nutmeg. Can't risk it. Stay here for a while." His voice was flat as cardboard. "Here in the widow's walk, till I…" He stopped. "He's dangerous, even to you," he said triumphant and cold at the same time.

When I didn't answer, he pushed. "You see that, *don't* you! I'll take *care* of him. That's what big brothers are for." Flashing teeth, he tugged out the emergency kit with effort, waggling it before my face.

I shoved it away. "Trapped you mean, Lan!"

"You still think *Zak* walks on water." In the dark his words hung a poisonous vapor.

"No. It's happening too fast to think, to—to plan! Wish I'd never found those—*things*. I *do* believe. Let's keep away from him. Act normal. We're not sure that…"

"I think we tried *that*," he said with a sarcasm making me cringe.

"I can't! I won't, Lanny." Being locked in this glassy mausoleum of the widow's walk was not on.

"You will!" He ordered striding the small space with new energy. "I'll strike first. Christ, I'm not even hungry anymore, thank God. I see things clearly now." I was too aware Lance still watched me like a starving cat with a bird, waiting to see which way I'd flutter with my "broken wing."

I made light. "In the dark? Come on, Lanny, let's go! We are stronger together. Like old times, right?" He cocked his head, eyeing me in a manner disturbing. There was a birdlike quality—a crow or raven eyeing its next meal about his fixed stance, collar up, black hair sleeked to meet his back, and hunched in a crow-like curve, so like my first image of him outside the French doors, a million years ago.

"Cellar then," he finally demanded. "Till it's over."
I shillyshallied. "Cellar? What about you?"

"Do I look the hero? First sign of danger, no fear." I
heard the smirk. "I'll beat you to the bottom and be
cowering under the coal scuttle."

A *screeching* came from below, like chairs scraping
the floor. Lance placed a hand over my mouth.

"Too late. You in? All the way?"

I kenned what he meant. *Zak's death.* I gave a short
nod. He released my mouth.

Glass smashed somewhere in the cavernous house.
Together we eased down the back way. Lance put a hand
up, before slipping into the dark silent kitchen. A frigid
breeze swept the room. The door was swung open.

Behind him, I stepped on a decorative, "*Season
Everything With Love*" plaque…hanging on the wall by
the old Kelvinator like since forever, now shattered on
the linoleum, shards crunching beneath my feet.

"Dammit, Meg! Shhh!"

"It was wind!" I whispered nodding meaningfully to
the door. "It wasn't latched."

"Like hell! He was here! Is the gun still there?"

"Over the mantel? Doesn't work, Lanny, even if we
had shells." *Oh, please, if there is a God, no shells. I felt
split in two.* One half fearing Zak, the other, yearning to
stand before him, taking the bullet, the knife, the
accusations…

"Is he aware of that—for sure?" Lanny fidgeted
about the kitchen, peering out windows.

I jerked a shoulder in answer. "No. He was never
into guns. May have. But it'll blow up even if we did!
Wait. Your archery set! You had it!" My heart broke

even as I suggested it, but I wanted his thoughts well away from the gun over the mantel, and Lance never could hit a barn door if an arrow had a missile guidance system attached to it.

"Judas priest. Hiding in plain sight." He thwacked his forehead and dashed up the back upstairs, calling behind him. "Believe me. I aim real good when Zak's in my sights."

****

Lance stared at his sad archery set. Loose string, fletches ragged, and the shafts a joke, all cracked and warped. "Hell!"

Chapter 33

Polar Express

"Where's your bow?"

"Piece of crap…strings broke." Lance grunted sulky with a face that said—*don't ask.* "I'll find somethin'." I ignored his mood, and at my brother's insistence, jerkily chucked a rolling pin, ball of twine, a meat tenderizer, and a broken screwdriver down the cellar steps making a great clatter, but could not stop my manic activity.

Where was Zak? I had to see him first. Read him. Look in his face for the truth, no matter what. If I had not seen those tools, those videos…?

The blue clad knee? The bloody cuff?

"Christ, Meggie! Can you make any more noise!"

"Oh, Lanny," I wailed. "We're lunatics!"

"Good word. Lunatic!" He stamped up from the cellar. "Like I said. *Anything* that might be a weapon. More for us, less for him. The sick bastard."

"Where is everything!" *Where is Zak?* Fingers shaking so badly rummaging drawers, empty but for flotsam—brittle rubber bands, one thumbtack, scattered mystery keys and a herd of dead batteries rolling about the back of the drawer, I dropped things. "Nothing's left," I wailed. "Even that broke scissors. Knives! Everything gone." I wasn't even sure why we were hiding weapons in the cellar. Unless Lance still meant to keep me there.

"The big cleaver. Where the hell's that? That damned thing we played pirates with. Where's the ax?"

I saw the ax in Zak's belt; why bother telling him? Holding up a bent corkscrew, I lobbed it at him, followed by a hefty serving spoon, feeling stupid. A serving spoon against a determined killer?

"Wait. The fire poker."

"Fastening veranda doors. And I can't find the tongs. What do I do with this?" Lance held up the bent spoon. "Garage sale?"

"Don't be silly!" I snapped harshly for me.

"Okay, okay! That all?" Lance rubbed his thighs with nervous energy.

I opened another drawer, cynically holding up frayed towels. "Smother him?"

Suddenly, I slumped, weary and defeated.

"Cellar now, Magpie!" I stared at the abyss. He held the door open invitingly, to a black oblong slanting down like a tunnel, to an underground tomb. The fragrance of mold, earthworms and grave chill wafting up, had never been so pervasive.

"Lanny, this is nuts. I can help." *Warn Zak?*

Lance looked significantly at my gimpy leg and away. "Sorry Magpie, not with *that*. Can't worry 'bout you *and* him." He gave me an awkward hug. I stiffened despite myself. "Sorry I yelled. Now hurry, Little Nutmeg. Could be the end for both of us, if ya don't. Now scat!"

He looked over his shoulder and fingered the cellar door open wider. "Now, I said! Bastard's probably sniffin' us out now!"

I peered over his shoulder into the dim flickering

kitchen, delving in shadows our lone stub of candle created. *If he wasn't here already.* Somewhere. He was late. The moon was over the trees. I celebrated. Then, my heart hurt. Had he fallen? Was he sick? Feverish? Had he fallen victim to whoever hung the man in the tree?

I had consigned the image of frozen shanks, and horny feet dangling like pendulums before my face, to the chilly pits of oblivion. Now it was back. *Zak where are you! I need you,* I fretted irrationally. "But, Lanny, he won't know we found those—" I choked, "tape things."

"Our dear cuz will, by the look on your puss, Magpie!" he said with ferociousness verging on hate. I clung to the frame, checking the black hole. "Colder down there. It *smells*."

"Quit stalling!" Lance's face twisted in a snarl showing yellowed teeth. I couldn't hold him off much longer before he tossed me down the steps. It locked on the other side. *I'll be trapped if Zak gets you first. And then, what?* "I want to take my chances *here, Lanny*! He'll suspect something, if I'm not—"

"Too effing late." Prying my fingers as he spoke, black glittering eyes set deep in cottage cheese flesh, between shaggy brows and dark beard stubble; Lance's face was a study in contrasts, martyred saint, or inquisition monk.

We both heard the distant crunch of boots and stared at each other as if for the last time.

"I'll come when it's safe. I swear."

Lance surprised me, grabbing me, fiercely hugging, kissing my hair. He placed his forehead on mine. I felt him tremble as he moaned, "Help me, Meg. Ah, Jeeze. I'm scared. Those tapes! Ah, Jeeze! Now, go! Go. Before

I change my freaking mind."

Lance pushed me through the doorway, *hard* before I could stop him. I banged into, and slid down the wall half way to the bottom, scrambling back on all fours as the lock *snicked* closed. "Lanny!" I pounded futilely as footsteps faded. He seemed so vulnerable. Ghost pale and pathetic in his oversized black coat.

****

Lance, haunted and frail in the candlelit kitchen pocketed the key. His fingers pinched the flame. He fondled the faded red round cylinders—*the shotgun shells,* thrust deep in his pocket and stalked grimly toward the Great Room.

****

I pressed the cellar door. Dim candle light extinguished. I wanted to pound, but some scared little-girl part of me didn't. I wondered if I could batter my way out the slanted storm door when all I wanted to do was huddle at the top of the stairs, squeeze my eyes tight and make the demons go away.

That got exasperating, way soon.

Feeling my way back down, the cellar was pitch, until dirty light seeped from below, via grimy windows lining the dirt ledge. The moon bouncing off the snow created a soft pale glow. Brushing rough clammy walls, the way down, picking my way in the gloom I crept past the furnace mastodon. Dragging a plastic crate and levering a knee up, I gained the dirt ledge; tearing webs entangling my eyelashes aside, I crawled to the first window. Moldering earth penetrated my knees. A spider scuttled over my nose. I brushed it heedlessly; crouching with my neck bent peered through century-old dirt at a narrow slice of moonlit yard.

Steps *critch-crunched* brittle snow. A shadow moved past filthy panes. I saw Lance—black coat flapping like a crusader's cape—carrying something long and gleaming dully against the dirty snow. He halted and glanced toward the boat house and once down at the window I crouched behind, then scanned the lane beyond the white mound of my car, partially concealing him.

I breathed out. Hard to miss the bright fuchsia blot of Zak's garish cap and ghostly figure in the dark maroon Patagonia. Broad-shouldered, tall, he lurked in the tree line, but looking to the house. I rapped for Lance, *or Zak*—I wasn't certain which one, sucking in; then, withheld my fist. Yet, Lance must have made some noise. Zak crouched slightly but made no move to hide as Lance slowly raised his arm and with it, to my shock, the ancient shotgun from over the fireplace. A grin split his black beard. Not the grin of a hunter stalking a killer.

This was revenge killing, for not being as good, as clever, as handsome.

The long barrel with the end of the muzzle tracking Zak as he moved to one side stepping from the shelter of the wood, if anything, calmly lifting his gorgeous bow, the arrow, red feathered, notched, and ready, until it twanged, and let fly with unsurprising force and aim, the shaft soaring across the space between the tree line and the boat house.

I now saw he had edged from the wood to get clearance for his pulling arm.

Clever Zak.

The shaft rocketed through the air, making a *sizzling* sound, even through the glass simultaneously with a burst of smoke, as Lance's old blunderbuss's muzzle-flash, sparked orange against the blue-white background with a crack that split my world.

Zak's arrow sank deep in Lance's side—sickeningly, I saw the shaft and arrowhead punch through the back of his coat.

Lance's blast pierced Zak high on his left shoulder slamming him back into the tree line onto a broken-limbed trunk. Zak threw his head back, gasped once in soundless agony, then, head down, bulled forward before Lance could reload.

If Zak wanted to make a killing shot, he could have easily done it. Zak, the archery star could have sunk a shaft in Lance's heart, or head, easy as slicing butter. Sugar, he could put one square in his eye had he wanted. "Bless you, Zak," I breathed.

Lance and Zak both staggered before they reached each other. Lance to his knees, holding his side; cried out, dropped, and rolled. The old gun skittered away. Tugging at his side his pale, pained, shocked face, white against white, looked across the yard at me as if for help. I yelled, *"No, don't pull it out."* Instead, he staggered to his knees, locked together for balance. Then I saw the shaft dripping trailing blood, as Lance grimacing and howling, seemed determined to yank it out.

Shuttling to the next window, I hollered till my throat was raw, and pounded the pane. Lance got to his feet like a child learning to walk, groping his pockets and shambling determinedly to Zak, leaving the shotgun sunk in the snow. He still clutched the arrow sticking from his side, perhaps keeping it steady.

My eyes scanned the yard as if seeing a tennis match, back and forth—

Zak.

Then Lance.

I barely made out the hypodermic's weak glint, held low to Lance's body.

Zak lifted his bow with his left-hand, fumbling weakly with the string, holding his arm close to brace it. He seemed helpless. No way he could draw the bow with his injured shoulder, even if Lance wasn't haltingly staggering and holding his own side. Still, he was closing in.

Nevertheless, before Lance reached him, Zak again barreled into him, clumsily bear-wrestling, before Lance, furiously attempting to jab the needle, could raise his arm. Zak's motions were sluggish. Lance, looking no fitter, broke free. Both plummeted to their knees.

I had to help. But which one—if I could? The windows were too narrow, even for me to wriggle through. I batted the pane. Useless…old glass, thick, strong and wavery. So, helplessly sobbing, I observed the terror play out.

Lance crawled on his knees, circling Zak. Zak desperately thrashing, rolled, and twisted to avoid the hypo. Lance, relentless, slithering this way and that, trailing blood; once, facing me, I saw the feral gleam as he held the needle like a knife in his fist, feverish to stab at the least opportunity. Then, Lance, tripping on his own coat, pitched forward, coming up with a face full of snow, spitting and grimacing, showing his teeth in an enraged snarl. Propping on one arm, he raised his other arm high, howling and lunging in desperation before Zak got to his feet.

I saw the gleam like an evil eye glittering under the moon—Lance's pinched determined mouth as he swung the hypo down in a brutal arc aimed at Zak's neck. I screamed as the hypo slid past Zak's Mandarin collar. I could feel the piercing on my own neck, sinking in my flesh and release of cold poison coursing my veins, moaning, "*Nooooo,*" sucking in a hiss as Zak thrust a hand up, bracing Lance's quivering arm as he attempted another desperate jab.

Still gripping my brother's arm, Zak rolled aside. The hypo sank in the snow. With an insane angry cry, Lance groped for it on his hands and knees. As Zak looked to crawl away, my brother frantically scattering snow, spotted and lunged for a felled arrow, visible by its bright red fletch.

Raising it, triumphant, he swiveled, lurching aside as he fell, plunging it without aim, only murderous intent, his whole weight behind it, apparently aiming for Zak's heart—deep, deep through the puffy Patagonia jacket. Instead, the arrow with its sharp tip, rammed in the small of Zak's back as he hurled himself aside at the last minute. Yet, they were both flagging.

I pressed my face to the window pushing the pane so hard it might shatter. I didn't care. I wanted out, to shout at Lance. Lance still gripped the arrow, wriggling it whether to cause Zak maximum damage, or wiggle it loose to jam it again, I couldn't tell.

Heart breaking, I heard Zak's howl. Who would have guessed Lance might get the upper hand in a battle to the death? I realized with sick awareness; Lance must have guessed the shotgun still worked. He *must* have squirrelled away the shells.

Only three inches of the arrow showed between Lance's fists, then he put his palm on the end, ramming the shaft deeper, pinning Zak to the ground. Still Zak fought, lifting himself off the snow, thrashing side to side as far as the arrow allowed. I could hear his screams. Managing to loose the shaft from Lance's hands; God knew what pain and destruction that action caused, Zak rolled frantically, struggling to his knees. I saw the arrow plain now, dripping a substance black against the snow.

Then, I grasped that the arrow in Lance's own side kept him from getting close enough to Zak, even though grappling him in a clumsy tussle. Helpless, I endured Zak's cries as the shaft that seemed to be closer to his hip, jostled, matched by Lance's grunting moans. The two staggered to their feet, clinging like drunken lovers. Swaying in and out of view, they danced clumsily about the yard, two wounded bears in combat, one thin and shaggy, weighted by a coat, the other badly damaged.

As I lost them, I crawled through dried insects and webs one window to the next, then Lance reeled backward holding his side, leaving Zak to drop face first...I watched him crawl in circles tossing snow aside like a dog after a bone, still searching for the hypodermic, oblivious, as Zak dragged the ax from his belt and using his last strength, gave a mighty heave, tumbling it end over end, before sprawling again and laying very still.

Shouting uselessly, I tracked the ax arc and circle, sinking through Lance's black-coated back. Lance arched, his howls near shattered the glass, reaching behind him, but his elbow could not make the awkward bend. I pounded so hard the rotted frame finally cracked; I tugged jagged glass wedged in tight with ancient putty, and a hundred years of paint. Sobbing mad, I studied the lethally sharp opening. I could never squeeze through without slicing my gut to ribbons.

I hobbled upstairs banging my hip into the lead pipe

railing, crashing into the wall; my leg ached worryingly from kneeling on the clammy ledge. Now, after the bruising fall, refused to do the proper duty of a leg, by *moving*. Gritting my teeth, I grabbed under my knee and heaved my leg up to the next step, and the next, hurling myself at the door, but it was from below that I heard a voice calling, weak and drained of spirit.

I dropped my head to my hands sobbing for real, and bumped back down the steps on my bottom, hobbling over to what appeared a gargoyle through the broken window; Lance with his head thrust past the broken frame, reached for me, his hands smeared with blood.

"Open the door, Lanny! I can't help you out there." I pointed up. I did a quick scan. The yard seemed empty and scuffled as if a great battle had been fought in place of two exhausted warriors on the edge of starvation.

Where did Zak go? Would he kill me too, in his certain rage? He wasn't aware I was locked, or if I sided with Lance. My eyes tracked back. The fuchsia hat flung aside, blindingly brilliant against the monochrome background, but no body lay beside it. I searched the featureless expanse. No Zak.

Lance nodded weakly, backing out and heaved to all fours. I stood on the box watching him crawl to the lattice porch leaving trails of reddish black until the billowing white resembled a Pollack painting. The silhouette of the ax still protruded from his back. If I could simply make it back up the stairs. Strength returned along with pain. I felt my scar taut as a bowstring, my calf throbbing to my heartbeat. Sensing the hulk of the furnace looming beside me in the dark, I made the stairs; groping for the railing, drew myself up hand over hand.

****

After a long, too-long time, gasping, and draped over the tiny landing with my head butting the wood, I heard fumbling lock-clicks. I shoved at the door. It opened a wedge—and stopped at the sound of a thud and a moan. A thatch of black hair showed beyond the crack.

"Lance move!" I pushed and wriggled through, edging past my brother sprawled on the old linoleum in a pool of already collecting blood.

He slurred, "Wasn't fast 'nough, Meg. Waitin' f 'me."

I darted looks to the wide-open porch door through which a chill miasma wafted through like a ghost of freedom.

"Yes, you were, Lanny." I heard the catch and sob in my breath. I must remain strong. Gimpy as I was, I was whole. "Y-you got him good."

Could one die of a broken heart?

I braced, hardening like forged steel. Any second, Zak would roar through with fire in his eyes. I'd seen him thwarted before, rarely angry perhaps but when he was—? Yet with the pain of the shaft and the shotgun blast doing God alone knew what…? Stop it! *He might be dead or dying out there alone in the cold.*

My mind ping-ponged—his anger would be deadly if still alive, but his wounds would bring a long lonely death bleeding out in merciless cold; my heart lurching like a long-caged bear from bar to bar I wished for a shameful time, it was Lance lying bleeding somewhere in the cold barren yard. But Lance was here, right before me. I gingerly turned him. He was half-lying on the ax, still stubbornly caught in muscle and coat fibers. It had not struck his spine I thought, or he could not have moved his legs.

Thank God for small favors.

I would not thank God later.

"Hang on." I flinched and gripped the handle, then halted, stuffed a towel in his mouth and, gritting my teeth grabbed hold of the arrow: with hands on both sides bent it hard as I could, enduring Lance's muffled howls, managed to snap it off before I could lay him straight on his stomach.

"Owww! Stop!" Lance howled.

"It's over, Lance. The worst part," I lied and groped under the coat. The blunt blade pierced his muscle, slightly, not his spine. Using my skimpy acquaintance with medical issues, I hoped it was safe to draw it out, shut my eyes and yanked. I slung the axe, skittering it across the linoleum as Lance howled protests. "Payback time, Doc." Then attempted easing him from the coat.

"No joke! *Aahhhh!*" At least he did not admonish me for doing the wrong thing. Lance never stoic, yelped as I twisted his arm out of the sleeve.

And Zak is out there. Zak is dying. Darling precious Zak. My beloved. My life.

Tears ran down leaking onto Lance's face as I probed to see if cloth was imbedded and Lance kept howling—"Je-sus! Meg! Quit dripping all over me!" On inspection, the ax sliced the thick coat, nipping the long muscle beside his spine—a bleeder but not painful enough for his outburst.

"Not bad, Lanny. Let me see the other." Impatiently dragging his layers of sweaters up appalled at how thin he actually was, I saw Zak's arrow pierced the fleshy part, if Lance had a fleshy speck of fat on him. I ripped a towel, tying strips around his chest and back, once again, pondering Zak's puzzling lack of accuracy, my mind not on the task, but out in the barren yard under a pitiless moon, where my beloved lay bleeding out.

My hands had a life of their own, moving rashly, bluntly transcribing my bitter thoughts to action. Another yelp of pain when I tried to maneuver his sweaters back down. Lance thrust me aside. I was more than ready to do so, gritting my teeth to keep from telling him.

"Like I don't go through this shit," he grunted. "Gotta PhD in knife wounds!"

"Okay! Lanny. Stay there." I ordered him.

"I'm fine, now! Get me my shotgun!"

"Where'd you leave it?" I snapped. *Please don't find it.* If he cottoned onto my need to tend Zak, he'd stop me—if he could. I calculated the distance to the door.

Struggling to rise, he looked about, belligerently eyeing me with chilling paranoia while his wheels, though weak and rusty still churned in his head.

"Outside!" he ordered. "You go. I follow. Go! GO! Dammit! Hurts. Ain't dead..." His grimacing face made him wolf-like—lean-jawed, black-bearded, bloodshot eyes coldly studying me.

I shrank as it sunk in. "Oh! You mean—like *bait*?"

Lance creaked up, groaning, holding onto a chair. "Used ta win prizes," Olympic material!" Chortling with slitted eyes, and his lean bristled face he looked even more wolf-like.

"I'll get him!" It was a howl and a moan of pain.

Abruptly, Lance half-swooned over the white enameled captain's chair, giving me a thrill of hope. His knees buckled. He slid to the floor. I looked apprehensively at the door, half rising, when his hand shot out, the good one, grasping me in a bony vice surprisingly strong.

"Don't leave me, stupid bitch! If he ain't dead, he's dangerous! Help *me*, Meg! Don't go soft on me!" Lance's lids fluttered, but his teeth bared. I watched his mouth ridged with pain between a straggly black beard. "Trees," he hissed yanking my close. "He'll follow, if any life's left in him, the murdering bastard. He'll follow you to the grave!"

He chortled at his joke. "Like old times. Hide go seek. 'Member Magpie? I'll find him *good* this time!" He tossed his head back and gobbled a handful of pills from his kit. Pain killers I guessed.

"I remember." My voice had the dullness of lead while his seemed stronger. I looked in his eyes. My brother's once more as he got to his knees, but wincing, out-crying still holding on, as if I were a prisoner, not a lifeline.

I had no choice. But at least we would be outdoors.

We hobbled like a three-legged race, with Lance hanging on to the lattice screened porch, resting as we watched the yard.

No Zak.

"Where's that freaking shotgun?" He squinted. "Hah!" With an excited *yip,* Lance gripped me painfully. "Guess old Zak ain't so lucky. Look what I spy." I sought frantically where he pointed. No shotgun, but Zak's gorgeous bow stuck out of the snow like a golden harp, the quiver flung beside it. Arrows, showed by their red fletches, scattered the ice like pick-up sticks.

"You see what you havta do? Be real bad, if you don't!" He half threw me outside. "Go get'm. No!" He jerked me back. "Don't trust you! Let's go." Lance shoved me. I wanted no one behind me. I tried to wriggle away. We lurched, with him hanging on; me on my bad leg, and feeling a shaft of pain arrowing from ankle to hip, we made it across the white blanket churned up with signs of struggle as after a sleepless night.

Holding his side, he hobbled over, scooped up the bow, snatching arrows, *then* swerving to the moon shadow of the boathouse.

Running on adrenaline, making a great fuss as Lance instructed, I limped to the tree line, all the time searching for Zak. *I* could *warn him.* As I faded in the woods— *free!* I looked back and watched Lance keeping to the purple moon-shadows. Invisible. Stalking.

Opening eyes wide, holding my mouth to keep from yelping, I detected Zak's boots crunching the snow, uneven, halting. Snow muffled the direction of sound. I spun in place, blundering deeper in. *Where was he!* "Zak!" I hissed, "It's me! Don't shoot!" I kenned he must have the shotgun, if he couldn't draw the useless bow even if he had it, imaging the blast shattering the cold, braced for the pellets ripping into my body.

Making noise, scraping bark, scrunching leaves under the snow crust to alert him, whispering his name, I found myself back at the tree line overlooking the boathouse. All was lost, if I couldn't find him. Zak could not survive out here alone. "*Why do you care? He might be a killer? Lance is hurt bad,*" my lesser angel warned. A movement. A flash of dark maroon.

Zak backed from a clump of straggly cedars in a half spin holding his side. Blood leaked from his shoulder peppered with black dots around an ugly wound seen though the Patagonia's insulation.

"Meggie?" He breathed, staring as if not understanding what we were doing out here in the barren wood. He reached out. Then I saw Zak indeed had the shotgun clutched in his bad hand. It held two shells in its double barrel.

Lance eased from behind the boathouse holding the bow steady enough, aiming at Zak's back. I shouted a warning dragging him down. Even so, Zak heard Lance's unsteady progress, through the snow crust eager, ready for the kill of weakened prey. I saw it in his twisted face and long-toothed grin. Zak managed a half swivel, shakily holding the shotgun one-handed against his good shoulder, finger on the trigger. "Brace it, Nutmeg," he begged. "Help me pull." I looked up as…

…an arrow swished overhead.

Falling flat, spread-eagled the shaft whizzed home with a *slashing* of air felt more than heard, then the solid *punch* like a knife through melon. Zak's breath exploded in a tortured cry. The arrow thunked low in his side. Even then, I marveled that Lance, the weakest of us all in the art of archery, should have gained the upper hand.

Zak swiveled, corkscrewing from his knees into the snowfall littered with shed needles and dead oak leaves; unsteadily aiming the old rifle from where he fell. Lance stalked over giggling and pointing like a madman. I saw the barrels waver—and another shot heated the night with a scorching orange blast.

The shot fired wild over Lance's head.

Lance kept coming, with a sulky expression, black coat flapping in the wind night, a giant crow ready to peck Zak to death and sail off with his prey. He stretched his elbow back, the bow taut and humming, another arrow nocked, arm trembling with desire to let go like a finger on a trigger. I couldn't stand it. I dashed out yelling—"Enough!"—tumbling back beside Zak, half-shielding him.

Zak focused, breaking my heart over the unaccustomed fear in his beautiful wounded eyes. Lance stood ten feet tall over us, legs apart, spreading his mouth in a long-toothed smirk. He booted me, snarling his impatience. "Move, *Nut*meg! If you don't want this arrow through you, too."

"No more!" I crouched over Zak. "End it!"

"We won! Let me finish this, dammit!" His eyes glittered with wetness. I put my hand up soothing, calming. "He can't hurt us, now, Lanny. Don't be like him."

Lance glared, furious. He propped the bow in the snow, leaned on it, snorting, "Yah, looks like from all that blood, ain't gonna make it, anyway." He sniggered. "Tough breaks, Magpie."

I held back anger and attended Zak, prodding the arrow piercing the Patagonia jacket, ripped, stained beyond redemption, hearing Lance clucking behind me. "Hey, Nurse Ratchet!" He snickered referencing the old film. Shutting him out, I breathed, "Sorry, Zak. So sorry!"

Aware of Lance's scornful eyes and dangerous mutterings, I dragged the point back out with my fingertips, until some of shaft emerged. Using my last strength, ignoring Lance's angry breathing, *flinching from the slap, the knife in the back, the shotgun blast to my head,* tugged the slim rod, while Zak, biting his lip to keep from moaning, thrashed beneath me.

"Lie still, my darling," I whispered and snapped the shaft short, trying to jostle it as little as possible, leaving it in place. *I was getting quite good at it.*

"Go on, Magpie! Yank the sucker out!" Lance

chortled.

I looked to my brother. "Help me," I asked simply. "I haven't a clue what to do now. You are a doctor. It's *over.*"

Lance smirked. "You got that in one, *bitch*!" Holding out bloody hands, he showed me the shaft he had pulled from his own side. "I hurt too, Meggie," he whined. "Bleedin' here!"

I had no idea until now how deep the river of acid resentment flowed in Lance. His hatred of me. His sugar-coated sympathy, all vinegar. He did seem ghastly though. Perhaps his back bled more than I figured. Fresh blood dribbled down his hand. Under the chalky moon, Lance's face, between his mob cap and disheveled beard, gleamed with cold sweat like phosphorus.

I was crazed, undecided between Zak holding his side, striving to rise, or Lance dripping blood on the snow crust. Zak swooned resolving any guilt left. I held my cheek to his face. *Still breathing...*"*I'll hurry, dearest.*"

I never spoke these words of endearment before, afraid of taking the liberty, *afraid of what?* I would scare off our tentative bond like a frightened mouse, or he'd mock and make light comedy of my affection? Too late. If we ever escaped, he would be tracked down like a rabid dog perhaps shot without warning or trial. Half my mind fixated on those intimidating videos, and Lance's fake damning reports.

Please God. Please fate. It was not too late. I can burn them, I savaged. They will make a lovely pyre.

Lance's braying startled me out of sad reflections. "Dammit, Meggie! I'm dyin' here!" He let go the bow still quivering upright in the snow pack, and crumpled beside it.

"Coming!" I crawled over, and packed snow beneath Lance's bandage come loose while he cursed me at its coldness. Blood was still trickling from the wound in his side. Just a flesh wound. I glanced back at Zak. *Was he lying too still? Still breathing?*

"Hold still! I'll hurry." I hobbled to the kitchen rummaging towels, ripping strips as I hitched back as fast as I could. Funny, I wasn't hungry anymore either. My strength fed on adrenaline…

I must tend to Zak no matter what. Lance always exaggerated. However, when I flung myself out the lattice porch…it was to a peculiar sight making my bones turn to chalk, and my blood to ice water.

****

Lance stood still as a pagan statue, head thrown back, wild black mane thrashing in the wind as he gazed at the star-drenched sky. To me he seemed a feral animal senselessly contemplating the moon. He began *howling*.

No. I was confused. Not eerie high-pitched howling. Instead, *singing*…

Yet, that wasn't it either, when I made out words of a queer *sing-song*, like a child's cruel counting game. My brother seemed like a four-year-old, prattling nursery rhymes, piercing the air like a knife made of ice, not a grown man, captivated despite myself by his prolonged warbling, in an eerie high-pitched tone that screeched in my head…

"Four little girlies sittin in a tree…"
One little girlie hung her little self…
Then there were three…"

Ripples quivered down my legs…my hands shook.

"Lance?" I softly approached my brother. He kept

burbling…chanting in his weird falsetto setting my teeth on edge.

"Three little girlies huddled by the flue.
One got her little self, asphyxiated…
then there were two…"

Lance threw back his head until his spine arched and shrieked at the stars, quite mad, arms outstretched, hands in fists, bawling, *"…little girlies sittin' on a stone—!"*

His head turned a fraction, like a stone idol, ancient as sin eyeing me sideways from under lowered brows, with a speculative chilling gleam—*you are next…*

"One got her little face bashed in…" Lance cooed the last. An alien sound…drawing the hateful words out in gooey sweetness.

"…and then there was…
ONE…"

His head creaked round full-on; features twisted in a gleeful mask nailing me with a wet red gleam calculating as a starving, slat-ribbed wolf.

Then, I heard something I comprehended would chill me forever if I lived past this night as Lance minced in falsetto—

"One little Meggie hitching' up the stairs…
was hacked to death…."
And then there was—
Lance…"

He brayed the last line with triumphant exultancy, with an expression I thought I'd never see on a human. Then, behind him, Zak moved his arm and made a low distracting noise. Frantic, Lance spun as if he had lost him. Drawing his leg back, viciously kicked his hurt side. *Thank God! Zak was alive.* He groaned and tried to move off, fingers grabbing nothing but mush.

I searched the snow for a branch—*anything,* scanning the chopping block with its baker's hat of snow. Of course, the ax was missing—*where was my mind?*— racing over possible weapons. *Tossed in the cellar, thanks to my brother.* Where *was* the shotgun? Somewhere over by the tree line where Zak dropped it. I wasn't certain if it was still loaded. As I made my move, alerting him once again of my existence, Lance swiveled, fixing me full on from two black holes for eyes.

He *despised* us. Perhaps he had all along since we were kids. Hiding it. Building on resentment until the fragile barrier of relationship corroded with each acid drip, until the *real* Lance lay exposed like an open festering wound.

Lance lowered his head intently tracking me as I hobbled across the snow crust beneath his mob cap. He resembled a wild animal spying from the bushes. Never regretting my gamey leg as much, Lance commenced stalking…teasing me by feinting. Apparently, his wounds did not slow him. I noted the bleeding ceased; the churned snow was pristine— I saw all that as my numbed brain demanded—*Move—move!* Frantic I searched the surroundings…

A mass of depressions. No shotgun. Where was the gun!

The stag head poker was still jammed through veranda door handles. But I can't backtrack. Lance, is almost upon me, relentlessly nailing me with his dark cratered look. Wet snow cemented my feet in place. Futile anyway. Even in his damaged state which seemed not to hinder, but to energize, I could never outrun him. I risked a glance at Zak, still where I left him. The stain of red only a little wider. His heart still beat.

Move! Run! Awkwardly, I tried to lift my bad leg. It was frozen meat.

My mind screamed, breaking the spell.

Yanking my foot out of snow like frozen mud, I backed slowly around Lance as if he were a rabid dog ready to spring, making for the porch. He made no move; a puzzled look, his wet gaze flickering between me and Zak, head lowered curiously watching me, wondering what I was up to, or merely making sure both of us were yet *his* to kill.

He had all the cards.

Even so I made it, nipping inside. Lance finally moved with a mouth in a rictus grin of triumph. I tried desperately to latch the screen with fumble-fingers, dropping the hook. He could rip the rusty old latch from the rotten wood frame like child's play.

Scarcely long enough to get the poker.

I hobbled to the Great Room yanking the stag-head poker from the handle.

Minutes dragged with me gripping it, tense and waiting.

The screen door rasped from its sockets. The kitchen door slammed. Sneakers squeaked across kitchen linoleum. Then I heard...

"Got him good, Meggie!" Lance warbled. "For you!"

Jovial, full of fun.

I almost dropped the poker.

I tiptoed, easing the swing door. Once again, my brother's unpredictable mood, shifted. I was dizzy with it. Carefully entering, poker behind my back, I tried to divine this new disposition; hating the quake in my voice, I swallowed. "What do you mean? D-dead?"

The only light in the kitchen was through the window.

Lance giggled childishly. "Good as."

"You can do something." My lips felt like wood. "Help him, Lanny. He's out there, freezing."

Lance's manic white grin wavered. His face crumpled in a withering scowl. He reeled dripping fresh blood on the linoleum. "You'd *save* him!" He wrenched the poker away, hurling it to the floor.

Oh, dear God, he had the ax.

I kept coming, not giving in, trying to skirt him. "He's ours, Lanny. He belongs to *us*. What's *wrong* with you?"

"What's *wrong*?" He howled raising the kindling ax, swishing it in the air. It whizzed past my sunken belly, as he backhanded my face. "Lanny!" I yelped, holding my cheek.

"Scared little sis? Now maybe you'll be good. Not ask *bad* questions!" I smelt his breath. It smelt of copper. Had his stomach been hit? No, it was fear and ketones.

"What's wrong?" "I've had enough! That's what! I've done *everything* for you! Cheered you on! Listened to you *bleating* over Zak as if he walked on Olympus! It *sickened* him, you fawning over him, like some sloppy twelve-year-old! He *hates* you, you dumb cripple! He's the one *made* you that way if you weren't such a stupid, blind slut, you'd see that! Pity, if anything is all he feels for you!" He slammed the ax in the wooden drain board.

I reeled. "No, Lance." I put my hand up as if warding off a blow. *Deep down, was it true? Was it only pity? But he used present tense.*

Zak lives.

Spittle hung from Lance's mouth. He looked wildly

about, snatching a cup of cold tea little more than gray water now, that I left behind a lifetime ago.

"You need this, sister mine."

I watched with anxious eyes, took the cup with one hand, dutifully sipping, hardly aware of what I was doing, looking beyond Lance blocking the porch door.

"Funny how people trust each other."

Lance indicated the cup.

"That could be anything."

I looked at him stupidly. With a shaky hand, I set it carefully down, wanting to hurl it at him.

"*Heee-heee!*" He chortled like a four-year-old. "Look at *you*! Gotcha! Look at your *face*!" Lance snickered. "Nutmeg—Slut-Meg. Just like Mum! So *dumb*!"

"Lanny don't say that. You—you're not well."

Lance cocked his head. Then, ask conversationally, "Meggie? I ever tell you how very-very much you look like our dear old mum? The *slut* of Pole Town, De-troit, Michigan? Yup! Florence Lodge, and her ugly tap-dancin' slut-meg daughter—"

He studied my feet. "'Cept you don't *tap dance* so good no more."

"Lanny, you're bleeding again."

I watched the slow drip on the old linoleum. "Let me take care of it, then I must see to Zak. You see that don't you?" Lance, in some interior dark cave he had returned to, wasn't heeding me.

"Used to watch Mom smear on her lipstick."

"What?" I looked at him uncomprehending.

He spoke slow, in a trance of recollection. "Glistening. *Re-e-ed.*" Drawing out the word like a slow-moving train. "Like a *wound.*"

His face was beatific.

Eyes wide staring unseeing.

Now was the time.

"Like fresh—wet—*blood.*"

His expression twisted with excitement, then darkened.

"For *him.* She made herself pretty for *him!*" He bit off vehemently.

"Who? Lanny *who*?" My curiosity stayed me. Important somehow to understand.

"Zak's dad of course! Not *me*! Never pretty for *me*! After she left, I put on her lipstick and saw what she saw. Once, she found me and screamed, "you filthy little bugger! My expensive lipstick!" She took it and smeared it all over my face till I looked like I was bleeding! It broke off, and fell on the rug and I smashed it with my foot and rubbed it in—I *hated* her!"

"Lanny. Don't."

He turned cold pale eyes on me. The moon, bright enough to read by, shone on his face. His pupils were tiny dots. Dark rims about pale irises, more pronounced, as if his eyes had no color, blind to surroundings…only his deep sick thoughts.

He had changed again, like whiplash. One second a cloying little child, the next a calculating madman.

"I used this white elephant whenever I wanted." He threw a belittling look at my puzzled stare. "Did ya guess? Probably not. Too concerned old Uncle Dez might not leave you the lot, to abandon the old fart."

I looked at him confused. *How*?

He chuckled. "Sorry, Meg, to stomp on your pathetic *dreams!* Truly." He smirked. "Yet you comprehend with you *dead,* I'll retain my secret. *Oops!*"

He put his other hand—bloody I noted, to his mouth, staining his lips leaving a weird imprint much like a lipstick as he complacently continued. "A *private* surgery? The *divine pattern* here? A scientist *needs* to experiment. To have space and solitude to perfect his brilliance—his technique! His signature!"

The senseless tirade he spewed was surreal. Was it the slow starvation? Or something deeper-rooted than a famished brain. Then, recalled the glass in the sink. The other signs—the recent newspapers in the kindling box. The hard rock of cheese in the old Kelvanator.

He had been here. Doing God knows what. In my house! A small part of me angered.

"Technique!" I exploded. "That was butchery! Sadistic torture! You aren't a revolutionary scientist. You made no more breakthroughs, than—than Dr. Mengele!"

His face flooded with resentment and flashing awareness of whom I meant. Dr. Mengele...Doctor Death, notorious Nazi pseudoscientist with his hideous experiments on twins and prisoners, all kinds, all races, culled from death camps to add to his notorious resume.

"The world will never miss my subjects in the name of science!" His spittle was on my face as he tried to hold me in thrall with words tumbling out, eager for freedom like sick birds too long caged. Zak was still out there slowly freezing to death. This conversation in a dark kitchen was surreal as he kept babbling on.

"It seems despite my best care, too many little mums went to their reward. Ah well. One less hooker. That bitch at the clinic? Her brat? If it survived and believe you me, I made sure it passed from this coil of intestines, called *life*...would be a cheap *whore* exactly like Ma...!

Her ma!" He corrected. "Two for one, I'd say." He giggled a high-pitched whinny, winked, and looked to the Great Room.

Mercurially his face clouded over like the bitter sky outside.

"And then, *they* sent someone *after* me! Me! I took care I of *him*. Filthy meddling cop!"

I scowled. "Lance! What filthy cop?" He made negligent wave, muttering cryptically, "Animals..."

I pried fingers from my arm. In his tirade he did not notice. I backed, hardly caring where my feet took me, swiveling to keep him in view as my brother paced. Lance somehow steered me from freedom. I edged past the table, realizing he herded me to the cellar. Maybe I could latch it and crawl out the coal chute, or get the slant door open. But then he'd be waiting. I looked down. The bleeding had stopped again, but then I thought with resentment, all he had were two painful stab wounds.

I did not see Lance haul off with his good hand, walloping my cheek. "Are you listening!"

My bad leg gave way. I staggered. My feet tangled. I crashed against the old Kelvinator fridge hardly feeling my head bouncing off the old icebox, solid as Mount Rushmore. Red stars, white zigzags pulsed behind my eyes. Scarcely felt myself slipping, or my neck bending, or cheek burning as it slid down the slick enamel until I slumped, nearly oblivious, bloodied and still with my neck unnaturally twisted.

When I came to in a red fog, all came roaring back. Lance collapsed to his knees. Skidding across the linoleum, shook me, then jumped up, spinning in wobbly circles, tearing off his cap, ripping at greasy hair. He returned, jostling, and poking, like a mean child wanting someone to play with. "Magpie! Wake up. Don't leave me. Meg-*giiiie*! Dammit! You all *leave*."

He flung me back on the floor. My head bounced. I had to get away. I had to check Zak.

I felt light behind closed eyes, heat on my face, frightening no matter how welcoming. Fluttering my lids, I groaned even as I told myself to lie still. *Too late.* Lance held a candle to my nose. He touched my forehead coming away bloody.

"Hey!" Lance grinned all foolish and sloppy. "You're awake! Hey, Magpie! Didn't mean to jimmy the brakes! I'd *never* hurt Ma!"

Gibberish again. *"Brakes?"* I slurred. I shifted away using elbows, heels, and skinny butt. Lance investigated something in the distance seeing only what he could see. "Only four," Lance chuckled.

You are only four now, I thought groggily. *Where's Zak? Oh God, had to get out to him. Get away from this madman who used to be my brother.*

"Cute as a button, sharp as vinegar, Flo always said. That's me." He grinned happily. "Little Lance. Named the car after me. Ma was so pretty. All the men watched her, Meggie Anne."

My head thumped in rhythm to my blood. Going all woozy again, fighting to stay sentient. Lance struck me. My bruised temple hit the stone wall of the fridge once more. Lance knelt turning my face this way and that. I sensed a slow trickle of warm blood from my ear. I kept my eyes closed. Maybe he'd leave. Get bored—distracted.

"Wake up! Wake up, Meggie!" I felt my body lifted. Unable to do anything about it.

"Damn it. You ruin *everything*!" The thin wolfish

face had a curious mixture of childish petulance. "You kept that old bastard alive even when I took his puke-y, smelly dog!" Lance's words burned like acid.

"You killed Lolly? You fiddled the brakes?" I mumbled, numbed with the ringing in my head. "Mom and Dad, they all died because of—you, Lanny?" Lance's words burned like acid. My head hurt as if a hammer pounded my skull. Had to stay awake. In my grogginess, I calculated how far the door, how near Lance. The ax in the drainboard sunk deep. It seemed an impossible equation. Zak in the snow. Dying. Surviving meant moving, for both of us. So easy—*just lie here*, fighting my eyelids closing to blessed oblivion, but could not help hearing the ugly words. My brother's voice—a buzz through cotton.

"Years from now they'll place a plaque!"

Between my lashes I could see Lance parade around the kitchen table in triumph, I willed myself to move.

"Pilgrimages in my honor!" How could he be so active? He *must* be weakening. Feeling *pain*. Then, remembered his pharmacopeia, thinking bitterly of the medication he had accesses to. Pain stoppers, stimulants, and antibiotics somewhere in his stash. Tediously, I slid up the white wall as his back was turned, bracing against the old fridge, sucking a breath at throbbing shooting down my leg. I had to move. I could not wait for his next mood swing.

There. The spike of ache even helped.

Lance lasered those pale ghost eyes suspiciously on me.

"Yes. So right, Lance. No one gave you credit, Lance dearest. Your head. Rest," I soothed. "You didn't kill that mother. She died in the hospital. You wouldn't kill our mom and dad…"

He smirked. Eyeing me closely, he went off on a different tirade, lips curled in outrage. "Bed and breakfast! I can see it now! You and Zak raking in the dough, *laughing* at me behind my back!"

My heart thudded. With no strength in my legs, I slipped back down.

"….rich trash!" I heard the words roaring through my head. "Slumming the backwoods, guzzling vintage wine costing more than the clinic scams in a good month! I don't think so! You *dense*! Think I'd really let you do that!" He kicked me. Thank God he was so attached to those old sneakers, I thought, groggily focusing up the white glacier of the old Kelvinator. Drawing on a will from no place I recognized, I hitched away on my elbows, while Lance paced, still raging. I could not placate him. Hopeless even if he stayed on the same subject. If Zak and I had any chance at all, if Zak were alive, or—*dead*, I must see to him. Gain an ally no matter how unlikely. *The devil you know…*

Almost at the door.

I winced at Lance's enraged bellow, followed by racing sneakers, squeaking across the linoleum as he rushed over, kicking at me. My arm shot for his ankle.

He stomped on my hand. I yelped, wrenching it free.

"Ain't going far, Maggoty Anne! *Morgue maybe!*" His giggle sent new ice down my spine like the claws of skittering frozen rats.

"Gotta makeshift morgue inna boathouse. Keep Zak company," Lance chortled. "Only he don't look so *hot* now. May not fancy Old Zak no more. May not have the *hots* for old Zach-er-y when I get through! Don't go nowheres now, *Maggoty Anne*."

He banged out the door catching my side. I curled my knees to my chest willing myself up.

"I'll be back for ya!" He giggled and barged through the old screen ripping it from hinges. I watched him lope across the yard to the boathouse.

I moaned clutching the frame. *Dear God, what had he done while I was out?*

Chapter 34

Squall Lines

Zak lay flat on a plank trestle table littered with old fish scales as if he were an ancient king set on his funeral pyre, surrounded by elderly cross-country skis with rusting clamps and dried leather straps, frayed rope, empty tins, a splintered oar, broken creels, a cracked Coleman lantern hanging overhead and from boathouse walls.

He eyed them where he lay in and out of torpor wondering if they could be of any use. His chest leaked frothy blood welling around the broken shaft that dripped onto a canoe in a steady *plink-plink;* not used since childhood a thousand years ago, upended and stored beneath the scaling station.

Lance watched carefully until the tortured rise and fall of Zak's chest resumed, reluctant as a cart pulling a load of iron ore.

Lance hopped foot to foot blowing on his hands. "Hot damn! I'm good."

Fog crystals leaked from Zak's mouth. He whispered, *"Meg...?"*

Lance, admiring his handiwork muttered distractedly, flapping a dismissive hand. "Dead, departed, gone, history..." Zak breathed a shuddering sigh, until Lance twisted the shaft, releasing more blood and Zak too, at least from pain, as his body stiffened and slumped.

****

I crouched beneath the boathouse window facing the house. How I got there, I couldn't say. Yet, the outrages of mind and body lent fire to my soul; I no longer cared if Lance was sick or dangerous. My rage was incandescent. I would end his reign of horror.

I ducked, fearing my haunted face showed through the dirty window as Lance banged out heading to the house, muttering as if he'd forgotten something.

Groping the dark, I slipped inside.

A bloody hand shot out.

Silencing a shriek, breathing joyful thanks with the memory of that strong hand ingrained in my flesh, I made out Zak curled on his side, *and alive* on the old fish-scaling table. He gazed up. I did not comprehend if he saw me or the other world he would soon enter. His striking face held the wounded pain of a martyred saint.

"Go. Go. Hurry. Get outta here," Zak hissed between gasps. His hand dropped as he half-rolled. "Gimme somethin', Meg. Weapon…anything," he cried fitfully tugging at the broken shaft. "The arrow! I can…"

I stayed his hand. "Don't be silly! You'll bleed to death. Stop it!" His head wasn't right. Too much blood lost. I checked the glistening pool, black and spreading. I was stepping in it.

"Sweet little Nutmeg," Zak slurred almost incomprehensibly. "Run. Anywhere. Tried to hide all weapons…"

"And the rest are in the cellar my darling. I can't get them!" My mind scrambled to find a way. *Enter the house, run into Lance. Or make it to the cellar, maybe I could not get out the slant door. Snow maybe piled…*

Lance could lock the kitchen door. All these thoughts tumbled through my head like ping pong balls.

Damn my brother!

Zak's eyes closed. I leaned closer hearing the *plink-plink* on something wooden. As my sight strengthened, I scanned the flotsam hanging on boathouse walls. Surely there was something. A weapon. I scanned a broken oar, cursing. It lay across rafters far above my head. I would need to disturb Zak to reach it.

I scarce heard him.

"Girl. More'n one. Dead in...woods," he gasped out.

"Shhhh, darling, save your strength." The moon slanted a glow, white as artic breath wafting too faint from Zak's lips. I closed my eyes after seeing a widening pool of froth on his chest. *A stupid thing to say.* Lance pierced his lung. He was dying. Nothing I could do. Vaguely, I understood compression worked but would that help, or hurt if I bound his chest, or was that specifically with a bleeding wound? Keep him talking. My thoughts skittered like mice in a maze. I checked the open door expecting Lance there gloating. He'd be back soon.

"I know. Lance is sick. Debbi. He took her somewhere...and..." I was babbling and every second, brought us closer to Lance's madness and final solution. I dared check the house. Was he outside listening?

"No. Sweet Meggie. Me. Least—did that much..." His words were so faint I needed to put my ear to his lips.

I jerked my head back. "What? But where?" I watched him befuddled. And why now... when there was so much...? Then, impatient—"Oh, don't talk!" I nuzzled his forehead, smoothing his hair. "We *have* to go, darling. Can you sit?" *Where? Where would we go?* I ran to the window. Still no Lance. A blessing. Perhaps he forgot us! In passing I registered the dark blur of the old hunter's blind smudging the lake through the dusty window, but my mind remained blank as mounds of snow, yet chaotic as the interior of the boat house.

I tried lifting Zak. *If I could sneak him back into the house...* A dead weight. The arrow kept him half on his side. I dared not roll him off. I could never catch him.

"She was so worrying you..." His whisper was a snowflake caught in the wind luring me back. "But—where? We looked."

Zak managed a crooked smile turning my knees to mush. "Under the canoe. Under me." His arm swung down. "Not even Lance knows."

"You put Debbi's body under the canoe?"

He grimaced and moaned. But weaker. His breathing hitched like a broken wagon dragged by a child—then stopped. My heart stopped too. No!

His breathing resumed with a strangled wheeze.

"My darling, shhh. Don't say more. Doesn't matter." *My dearest love.* I murmured pressing cold lips against his shockingly chill forehead. I wanted to give him a lifetime of love. All his heart could hold these last precious seconds, if that was all allotted us.

"Where else are you hurt?" I asked stupidly. Frenziedly roamed my hands over his body. Perhaps I could still stem the low tide of death. They came away bloody from his side. Where was the other wound, again? So cold. So hungry… I searched the walls for a bludgeon, raking the interior, wailing, "I have to find something to stop him."

I felt a touch and looked up. Zak caressed my

wounded forehead. His hand dropped. He coughed reddish foam and went silent.

My own face twisted in anguish as my beloved slumped with a horrible indrawn breath—*saws on files*—at the same time, my ears tuned to a door slam. I watched my beloved's white agonized face, waiting for him to take another hitching breath long costly seconds. His face smoothed like a sleeping angel.

Lance's crunching footsteps neared.

Zak's face remained still. His chest didn't move.

"Love you too, Zak. Always have," I whispered. "Always will."

****

I listened with senses quivering like a bloodhound on a short leash.

Wind shrieking between the boathouse and my monster of Victoriana, masked sounds, *but I knew. I knew.* I ran to the window. Still wearing his heavy black coat, Lance dragged the yellow plastic bag with saws and tools of death. His pocket drooped. I saw the sharp fins of the heavy brass Lancette replica poking out, dragging the pocket down. It must weigh ten pounds at least.

I braced for what must come. What I *must* do.

"He can't hurt you anymore, my darling, my dearest Zachary. Zak my darling, my love..." Tears froze as I kissed his already chilling face for the last time. "It's me, he's after. I will get him! I will get him for you, my *darling!*" I drank in his arresting face one last time as if packing in a lifetime of memories, even if those were only to last a few moments, a few more hours.

I had few options. Hah, that was a laugh, yet from my last reserves the strong force of life took hold. I dug deep without realizing. I would *not* give the final victory to Lance, already searching—searching, my gaze desperately roving the walls.

Frenziedly, I raked broken creels and bait buckets for what I half-noted earlier. *Where were they!* As if waiting all these years for precisely this one time. My gaze tracked back. Ancient cross-country skis and poles, hung half concealed, tangled in fish net—the tip of one was cracked, I recalled Uncle saying long ago, "*digging the snow gliding forward if you don't keep your toe elevated*"— One pole had a broken leather strap. Somehow, the dry old skis escaped burning. A wisp of hope lifted my despair.

Yanking them from dusty moorings, stifling a sneeze, I rummaged a rusting tin of wax from among frozen paint cans, and shoving against the small side exit nipped out as Lance banged through the other door; immediately blown sideways in a wind slamming across the lake clean from the prison camp. I crouched, pressing the door closed, prying frantically at the tin with a rusted-in-place key. It snapped off. *Seconds ticking.* I dug nails under the brittle metal rim. With a mighty pull, the lid popped in a spray of rust; desperately scraping the withered pad across the old wax, I furiously rubbed it along the length of the desiccated old skis, that hadn't seen duty since Uncle Dez was young.

The wax was hard and dry, slowly warming with friction caused by my tired arms feeling like they would drop off, but I kept sweeping the whole long length. My heart fluttered a beat at the notion I might not be able to use them. They were too long. Longer than my body. Thin. Racing skis. The narrow, curved tip *was* cracked. I'd need to lift my foot higher than the snow with each lurch forward. I felt sick at my stomach. I had no choice, aware Lance raved unintelligibly inside, banging into things. I had to try. Clamping the stubborn clasps over my shoes with trembling fingers, I backed into a shapeless mound with a sharp metal edge, realizing with a pang it was the Ranger's truck poking out of the drift, forgetting it, as I swung the too-long skis over the sea wall, and slithered on my rump to the broad icy plains of Convict Lake.

Crouched below the rip-rap wall, I heard Lance's voice, querulous, then with increasing panic and rage against a background of cursing and crashing of old paint tins and breaking lantern glass. He bellowed, demanding me show myself. "*Meeeeggggie!*"

I thrust my good leg forward; the lake boomed, creaked, and thundered its welcome or warning. At first, the skis wouldn't budge…then friction finally took hold sliding me in fits and starts. My bad leg already protested. Blessedly the wax warmed and the cracked tip didn't seem to hinder as I seamlessly slid twenty feet out.

I paused and looked at the endless expanse, of glittering, windswept ice, ridged with waves of frozen snow evaporating into the mist before me, to see the best route. I would have to ski between valleys of ridges, at least when the track was long enough to accommodate the man-sized skis. Uncle was a big man, I mourned. These were meant for a body at least six feet, and I barely five four, changing direction with the too-long skis in a rough zig-zag as wind had arbitrarily scoured the ice refreezing into dagger-sharp peaks.

Yet night was a friend. Darkness and mist would swallow me up.

I hoped.

I looked behind me.

Good! Lance stormed back inside. I was seemingly forgotten. *Don't think what he was doing.* I had no time. I must hide myself, vanish into snow fog rising from the ice.

****

Lance halted, distracted. Ripping the Patagonia jacket, slicing the sweater beneath, teased a scalpel up Zak's throat and down his chest, and back, admiring his work when a scarlet line trickled when he misjudged, lingering the blade over Zak's model perfect face, even in privation.

Perhaps sensing the alien coldness, Zak stirred, widening his eyes, batting the scalpel away and trying mightily to rise.

"Oh! You awake? Fan*tas*tic!" Lance clapped his hands, chortling and hopping about as if unable to contain himself. "What'll it be, Zak! Plastic surgery? No time like the present! Hey, I got it! An autopsy! How 'bout *that*? Never done autopsies before!"

Lance inspected Zak on the table with great satisfaction.

His face drooped beneath the mob cap.

"Oh wait, you're not dead, yet." He spoke as if pondering a weighty problem. "I can fix that—or, maybe not."

Knocking his bloody fist against his chin, Lance chuckled. "Might be fun, though— performing a *premature* autopsy, at that. Too bad I ain't got no anesthetic."

****

My elderly skis hit a patch of mush-ice stopping my forward slide *cold.* Not to pitch arse over teakettle, I favored my bad side falling instead, twisting my leg, and in doing so, out-cried; I clapped a fist still gripping the pole, over my mouth, but not soon enough.

Ginger! Another wrist strap broke, too. I stifled a cry. I had to grip extra hard, not allowing the pole to fly free as I swung it ahead of me, to dig in.

****

In the boathouse, Lance held the scalpel aloft; turning with elation, eyes wide, he rushed the door, calling out gleefully.

"Me—eg? Is you is, or is you ain't? Clever little *slutcunt*! *Where are you*!" He sing-songed. "Let's pla-*a-a-y*!"

Light shone like mercury off Lance's scalpel. Mesmerized by its unholy gleam, Lance's face turned beatific; raising it high as if a devotion. His face darkened. Reluctantly slipping the sharp blade next to the Lancette replica sticking from his deep pocket, he stalked the seawall. His face took on a crafty cast.

"Hey, Magpie? Maggoty Anne? NutMeggie, Scut-Meggie," he sang out. "Come back. Let's play. Remember? *I cut off their heads*!" Lance chortled as if that were the cleverest joke ever.

"I CUT THEIR HEADS OFF!"

Still holding the scalpel, Lance raced out, avidly searching the endless shimmering lake—at last spying Meggie as she dug poles in and clumsily regained her seat above the skis.

"I spy!" His voice rang over the lake until it snuffed out in muffling layers of cold mist.

****

Hitching and dragging, I thrust my poles deep, hitting hard smooth ice, I sprang forward as much as the dry old skis allowed, thanking God I had not worn my fur but traded it for one of Lance's bulky sweaters over my own collection. Snow mist might hide me the deeper I traveled if I could outrace a moon threatening to peep beyond the cloud cover. I might be invisible—*and forgotten?*

Lance was that unpredictable.

Too late. The full platinum moon slid from clouds spotlighting me.

Lance's renewed entreaties skated across the glassy surface. I flinched but renewed thrusting and gliding with the broken poles with a vigor I had to reach deep for. Harder with each push, weak from hunger and with slush build-up forming crusts on the bottom of the runners, I had zero reserve. Even so, half my thoughts were behind me.

WasZakdarlingZakbelovedZak dead? Left to die alone at Lance's whims? Lance was truly insane, not from privation but cracked like a nut. I had no idea how cracked.

Thanks to dried-out runners I continued to ski clumsily, with intermittent drag stopping me cruelly short. My arm sockets took the brunt. It took every ounce of waning energy to force one foot ahead, and dig the poles, sometimes into crust, ofttimes into tooth-jarring wind-ridges of refrozen slush—still I poled, keeping prison lights in view, my only hope now, even if I expired on the lake. How far, I could only guess, shamed I hadn't tried for the prison long ago while I still had strength, *storms be damned.* But then, privation caught up with us all with the inrushing tide of whiteouts.

****

The hunter's blind, spiky with firs, was dead ahead. A wee bit closer with each shushing sound beneath my reluctant feet. My leg had transformed from searing throbbing pain to dull aching numbness, but still working, loosening up even. A brief hope of refuge—the black foreboding blot loomed, yet was it far enough off from Lance, even if I made it? Would Lance be fooled? Of course not. He'd need rest, as did I. He'd tear the place apart. If he came after me. I dared not look back, for that would make it so.

A minute or two stop can't hurt. Sucking in searing air, I drooped over the poles. The dark, as the moon once again slid back into its envelope of cloud almost swallowed my dwindling figure, *but not quite.*

Lance is coming.

Floundering, slithering in his sneakers off the seawall, insane rage lending him strength, he plowed relentlessly through drifts. I could *feel* him. Then hear him.

I looked back once. Broad curving windswept swatches where ice scoured bare, lay in random patterns ahead of him, too. If I thought that would stop him in his slick sneakers, I was wrong. Lance struggled in pursuit. No finesse, legs sliding apart, black coat flapping, dragging at him had he presence of mind—the sanity or logic, to shrug it off.

Savagely thinking—*that coat could slow him down*—I plunged my poles, with new vigor, feeling my heart's rapid thud in my chest and cold sear my lungs shoving, dragging the heavy skis, picking up more slush no matter how I veered around gray spring-fed mush holes, dreading those small detours. My feet were pounds heavier. My bad leg ached like a tooth now. I could go faster if I *removed* the skis. Kneeling on snow crust, like kneeling on a tray of ice-cubes, I wriggled the rusty fasteners. Any other time, they would fall off, now they stuck to boots like crazy glue.

Looking over my shoulder, I made out my brother's slipping flapping approach, audible curses, and labored breathing. He hunched once holding his side. I wondered at his forbearance. It must be like mine, born of desperation.

I gave up the fasteners. My limp was pronounced now, lurching with one foot, dragging the other, hands welded with cold to the poles. Slurry added two more inches to my poorly waxed runners, then a patch of slick ice gleamed lavender ahead where refrozen slush formed gritty ridges, sharp as sabers. I scraped the skis back and forth breaking off chunks.

Renewed, I slid forward with a satisfying, *whoosh swoosh*...wind blessedly veered behind me, as if a strong hand pressed my shoulder blades shoving me ahead.

"Damaged goods, Maggoty-Anne!"

I lurched.

Sugar! Too close!

"Ya won't make the blind! Bet your leg's fallin' off, *Nut*meg!"

Furious I didn't give up; Lance's voice rose to a screech. "It's *over*, bitch! I'll cut you up right there on the ice! You see I will! Can't ski worth crap. Your leg burns like hell-fire! Think I don't get it! Don't ya feel it!" Followed by an insane cackle.

Too well! I risked a look. Lance resembled a giant bat, black coat sailplaning behind him above the lake's sharp shadowed ridges.

I felt a *snap*. My foot lightened sinking in cold mush, while a ski flew off skittering across a slick. I pitched grimly on *with no wings at all*, skied with one leg and trotted desperately with the other—yet heartened. Behind me, random ice patches made Lance's sneakers treacherous, his swearing lightened my burden as he slid in leg-splitting dances and sideways listings.

Even as I looked back, one leg went out from under, feeling the shudder of ice radiating toward me from his hard tumble. Not in danger of falling though, *nor was I, I hoped,* yet with icy water and freezing mush encasing his sneakered feet, it might even things. For once he seemed too occupied to hurl curses. I curved a frozen smile.

Blessedly, the wind still sheered from behind pushing me along with its welcome hand on my back. I could not see beyond the derelict hunter's blind, it was that close, *making love to the dark lumpy shape, no more than twenty feet off now.* Here, at least I could make a stand.

I bit my wooden lips. Perhaps I *should* circle and make for the camp. It would slow him perhaps a precious half hour, while he searched. If he did not spy me going round. Maddeningly, the prison lights glittering off to the right seemed no closer. I'd never make it without a rest.

Oh, and you can now?

Abruptly looming out of the snow fog, I made out the car-sized boulders sheltering a ragged, roughly round shoreline making the decision for me. My haven boasted clumps of half-dead wind stunted trees thrust like skeletons through a silken veil of mist. In the snow-blasted log shack, surrounded by the detritus of hunters and squatters, I saw not a trap, but possibilities. Hope against hope, Lance can't make me out against the dark island.

But where else would I go?

I froze, dispirited. *Feet slapping ice behind me had a more determined sound.* With my last strength, I poled to the rocky limb-strewn shore. By my brother's heavy wheezing, slick sneakers and flapping coat, my only hope was he was handicapped as me as I clawed and clambered the rocks, brittle cold beneath my bare hands, keeping my profile low.

Scrambling behind a boulder the size of a Volkswagen, I rid myself of the clumsy ski, dragging it as a weapon. Spying a discernable cleft, I wriggled through and up the slight rise to the listing cabin with bark scaling off in leprous spots, surrounded, save for the front, by ragged wind-worn firs scratching out messages in the wind.

"Meg-gie!"

It was almost Lance's voice again. *My brother, whom I knew well, had played with, my ally...He seemed to need help in his old way. Like when he fell from trees—or cut his finger.* Then, I heard the thud and wail of pain and fury.

****

Stunned, with sludge weighting wet sneakers and his legs still covered in soggy navy corduroy and numbed to the knees, Lance willed himself up, his rage incendiary, overriding any weakness, his thoughts black and cold as ice. *All Meggie's fault!*

Fall forward, crawl a piece, slither up, stagger to his knees. His feet were bricks burning with frostbite. Hands like hamburger set out to thaw, aware too of his freaking coat. Wet and heavy from falling and the hefty Lancette replica weights him too, making him veer left and he can't wriggle it free from his ragged pocket lining.

In short, miserable, and misery rekindled Lance's

fury. A mindless beast with claws and teeth slavering to rip and tear...*and his prey in up there*! In that cabin. Gone, nostalgic memories of sailing out on their little skiff, playing pirate and pioneer trappers, or fighting Indians. With wrath spurring him, keeping the derelict hunter's cabin in red-eyed focus, Lance finally reached the boulder-blocked shore.

Maggoty-Anne thought she could outfox him. He saw her puny figure drag up these same boulders. Thought she could barricade the blind. He recalled how rotten it was. Even more so now, these years later. He chuckled at her stupidity. Her trust. She made it too easy. How much fun was that?

Maggoty-Anne, the boring.

Chapter 35

Black Water

I dragged the door, hanging on leather hinges, closed, one dangling so it swung aslant, dropping the bar into the wooden slot anyway, and frantically raked the one room for anything to defend myself, besides ski poles.

Moonlight pierced a gap in the roof sadly revealing a crumbling river rock fireplace, litter of broken ammo boxes, a single chair, moth-eaten fur of some kind before the hearth and a badly listing dusty table, holding a battered tin plate. Evidences of raccoons, possums, rats, and birds littered the floor with scat and tufts of fur and feathers.

I rammed the rickety chair under the latch realizing the hut was holey as a colander, but stacked mossy ammo boxes over the two windows across from each other anyway, not glass even, but covered with rotting shutters. A baby could break in. Sugar! I should have dragged the ski in too. Where was it? Must have left it, I feared, as I opened the door searching for it. One more weapon for Lance.

I dropped the warped shutter bars in place, even as Lance *thumped* the same door, heard a fumbling of the latch, followed by a sharp *clunk*; Lance apparently chucked a rock at it. I grabbed my own stone tumbled from the fireplace to the hearth, waiting with it in hand, crouched inside the fireplace with the ghost of old ashes acrid in my nose, listening to Lance sniffing about the cabin, like an animal. The shutters rattled, viewing his passing figure, the great coat, through chinks. I heard whistling breath.

I am his prey.

The crisp crunch of snow over dead weeds halted again at the door.

A minute—two long minutes passed as I counted heart beats thudding against my ribs, then the old door shook, but the chair, that *beautiful* chair shuddered and held fast against the splintered floor.

"Magpie! I know you are *in* there! Might as well give up. It'll be worse for ya!" Heavy breathing, a chaffing of rough dry hands. "Nah, only kiddin'. Come on. You know me! I'm your bro for Crissake. We're playin'! Bout time, right! Let me in now! Way too serious."

Like a heart attack.

A fist or chunk of wood thudded the old logs. I detected a resumption of footfalls tromping the perimeter, jumping away from shutters; wood rendered with a *squeal* of nails—wouldn't take long for bars to snap or damp wood slots to wrench free of rusty brads fixing them to the logs—*ending in silence.* More tramping feet and snuffling, like an animal sniffing for a way in, when *squealing* renewed at the other window. A muffled *crack* of wet wood and a slat ripped free.

Bracing the remaining slats, I jerked back. An eye glittered between the crack. Spying me, Lance giggled, high pitched, wound-up, followed by renewed pulling sounds, but the shutter held fast. I retreated deep into the blacken maw of the fireplace. Ashes wafted up, soot pattered down, acrid clouds made me sneeze. I heard muted evil laughter, but I couldn't hear from *where* or where stealthy scrabbling came from next, either, until dust drifted down. Clods of earthen matter; damp moss and dead leaves pelted the rough floorboards like dirty rain. I scanned the ceiling. The ceiling *was* the roof. I could see stars. *He climbed the logs like a ladder.* I detected the muffled scrape of knees and feet on rotted spongy moss shingles overhead.

My hands scrabbled through the ashes, feeling another fist-size rock fallen from the shaft and a rusted rebar most likely used as a poker.

"*He's up there, stomping the roof,*" I muttered. "*Jumping* on it."

The roof shook. *Thud! Thump! Thud!* Chaff fell on my face, in my eyes. For a moment, I visualized him crashing through the flimsy bowed rafters. Hefting the rock, I hoped I didn't have to use—that Lance woke from his homicidal rage and saw me for his sister, and not prey.

All quiet. *Calculating quiet.*

I spun to the door at another sound, where I did not expect one. A tiny *chink*. Did the bar slightly lift? I tiptoed over clutching the stone wincing as my foot hit a bent fork, skittering it tinnily across floorboards. I heard giggles. I put my face to a crack. A sharp blade probed the same split in the old weathered wood. I fell back, chilled with sweat, right before the blade pierced my eye, actually nicking my eyelid. Lance meant business despite his jolly childish manners. Well, so could I, the business of staying alive. Wasn't that what Zak said, a thousand years ago? My heart broke at the thought. Zak, alone, cold, and dead. *Yes, he would leave a good-looking corpse.* Tears streaked my face.

Can't cry now...

Shaking with dread, I clumsily backed, ducking as the tough leather hinges shot rusty nails to the floor.

The rickety chair exploded, shooting splinters across the room... and Lance burst through.

His hollow eyes stared from murderous black holes. Knees bent, arms crookt, hands flexing for the kill, he spat, "Bitch! Got ya!"

"Lanny. Please. Don't! Think what you're doing! It's me. Meggie...your *Nutmeg!*"

With an animal growl deep in his throat, or a mind gone primitive, Lance responded. "Been thinkin' about you for years...*watching* you'n Zak cut me out. Always *you! Poor little Meggie.* Let's give Magpie a sweet place to *live*—a cushy *job.* A generous *stipend* from old Uncle Dez!" Lance snarled. "Oh, *so sorry.* Did you want to attend *college*? No moolah left for college, *Lance Boy!* And that last loan to Zak... "

Before I could back far enough—I had nowhere to run, I tore from Lance, stumbling back into the fireplace to peer, out of desperation, up the narrow black hole of crumbling river rock forming the chimney—too small even for me to wedge myself up.

Lance laughed like a clogged drain and launched himself, hands in claws with nails grown long and jagged in our confinement, and ready for the slaughter. One rake would cut my cheek open.

I realized I still held the rock. I raised it. He stopped. His face held fiendish amusement *this should be good*—and looked at it scornful. With his longer arm, he dashed it aside, fumbling his pocket with his other hand for the scalpel.

As I pressed deeper, I watched the arc of his glittering lethal instrument slash the air in short quick jabs, and wild side-swings, closing my eyes, awaited the unescapable, trapped with my back to the sooty fire wall. He sniggered in triumph. How stupid I was. Not only my leg was lame. No wonder Lance had no respect. "Please, Lanny," I whimpered. "Please!" How pathetic even to my ears, yearning to take back my bleating words.

He was almost on me, making swishing stabbing motions, with great theater—*he was savoring this* and a mouth stretched in a lip-splitting grin, teeth stained as a rat's, I saw. How appropriate.

Abruptly with a cry from Lance, I watched him uncomprehendingly trip forward as if flying, with his hands out-spread. Then, bemused I saw one of my brother's sneakers caught on a rough-cut floorboard. As kids we trod upon them for so many summers, we always managed to avoid those, all aware of lethal planks with rusty nail heads sticking up to snag a bare foot, or cut a toe, with vague warnings ringing in the back of our juvenile brains, of ugly tetanus shots to come.

My brother forgot *Old Nasty*, sticking up a full inch, more so than long ago, the nail even rustier, and more snaggled. Lance tripped, *hard,* overcompensating, thudded heavily sideways on his hip. His other foot, crossing over to balance himself in a lost cause, plunged through the broken chair's rush-bottom seat with a vengeance. The chair and Lance hopelessly entangled, tipped sideways, crashing to the floor.

I coughed from dislodged soot flaking down and struggled out of the cavern, edging sideways along the rough walls.

Lance struggled to his feet, frantically striving to kick the chair loose, but the old rush webbing ensnared Lance's leg like a bear trap.

I giggled pointing as he hobbled furiously dragging it. *The shoe was on the other foot now.* Lance hopped about, snarling, cursing, shaking his foot like a dog attacked him with the chair still cumbersomely gnawing his leg. Tromping on it with his free foot, he tried to walk the other out, instead, fatally stumbled over the remaining three legs, and the one broken rung.

After a period of suspension, with arms windmilling, Lance crashed heavily to the floor with the chair bottom rammed deep in his midriff. I heard the brittle rush break free. Heedless, never taking mortified yet deadly eyes, off me, Lance lurched up without thought—and that was his fatal undoing.

In place of dropping, and releasing his leg, the chair twisted, skittering sideways, striking his shin as he stepped over it, and snagging a high-top sneaker's rubbery toe.

Curious, so humble a defense should be part of his undoing.

If we had a crystal ball, I'm certain, Lance would have made a bonfire out of that lethal chair, lying in wait all those years long ago, for—at this second tumble, the splintered shaft jabbed deep in his inner thigh. So focused on me, Lance ignored the jagged shard sticking from his groin and hot blood pouring down his pant leg until I pointed, one hand over my mouth to stifle—not *horror,* dear reader, if any should peruse *my* diary…but *a laugh.*

****

A laugh, instantly chilling with its pitilessness, I am

certain, looking back.

Distracted, distantly puzzled, Lance looked down at the jagged splinter with part of the chair leg still attached forming a jagged *T*, and jutting rudely between his coat flaps. Perhaps puzzled because he could not walk.

His right leg could not move forward without jamming the rung, attached to the wreck of the chair, deeper in his thigh. He howled in the torment of frustration, more than pain, it seemed, as he mindlessly tugged, gripping the rung in a race against pain—against reason. He knew better. He was a doctor. Of sorts.

I was still laughing *and pointing!* Not hysteria or horror. I saw him look at me with his face twisted in befuddled torment. Didn't I comprehend all too well! Lance looking bewildered, hobbled toward me holding out his hand, beseeching.

Then, the medic took over; he realized he could not release the flood, clearly as Zak could not yank out the arrow. He can't free the rung or he'll die.

"I'm in trouble here, Meggie! Get your butt over here!" It was a strangled demand. I watched him lurch doggedly after me, when I, still laughing, didn't back-peddle fast enough. He shambled after, leaking blood, hauling the fragments of chair with him bellowing in torment as his leg, with the spiky rung, hit all surfaces, as I danced around him.

Still getting my own back, I skirted one last time, then made for the door.

Lance striving to change directions, took another tumble, landing the last minute on his good side, but heavy, on his shoulder; fighting to rise—to reach me without knocking the ragged shaft against *anything*—whimpering, crawling, he couldn't keep the splinter from scraping and banging the floor, howling at each contact. Through all this, Lance still clung to the scalpel; using the tough steel, he stabbed the rotted old boards to haul himself toward me.

Lance made it to his knees. Trapped inside his coat, he yanked it out from under with another howl. The last part of the chair broke away, leaving the rung-sized spike, still embedded in his groin. He grinned wolfishly, one fist around the rung, like he was itching to jerk it out and use it on me. He hobbled ungainly—as *I* was forced to do for all my good years—*my young innocent lost years*.

To my consternation the rung hadn't hit the femoral artery. No spurting, scarcely a steady leaking and this all but stopped. Time to go.

I turned, but reached back at the last moment, savagely twisting the shaft, dancing away. He grabbed at my hand. "Meggie!" His cry was one of loss and incomprehension.

I wasn't sure I comprehended myself. I was running on fumes of hurt and revenge. I snatched my hand back in a game of keep-away, kicking at the shaft—gauging the distance, always dancing, *hobbling* rather, a hair out of reach, as I led Lanny a deadly chase to the door.

" *'Meggie?'*" He mouthed in a rictus of agony.

"Whose leg now, Lance! Who looks like hamburger? You did it to me! You and bloody, Zak!" He stopped. We stared at each other across a divide of more than the room, but years of hidden obsession, I did not realize I possessed.

"Meggie, I didn't mean it to happen that way. How could I? I wanted to *be* Zak. Kids! Just dumb kids, dammit!" He bent forward. I thought it was to catch his breath. "I felt so—bad over the years. I tried…" Lance was slowly advancing, I realized with a chill. He wasn't sorry. His face didn't match the words.

"Who needs your sympathy, loser!" I limped tantalizingly in reach. He lunged for my bad leg; landing on one knee as I twisted away the last minute. The rung skidded across the floor. His eyes rolled up in their sockets. His mouth opened in a silent scream. He seemed to swoon. Rallying, never taking a murderous gaze off me, he sucked deep breaths. Trailing blood, my brother tried to rise, tried to avoid knocking the broken shaft, still holding onto it with one hand, against *anything*.

I kicked again at the jagged splinter. My foot connected this time, sinking it deeper in his groin. Lance's face wavered between disbelief, shock and calculating evil. He sank almost to the floor moaning. I could summon no pity.

"How's it feel, Lancer? What I lived with, for years! The operations. The splints, the crutch, leg braces, the months in bed! Uncle Dez's *pity*." *Only beloved Zak came to tell jokes and bring silly presents. And Lance killed him.*

I vanished outside in swirl of sparkling snow like I was in the midst of a snow globe. I was transfixed for a moment. A glimmer of an idea formed like ice crystals on a windowpane, spreading chilling patterns of wicked design through my brain.

How best to end this?

Hunched, Lance staggered over the threshold.

Standing aside, I came from behind, shoving him hard, gazing down as if he were a particularly disgusting insect. I gripped the dropped ski pole, jabbing it repeatedly in the snow and poking at him, railing at him as he crawled."

Those tapes," I sneered. "So *stupid*! Failure! Moron! Those lame *diaries*!" I twisted my mouth. "You're a wanna-be! You don't leave a trace, you stupid moron! Amateur! You don't *need* an audience. That's how it's *done*. Secrets are more—*appetizing*, more *practical* than *any* notoriety, you clown!"

Even my leg took strength from the satisfying words and emotions, so long held back.

I stopped abruptly. I had not appreciated until then, the resentment piled up behind me like a bad car wreck. I smiled bitterly. It did me no honor to vent like this. It was weak.

"Meg?" Lance rolled over looking up with bafflement and hurt cutting though his other pain, all the while snaking for the scalpel somehow thrust back in his pocket. I saw his hand brush the chill metal of the Lancette. He looked down at his abdomen. Aghast. I saw he stupidly realized he landed on the replica's sharp fins adding to his torment. No doubt, there were two small but deep punctures in his side now. How ironic. How appropriate!

"Please! You're my sis! Said I was *sorry*!"

"Hah!" I continued, ignoring him. "Wanna be doctor. Wanna be killer! You're only a butcher! The woods, the streets! The hedgerows, ditches, the alleys of Detroit are *filled* with my handiwork! Clean and neat! Some even here, right there in the woods!"

I nudged my chin, my voice choked with disgust as I paced about him.

Even then, I bit my tongue in chagrin.

Not entirely true.

I felt bad.

The Indian was messy. He wasn't in the same league at all.

He was only hungry.

I wouldn't let Lance have that juicy information though! Even under the stressing circumstances, I had to suppress an outright chuckle. "You boys thought you were protecting me, covering him up all neat and tidy!" I giggled again at the notion. "Thank you, guys. I owe you one," I laughed. "Maybe I'll even be gentle with *you*, Lance." I sneered down at him. "Clean kills!" I continued. "Straight as you might say—as *an arrow*!" I could not help but chuckle again at my last words and his expression.

"But this was *my* place..." He almost whimpered.

I scoffed. "What do you mean, 'your place'?"

"*My* place! It was *perfect*. S-secluded. N-no one could hear screams—or if they *escaped*, where would they run? Huh? Plenty of room and time. I would have been written up in medical journals—!"

I ignored his drivel as we both poured out our grievances. I could hear my own emotion as I looked across the shimmering lake, dazzling with moonshine bouncing off the slick platinum surface.

"All those pretty...useless...*beautiful—!*" I shook my head, choking, not wishing to reveal weakness, my insecurities. With that, I backed to the lake. *Enough!* Lance might die before I had a chance at him. Smiling inwardly, I grasped that my brother holding the now bloody dripping rung steady in one hand was hobbling after me.

This might work. If not? I shrugged, perhaps we all end here. "The three damaged *mousquetaires*" of childhood.

Lance seemed to feel no pain, now. Perhaps the body was the best anesthetic after an injury. But no, it seemed more than that, so intent on me, Lance was implacable.

"So *easy,*" I hissed, backing, luring him on and on. There was a gap in the rocks for mooring boats. Clambering down to the short, exposed beach, I was already on the ice.

He lurched inexorably down the shallow shelf. I saw what he was thinking by the triumph in his eyes. *Nowhere for me to go. All he had to do was reach me!* As anger blotted out my pain, my hunger, it seemed rage blotted out the agony ripping down *his* leg and blood freezing on *his* pant leg.

As my dear brother, riveted on me, slithered on the ice I judged him. Hollow black holes for eyes, the glint of cold hatred deep in back, never wavering. My brother...my *beloved* brother holding the honed scalpel, ridged and high like a downward slicing knife.

I hitched farther onto the solid ice, leading him on. I didn't need to. Lance seemed unstoppable, ignoring misery in his zeal to—*kill* me. Slash me to ribbons, staining the ice red with my blood mingling with his own. In the ambient light the scalpel glinted a silver wink.

I looked back.

Yes, still coming. *Good. But closer. I had to hurry.* Yet, between Lance's injuries, and my damaged leg, we were a match, both on the thin edge of starvation.

"Boring really." I taunted Lance, stepping carefully backward checking over my shoulder every now and then. "Who's scared of a *cripple!* All I had to do was pick'm up," I shouted across the ice. "Can find them

anywhere…*everywhere! E*ven in *school."*

My mind flew back to the girl in the pink sweater.

One of Zak's *trophies*

His prom queen if you will! Thought she was waiting for Zak. Still smiling at the memory of her face when she saw me. Then, the bow and arrow. The pretty girl swiveled to the target and back with a sneer and an— *are you kidding*! expression.

I wasn't, she found out. I smiled again with satisfaction, even after all these years…

One of my first.

Ooops! Almost too late. Lance crept up on me. I noted also the interesting spread of blood sinking into the snow. Soon he'd need help, or bleed to death, but first…

"The woods were perfect—till *you* showed up. You and—" I hesitated"—*darling* Zak." I heard the sob in my voice. *He was dead. I could feel the emptiness. Nothing left but vengeance.* His fault showing up like that. Despoiling my sanctuary. Briefly, I saw the swinging foot and the frozen man hanging in the tree. Didn't seem like Lance's handiwork. Who had done that? My faltering mind wandered back to the forest.

Oops—almost had me. "Ah-ah-ah!' I chided, prancing backward in and out of range. "Stuck-up bitches didn't even see me till *way* late for pity parties."

I leaned putting hands on my knees to rest— *almost over*— clinically watching my brother stagger like a drunk on the ice. He actually wept. With pain, contrition, or the crocodile variety, I didn't care; he was distracted between his hand on the rung and me, assessing both with a cunning born of desperation. He grasped he was losing. Antagonism prodded him on with a red-hot pitchfork.

"Well, I did care," I growled softly. "*Surprise!* Pathetic little Meggie! Couldn't harm a flea. Isn't it *nice,*" I mocked, "the way she looks after that dotty old uncle! What a queer *sweet* thing she is. Isn't it *quaint* how she fills her time with tatty old films? Too bad she doesn't have a *life!*"

When he halted, one elbow on his knee, the other hand holding the shaft steady, I slipped back making a grab, and kicked at the rung, skipping off in a way I hadn't done in years. I stopped, sucking in, feeling blood roar in my ears. The sprint across the lake leached the last adrenaline-born strength out of me. It had to be soon.

"I had no life," I rasped. "Why should they? Why should *you*? *You* and a string of clinics. An *empire,* raking in government rip-offs. How'd that turned out for ya?" I sneered, slithering sideways to him, where he slid to ground, prepared to kick again. "Keep up!" I snarled.

Lance glowered. Too late I saw he was curled over concealing the fact he released his hand from the rung long enough to snatch at me. I hobbled away, wincing. My leg acted up big time. Lightning bolts radiated, hip bone to shin. *Never mind. Keep going. It had to be soon. I kept goading.* "Sloppy butcher, that's all you are! And those diaries? Those tapes! What histrionic *drivel*! And you were going to sully my place with your sloppy *experiments*!"

"No. Not true! They were important research science!"

I stopped. "Why Zak's room?"

"Why not!" He sneered. "If anyone got nosy, all the evidence was in there. Get a clue!"

I jabbed his hurt shoulder with my ski pole, retreating with a hop back. "Get up!" I scorned. Pain and mortification prodded him as I hoped. Sure enough, Lance righted himself, lurching side to side hunched, looking down though, preoccupied with groping his pocket. Briefly concerned, I saw the dull glint of the metal replica of his namesake. The thing weighed twenty pounds. *The replica. The hated symbol for all our problems. Uncle Desmond's, our mother Flo. Zak's parents. My dad...*I twisted my mouth. Perfect. A perfect ending for the thing, as long as he could not get it out of his pocket. I watched with interest. The sharp fins snagged the lining.

I backed farther and farther from shore, leading him. The hut and island blended into a hump-back beast spiky with trees. I too was almost past my limit of course; *panicking if admitted...So close now to my goal! But then so was he.* When did that happen? I sensed the swishing of the blade slicing the biting night air to ribbons.

At last, searching behind me, I spied a darker splotch, a bit larger than most, actually twin spring-fed mush holes, so close they were one in a rough figure eight. Dark mouths filled with half-frozen slush from underwater aquafers over a thin layer of ice.

I smiled, edging to the ugly bruises making him veer; I slowed, backing, allowing him to catch up, then steering him *left-right*, as he slip-slid with his reddened eyes only for me. I concealed the bruises behind me, jagging the last second as Lance slithered faster—*he couldn't stop.* His sneakers glided on slick ice toward the gray-blotches, desperately lunging at me in a misguided tackle. Landing on one knee, he jammed the rung deeper.

Lance's wounded yowl reverberated across the lake. I glanced at the prison lights pondering if they heard it as he clutched his side, staring down his sunken belly in bewilderment, as we both watched black-under-the-moon rivulets of blood, spoil the pristine sparkling whiteness.

Then, laughing, I spied the sharp-finned Lancette sticking absurdly from below Lance's ribs. Lance tugged the replica, still wedged in his pocket, and the razor-sharp tail fin from his stomach. Thrashing, out-crying, he rolled heedless of the widening black mush hole, as freshets of new blood released, trickling into open water.

Jerking with shock at the cold liquid, his out-flung hand touched the slushy edge's bitter wetness. He tried to push himself back with his sneakers, but sludge beneath him so near the mush hole crumpled, dissolving into slush, gnawing at the space between him and glittering open water, as great sherbet-y bites melted into liquid, bitter-black as gall.

Shuffle-hopping back, I watched a manhole-size chunk break away under his weight.

Lance clawed at the edges to push himself away, yet his weight rolled him closer and the mush lost integrity. He was sideways now to an enlarging hole, no more a figure eight, but a ragged hourglass sloshing with water as the lake groaned and vibrated beneath us. Lying on his back, he clawed at slick ice beside him to end his downward spiral but now, his feet sagged in the hole.

His eyes rolled like a frightened horse. Instinctively, I almost reached out as his arm raised up to me. Slowly, his legs slued into the cavity as he tried to roll over. The heavy coat floated on the water. Then, only his top half lay on the surface. His legs and the heavy black wool coat and brass Lancette, weighted him as the lake slowly sucked him under.

Meggie? Why? I saw in his frightened eyes those last seconds. Scrabbling the sides, Lance looked up with horror as he realized his fate if something didn't happen—NOW. I pulled him part way out. His face turned hopeful, grateful, hazarding a weak smile.

"Why you, Lance?" I wrenched my eyes off him and studied the vast ocean of snow. "Guess we are both a little, *crazy*." I murmured, then laughed, as if it were a joke between us—*a family in-joke.* I knelt, still grasping his hand. His teeth clicked to the breaking point. "Didn't you always say, 'Crazy old Flo'? Guess we had more in common, than blood, Lanny."

I chuckled companionably, ignoring the fact he was chest deep again with his other hand digging furrows, trying to leap up, but each time, sinking farther. His face turned bloodless as if he himself was turning into ice. His teeth chattered with a violence painful to hear. He pulled his hand free. The motion made him slip deeper.

Only shoulder-high now, I noted calmly, with legs thrashing under water trying mightily to lunge up once more, but more slurry fell into the void. He had no purchase. I could easily press his head down—but I wouldn't—wouldn't be fair. That was cheating. I curled my knees sideways on the ice, well away from clawing hands, noting with each lunge, he plunged a little farther. I lay on my stomach pulling at him again, but carefully, by his cuffs, digging my toes in, not letting him sink.

"Going to freeze down there, Lanny. Why not tell me?" I teased. "Might haul you all the *way* up." His hands spasmodically dragged dead fingers through frigid mush as he tried for traction.

"Yeah, you're so s-s-s-smart," he chattered. His chest bobbed deeper as he raised his chin.

357

"No, didn't mean it!" Lance heaved a foot out of the abyss, only to plummet yanked by the coat. More ice broke with a snap—*solid ice* I detected, scooting farther back. He was up to his neck now with my hands still clutching his cuffs.

Lance chattered desperately. "W-we could make a g-go of it. You n-need me! You can trust me! Not that smart ass! Zak's lazy and—and…" He looked at me with slyness. "We could hunt together. All the pretty girls. You do yours. I'll do mine."

"Tell me," I cajoled. "Here. Grab my hand."

His face changed to triumph—a shared triumph. He seemed to forget the killing, the deadly cold, his coat sucking to him in icy embrace, or that his feet were dead to the bone. He felt no pain, I'm sure.

"I did, Meggie. I did! Killed off as many as I could. Just like y-you!" Lying flat, I dragged at him to stay his downward spiral. "Tell me. Maybe we could still work it out." I tugged at him hard as I could, grabbing his coat collar and an arm. He would not last long. I did not want to lose him—yet.

His face was gleeful in remembrance, as his chest flopped on the icy surface. "Garbage, filth, dumpster trash. All of 'em, Magpie, shatting out brats every year and let'm d-die—"

"So, you were a saint?"

"Yes. Y-yes, I was! I rid the world of *stupidity.* They w-were perfect for my experiments. No one m-missed them," He barely got the words out, his teeth clattered so. I left my comfort zone as I pressed closer to hear. My face hardened as I saw Lance eye my approach with desperate cunning of a man falling twenty stories, when out of the blue, he sees he wears a parachute.

I let go.

I was not like Lance.

I was a *winner.*

He was the one in icy water. *Not me.*

I stood triumphant, searching the vast lake shimmering platinum under the moon. I need not slog on to the prison camp still so far away, but back to my home…

My home. And Zak's. I choked a sob.

It would have been. I gave one last glance at Lance. This was getting boring.

Slipping, Lance mouthed a wordless cry—a gasp of shock, sputtering as water filled his mouth. I barely registered. Now, only the top of his head bobbed. Lance's long black hair floated on the water. The mob cap, sodden and heavy sank heavily beneath the ice.

What I intended, not even I identified; without warning my bad leg went out from under. One minute my boot was solidly planted in a chunky drift, the next, my foot hit a patch slick with recent wet and I landed on my side. I viewed the black hole spinning closer with icy horror, or was I swiveling like a kid in a dishpan with my bottom sliding across the surface, flying to the hole. Instantly, my hands flew back clutching at snow, crust— mush—*anything.* I grabbed an ice ridge, sharp as razors…

My body halted with a jerk. I felt my fingers sliced through my gloves, poor knit things as my body slued inexorably to the cavity. For one horrible second, I supposed black water tugged me like a strong tidal pull. As if it wanted *me,* not Lance.

I spun sideways, then whipped straight, whirling closer, feeling the grit of ice through my britches, then whooshing through slick spots like black mirrors. All was a blur of trees, endless lake, a glimpse of the top of my brother's head over my stomach, and Lance's long white hand, like a dead fish thrust from the ice clutching my foot in a death grip.

I struggled to rip my foot away. *So close. Inches away.* Looking past my flat stomach again, I saw my brother's exultant face as he made efforts with his last reserves, to heave up and out, using my weight as a fulcrum. *Oh no, you won't!*

I slewed myself double, biting his hand, cold and hard. I felt the bones beneath my teeth. The fist spasmed open. He looked at me. Fury, hate, realization flickered in his eyes. With one hand in the air, the other grasping at nothing, Lance sank silently, without further splash or drama. I watched bubbles break the water. A flap of coat whipped out like a shark fin and then, it too was gone.

I tarried, even as more ice disintegrated, until there was a bathtub-sized abyss awash with dark water where a gust formed small wavelets at my knees.

****

As I watched Lance drift below, black coat billowing up like a dark cloud, the Lancette replica finally loosened. Shimmering in ebony water as the moon bounced light off it, it dimmed as it plummeted, most likely sinking deep in the marl more feet than I was familiar with, below. Perhaps there was no bottom. For a second, I thought I saw the scalpel's shiny brilliance wink out too. Still, I stayed, not minding the cold.

I was at peace. I was safe.

****

Underneath the hole and three feet of ice, the moon hardly penetrated—all was gray, five inches in front of his face, then *nothing*. Lance madly waved his hands as if yearning to touch a solid thing. A wall, *a stairway to heaven,* instead of the bitter black hell beneath—untold feet of bone-killing death. No one told them how deep the lake. Forty—sixty—*a hundred feet*?

His last thoughts burned dry ice in his brain.

They played guessing games the three of them when young and innocent, diving deep as they could, but at the shallow end! The shallow end! his brain screamed— right off the dock, no more than five feet, murky with sand into marl and waving weeds. They could easily bounce off the bottom and resurface.

His brain called then—*urgently.*

Oxygen. Lungs must have oxygen!

Breathe!

The diaphragm commanded and obeyed sending off imperative red signals.

No! Lance's mind whimpered for that will be the end of him. Can't feel anything. His body is one thin icicle...his coat billowing before his face is a scratchy friend from a world rapidly receding, then he doesn't remember it at all.

Lance sank thirty-seven feet, bouncing lightly. He was lucky. His coat was shed by the pull of water like a chrysalis. But his limbs won't move and the water is bitter as death. Somehow, his weightless body floated to the top where he banged the gritty ice ceiling. He is already beyond capacity, still he crawled the ceiling like an underwater fly, grasping rough grit above him, propelling himself in desperate exertion.

His head felt swollen.

His lungs burned with fire.

Faint blueness...*The hole!* His fading faculties

rejoiced. Lance's hand thrust through floating slush like an odd lake creature that never sees daylight. I watched what must be dead fingers, grasp the ragged edge. It held. I could not move. Fascinated by his efforts.

His head popped up, hair streaming over his face like black seaweed, his breath a bellows hawking oxygen so fast his throat seized up. I approached on my knees captivated by how he survived on a sliver of existence. Too late, I saw the flash of fish-belly-white hand lunge desperately, *unbelievably* grasp my ankle!

I kicked sideways, renewing the flame of hurt searing my leg. I hated him. How could he live! His grasp slipped away. Only his hair floated lazily on top. His face was so savage before his head sank under the littered ice, I froze at the hatred and vindictiveness of it. I could not blame him. Somehow, deep inside I admired his tenaciousness, his gritty will to live. I would never have thought it, yet there was much I had not supposed of my brother!

Still waters run deep. I smiled, musing over the appropriateness. I jerked back to reality. One arm thrust up like the mast of a sinking ship. I stared in astonishment at the heaving of a miniature lake. For a frightening amount of time, it looked as if Lance, with herculean effort, might heave himself out again. Was there no end to his effrontery! I stomped on ice at the edge of the hole making it harder for him reach anything but floating mush.

He lunged with a swimming stroke scarcely fingertipping my pantleg, then with another desperate heave, snatched more cloth as I tried to scoot away, dragging me to my shock and fury, to the hole.

His hand clamped my ankle in an icy vice. My limbs

were so numb, I had no sensation of his touch, chilled as
it was. White tensile hands crawled my narrow bones
gaining my leg, my weak one of course! yanking me inch
by inch in herky-jerks to join him. I had been too cocky.
I couldn't kick with my other leg tangled beneath me. I
tried to roll, to twist, releasing his grip. It was cold steel.
Had he died? Was this an unbreakable death-grip?
Panicky I jerked my leg out and feebly kicked. I looked
back.

Then, Lance looked at me strangely for a suspended
moment, as if photographing me.

He was my brother again.

His face relaxed.

His eyes rolled. I saw the whites. His fingers slipped
leaving furrows in the slush.

Lance let go and feathered gently down with
underwater currents, into the bone-shattering abyss of

Convict Lake....

into darkness

white face looking up…

dwindling

down

darker

DARKER...

I fell back. I felt a giving-way as bruised, abused ice
rapidly crumpled into soft chunks, sensing bitter bone
numbing water soaking my pants.

Then, as my bottom plunged through, *nothing*
beneath me.

"No!" I howled to the night.

"No!"

No one could hear.

I'm going down!

It happened so suddenly, I hadn't time to grab the mushy edge, as Lance had, but not panicking—*not yet*. I thrashed arms wildly about to grab *anything*. I kicked my legs beneath. I felt my foot glance off Lance's head, instantly drawing my legs up; an icicle stabbed my heart at the thought of him snatching my feet underwater. I lifted my chin to keep my head above, but it forced my body down; my face dipped below. I gulped water. My throat constricted closed in a vice of freezing lake.

One free waving hand slapped ice, my arm reaching as far as my armpit allowed; I grabbed a frozen ridge sharp as glass, bobbing myself up, but Lance's sweater was heavy. Bitterness crushed my ribs, halting my breathing. I sank beneath weighted with my clothes. With eyes wide I open, I saw inky water with the moon shining through. The ragged hole dwindled as I looked up...

With my last effort, I jackknifed, wrestling the sodden sweater with frantic haste. The arms caught; the neck snagged on my hair. It didn't matter. It no longer shielded me from the biting chill. Free of the cumbersome weight, I bobbed up. I must weigh a feather. Instantly, I flung out my hands thrashing them about with my face tipped to an unforgiving moon watching me with benign indifference, the stars cold and silent as judges.

Fingernails scritched along the slick rime—I'm slipping in again! Plunging *down to join Lance...NO!*

****

Out of nowhere, a small gloved hand reached out, powerfully grabbing my wrist.

I scarce felt it, or believed in it, so numb was my wrist, like a bundle of sticks twisting beneath that firm hold, or the sensation of blessedly dry, scratchy wool. Warm, welcoming. Promising safety. *Life from death.*

I goggled up at the female deputy sheriff's petite figure, still slight in her bulky olive drab parka. She was from another world I left behind, a fantasy nightmare ago.

"Reckon you could use a hand and hot shower 'bout now, in that order." The small female rasped out, grinning. "I gotcha! It was close though!" Without thinking I shot my other arm to the wiry deputy, now plopped flat on the mush-ice hauling my weight, then yanking my unfeeling feet from the hole.

"You come on now. Here, I'll help ya. Gotta get you warm as a hot biscuit. Pronto." She frowned at the hole. "Sorry I can't help him, any." She shook her head. "He's gone, hon. I'm so sorry. No way we can find him."

Gone to meet the devil.

I stuttered though chattering teeth. "Y-you an angel?"

"That's right! A snow-angel!" The deputy hooted a laugh. Tossing a blanket around me, she supported me carefully away, talking cheerfully as she did so. I saw a small sledge. I couldn't wait to get on it and away.

"Talked to Aggie. Put two and two together and came up with some pretty interestin' calculus." She halted, as if thinking. "By the way. Ain't seen a Ranger have you? Feller about—? Ah! Never mind now. Don't see how ya could. Aggie thought he mighta come this away, but I guess not. You'da seen him."

I frowned and through chattering teeth, managed, "N-no…I wish I had."

"Ahh! Bet you do! Enough a that now. All will be told in good time," she grunted. She was busy bundling me shivering uncontrollably in her own parka. The deputy's earnest face was elfin and homely.

That was acceptable then, I thought.

We might even be friends.

I glanced sadly back at the black hole.

"Friend a yours? From where I sat, didn't much *look* like it! But time enough to talk about that later too. C'mon now."

Actually, I was checking.

"Guess he had a accident. Shouldn't skate on thin ice. Anyhoo—I got the Service to fix a plow on my snowmobile. Preggers woman down road a piece. I needed to get her ta the hos-pital pronto! You was a return bonus. Come on now, Princess. I got the sleigh."

I held back, fixated on the lake for what reason, even I did not comprehend. "Can't do nothin' now, luv. Was he kin? A friend? I'm so sorry for you loss, but I reckon he ordered his own tombstone."

The little deputy shuddered. "Wouldn't be my choice."

I whispered.

"Nor mine. Poor Lanny. We were *so much alike*."

Chapter 36

Black Ice

It was the first day of summer when Lance's body, washing back and forth cradled among snake-tail reeds, and brilliant purple loosestrife, bobbed to shore in the frothy wakes of classic wooden speedboats that ripped across Convict Lake, between lazily wafting sails and vintage canoes. An iridescent dragon fly flitted about his head. The antique wooden boats, canoes and rowboats, men in boaters, ladies with parasols, nosed the wide dock made for diving off into the cool spring-fed waters...

If his washed-out eyes could see, he would drag himself from the marl, marveling over the tarted up Victorian mansion with coats of spanking fresh paint—yellow, and forest green with gleaming white gingerbread trim. A true Painted Lady with dark maroon shutters and mellow gold fieldstone chimneys surrounded by aromatic summer beds of marigolds, poppies, jasmine, and larkspur. Rosy brick herringbone walkways wound through a vast lawn dotted with follies, nooks, gazebos, grottoes and two-person swings, all aiding a fulsome, retro ambiance under a dazzling sky and the season's first hot lashings of sun.

The location was *so deliciously old-fashioned, so retro, undisclosed, very expensive and exclusive.* Cell phones and all wireless gadgets strictly *non gratis.* The internet taboo and terribly *declassee*, the wines, and spirits rare and priceless, the waiting list guarded, and speedily filling up. The only jarring notes were the "*Keep Out*" signs bracketing the woods with fearsome icons of bears and rattlesnakes.

Yet, umbrellas and tiled tables, a large outdoor bar in a gazebo serving "Gatsby" drinks, Gibsons, and rye whiskey sours under a huge oak tree, were centers of joviality, offsetting that darker side, while servers in smart waiters' garb of the last century milled with frosted champagne in antique flutes and scrumptious canapés.

Moreover, if one looked closely, guarded by huge round dark glasses under masses of scrunchy cinnamon hair, sporting yellow diamond earrings and *very* little else, a fabled young actress with skin rich as cream laughed in the sexy breathless way for which she was notorious.

****

Zak and I strolled arm in arm greeting, laughing with the guests. I wore long tangerine silk palazzo pants camouflaging my leg, topped with a turquoise bust binder matching my eyes. My hair flowed behind me in a silken ebony storm. I comprehended I looked magnificent, though aware I was a bit pinched around the mouth at the moment.

For a second, as I roamed the crowd, deliciously content, I felt my eyes turn to chips of ice. Sullen-eyed, I narrowly tracked Zak as he openly appreciated the more toothsome female guests, particularly the flame-haired actress in her backless, low cut, lace dress, and sky-high heels that I could never aspire to…

She was so pretty.

****

Meanwhile, not too far from the Victorian house—ten miles as the crow flies—as if kicked from a car, Goth Girl, her leathered flesh, and yellowed bones lay scattered by the road side after road crews cleared the last of the seven-foot winter scrum of drifts, with an arrow sticking from her sternum —

A word about the author…

I write novels and scripts in Myrtle Beach, on ships at sea, the car, my arm, or anywhere there is a phone, laptop, or paper napkin - a skill using few tools beyond a doorstop thesaurus and blood-spattered laptop…

Thank you for purchasing
this publication of The Wild Rose Press, Inc.

For questions or more information
contact us at
info@thewildrosepress.com.

The Wild Rose Press, Inc.
www.thewildrosepress.com